For Ann

SHAWN SPRAGUE

Cover design by Heather Burlison

For Mom, Dad, Janine, Chris, and Stan

Prologue

The first time I saw Zach Hardy pitch was in the spring of 1977. I was nine-years-old and toiling away in the Minors of the Everton Little League. I'd heard about him, of course, as had everyone else I knew. But until the day I actually saw him with my own eyes, he was a little like *Sasquatch* or *Nessie* – a mythical creature whose legend got passed quietly from one nervous kid to the next. *Have you seen Zach Hardy pitch yet? He's 6'4" and throws it a hundred miles an hour. He hit a kid last night, and the doctor said he might not make it.* Yes, I'd heard all about Zach Hardy, but I still wasn't prepared for what I saw that day. It's been forty years since that beautiful, cloudless Saturday in the spring of 1977, but in a lot of ways – as the old saying goes – it seems like it happened yesterday.

Our game had just ended with another loss. You could say wins were hard to come by that year. In fact, I don't think we'd had that particular experience yet on what was either the sixth or seventh Saturday of the regular season. My team was The Elks Club, and in 1977 that meant gray pants and a hideous purple shirt with a matching purple hat. Actually, the hats didn't quite match, but they must have been close enough because no one sent them back. They might well have been the ugliest uniforms in the league, but it wouldn't have mattered if they were the sleekest. We still would have sucked. If we weren't the worst team in the Minors, we were painfully close to it. I can't remember the names of my coaches or even what they looked like, but I do remember they didn't take our team all that seriously. I think we had maybe three practices the entire year, and believe me when I tell you…it showed.

After the obligatory handshakes, I walked across the street to Barnell Field where a Majors game was in progress. My mom had to take her new boyfriend, Mark, to pick up his car, so I figured I could kill some time until she got back. I found one of the few empty spots in the bleachers and took a seat. There was a kid sitting next to me from the team we'd just played. I didn't know his name, but since we'd just done battle, it seemed safe to speak to him without a proper introduction. I asked him who was pitching, and he looked at me like I'd just asked the dumbest question that had ever been asked.

"That's Zach Hardy," the kid whispered. Clearly, he felt he'd be judged as stupid as I if anyone else heard him say it.

I felt the familiar stir of embarrassment in my stomach. I was apparently among the last few people on earth who couldn't immediately identify Zach Hardy by sight. I turned back toward the field, and it didn't take me long to see what all the fuss was about. Up to that point in my life, I'd never seen anyone more intimidating on a baseball diamond. Hardy stood about 6'1", which was as tall as my brother, Adam, and he weighed at least 170 pounds, maybe even 180. No question he was a big kid for eleven-years-old, but that was only part of it. To understand the aura surrounding Zach Hardy, you had to see the whole package. He wore these huge reflective sunglasses, so you couldn't see his eyes—not even a vague outline. They don't let kids wear that style anymore during games because of the reflective glare, but they were perfectly legal then. Not that Hardy needed any help. His fastball was clocked at seventy-six miles per hour, which translates roughly to a Major Leaguer throwing a hundred mile per hour fastball. Of course, Major Leaguers are throwing to grown men, not eighty-pound kids still walking the halls of elementary school. I'm not exaggerating, even a little, when I say he would release the baseball and almost instantaneously it was in the catcher's mitt. Making matters worse, everything he did—other than his actual pitch—was in slow motion. His windup, his delivery, even the way he walked around the mound was slow, smooth, and deliberate. It seemed his plan was to lull you into somewhat of a relaxed state before delivering a blurry white flash past your head.

As I watched him mow down the side without as much as an accidental foul tip, I heard some adults laughing behind me. I turned back and saw two women talking. They looked about my mom's age, so I assumed they had sons playing in the game. (In 1977 there were no girls playing in the Everton Little League, at least not in the Majors.) One of the women was recalling a scene from a movie she'd watched the night before. For some reason, that conversation—and more so the comfortable nature of it—stuck with me. Kind of like how you notice certain details when you witness a traumatic event. The smell of a nearby barbecue after a car accident or the color of a kid's book bag during a hallway fistfight. I wondered how the women could be so relaxed watching Hardy pitch while *my* stomach felt like it wanted to vault out of my throat. Sometime later, might have even been a few years later, it dawned on me why. *They didn't have to face him.* Neither of them would ever have to take the lonely walk from the dugout to the batter's box, raise a narrow bat over her shoulder, and stand motionless while he launched a baseball past her defenseless body. They, and all the other parents, could watch Hardy all day long from the safety of the bleachers and talk about what an impressive young pitcher he was (or what movie they watched the previous night), knowing full well there was no chance of one of his fastballs ever connecting with their rib cage.

There were other events in store for me the following spring that would help put Zach Hardy, and everything else for that matter, in perspective. But sitting there that day, the thought of facing Hardy was almost enough to make me quit baseball. I'm not ashamed to admit it. And if my mom had been there right then, I might have even floated the idea by her. Not the *why*, of course, but the fact I was considering it. I'm sure there were a few kids who saw his fastball and did just that. No doubt they came up with a handful of other reasons why they didn't want to play anymore. *Baseball's boring, I don't like my coaches, I like golf more, etc.* But I'd bet that not wanting to get within striking distance of Zach Hardy was pretty high on that list whether they ever admitted it to themselves or not.

1

Present Day, Wednesday

My name is Daniel Abbot. Everyone calls me Dan, except for my brother and a couple old friends who still insist on calling me Danny, probably because they know it annoys me. I've known for quite some time that today has been coming, but it doesn't make it any easier. I'm going to see my brother for what will be the last time unless God decides to grant him a reprieve, that is. Judging by the way he sounded on the phone last night (and his nonexistent relationship with God) I don't think that's going to happen. Adam told me it was the bottom half of the ninth, and he was down three with two outs and nobody on. He liked using baseball analogies with me. Our love of the sport was one of the things we'd always had in common.

The call came in last night at around 9:00. I'd just put my son to bed, for the last time in my old house as it turned out, when the phone rang. I can't say it surprised me. I knew Adam had been having a down week. The last couple months had been cycling like that—decent one week, shitty the next. He'd stopped the chemo treatments since everyone involved, I think three different doctors in all, said it wasn't working. Why take something that was making you vomit three times a day when it probably wasn't going to extend your life by more than a few weeks anyway? For Adam it was an easy call. He almost didn't even try it in the first place. In fact, if it wasn't for me and his wife, Jen, practically begging him, I don't think he would have. His motto was *When it's your time, it's your time.* So, yes, I knew Adam's final days were coming. I just didn't expect it to be so soon.

I'll spend tonight at my brother's house, and depending how things go, I might even stay over again, but then I'll come back for the first night in my new apartment. It's a basic one-bedroom flat above a bike shop, about a mile from the house where, until today, I lived with my wife and son. We all live in a town called Tremon, NY, which is just across the Susquehanna River from Everton. The owner of the bike shop lived in the apartment himself until about two months ago when he moved out to be with his new bride—

his third marriage, her first. An apartment is the last place I would have expected to find myself at the age of forty-nine. Then again, I would have never expected to come home and find my wife screwing our son's elementary school guidance counselor, but that's exactly what happened.

I should probably get that unpleasantness out of the way first. It all went down about six months ago. I'd headed out of town to visit Adam. He was still getting chemo treatments, and he liked to have me as close as possible, so he could bitch at me for convincing him to do it. He'd give me shit over the phone, too, but having me in the flesh was his preferred method. Actually, he was pretty funny about it in his own disgusting way. He'd make jokes that I'd be on bed pan duty soon or that I'd have to give him his sponge baths when Jen had finally had enough and left him. I'd forgotten what a good sense of humor he had, albeit a little crude. As awful as this disease is and has been for him over the last two and a half years, it gave us a chance to get close again. There was a time when we were very close, at least as close as two boys six years apart can be. But when our younger sister, Jess, died in a car accident and then Mom followed her two years later, things changed dramatically. You'd think it would have been the opposite. We should have grown closer, knowing it was just the two of us, but it didn't happen that way. I think there was almost too much pressure to be there for each other, and we both sort of just moved away from it. That's what most people do if given a choice, isn't it? Move away from pressure? Adam moved just outside Philadelphia and suddenly it was a bit of a hassle to get together. The visits, which had been frequent for a while, started getting further and further apart, and neither of us really liked talking on the phone much. Over time it seemed like our calls were getting more and more awkward, so we just stopped making them. We hadn't spoken in almost a year when Adam called to tell me they'd found a spot on his liver.

Okay, back to more pleasant thoughts, like my wife banging our son's guidance counselor. I'd gotten a late start leaving for Adam's on account of work being absolutely crazy. About a half-hour south of Tremon, I realized I'd managed to forget my cell phone charger. My car charger was broken and had been for three weeks. At work I try to be as proactive as possible, and do a pretty fair job of it, but in my personal life I'm a full-blown reactor. I wait until something is completely broken down before I take any steps to fix it. If I'm being honest, I'd have to put my marriage in that category, as well. Not that I deserved what happened to me—Christ, no one does—but I'm not a totally innocent victim, either. Anyway, I had no choice but to go back for the charger, so I turned off at the next exit and started back. I was going to call Laura and ask her to grab it for me, but in one of life's little (or not so little) ironies, the phone was already dead.

When I got back to our house, I noticed a car parked down the street, nestled alongside a group of pine trees. We live (or I guess I should say

Laura and Connor live) on a dead-end street we use as a turn-around, so I passed within ten or fifteen feet of the vehicle. It wasn't unusual for kids to park back there to drink, or to fool around, or whatever, but I didn't see anyone in the car when my headlights shined into the cab. I figured the occupants could have dropped below view when they saw me, or maybe they were already horizontal, but I didn't think so. I had gotten a good look into the car, and there was no one in it. Right about then an unsettling sense of dread came over me. It was a sensation I can't ever remember having before or since. There was no logical reason why the feeling should have been so strong. There were a million possibilities for why that car was parked there, but I was almost certain that whoever owned it was inside my house at that moment. And that realization spawned another. *My wife's in trouble.* I remember thanking God that Connor had gone out of town with a friend and his family.

I parked my car in front of the mystery vehicle, grabbed Connor's baseball bat out of the back seat, and began sneaking toward the house. It was already past dusk and almost fully dark when I reached the back door. Through the glass, I could tell all the lights were off downstairs except for the small light above the stove. I used my key to quietly undo the bolt and let myself into the house. I crept slowly across the kitchen and into the living room when I noticed a dim light coming from the stairwell. Right then I heard a noise. It sounded like a voice—probably a male voice—but I wasn't sure. I tiptoed through the living room and stopped at the base of the stairs. Looking up, I saw a light shining from our bedroom into the hallway. The light was dim, which told me it was the bedside lamp and not the overhead fixture. I waited there, listening. It was then I heard another noise, but this one's source I *was* sure of. The bed was squeaking. I recognized the sound, although it had been a while since Laura and I had generated the necessary energy to cause it. My heart began to beat even faster. I stood at the base of the stairs thinking my wife was being raped. The idea she might have summoned a secret lover to the house never occurred to me. I gripped the bat tighter and headed up the stairs, walking on the edges and hoping they wouldn't creak. I knew there were a couple that did—I just couldn't remember exactly which ones. My technique worked because I didn't make a sound. Sadly, it probably wouldn't have mattered even if I did.

I was almost to the top step, both my heart and mind ready to explode, when I heard Laura's breathless voice. "My God," she said, "I'm getting close."

I stopped cold, one foot on the top step, the other in the hallway. The bat was already raised above my shoulder. A devastating array of thoughts, images, and emotions flooded my brain. There were so many piling on in rapid succession, it was overwhelming. For a second or two I wondered if I was having a seizure. When my mind finally began to settle, amidst the dreamlike sounds of a squeaking bed and my panting wife, a horrible realization formed. *My wife's screwing another man in our bed.*

We'd been having troubles for the last year, probably more like eighteen months. I'd been battling depression and I guess what you could call an early midlife crisis. A mild one perhaps, but a midlife crisis all the same. I was in my late forties and held what felt like a dead-end job in a dead-end industry. Laura and I were fighting a lot and couldn't seem to see eye-to-eye on anything. She wanted to move into a bigger house. I wanted to save some money and start investing in a college fund for Connor. She wanted to travel and see the world as a family. I wanted to change careers. We couldn't do both. Neither one of us was wrong. Selfish maybe but not wrong.

Eventually, the list of things we agreed upon became dwarfed by the list of those we didn't. We had always been opposites. I was the classic steady influence, providing some sort of stability to her high-flying spirit. It worked for a while, a long time actually, until life finally asserted itself and managed to get in the way. Her father passed away and Laura got a taste of what it was like in the real world, working for someone who didn't love you more than life itself…and someone you couldn't manipulate. Not surprisingly, she didn't care for it. Then my brother found out he had cancer, and things only got worse. Naturally, this affected me. According to Laura, I was distant most of the time and moody the rest. I know she was right. Conversations beyond the necessary dialogue were rare, and sex had become nonexistent. If we hadn't had Connor, we might have called it quits and gone our separate ways. But we did have Connor, and I also think neither one of us wanted to give up on the marriage. We decided on counseling, and to my great surprise it actually helped. We started talking more, making love more, and it felt to me, at least, like we were heading in the right direction. We weren't quite back to the way things had been when Connor was an infant, but we were within shouting distance, or so I thought. All of these things and more rolled through my thoughts as I stood on that top step.

There are a handful of decisions I've made in my life that I wish I could take back and deciding to continue down the hallway to our bedroom is at the top of that list. I realize very few men (or women) would have been able to stop themselves, but I still wish I could have summoned the strength to do it. I sometimes wonder if things might have turned out differently if I had. It was obvious my wife was not being raped. She was in no danger, not from the new guy anyway. I should have just gone back downstairs or out on the patio and waited. I could have confronted them when they were done. Instead, I continued to creep down the hall as my wife hit the first stages of what sounded like a very strong orgasm. I recognized her gasps from the early years of our marriage. It hit me even then that it had been a long time since I'd heard them. I stepped into the open doorway of our room. The bedside lamp was on, as I'd suspected, and the sheets had either fallen off the bed or more likely had been kicked off in the heat of passion. My first thought was *Why is the light on?* She always made me turn it off, even when I explained that I loved her body and just wanted to see it. My second thought—more of a numb realization at that point—was that we usually had to have a sheet over us while making love, even when it was hot. She always claimed Connor could come walking in at any moment, even when he was fast asleep and our bedroom door was locked. Apparently, these two hard and fast rules didn't apply anymore. It was anything fucking goes for the new guy.

I stared dumbfounded at the scene before me. Picture Ben Stiller's character, Reuben Feffer, at the beginning of *Along Came Polly* when he finds his wife having sex with the scuba instructor. Now picture it a hundred times worse. Feffer knew damn well what was happening under those sheets, but he didn't have to witness it in excruciating detail from just ten feet away. I promise you it made the scene significantly worse. I could see the new guy was pretty big, and yes, I mean that in every way you might suspect. Of course, at that point I didn't realize I already knew him. He looked to be at least 6'5" or 6'6". My wife is only about 5'2", and they were handling the transaction missionary style. Bottom line, she had no chance of seeing me and neither did he. He was facing away from me and otherwise occupied. If you're not getting the full picture yet, let me put it another way. If every female virgin on the planet saw what I saw that day, the human race would be headed toward extinction in one generation. It was that bad. And they just kept right on going—bed squeaking and wife panting—as I stood there watching. I felt like I was viewing a porno flick, except this wasn't an actress manufacturing bogus sounds of pleasure. It was my wife, and the pleasure was as real as it gets. In the end I didn't even have the necessary presence to ruin her orgasm.

By some miracle I made it through the incident without killing either of them. I'm still not sure how. The new guy turned out to be the guidance counselor at our son's elementary school. It wasn't hard to figure out once I saw the front of his head instead of the back. After a great deal of screaming and a few threats with the baseball bat (I don't think I was all that close to actually swinging it), all the naked people got dressed and we headed downstairs. Alan McBride fell back on his training as a counselor and tried to smooth things over, as much as he could anyway under the circumstances. Not long into his parade of bullshit, I lifted the bat and threatened him again, and this time I *was* very close to swinging it. The most dangerous moment for him came when he mentioned Connor. He said something along the lines of, "Whatever we do moving forward, we have to think of Connor." I'm sure at that moment he was just trying to save his job and his marriage, but I don't think he realized how close he came to pushing me over the edge. My screaming response was, "You don't get to fuck my wife and talk about my son on the same night!" I thought that was sort of clever on my part, but it was that moment when a light burst on in my head. *He's right. The fucker's right.* I realized if it ever got out, it would ruin Connor's life. That might have been overstating things a bit, but then again, maybe not. At the very least, it would have been a terrible weight he'd have to lug around until adulthood. Anyone who's ever walked the hallways of a middle school, or any school for that matter, knows how cruel children can be to one another. This would have been like a razor-sharp knife anyone could use to cut him over and over.

It was the first in a long line of shit I've had to swallow since that night. Not only did I have to witness my wife having sex with another man in agonizing detail, I couldn't even make anyone pay for it, at least not if I wanted to protect my son. And the cherry on top? The guy who was screwing my wife was the one who made me realize it. I can't honestly tell you I mapped everything out right then, but one thing was clear to all of us. We couldn't tell anyone what happened.

The next day Laura moved in with her sister. She vowed to stop seeing him, and about two weeks later — which was about how long it took for the initial shock to wear off — we went back to counseling together. Our counselor, Eileen, was the one person I trusted, and thank God for her, or I would have lost my mind. Everything came out, either in or because of the sessions. I had a billion questions and Laura answered all of them. There were a few specifics like *Did he make you come?* or *Did he have a big cock?* that weren't necessary. Laura said she turned to him out of desperation. She was dying in our marriage and wanted the kind of attention I didn't seem capable of giving anymore. She apologized profusely and begged me to reconcile so we could try to salvage our relationship. After a few weeks of telling her it was over, I started having second thoughts. She was persistent as hell and more important, I could see she meant it. Two months after the worst incident of my adult life, she moved back in so we could try to save our marriage. For a while, things seemed to be improving. We were communicating again, and I was starting to have short periods where I didn't think about what had happened. She told me the time table for sex was up to me. I thought that was nice of her. She said when I was ready, we could do it as often as I liked. There was no pressure or expectations of any kind. Unfortunately, it never happened. We came pretty close a couple times, but I just couldn't finish the job. Some men fantasize about watching their wives doing it with another man. For me it was the exact opposite. Seeing my wife having sex with him literally ruined my desire for her…and for quite a while, sex in general. I don't hold my wife responsible for the mechanics behind sex itself. It wasn't her call when the blueprints got drawn up for what body part goes where or for that matter how big certain body parts might be. But having to watch it play out from point blank range while she's having a massive orgasm was too much for me to get over.

Eventually, Laura accepted I was moving out whether she liked it or not. To her credit she said she understood, but to be perfectly honest, what choice did she have? I think somewhere along the way she realized one day Connor was going to learn the full story of what happened, or most of it anyway. I couldn't see myself ever sharing the full bedroom details of that awful night. But whatever he got from me or whatever he surmised on his own wasn't going to make her look very good. Did she really want to compound that by turning into a nasty bitch just because I wasn't able to forgive her? Maybe I'm being too hard on her, but at least I didn't beat both of them to death with the Easton. That's something, isn't it?

2

The trip to Philadelphia took me just over three hours. I say Philadelphia, but Adam and Jen actually live in a town called West Chester, which is about a half-hour west of the city. Adam moved there from Syracuse after mom died when he took a job with UPS. At the time, Jen was running a small craft supply business out of her apartment on the north side of town and was constantly sending and receiving shipments. Adam was her delivery guy. After about a year, he finally worked up the nerve to ask her out on a date. She told him no because it took him too long. It was one of Adam's favorite stories, and he usually added an F-bomb or two to spice it up a little. They never had kids, although they did try for a while. They also tried the adoption route, but after running into numerous dead ends, they finally gave up. They just figured it wasn't meant to be. They had each other, plenty of nieces and nephews—Connor and a bunch more on Jen's side—and some close friends. I'm happy to count myself as one of them. This was always enough for them, and they were truly happy. And as far as I know, neither ever came home and caught the other one having sex with someone else.

It was just after noon when I pulled into their driveway. Jen had called about an hour ago to give me an idea of what I'd be walking into. I'd seen Adam in rough shape before, mostly side effects from the chemo, but this was different. She said he was bed bound now and didn't think he'd ever get out of it. I parked the car and stepped into the hot, muggy June air. It had been a mild spring so far, but the northeast had recently stumbled into a heat wave. I grabbed my overnight bag from the back seat of my Saturn Outlook and walked toward the door. I'd been preparing myself for this day for quite some time, but I wondered how I would hold up when I actually saw him. I'm a pretty emotional person, so when things hit me out of the blue, I don't always handle it well. Conversely, when I know something is coming, even something difficult like my brother's impending death, I can usually slip into a calmer state. It's almost like a shield forms over my emotions to keep them in check. With Adam, that shield had been building for a while now. It felt heavy as I stepped out of the car

Their house was a basic two-bedroom ranch that sat quietly on the crest of a small hill. Jen liked to garden, so the front of the home was bordered by a beautiful array of June flowers: purple Irises, pinkish Peonies and Hydrangea bushes in full violet bloom. I could smell their sweet aroma as soon as I stepped out of the car. The house seemed undersized compared to others in their neighborhood, but it was plenty big enough for the two of them. Jen greeted me at the door, smiling. I stepped into the foyer and we hugged tightly. Jen was forty-eight but could have easily passed for thirty-five. Adam once showed me a few photos from her coed days, and she was an absolute knockout. As far as I was concerned, not much had changed. At first glance, and probably every other glance, she was way out of Adam's league. I liked to ask him how he managed to land her. With any other topic he always had a bullshit comeback, but on that question it was always the same answer: "I have no idea."

"I'm glad you could come so fast," she said quietly. She closed the front door and turned to me. "Like I told you on the phone, I don't have a good feeling this time. I think he's preparing himself to go."

As soon as I heard those words, I felt a deep fissure forming in my emotional shield. It wasn't what she said that surprised me. After all, she'd already told me as much on the phone. It was more the way she said it. There was something in her voice. There's no right word for it, but I think the closest is *relief*. Relief for Adam, of course, but I also think relief for herself. It's a feeling I knew well and one you can't fully comprehend until you go through the slow death of a loved one. The toll it takes is impossible to measure.

"And he really wanted to see you again," she added. "He'll be so happy you made it."

It had been almost three weeks since I'd last seen him. That had been a good day, thankfully, and we were able to talk while we watched a couple hours of a Yankee game. But according to Jen, the good days had been growing fewer and farther between. "I'm sorry I haven't been able to come more," I said, hoping my voice wouldn't crack.

"Stop it, Dan. You've been wonderful through this, and we both love you for it."

I started to say more, but she cut me off. "No more of that. Let's go see if he's awake. He's been in and out all morning. He has a lot of drugs in him right now. The hospice nurse left about an hour ago."

From the very beginning of his illness, Adam insisted he wasn't going to die in the hospital. We'd both watched our mother suffer that fate. I can still see the tubes running in and out of her body as she withered away to nothing. I think Adam vowed that wasn't going to be him, at least not in a hospital.

We walked down the hall to their bedroom and Jen opened the door. Adam was lying in the hospital bed, motionless. The bed was here on my last visit, but some additional equipment had been brought in, including an

IV drip. A clear tube ran from the bottom of the IV bag down to a receptacle taped near the crook of his elbow. As I looked at him, my first thought was he'd already died. While Jen had been waiting for me to arrive, he'd simply slipped away and moved on to the afterlife. Only the faint rise and fall of his chest finally convinced me otherwise. He was incredibly thin, easily ten pounds lighter than when I'd last seen him. The second thing I noticed was that his color was all wrong. It hadn't been great three weeks ago, but now he was an ashen, unnatural shade of gray. Again, I felt a sharp stab of guilt for not getting down here sooner. I almost said it again, but I knew Jen didn't want to hear it. What mattered to her and I hoped to Adam, as well, was that I was here now.

Jen stepped into the room and walked over to Adam. I saw there was an armchair beside the bed. She stood in front of the chair while I moved in beside her next to my brother's head.

"Should we let him sleep?" I asked.

"No, he'll want to know you're here." She reached out and touched his hand. "Adam, there's someone here to see you." Adam didn't respond. Again, I had the feeling that he'd already passed. "Adam, honey, Dan is here. Wake up and say hello."

I saw Adam's eyelids flutter, and then he opened his eyes. He stared ahead for a moment, and I was sure he was going to close them again. Instead, he turned his head toward us. His eyes found Jen first and then they settled on me. His movements were slight, yet the effort he was exerting seemed great. *I should have come sooner,* I thought again. In that instant, what remained of my shield was ripped away by some unseen force. I was naked and there was nothing to support me. I think if Adam hadn't smiled so broadly, I would have fallen apart right there in front of them.

"Hey, little bro," he whispered. "How's it hanging?" His words were slow and labored, but it was vintage Adam.

Jen let go of his hand and stepped back. I slid down and grabbed it, my feet feeling anything but steady. "I'm good, Adam, how about you?" It was a stupid question, but it just came out. Right then it was either a programmed response or a complete breakdown.

"I'm doing good, bro—thinking about getting in eighteen holes later." Golf was another thing we'd always had in common—a byproduct of growing up within a hundred yards of a golf course.

"That sounds good," I said. "I'll caddy for you."

"Sounds like a plan." He followed it up with another smile. It was all teeth, but it was good to see anyway.

I watched Jen lean down and kiss my brother on the forehead. She pointed toward the chair behind me, then smiled and left the room quietly. When she closed the door, I sat in the chair, still holding Adam's hand. "Jesus, how the fuck did you land her?"

He smiled. "I have no idea."

We talked some more golf, then jumped to the Yankees, *our home turf.* They were riding a four-game winning streak and were playing a lot better than anyone expected. After about fifteen minutes of slow conversation, Adam had closed his eyes, and I thought he'd drifted off. When he spoke again, it startled me.

"Like I told you last night, Danny, I'm winding down fast. There's two outs, two strikes and nobody on in the ninth." He smiled again, but this one ended in a grimace. "I'm sure you can see that for yourself." I squeezed his hand but didn't say anything. "I think I've got maybe one more week in me and maybe not even that." He paused and took a few breaths. "I've never been on death's doorstep before, but that sure is what it feels like."

On death's doorstep. That had been one of our mother's many expressions.

As if reading my mind, Adam said, "Mom used to say that one, remember?"

"I do, along with *barking up the wrong tree* and *don't count your chickens before they hatch.*"

Adam laughed. "Funny how that shit stays with you, isn't it?"

"Yeah, it is."

There was another long pause. "You know I don't believe much in the afterlife, but I hope I'm wrong. I'd love to see them, Danny…Mom and Jess, I mean. I miss them so much."

I'd like to say I wasn't feeling sorry for myself at that moment, but I think I was. Ninety-five percent of it was because I was about to lose my older brother, but the other five percent was because I was about to be the last surviving member of our family—aside from our dad, that is. I started to say I missed them, too, and that was when I lost it. My words got caught in my mouth, first stuttering and then stopping altogether. I lowered my forehead and rested it on the edge of the bed. When the tears came, I felt Adam slip his hand out of mine and rest it on my head.

When I finally stopped crying, I looked up to see that Adam had really dozed off this time. I stood slowly, being careful to keep my chair from sliding on the hardwood floor. I could see how much it took out of him to talk, so I wanted him to sleep. I took one step toward the door when I heard his voice again.

"You done bawling yet?" he asked, smiling.

I couldn't help but laugh. Adam had never been one to cry. I could remember a couple times, like when Mom and Jess died, but as an adult that was about it. "Fuck you, you cold-hearted bastard."

He laughed, then winced again. "Don't make me laugh, bro. It hurts too much." I sat back down and waited. It took him a minute to gather his strength. "When you talk to Jack, I want you to tell him something for me."

Hearing Adam mention our father surprised me. I'd reconciled with him years ago after he began reaching out to me. It was about a year before Connor was born. I guess he finally realized his time here on earth was limited, and he wanted to get to know his sons. I can't say we had a great relationship, but it wasn't terrible, either. He came up a few times from Delaware, and I worked in a visit to see him during a family vacation. That had been just over two years ago when Laura, Connor, and I were still a happy family...and Adam was still feeling as good as he ever had. Since then, we'd kept in touch with the occasional email and the even more occasional phone call. I'd forgiven him for leaving our family, but the truth was I just didn't like him all that much—not the way a son *should* like his father. I knew we would always keep in touch, but we'd probably never be close. Adam never even gave him a chance to get that far. I didn't blame him, and after one half-assed attempt to get them talking, I never pushed it. Adam was a lot older than me when our father left. For him, it was a much harsher betrayal...one he never got over.

"Of course, Adam, whatever you want."

"Tell him I wish I could have forgiven him. Say it just like that. Don't say I'm sorry about it, because I'm not. Just say I wish I could have forgiven him."

"Okay."

"And if he makes some kind of asshole comment, tell him I said he can fuck off."

I laughed and Adam smiled. "There's one other thing. Pretty soon I'm going to take a nap because talking to you is exhausting." We both smiled again. "Seriously, Danny, when I fall asleep, I want you to leave."

"Adam, I'm not—"

"I know I'm not much to look at right now, but at least I'm still here. I don't want anyone to see me dead, other than Jen. Obviously, I don't want her to see me like that, either, but there isn't much choice there. Plus, it's different with her. You'll understand what I mean someday with Laura." I nodded, but he knew what I was thinking. "Maybe you won't. I'm sorry I said that."

"No worries, Adam." Adam had no idea what had happened. Like everyone else, he just thought we were going through a rough period. "Who knows, maybe we'll get it worked out."

"She's a spoiled brat, but I always liked her."

"I know. She sends her love by the way. She offered to come and would have, too, but I told her not to."

Adam nodded and looked at me. "Danny, other than Jen, I love you more than anything in this world, and I'm happier than hell we became brothers again."

At that, Adam turned his head away. And then for just the third time in my adult life, I watched my older brother cry.

Mr. Holt

3

1978

It's kind of funny to look back now as a forty-nine-year-old and admit this, but I was very much in love with my fifth-grade teacher. It was a primitive version of love—one that only a ten-year-old boy could fully understand—but it was love, nonetheless. Ms. Becker was pretty and she had gorgeous legs, but that wasn't why I loved her. Those traits were enough to cause the infatuation, certainly, but I loved her because she was kind. You could see it in everything she did. The way she treated you when you didn't understand something, the way she treated you when you did, even the way she handled the assholes (also known as *the problem students*). Without question, she understood kids better than any other teacher I ever had, before or since. Maybe it was because she was still young, late twenties at the time, but I don't think so. I think it was mostly because she was smart and also because she was tough as hell. She could outtalk, outwit, and outmuscle every kid in the school if she needed to. This was proven for all to see on the second day of classes when she broke up a fight between Big Mike and Elliot Holloway—the two toughest kids in the school—and then escorted them both to the main office.

Fifth-grade, with its drama-filled girls and unruly boys—many now as big as the female teachers themselves—kept all but the toughest of women away. Most stayed down in the first and second-grade where the children were still sweet, and they couldn't look you directly in the eye. Not Ms. Becker. She wanted to teach fifth-grade, so that's exactly what she did.

As I walked toward school with my younger sister, Jess, beside me, my thoughts jumped back and forth between Ms. Becker and baseball tryouts. The following day was Saturday, March 20th, the day I and all the other hopeful Minor Leaguers would audition for the big time. I'd known for weeks that baseball tryouts were approaching, but somehow it still snuck up on me. The truth was I wasn't ready. I'd played catch a couple times with Adam and once with our mom's boyfriend, Mark, but that was it. I hadn't hit a live pitch or fielded a true grounder since the previous summer. The last two days had been unusually warm for March and would have been a perfect time to reacquaint myself with the sport, but Adam had been too busy and Mark hadn't been around to ask. Unfortunately, Jess wasn't an option. She liked watching baseball on TV but had absolutely no interest in actually playing it.

We walked into West Everton Elementary together and headed down the hall toward our classrooms. I stopped outside my room and said goodbye to Jess as she continued down the hall. I always waited until she entered her classroom before entering mine. The ritual was a holdover from the days when Mom insisted I walk her directly into her room. As I stood there waiting, it dawned on me that it was Friday, which meant *Friday Kickball*. Weather permitting, Ms. Becker usually let us out around 2:00 for a quick game. It was an activity she used to help keep us focused throughout the week, and it worked pretty well. We'd actually been talking about it the last two days since it had been so nice.

As I entered my classroom, any thoughts of kickball quickly evaporated. I sensed right away that something was different, and I had the odd feeling I wouldn't approve of the change. For starters, Ms. Becker's desk had been moved from the front of the class to the back corner, just inside the door. I noticed the polished brown wood to my left as soon as I walked in. The second thing I noticed, and this was the far more disturbing of the two, was that Ms. Becker wasn't sitting at it. Not unless she'd turned into a man and aged twenty-five unkind years overnight. At first I thought I'd mistakenly wandered into the wrong room, but I saw several classmates sitting exactly where I would have expected them to be. I turned back to the man sitting at Ms. Becker's desk, and after a few stunned seconds, I recognized him. *Mr. Holt*. He'd been a substitute teacher in the school several times by my count even though I'd been lucky enough to avoid any firsthand experience. Stories about Mr. Holt, mainly of the *That guy is really mean* variety, spread throughout the school like a nasty flu bug every time he showed up. I'd never been within thirty feet of him before that moment.

They say you can't judge a book by its cover or at least that you shouldn't. Likewise, they say you shouldn't judge the character of a person by their appearance, but Mr. Holt turned out to be the exception to this age-old rule. He was like that old *Twilight Zone* episode where the relatives of a dying man were forced to wear hideous masks as a condition of their inheritance. When the veneers were removed at the stroke of midnight, they'd each taken on their mask's appearance, revealing their true inner nature. I believe Mr. Holt's mask formed slowly over the years as a stern warning to anyone unlucky enough to stumble across his path. As I stood there, I realized he reminded me of a cartoon character I knew, although I couldn't quite place it.

"Hello," he said in a voice that sounded like sand running through a meat grinder. It also sounded like he had a bad head cold even though he didn't. His expression was friendly enough on the surface, but to me it looked (and felt) like bad acting. He was expected to be nice, especially as a substitute, so he was giving it his best shot.

"Hi," I replied, my feet locked in place. I was still staring at him when it came to me. He looked like The Creeper from *Scooby Doo*. His hair was gray instead of brown and his skin wasn't green, but other than that it was a solid resemblance, especially to a fifth-grader with an active imagination. His mouth hung open a little, adding to the illusion. I just stood there, hoping he wasn't a mind reader.

"Why don't you take a seat," he said. "I'll introduce myself to the class in a few minutes."

A sense of dread enveloped me as his words bounced around in my head. *"I'll introduce myself to the class..."* The implication was this wasn't going to be just a one day gig but some kind of extended stay. We'd already had two subs that year, but in both cases Ms. Becker had let us know the day before. This time she hadn't said anything. I think it also bothered me that her desk had been moved. I figured it was possible she'd decided to rearrange the room herself after we'd all gone home, but it certainly wasn't likely. What did seem likely was that Mr. Holt had done the rearranging himself when he came in that morning. I looked down at the top of her desk, hoping to see her usual things. I eyed her wooden apple pencil holder and her large gray teacher's stapler. The words *Becker Fifth-Grade* were still visible on the top of the stapler. Seeing these items made me feel better, but the desk still seemed different somehow. Something was missing. It came to me like a cold slap to the face. *Her vase is gone!* All that week there'd been a bouquet of yellow flowers sitting front and center. She'd even told us what kind of flowers they were, but I couldn't remember. Just the day before, she'd commented they were starting to wilt.

I turned and headed toward my seat, hoping she had simply come down with the flu. Jess had had it a couple weeks earlier, as did plenty of other kids. It wouldn't have been unusual if a few of the teachers had picked it up, as well, but my gut was telling me different. My gut was telling me Ms. Becker hadn't picked up anything. Substitutes don't move teachers' desks around, nor do they remove glass vases, even if the flowers are wilting.

I took a seat at my desk and looked around the room. Jess and I had been running late, so almost everyone was there already. A few of my classmates were reading or organizing the previous night's homework, but most were conversing quietly with a neighbor. In their faces I could see the same nervous tension I was feeling. *What happened to Ms. Becker?* they all seemed to be asking. I remember having another question. *When is she coming back?* I glanced up at the blackboard and my heart caught in my chest. Written in large letters, spanning almost the entire width of the room, were the words *Fifth-Grade, Mr. Holt*. I'd grown accustomed to the flowing, feminine cursive of Ms. Becker. The printed words staring back at me that day were scraggly and abrupt. Masculine. That isn't what bothered me, though. What bothered me was that these were words you'd typically see on the first day of school. The fact they appeared that day, the 19th of March, did not sync in any way with my hope we'd see Ms. Becker back on the following Monday morning.

None of the things I'd observed thus far were absolute proof of anything, but I'd had quite a few substitutes in my five years at West Everton Elementary, and not one of them had ever used the entire blackboard to write their name, nor had they moved the regular teacher's stuff around. I looked around again and caught the eye of a quiet girl named Kathy Anderson. I didn't know her very well even though we'd shared three classrooms together over the previous five years, including kindergarten. She looked nervous, maybe even a little scared. And when she looked at me, I could read her thoughts as clearly as if she'd screamed them across the room. *Ms. Becker isn't coming back.* I was pretty sure my face was reporting the same. It was then I realized Kathy and I were at a deeper level of understanding. While there was some unease in the air, it was clear not everyone had put all of the clues together...probably because they didn't want to.

Our eyes were still locked when the 9:00 bell rang. We were like two earthquake survivors, staring at one another across a newly formed chasm. The bell was followed by a fellow student's voice, asking us to stand for the Pledge of Allegiance. Once we finished the pledge, we sat back at our desks and listened to a handful of brief announcements and reminders. When that was done, Mr. Holt stood from his chair and walked toward the front of the class. He was around six-foot-two and walked with slumped shoulders. He wasn't fat, exactly, but he carried an extra twenty or thirty pounds around his midsection. When he reached the blackboard, he turned to face us. An image of The Creeper filled my head again, this time chasing Scooby and Shaggy through some bleak, barren countryside.

"Hello, class, my name is Mr. Holt. I'm going to be your teacher for the remainder of the fifth-grade."

A collective gasp echoed throughout the classroom. I watched him pause and survey our shocked faces. I got the distinct impression he was enjoying the moment.

"Ms. Becker was in a car accident last night and broke her leg." Jaws literally dropped all around, mine included. "She's okay from what I understand," he added quickly, "but she won't be able to come back this year, so I'm going to finish it out for her. I have a paper that you'll need to take home tonight and get signed."

In 1978 there were no personal computers or cell phones—no websites, emails or texts. Communications between parents and teachers were usually handled with pen and paper and transported in book bags and back pockets. Only the most severe situations warranted an actual phone call.

Mr. Holt moved seamlessly from his brief announcement on the circumstances surrounding Ms. Becker to his plans for the rest of the year. To be fair, who could expect the man to dwell on the beloved teacher, with whom we had all spent about half of our waking hours over the preceding seven months, when his future plans were still unknown? Three kids raised their hands, but he told them he wanted to finish going through the upcoming schedule before answering any questions. It was simply too much to take for a couple of the girls, including Kathy Anderson. The shock of Ms. Becker being replaced by a man with a reputation like Mr. Holt's—coupled with actually seeing him in the flesh—was more than she could handle. I watched her trying to fight it, but it was like watching a rogue wave roll over a bamboo fishing boat. She never stood a chance. Her face contorted and she raised a shaking hand to her mouth as a muffled cry escaped her lips. A few seconds later another girl joined her. Mr. Holt continued talking, although it was obvious he was becoming annoyed by their display. When the crying continued, he stopped talking and glared at the two girls, his mouth hanging in its usual position. Even though I could tell he was angry, I expected to him to offer some type of comfort. I was wrong.

"Are you two serious?" he asked, his voice only a decibel or two shy of a bellow. "You're in fifth-grade now, not kindergarten!" The crying intensified. I scanned the faces around the room and saw another girl about to embark on the slippery trek from composure to tears. Mr. Holt's cheeks and forehead had darkened to a deep, rosy red. I expected him to take the chastising to a whole new level, but he surprised me again. He let out a long, heavy sigh. "Okay," he said, "Why don't you two head down to the nurse's office?"

The girls looked at each other. I think they would have hugged had they been close enough. They left their seats and scurried out of the room together. Mr. Holt started in again with his plans but shifted gears soon after. I think he realized he was about to lose half the class. He announced he'd answer any questions we had even though it was obvious he wasn't happy about it. Naturally, every question that followed had to do with Ms. Becker. *Was she okay? Was she in the hospital? How bad was her leg broken? When would we be able to talk to her?* To his credit, I thought Mr. Holt did the best he could. He seemed to realize he'd underestimated the level of concern we had for our teacher. It became clear early on he didn't know a lot about what had happened. The accident had occurred in a town called Owego, which was about fifteen minutes away. Apparently, a car ran a red light and struck the passenger side where Ms. Becker had been sitting. Her leg had been broken in a couple places, but he didn't know if she had any other injuries. She'd spent the night in the hospital—he didn't say which one—and he hadn't spoken to her yet, so he didn't know when she might be well enough to see visitors.

I wondered if she was in Arnold Hospital where my mom worked as a nurse. I figured there was a good chance because as far as I knew, it was the closest hospital to Owego. I even considered the possibility that Mom was taking care of her at that very moment. I think I might have almost been smiling when I heard Mr. Holt's voice again.

"Okay, last question for today," he said.

I raised my hand along with six or seven others. To my great surprise, he pointed at me. "Are we still gonna play Friday Kickball?" I asked.

He looked at me like he had no idea what I was talking about, and I'd suspect at that moment he really didn't. I was about to dive into a detailed explanation when the veil of confusion lifted from his face.

"Yeah, we can do that," he said.

He immediately shifted topics to mathematics where he would spend most of his time (and ours) over the next three months. I opened my desk to search for my math book when a strange feeling came over me—a sudden sense of heightened awareness. *He's lying.* It was the first time in my young life I consciously realized an adult had lied to me. He was giving us the simplest answer so he could end the discussion and move on. It was only a gut feeling, mind you, but it was a strong one. And after what had just happened, namely discovering that my instincts were right about Ms. Becker, I was already starting to trust my gut feelings. Unfortunately, I turned out to be two for two on that unusually sunny day in March of 1978, because despite his assurance, we never played Friday Kickball again.

4

When the 3:30 bell rang, I grabbed my backpack and followed my classmates out the door. Everything was done in an unusually orderly manner. Not that we were unruly for Ms. Becker, because she certainly never put up with any bullshit, but I thought we were being especially good. There were the usual Friday afternoon giggles, but very little talking as we filed out. I think some of it was the lingering concern over Ms. Becker, but most of it was because we were afraid of angering Mr. Holt. I know I was. Things had gone smoothly after he'd sent the two girls to the nurse's office, but I think everyone saw his temper could turn ugly fast.

I left the calmness of my classroom and entered into the chaos that was the main hallway on Friday afternoon. I glanced back, looking for Jess, as I worked my way through the crowd toward the front door. Our daily routine was to meet on the steps outside the school. From there we would make the three-quarter-mile trip back to our house. Sometimes Jess walked part of the way home with a friend, usually a little ways behind me, and sometimes it was just me and her. But we always walked home together. Mom insisted on that, and there were no exceptions. I stepped outside the school and saw her at the bottom of the stairs, talking with one of her girlfriends. I was heading toward them when I felt a hard slap on my back.

"You trying out tomorrow, Abbot?" a voice asked.

I turned to see Jason Billings pass by on his way to the bus. He was a fellow fifth-grader but in another class. My back stung where he'd slapped me, but I didn't say anything. "Yeah, are you?"

"Of course." He smiled at me and said, "Good luck," then hopped onto his bus and disappeared.

Jason was typical of most of my relationships in fifth-grade—with the boys anyway. We knew each other's names and got along okay, but we weren't really friends. There were the occasional slaps on the back and the even more occasional high fives after a good play during kickball, but that was about it. Ever since my best friend, Evan, moved away the summer before fourth-grade, I hadn't made any true friends.

I walked over to Jess and her girlfriend who were still gabbing away about their plans for the weekend. After promising to call Jess later, the girl hopped onto a bus. Jess watched her for a second and then turned to me.

"I have to ask you something," she said. The concern was immediately evident on her face.

"Go-head."

"Wait," she said, looking around. "Let's walk for a little while." We walked up the street, past the last of the buses. They were lined up in front of the school like massive yellow tanks preparing for battle. She looked around again, making sure there wasn't anyone within earshot. "I heard Mr. Holt's your teacher now."

Her cautious approach struck me as funny. It was like she thought Mr. Holt might come running out of the school if he heard someone mention his name. "Yeah, Ms. Becker broke her leg, so he's subbing for her until she gets better. She'll probably be back by the end of the year." Mr. Holt hadn't said that. In fact, he'd said the exact opposite, but I wasn't ready to face that yet.

"I don't like him, Danny," she said, lowering her voice even further. Jess was a happy, good-natured kid. She hardly ever said anything negative about anybody.

"Did you have him as a sub?"

"No, but I saw him yelling at some girls last year during lunch, and they weren't even doing anything. He's really mean. I don't want him yelling at you like that, Danny."

For a second I thought she might cry, but then it passed. "Don't worry, Jess. He doesn't bother me." I thought I sounded convincing, but the truth was he did scare me a little. Thankfully, Jess changed the subject.

"I heard some boys talking about baseball tryouts tomorrow," she said.

"Yep. Tomorrow at eleven."

"Do you think you're gonna make it?"

"I don't know, Jess. We'll see." With school over for the day, the shock of losing Ms. Becker was starting to fade, and that anxious feeling was returning.

"Are you nervous?"

"Yeah, I guess I am a little nervous. Can we just not talk about it?"

"Sure." She grabbed my hand and held it. It was something she still did once in a while, but not like when she was younger.

We walked up Griffen Avenue past Our Lady of Sacred Heart Church and eventually crossed over Main Street. Adam once told us Main Street was the halfway point between the school and our house. I'd always thought it was quite a bit closer to the school, but I think he was just trying to give us a landmark. As we walked, I turned to the right and looked down a side street toward Valley View Golf Course. The tenth fairway was visible through a ten-foot chain link fence. Mark had taken me there once the previous summer. It was my first time ever playing golf, and I wasn't very good at it. When we reached Marcell Street a few minutes later, I looked onto the golf course again and saw a small group of men in the distance.

"What are those guys doing?" Jess asked. "Are they golfing?"

"I don't think so. I think they're just workers, trying to get things ready for the season. Maybe one of them is Billy." Billy was one of Adam's best friends, and Jess liked him because he always teased her. He called her Quarter-Pint instead of Half-Pint after the Laura Ingalls character on *Little House on the Prairie*. It was Jess's favorite show and one of mine, too, although I wasn't about to share that with Billy.

Jess's eyes lit up. "Billy works there?"

"Yeah, Adam said he got a job mowing greens on the weekends."

"Oh, cool."

We turned left onto Marcell Street and headed up the hill toward our house, a white two-story on the right-hand side. It was the fourth one up and probably the smallest house on the street.

Jess turned to me. "Yanks start next month," she said, smiling.

I smiled back at her. I could tell she was proud of herself. She'd remembered the season was starting soon and had brought it up to me first. Adam and I had been watching the Yankees together for a couple years, but Jess had just started showing an interest the previous fall. "First game's April 8th. We play the Texas Rangers." Somewhere along the line, Adam and I had started saying *we*, like we were actual members of the team.

"Think Thurman's gonna have a good year?"

"Of course. Why wouldn't he?" Thurman Munson was my favorite player, and I think he was Jess's, too.

"I hope he does."

We reached our front steps, and I saw our red truck in the driveway, which meant Mom was home. She usually didn't get home for another ten or fifteen minutes. I figured she must have gotten out early.

"Mom's home!" Jess yelled, and took off running.

She bounded up the hill, climbed the front steps, and disappeared into the house. I took the same path, walking instead of running, and followed her through the front door and into the living room. Mom and Adam were sitting beside one another on the couch. Mom was still hugging Jess, but as soon as she looked at me, I knew something was wrong. It should have dawned on me what it was, but it didn't.

"Jess, go on upstairs for a little while," Mom said. "I need to talk to your brother."

Jess wasn't one to question a direct command from Mom or any other adult. She grabbed her book bag and ran up the stairs toward her room. Mom looked at Adam, and he stood up and walked toward me. He smiled and slapped me lightly on the back before following Jess up the stairs.

Normally, he greeted me with "Hey, loser" or some similar term of endearment. I already suspected something bad was coming, but his greeting confirmed it. I looked again at Mom's solemn face. I thought something must have happened to our dad, but then it hit me. *Ms. Becker.*

"Come sit down, honey," she said.

"It's Ms. Becker, isn't it?"

Mom nodded. "She was brought into the hospital last night."

"Mr. Holt told us she broke her leg."

Mom nodded again. I can still see the look on her face — equal parts dread and sympathy. "She took a turn for the worse late last night, honey. She was in pretty rough shape when they brought her in because the car hit the passenger side where she was sitting. But during the night she had a heart attack. She's in a coma now."

I could feel the tears coming, and Mom must have sensed it, too, because she put her arm around me. "Is she gonna die?"

"I don't know, honey. I really don't."

I got that same feeling I had when Mr. Holt said we'd play Friday Kickball, although it wasn't quite as strong. I could tell Mom was trying to protect me, but it didn't change the fact she was lying. I could see it in her face. She didn't think Ms. Becker was going to make it. If it had been Mark telling me, or even Adam, I might have held onto some hope, but it was our mom and she was a nurse. If anyone knew who was going to make it and who wasn't, it was her. She saw I was about to lose it, so she put her other arm around me and pulled me to her chest. We sat on the couch in the exact same spot we'd sit just a year and a half later when Thurman Munson died in a horrible plane crash. And just like she did then, she held me close while I cried.

5

Later that evening I heard a light knock on the bedroom door and opened my eyes. I stared up at the bottom side of the top bunk, realizing I must have dozed off. The top bunk was mine and the bottom was Adam's, but he didn't care if I laid on his bed. I lifted myself to an elbow and watched the door creak open. Mark pushed his head into the room, smiled, and then stepped all the way inside.

"Hey, Danny," he said, "mind if I come in for a minute?"

"Sure." I was feeling groggy, but I wanted to wake up. I could tell by the light coming through the window I hadn't been sleeping long. I sat up and swung my legs over the side of the bed. I noticed Adam wasn't there and wondered if he'd gone over to his girlfriend's house. That particular spring, it seemed like he was there more than he was home.

"I heard about your teacher," Mark said. "I'm really sorry."

Mark made it sound like Ms. Becker was already dead. In my daze I wondered if maybe that was true. Maybe it had happened when I was sleeping, and Mark had heard the news from my mother. "Thanks, Mark," I said, praying I was wrong.

Mark walked over to the bed. I thought he might sit next to me, but he stopped a couple feet away. He reached his arm out and grabbed the bunk-post. He was just over six feet tall and had a muscular build. Adam said he was "built like a brick shit house." According to Mom, Mark was an accountant and worked a lot of hours, but she said he still made time to work out almost every day. He was still wearing a suit, so I assumed he must have come right from work.

"Danny, I guess you're old enough to know that sometimes bad things happen to good people for no reason at all."

Even half-awake, his comment rubbed me the wrong way. I felt like saying, *I know, Mark. My dad left when I was three-years-old, remember?* I knew he was only trying to make me feel better, but it still bugged me. I was glad Adam wasn't there because he probably would have said it or something close to it. Adam was a lot older than me and Jess, and he hadn't had a father for a long time. I think he resented it whenever Mark tried to act like one. "I know, Mark. I just really liked Ms. Becker. She's the best teacher I ever had."

"I met her at the parent conference last month. She's a nice lady. Maybe God has a miracle in his plans. It wouldn't be the first time."

That was another reason Mark got under Adam's skin. He was always mentioning God. I didn't care, but I think Adam thought he was trying to push religion onto him. I think Mark thought Adam didn't believe in God even though he did back then. Adam liked to keep certain things to himself, and his religious beliefs were one of them. "I hope so," I said.

"Do you want to pray together?"

"No thanks. I'll pray tonight when I go to bed."

"Okay, I will, too." Mark bent over and slapped my leg and then looked at me with a big smile on his face. "Baseball tryouts tomorrow. Are you getting excited?"

That same nervous feeling returned, but right then it made me feel nauseous. "Sort of. I'm just not sure I'm ready. I haven't played that much."

"Yeah, sorry I haven't been around lately. I'd go out with you right now, but I promised a guy from work that I'd help him move. His wife kicked him out." He smiled at me like we'd both been through the experience. "Don't worry, you'll do fine. I don't think *anyone's* been playing much, and the coaches know that. Just go out and throw hard and take good swings. That's what they're looking for anyway. Trust me. I used to be a coach."

I remembered Mom telling me Mark had a son from his first marriage. She said he was in law school somewhere. "Okay, I will." I looked back at the window and saw the sun was still shining. I wondered if Adam would play catch with me. Maybe we could even go down to the school for some batting practice.

"Okay, Danny, if you ever want to talk about Ms. Becker, or anything else, just let me know. Okay?"

"Okay, thanks, Mark. I will."

He ruffled my hair and then left the room without looking back. I heard him say goodbye to our mom, and then a minute later I heard him start his car and drive away. I got up and walked to the top of the stairs. "Mom, is Adam down there?"

"No, he went to Julia's, honey. How are you feeling?"

I guess there won't be any practicing tonight. "I'm fine, Mom." I walked back toward my room before she could say anything else.

I was still awake when Adam got home that night. It was just after midnight. I couldn't sleep because of the nap I'd taken earlier, but I was also worried about tryouts. While my subconscious had probably been kicking it around for a couple weeks, I chose that night to face the realization I didn't really want to play in the Majors. The truth was I didn't think I was ready. For starters, I had no desire to step into the batter's box against Zach Hardy. The thought of getting pegged by one of his fastballs was enough to give me nightmares. And he wasn't the only one. There was a kid named Will Russo who threw it almost as hard and a few others who weren't far behind him. There was no one pitching in the Minors who even resembled those guys. On top of all that, I wasn't sure I was good enough. The last thing I wanted was to make a Majors team only to embarrass myself on the field. There were quite a few kids in my school who played baseball that season. Jason Billings was just one of them. He would've had no problems making fun of me if I played poorly, and he *liked* me. There were a couple other kids who would have loved to make my life a living hell if I wasn't able to hack it in the big leagues.

As I laid there in the dark, I began leaning even more heavily toward staying in the Minors. My reasoning went something like this: If I decided to stay put, I wouldn't have to try out at all. I'd just be placed on a team — maybe even The Elks Club again. There were some obvious benefits to that scenario. For one, I would be a stud or certainly one of the better players out there. Second (and this one was probably the stronger of the two), by the time the following season rolled around, Zach Hardy and Will Russo would be long gone. They'd be in Teener League, or the pros, or who the hell knew where. The point is they wouldn't be in the Everton Little League anymore.

I think I had just about closed the door on the one-sided debate when I heard Adam enter the house. A few minutes later he walked into our room. Because our house only had three bedrooms, and because Jess was a girl and needed her own room, Adam and I had to share. For the previous eight months or so (ever since Adam had met Julia) the only time he was in our room was when he slept, so it was almost like having my own bedroom anyway.

Adam noticed right away I was awake. "Hey, man, you better get to sleep," he said. "You have tryouts tomorrow, remember?"

I hesitated, knowing he wouldn't approve of my recent decision. Finally, I decided to just come out with it. "I don't think I'm trying out."

"What do you mean you're not trying out?" He sounded confused rather than angry, so I knew he wasn't fully grasping the situation.

"I think I'm gonna stay down in the Minors for another year. I don't think I'm good enough to play in the Majors yet."

"You're fucking kidding me, right?"

Now he's up to speed. "There's a ton of good players in the Majors, Adam."

"Yeah, I realize that. Who do you think you're talking to? I played baseball, remember?"

Adam had just turned seventeen, and I knew he'd played Little League when he was younger. And as a general rule, if Adam participated in something, it meant he knew everything there was to know about it, whether that was true or not. I vaguely remembered him playing at Barnell Field, but I couldn't have told you which team he was on.

"I just don't wanna get made fun of at school if I don't do good," I said.

Adam shook his head and walked toward his desk. For a second it looked like he might just drop it, but I knew better. I knew he felt bad for me because of what had happened to Ms. Becker, but there was no way he was going to let that slide. He walked back to the top bunk and looked me in the eye. It was dark in the room, but there was enough moonlight coming in to see each other.

"You think they'll make fun of you for not doing good?" he said. "Wait until you're the only eleven-year-old in the Minors." I was about to remind him I was only ten, but he charged on. "I know you had a shitty day, but let me tell you something, bro. Next year at the draft, nobody's gonna want an eleven-year-old coming up from the Minors. When the coaches see a big fat eleven next to your name, they're gonna wonder why you didn't get drafted *last* year, like all the other *good* ten-year-olds. You wanna know what else they'll be thinking? That they'll only have two years to work with you instead of three." I didn't like where this was going, but he had a point. "So, unless you light it up next year at tryouts, which is hard to do because you're nervous, right?" I nodded and he leaned in for the kill. "Unless you light it up, you'll probably get left in the Minors again. And I'll tell you straight up. You don't wanna be the only eleven-year-old at your school in the Minors. They'll crucify you." He said the last part like he had firsthand experience, and I knew which side of the equation he'd been on. Adam was never a victim. "Besides, there's no fucking way my little brother is only gonna play one year in the Majors."

He made it sound like my well-being was his chief concern — as if there was no way he could stand by quietly while I experienced just a single year "in the big leagues." Of course, what he really meant, and I think I even knew it at the time, was that there was no way he was going to endure the embarrassment of his little brother playing only one year in the Majors. Not after the legacy he left behind in the Everton Little League.

Adam continued on. "So, you're gonna try out tomorrow, right?" He stood there, staring at me.

I thought about it, but I didn't have to think long. Adam could be very persuasive when he wanted to be, and he'd touched on some things I hadn't thought of before. I wasn't sure *how* he knew the inner thought processes of the coaching establishment, but apparently he did. Bottom line, I was more scared of being the only eleven-year-old in the Minors than I was of facing Zach Hardy. It's funny how quickly viewpoints can change when you're presented with something worse. "Yeah, I think you're right, Adam. I'll try out."

Adam smiled and patted my leg. "Good. We'll practice in the morning. Now get to sleep."

6

Wednesday Evening

When I rolled into Tremon, it was a little after 7:00 pm. After Adam fell asleep, I spoke with Jen in the kitchen. She didn't try to convince me to stay because she'd known Adam's plan all along. She did offer to put me up in a hotel for the night, but I told her I had to get back anyway. There were issues at work, and I knew my boss, Carolyn, would be happy to have me back early.

I decided to stop by Saxon Field, hoping to catch the end of Connor's baseball game. I pulled into a spot and texted Jen. *I made it Jen. How are things?* For some reason I didn't want to ask *How is he?* It was as if simply asking the question could somehow affect the outcome.

Jen texted back right away. *Good, glad ur back. He's been sleeping, woke up once since u left. He was so happy u came down. Me 2. I'll text u later tonight. Luv u, Jen.*

I texted back. *OK, love you too.*

I was about to get out of my car when I saw Laura and Connor walking toward me. Connor had his head down, doing the *We just lost shuffle.* Some kids were literally just happy to be there. Wins and losses or even how they performed in the game were secondary considerations. Connor was the exact opposite. It didn't matter what sport he was playing. If he lost, he wore it all over his body like the team uniform. Considering games usually lasted until close to 7:30, I figured we'd been *mercied,* which meant we were down by at least twelve runs after four innings of play, so the game was stopped. The idea behind The Mercy Rule is the team that's losing isn't going to come back from that kind of deficit, so it's cruel to subject them to further punishment. Of course, the other consideration is the games could go on forever because one or both teams can't make an out. And no one wants to endure that...especially the adults.

I turned to Laura. She looked fantastic. She had always been an attractive woman, but in the last couple months, she'd elevated her game. She'd been working out, so she'd lost weight and everything had firmed up. I know I said catching her with McBride had killed my desire for her, but there were still moments I wanted her as much as ever. And those moments seemed to be growing in both intensity and frequency as the days without having sex stretched on. This particular moment was probably the worst one yet. If she had told Connor to go back to the bleachers to watch the next game and then climbed into the back of my Saturn, there is no way I could have stopped myself from following. I would have had sex with her right there in the parking lot, tinted windows or not. If it wasn't for that massive wall between us—the one that stood about six-foot-five and spent its days teaching kids how to be nice to one another—I would have begged her for a late-night rendezvous.

I climbed out of the SUV and walked around to the front. I leaned against the headlight, the heat of the engine pressing against my back. The smell of hot metal and burning oil filled the air.

As they approached, Connor lifted his head and smiled. "Hi, Dad," he said. His front teeth had come all the way down, but there were still a few gaps that wouldn't be there next spring.

"Hey, bud," I said, smiling back. He walked up to me and gave me a quick hug. Normally, he wouldn't do something like that with other people around, especially his peers, but he knew I'd been to see my brother. Connor was only ten, but he had a strong sense for those kinds of things. My mom used to say the same thing about me. "How'd the game go?"

"We got killed. 13-1."

"That's okay. There'll be other games."

"I know."

"How'd you do?"

"I struck out once and I got a single."

"Nice!" Connor had been slumping badly. I think it had been three games since his last hit, maybe four. "Who'd you get it off?"

"Sean Rice."

"That's awesome. If you can hit him, you can hit anybody."

"Then I stole second and scored when the right fielder dropped the ball."

"You scored the only run?"

"Yeah." I gave him a fist bump. Normally, it was all about the team, but he'd been struggling so badly we had to grab onto anything we could. Connor looked up at me. "Uncle Adam isn't doing so good, huh, Dad?"

"No, he's not, buddy." It's not like he saw Adam all the time, but over the last couple years, they bonded over baseball and the Yankees. I'd been trying to prepare him over the last few months, but I wasn't sure how he'd handle it when the day finally came.

"I'm sorry, Dad."

"I know you are, bud."

"I'm not gonna see him again, am I?"

I'd already told him he probably wouldn't, but the simple honesty of his question hurt. "No, probably not, Connor."

"This sucks, Dad. I love Uncle Adam."

I could hear his voice beginning to crack, and I was engulfed by a massive wave of guilt. Why hadn't I taken him to see his uncle more often? My rational side knew that would have only made things harder, but that knowledge wasn't making me feel any better right now. "I know, Connor. It does suck." I could see he needed to talk about it, but I didn't want to do it here. In fact, I wanted to leave before any of our other coaches saw me. There was one in particular who liked to talk about the game afterward, and since I wasn't here for it, I'd be his prime target. There was no way I was doing that tonight. "Connor, why don't you ride home with me? We'll get an ice cream, and then I'll drop you off."

We both looked at Laura for approval.

"That's fine," Laura said, "but remember, Connor, you have to finish your homework, so not too late."

"I'll get him home quick."

Connor threw his bag in the back seat and then hopped into the Saturn. I watched him close the door and then I turned to Laura.

"How is he?" Laura asked.

It's funny. A few seconds ago I was dreaming about having sex with her in the back of my SUV, but after hearing her voice, I just wanted to get away from her as fast as possible. "Not too good. I was able to see him and we talked, but I don't think he'll make it too much longer. Maybe another couple days."

"I'm sorry, Dan. I really am."

I knew it was genuine, but her words just didn't mean anything anymore. "Yeah, it sucks."

"How's Jen handling it?"

"You know Jen. She's strong."

Jen and Laura had become closer over the last two years. Laura had asked to go down with me when things first started getting bad. I told her no. What right did she have to be a part of this? She'd forfeited all that when she decided to get comfortable with our son's guidance counselor. I knew it was petty, and I suspected I'd regret it someday, but right then I didn't. Right then it felt good.

"Yeah, she is strong," Laura said. I could tell by her voice she was sensing my anger. She'd seen and heard enough of it over the last several months to become almost clairvoyant. "Okay, let me know if there's anything I can do."

"I will." *My God, get me out of here.*

She turned around and headed back toward her car. I got in the Saturn and drove off before anyone else spotted me. I took Connor to an ice cream shop down the street. There were a lot of people sitting outside but only a couple waiting at the counter. Connor ordered a medium cookie dough in a bowl, and I got a small chocolate on a cone. In the old days, Laura would have told me I was boring. It was strange—even when she wasn't around, I was still hearing her words in my head. Just to save some time, Connor and I decided to eat the ice cream on the way home. We talked about the game, but other than his single, there weren't many highlights. As we neared our house, he started asking questions about Adam. I did the best I could answering them, but it wasn't easy. Talking to Connor about it made it more real somehow. Not that it wasn't real when I saw him lying in the bed, but everything took on a deeper dimension with Connor. Again, I felt tremendous guilt for not taking him to see his uncle more often.

I pulled up to the side of what used to be our house and kissed Connor on the forehead. He got out and walked toward the back door. When he reached the top step, he turned and waved before entering the house. I glanced back toward the pine trees where I saw McBride's car parked on that horrible night. Not for the first time, or even the fiftieth, I thought about meeting him on curriculum night. The bitch of it was I liked him. I remember thinking we had a lot in common. He actually reminded me of my mom's old boyfriend, Mark. He had that same inner confidence. He was a decade younger than me, but I felt like we might have been pretty good friends under different circumstances. Hell, at the time, I thought maybe we would *still* become friends. We were both into sports, both liked the Yankees and Giants, and both still played pick-up basketball. In truth, I'd stopped playing a few years earlier, but I remember saying, "I still lace 'em up once in a while." It seemed like a white-enough lie, and Laura let it slide without correcting me, although she did shoot me a quick glance. Looking back, I think it was one of the last moments we had like that, at least the last one I can remember. The kind of moments you see in a solid marriage when you're trying to impress someone you just met (or maybe you just don't want them to know the full truth about something) and your spouse covers for you. Maybe deep down they'd love to call you on your bullshit and embarrass the hell out of you, but they don't. Somewhere inside, there's a little voice whispering *We're a team*. I think when that voice goes silent, you know you're in trouble. Sometimes you're in trouble even when it doesn't.

What I remember most about that night was Laura's comment on the way home. I was rambling on about what a great guy he was while Laura stared absently out the window.

"I don't know," she said, "he seemed pretty cocky to me."

You might think she was trying to throw me off because she found him attractive, and you might even be right, but I don't think so. I'm pretty sure she didn't like him, which summons the question decent guys have been asking themselves since the beginning of time. If women think these guys are such jerks, why do so many end up sleeping with them?

In the weeks and months that followed, I fantasized about calling the school. I knew I could get him fired or at least transferred. Last time I checked, breaking up families wasn't part of the school curriculum. Maybe I'd just have a placard made up for the main office. *Here at Jackson Hills Elementary, we focus not only on the individual student but also the parents. Need to find a tutor? We can help with that. Horny wife looking for some action on the side? We can help with that, too. In fact, we have just the guy. At six-five, you might say he's a tall drink of water, and trust me when I tell you, he aims to please.* I came a lot closer to doing something like that than I care to admit, but I would've had to tell the school administrators what I saw, and that wasn't going to happen. Even if they were the finest people on the planet, the story would have gotten out eventually. Talking about scandalous secrets is what people do best, even when they know it's going to be damaging — maybe especially when they know it's going to be damaging. Ultimately, I had to protect my son, which meant I had to leave it alone.

The other big reason I didn't push for McBride's dismissal was even closer to home. Simply put, I was embarrassed. I didn't want the world knowing my wife had cheated on me. I don't know if women view affairs in the same way, but I think I can speak for a lot of men when I say good old-fashioned embarrassment is right up there with the worst of it. Obviously, I wasn't satisfying my wife. Why else would she cheat? Rationally, I know there are plenty of reasons why men and women stray, and a lot of times it doesn't have much to do with what the spouse did or didn't do. But that's a hard thing to tell yourself when you're at the grocery store or the movies, and you feel the eyes upon you like you're some sort of circus sideshow.

Over time, I came to view some of these recurring thoughts as old friends. It seemed appropriate since many of them visited me on a daily basis, sometimes even several times a day. The truth was I spent more time with them than anyone else. As I turned off my old street, I began conversing with the one I considered to be my oldest and dearest. In fact, she'd been with me from the very first moments. *I'll never look at my wife in the same way again.* Of course, there was the visual of the act itself, burned into my consciousness for eternity, but that was only a part of it. The bigger and more meaningful part was that I would never be able to look at Laura and not think on some level that she had betrayed me and Connor. This wasn't some unplanned, drunken hookup. Not that that would have been okay, but it does happen. We tell ourselves it can't or won't happen with us or to us, but the truth is it can and it does. People get caught in unexpected situations all the time and do things they normally wouldn't. I think I might have been able to get over something like that. At least I would have stood a fighting chance.

When I came to terms with that realization, I knew my marriage was over. I told Laura I needed some time apart to sort things out, but I'd already done all the sorting I needed. What Laura and I had together was gone, and it wasn't coming back, no matter how many sessions we had with Eileen. I knew once I made our break official, Laura would tell our friends it had been leaking away for years. Of course, I knew she was right.

I think that bothered me as much as anything.

7

It was after 8:00 by the time I reached my apartment. One of the perks of living above the bike shop (perhaps the only one) was that I got to use the parking lot. I pulled into the lot and turned off the engine. I sat there for a few moments, realizing I was totally spent. Finally, I summoned the strength to get out of the vehicle. I'd already been inside the apartment several times, including a few hours last night, but climbing the steps in the dark, it felt like the first time. I unlocked the door and walked into the kitchen where several boxes were scattered about the floor. I'd dropped them off last night but didn't have time to unpack them. Sitting atop the kitchen table was the brand new coffee maker I'd bought at Target. I had a feeling I'd need it in full working order just to get out the door tomorrow. I remembered throwing some coffee grounds and a couple filters into a Ziploc bag, but I had no idea which box I'd put it in.

I turned on the light and surveyed my new kitchen. On one side of the room was a gas stove, a double sink, and a Whirlpool dishwasher. On the other was the refrigerator and the entranceway into the living room. Everything in the room, including all the appliances and the wooden kitchen table, was some shade of white except for the tiled floor, which was an odd mixture of gray and blue. According to my landlord, he'd put the floor in less than a year ago.

I placed my overnight bag on the kitchen table and sat in a chair. I stared at the bag, realizing I hadn't even opened it since packing it around 5:30 this morning. *The best-laid plans,* I thought. The comparison, clumsy as it was, was staring me in the face. While I'd never mapped out the exact stages of my life, as far as where I expected to be by what age, I definitely wasn't supposed to be here. By forty-nine, I thought I'd either own my own business or be an executive at a successful, growing company. I wasn't supposed to be a customer service rep at a struggling printed circuit board factory. Nor was I supposed to be living alone in a three-room apartment over a bike shop while my wife and son lived in our home a mile away.

The familiar anger began building inside, but I thought of Connor and it dampened immediately. It was a trick Eileen taught me. She reminded me to focus on Connor whenever my thoughts began spiraling. He was the most important thing in my life. He was what mattered. I knew he loved his mother and always would. Someday he'd learn the truth about what happened, but right now he just thought his parents were going through a rough patch and needed some time apart. When he did finally learn the truth, ideally as an adult, and saw how I handled it, he would respect me all the more for it. That was my hope anyway.

I picked up the box holding the new coffee maker and began removing the tape when my cell phone vibrated. I checked the incoming number, fully expecting it to be Jen. As I stared at the phone, a clear thought formed in my mind. I was suddenly sure Jen had just gone in to check on Adam and discovered he'd died. I could see his gray, lifeless face, his eyes staring right through me. As the vision faded, I saw it was Laura's number. *Please be Connor,* I thought. "Hello?"

"Hi, Dad."

Over the phone, his voice sounded eerily like Laura's. "Hey, bud, what'd you forget?"

"Nothing, Dad. I guess I'm just worried about you."

"I'm fine, bud."

"I guess with Uncle Adam dying and then you moving into an apartment...I just want you here, Dad."

I could tell he was on the verge of tears. "I know, Connor. Mom and I just need some time apart." It hurt telling the lie, but I couldn't tell him his parents were never getting back together. Not right now.

"Like a couple weeks, Dad?"

"Maybe, bud. I'm not sure." *That bitch.* I hoped she could hear every word he was saying. I hoped it was killing her like it was killing me. I don't think I ever hated her more than I did at that moment. Even when I was standing outside our bedroom that awful night. I had to get off the phone. If I didn't, I was going to come apart. "How about you stay over here with me tomorrow night?"

"Really, Dad?"

I wasn't planning on letting him stay over right away, but it was the only thing I could think of. "Absolutely."

"That'd be awesome, Dad."

"I'll call you after work tomorrow, okay?"

"Okay, love you, Dad."

"Love you, too, Connor."

I walked back into my new kitchen, took several deep breaths (another trick Eileen taught me) and stared at the boxes on the floor. One of them was hiding a bottle of gin. I was exhausted, but I wanted a drink. I walked over to the closest one and opened the top. As I searched through the box, the thought of ordering a pizza danced in my head and was gone. I was too tired to wait for delivery. Suddenly, finding the gin and making a drink seemed like too daunting a task, as well.

I turned off the kitchen light and walked into the living room where I'd placed a single mattress along with a pillow and a comforter. Dusk was taking its slow, awkward turn toward dark, but I could still make out the flat-screen television sitting in the corner. As I glanced around the room for the remote, I had a brief vision of falling asleep to the Yankee game. *Should be the fifth or sixth inning by now,* I thought. I slid out of my jeans and sat on the mattress, realizing I wasn't getting up again, even for the Yankees. I laid back and pulled the comforter over me. *Forty-nine-years-old and I'm sleeping on the God damn floor.* I started thinking about Adam again but turned my thoughts to Connor and his base hit off Sean Rice. I smiled as I replayed Connor's expression in my mind. Before it could slip entirely from my face, I was asleep.

The vibration of my cell phone startled me awake. I groped around in the dark until I found it in the pocket of my jeans. It was Jen. The digital clock read 10:23. For the second time today, I was all but certain my brother had died. I raised the phone to my ear. "Hello?"

"Hey, little bro," Adam said, his voice sounding stronger than earlier.

Relief washed over me. "Hey, Adam."

"Sorry to wake you…I just don't know how many more times I'm going to be able to talk to you."

It wasn't the first time Adam had said that, but this time it hit me especially hard. "It's no problem, Adam. Call me whenever the hell you want." I thought I heard him chuckle.

"Thanks for coming down here today. I really appreciate you doing that."

"Of course. I'll come down again tomorrow if you need me."

"No, don't worry about that." Adam paused for a minute and I waited. I thought he was just gathering his strength, but when he spoke again, I realized he'd been debating whether to continue at all. "Listen, Danny, I was going to bring this up when you were down here, but I guess I just couldn't do it. When you don't talk about something for so long, it becomes harder and harder. You know what I mean?"

Suddenly, I could smell aftershave. I knew what was coming next. What *had* to be coming next. "I do, Adam."

"You know that thing that happened…that thing when we were younger?"

Jesus. Knowing something is coming and actually hearing it raised from the dead are two different things. I don't know how I kept my voice steady. "Yeah, I know, Adam."

"Well, I just wanted to say I'm sorry about all that. You were just a kid, and I never let you talk about it. That wasn't right. I should've—"

Adam started to cry, and a second later I was crying, too. "Adam, stop it. We were *both* kids." Right then the lie popped into my head, and I knew I had to say it. "And don't worry. I never wanted to talk about it anyway."

"You saved my life, Danny. You know that, don't you?"

I think I did know that even though I didn't think about it that way. Over the last thirty-nine years, I tried not to think about it at all.

"I love you, Danny."

"I love you, too, Adam."

"I have to go, and you need to get back to sleep. We'll talk tomorrow."

"Okay, sounds like a plan."

I hit end and set my phone down. I wish I'd kept him on longer because it was the last time we ever spoke.

Tryouts

8

The next morning I opened my eyes and squinted at the brilliant sunlight streaming through the window. I'd been dreaming about something pleasant, but it was slipping away quickly. I closed my eyes, hoping I could fall back into the dream. Then I remembered Ms. Becker's car accident. My heart sunk as my mind began running through the events of the previous day. The awful question of whether or not she would live began forming again in my mind when another memory came. *Tryouts are today!* I felt a quick pang of guilt that I was turning my thoughts from my beloved teacher to something as trivial as baseball, but the truth was I welcomed the escape.

I raised myself to an elbow, feeling like a bundle of sudden nerves. *I've overslept!* The thought jolted me fully awake and I sat upright in bed. The light in the room was much too bright. It had to be 10:00, maybe even later. I was about to slip into full-blown panic mode when I saw the clock on the desk. It was only 9:10. I took a deep breath and headed downstairs, thinking about how fast your thoughts can spiral when you're under some stress and there's no one around to stop it.

I was halfway through the living room when I saw my family sitting at the kitchen table. Mom was dressed in her nurse's uniform, so I figured she must have been asked to come in to work. Adam was wearing a pair of shorts and nothing else. They were both were reading a section of the morning paper. Adam had the Sports, and I didn't have to see it to know that. He lifted a spoonful of cereal toward his mouth as he read. Jess had her back to me, her blondish-brown hair hanging down past her shoulders. She was still in her pajamas, eating a piece of toast covered with a thin layer of grape jelly. That was another detail I didn't have to actually see to know. In those days it was all she ever ate for breakfast. It was a little unusual that three-fourths of our family would be sitting together at the kitchen table, but it was nothing short of remarkable that it was being done in near silence. As I approached, I could hear the crinkling of a shifting paper and the clinking of my brother's spoon against the ceramic bowl. The smell of sausage filled the air, but I didn't see any evidence of it on the table.

"What's going on?" I asked, stepping into the kitchen.

"Nothing, douche," my brother said, his eyes still fixed on the paper. Apparently, the grace period from Ms. Becker's accident was over. "What's going on with you?"

"Adam," Mom said, staring at him.

"What's the problem, Ann?" He held a straight face as long as he could before finally breaking down and laughing.

A year earlier, the interaction might have led to an argument, but by then Mom had mostly been letting it pass. I think it was a battle she just didn't want to fight anymore. Plus, she was a lot happier since she'd met Mark, and certain things just didn't bother her like they did before. She turned to look at me. "Good morning, sleepy head," she said. "We were just about to wake you."

"I know. I didn't mean to sleep this late."

"I'm gonna take you down to the school to warm up," Adam said, "so get something to eat. There's no way you're playing in the Minors again. Your team sucked."

Mom looked at Adam again but didn't say anything this time. If Mark had been there, he would have said something, so I was glad he wasn't. He didn't like it when Adam talked like that, mainly because our mom didn't. It would have probably led to an argument or to Adam storming off, and that isn't something I would've needed on the morning of tryouts.

"Well, I don't think that's going to happen anyway," Mom said. I walked over to the table and sat in the empty seat between Jess and Adam. At first I thought Mom was just offering some general encouragement, but she continued on. "I saw Vic yesterday and told him he better pick you if he knows what's good for him." She flashed me a little smile.

"Who's Vic?" I asked.

"He's an administrator at the hospital, and he's a friend of mine…and he coaches one of the teams."

The concept of our mom having male friends hadn't occurred to me up until that point. There was Mark, of course, but they weren't really friends. "So, he's gonna pick me on his team?"

"Well, there's no guarantee, but he said he's going to try. And like I said, he better pick you if he knows what's good for him." She flashed that same playful smile.

I felt my brain mulling over Mom's words. It was like it was working on its own again, without any input from me. It had never occurred to me a coach might pick a player for a reason other than their talent or how well they did in the tryout. This guy might pick me because he and Mom were friends and because she had asked him to. While the concept intrigued me, I had no idea I was being exposed to one of life's most important truths. I suppose it's something I should have learned earlier, but with Dad gone and

Mom working hard to support the three of us, there wasn't much time for in-depths on how the world works.

"What team does he coach?" I asked.

"Jackson and Franklin," she said. "He coaches it with his brother, Ted, and I guess one of his nephews plays on the team. You know the Baxters, right? They live over near the school."

The Baxters were a family of four boys, one older than me, one in my fifth-grade class, and two younger. I wasn't good friends with any of them, but they were nice kids. In those days it seemed like there was no middle ground. Boys were either nice or they were total jerks, and it was basically the same deal with the girls. They were either nice or nasty spoiled brats. Matt was the one in my class. I knew he played for Jackson & Franklin (J&F to all the kids in the league). He was only a few months older than me, but in baseball years, he was a full year older.

Unlike a lot of the boys I knew, Matt didn't brag about baseball or anything else. And that was a good thing because J&F won the championship the year before, and it would have been annoying to listen to. Matt did say, though, they were getting most of their team back. In 1978 there was no such thing as a redraft where a coach picks a new team every year. Once you made the Majors, you stayed on the same team for the duration of your Little League career. For a lot of kids that meant three years, and for a handful of the more skilled kids, it meant four. There were exceptions here and there — and one notable example would provide yet another of life's great lessons — but for the most part, players stayed with the same team until they moved on to Teener League. That meant J&F was going to be good again, and my chances of making the team weren't, regardless of what Vic was telling my mother. The math wasn't exactly complicated. If they were getting most of their players back, there wouldn't be many picks available. If I was going to make the Majors, it probably wouldn't be on J&F. On top of that, the talk on the playground — especially by those of us still in the Minors — was that there were quite a few good ten-year-olds trying out that year.

I turned to Adam. "Okay, when do you wanna go?"

"I'm ready right now," he said, getting up from the table. He placed his dish in the sink and turned back to me. "And we better hurry up," he said. "We don't have much time."

9

We dropped Mom off at the hospital before heading back to the elementary school where we spent the next hour warming up. The playground had a rudimentary baseball field, consisting of a weather-worn pitching mound, a backstop, and oval-shaped dirt patches for bases. Jess came along and shagged fly balls to help us save time. Normally, the three of us would have found some way to turn the outing into a huge fight, but both Adam and Jess knew how important that day was to me. When we dropped Jess off at her friend's house, it was 10:44 and we made it to Barnell Field by 10:53. That was one of the great things about living in Everton. You could get just about anywhere by car in ten minutes or less.

As we drove into the parking lot, there were roughly thirty kids standing near the third base bleachers. I scanned their faces and recognized most of them as ten-year-olds that had played with me in the Minors. I saw Jason Billings standing near the back of the group. He was off to the side, looking out onto the field. I followed his gaze and saw a handful of men scrambling to get the field ready. If the weather was bad, which it typically was in March, they held the tryouts at a nearby school gymnasium. But since it had been so nice, they decided to hold them at Barnell Field.

I grabbed my bat and glove and opened the door of the truck. I was about to climb out when Adam grabbed my wrist. "You're gonna do great, man," he said. "I'll be watching from the stands." He gave me a quick nod and a smile.

Adam spent a lot of time torturing me, but when it really mattered, when it was something I truly cared about, he was right there for me. "Okay, thanks," I said, and closed the door.

I immediately noticed the smell of fresh-cut grass in the air. I assumed someone had mowed the field, undoubtedly for the first time that spring. It had been chilly when I was practicing with Adam at the school, but the sun had come out, and it was growing warm. Even though it was only March, it almost felt a little like summer.

As I approached, I saw that most of the kids were standing around motionless, looking like mannequins with their gloves tucked under their arms. A few kids had slipped their glove onto the barrel of their bat, so they could rest everything on their shoulder. In those days no one had their own helmet or equipment bag. I nodded to a kid who'd suffered through the previous season with me on The Elks Club, but I wasn't sure of his name. I took my place at the back of the huddled mass, trying to appear relaxed. Inside, I was feeling anything but. Mom told me I'd probably have some butterflies, but she didn't say anything about needing to throw up. Just then a friendly male voice called out from the infield.

"Hey guys, come out onto the field. We'll have you play catch for a few minutes before we get started. Leave your bats along the fence in the dugout."

I recognized him from my season in the Minors. He was a coach for one of the other teams. I remembered him because he talked to his players a lot during the game and seemed like he actually wanted to be there. I noticed he was wearing a Yankee shirt with the number fifteen on it. *Thurman Munson's number.* After that, he became Thurman in my head.

We shuffled single file through the gate leading into the third base dugout and then through a second gate and onto the field. It wasn't my first time on Barnell Field but close to it. I think we'd played one or two games there the previous season. Unlike the Minor League field across the street, which didn't have an outfield fence or even real dugouts, this felt like an actual baseball field. The two-story clubhouse was painted a dark green, as was the fence that protected it. The two covered dugouts — painted the same dark shade of green — loomed over the home plate area like the jaws of an enormous crocodile. It created a brooding, claustrophobic atmosphere that made you feel like you were stepping into a gladiator cage whenever you walked to home plate. An elevated fence continued past the dugouts and bleachers before giving way to a standard waist-high fence that extended down the baselines and around the outfield. Wooden signs promoting local businesses hung on the outfield fence. I saw signs for Everton Plumbing, Mason's Auto, Stapleton Athletics, and Maine's Formalwear.

"Pair up with someone and head out to the outfield to play catch," Thurman said, smiling. "Grab a ball from the bucket there."

I looked around for Jason, but he was already heading out with someone else. I ended up getting paired up with a skinny kid I didn't know. We headed out to right field where there weren't as many kids.

"Don't get too far apart yet," Thurman yelled. "You're just warming up your arms."

I turned back and saw that he'd returned to the pitcher's mound where another guy was feeding baseballs into the pitching machine. There was also a third man standing off to the side of the mound, looking at a clipboard. I glanced into the stands on the first base side and saw a handful of men sitting in the bleachers. I figured they had to be the Major League coaches.

A few minutes later, the coach I'd seen with the clipboard told us to move a little further apart, and shortly after that he yelled, "Bring it in." This guy was shorter and stockier than Thurman. He was wearing a white tank top, so naturally he became Tank Top in my head. His dark brown hair was slicked back and his face sported a neatly trimmed goatee. I'd never seen him before that day, but I could already tell he wasn't very friendly. I got the feeling it was him (and not Thurman) who was in charge of the tryout. The butterflies, which had faded to a distant flutter, mounted a serious comeback. As we walked in from the outfield, Tank Top yelled, "Run it in!" He said it in a pissed-off voice that was probably closer to a scream than a yell. I saw a couple of the other coaches look up in surprise, including Thurman, but no one said anything.

We gathered around third base while Tank Top ran through what we could expect for the next hour or so. We'd start out fielding ground balls with stations at short, second, and first. After our turn, we'd rotate to the back of the next line and so on. Tank Top might not have been the friendliest guy in the world, but he was pretty good at explaining things. I looked toward home plate and saw Thurman standing near the bucket of baseballs. He was holding a bat in one hand and a baseball in the other, and as we'd just been told, his job was to hit us ground balls.

"Okay, let's spread out to all three positions," Tank Top said. "It doesn't matter where you go. You're going to play 'em all." A few kids ran toward first and second, but most acted like they weren't sure what to do. I could tell Tank Top was growing more and more agitated. He began pointing here and there, his voice barking out orders in frustration. By that point I was already standing at shortstop along with a handful of other kids. He looked right at me and said the four words most of us didn't want to hear. "You can go first."

Shit. This is it! Everything thus far had been strictly for fun. My quest to get out of the Minors was about to start for real. It never occurred to me the coaches had already been watching us play catch. I walked forward to where I thought the shortstop was supposed to stand. I noticed the other kids, standing right beside me just a second earlier, were now backpedaling hard—terrified there might be some horrible mix up and they'd be thrust into the opening slot.

As Tank Top was busy organizing the groups at second and first, I looked over at the first base bleachers. I noticed a few more coaches had climbed up, joining the others. There were now about fifteen men sitting there, most holding notebooks. I didn't see any women. I looked back toward the other bleachers and saw the exact opposite—all moms, no dads. When it came to sports in the 1970s, especially for something as nerve-wracking as baseball tryouts, the sexes didn't often mix. I scanned the fence for Adam and found him standing near a utility pole about thirty feet away from the bleachers. He nodded at me and gave me the thumbs up.

Just as I was turning back toward Thurman, Tank Top yelled, "Your mother can't help you now!" He was still using that same miserable tone. I realized with mounting embarrassment he was talking to me. A couple kids, probably the ones destined to be future Tank Tops, laughed at the comment, but most didn't say anything. I think they realized it could have just as easily been them. I had the urge to defend myself, to tell him I was just looking for my brother while he was busy acting like an asshole, but instead I just pretended I didn't hear him.

I turned toward home plate and saw Thurman staring at Tank Top, but he didn't seem to notice. Finally, Thurman looked back at me. "Okay, back up a little," he said. I took a couple steps back and dropped into fielding position. "Okay, here we go. Play's at first."

My heart was suddenly hammering away in my chest. Thurman held the bat up in his right hand and flipped the ball into the air with his left. Both hands reunited on the bat handle and he swung. As the ball bounded toward me, I realized it was closing the gap in record time. The only good news, if it could be called that, was that he hit it right at me. I wouldn't have had the nerve to get in front of it otherwise. The ball approached and I bent down. I knew I was supposed to lower my glove to the dirt and then use my body to block any bad hops, but the possibility of the ball bouncing up and taking out my front teeth was too much to take. The ball hit the infield dirt and somehow stayed down—defying all known laws of physics—and skidded under my glove before traveling into left field.

There are certain people you can always count on to make a situation worse, and Tank Top was one of them. "You have to stay down on it!" he yelled. "Next!"

Unfortunately for me, most of the next hour followed a similar path, and it didn't help that Tank Top was storming around the field making comments. My confidence was shot, and it took me a long time to recover. My fielding was atrocious, and my hitting wasn't much better. I managed to hit one ball hard, and I also made a couple good throws from the outfield, but I didn't think it would be enough. Most of the other kids had performed better. It was that simple, or at least it seemed that way to me at the time. I was apparently destined for another year in the forgotten chaos of the Minors.

The coaches released us after a quick pep talk from Thurman. He told us we'd get a phone call from our coach, either Majors or Minors, in the next day or two. I headed off the field, literally hanging my head. I didn't want to look at Adam. I figured he'd be pissed at me, and I just didn't want to hear it. About halfway through the tryout, I stole a glance in his direction and found him staring at the ground. I made my way into the third base dugout, found my bat, and then sulked into the parking lot.

Adam was waiting for me when I got there. As I approached, he put his hand out and lifted my chin. He was smiling. "Keep your head up, man," he said. "You made some good throws out there, and you hammered that one ball. That was one of the best hits all day."

I wanted to smile, but I knew he was just trying to make me feel better. I had a terrible tryout, and we both knew it.

"Let me see your bat for a second," he said. He took it out of my hand. "Go to the truck. I'm parked right there." He pointed behind him, and I saw our red truck parked about twenty feet away.

I was happy to see Adam wasn't angry, but I was still in a depressed daze. I never even wondered why he'd asked to hold my bat. I scuffled toward our faded red truck, a massive double-cab Ford pickup. *Big Red*, as our mom called it, was one of the things our dad left behind...along with us, of course.

I opened the door and pulled myself up into the cab before closing it behind me. Almost by accident, I noticed Adam walking out onto the field. He was heading toward the pitcher's mound where Tank Top, Thurman, and another coach stood talking. All at once it hit me what Adam was about to do. I thought about yelling for him to stop, but I couldn't move. A strange feeling of otherworldliness had come over me. I wasn't in the parking lot of Barnell Field anymore. I was a thousand miles away at some daylight drive in, watching this soon-to-be ugly scene unfold on the big screen.

The three men were looking at a clipboard, probably making note of who hadn't shown up. Adam approached them, stopping about four feet in front of Tank Top. He held the bat casually in his right hand. The men looked up in unison. I couldn't see Adam's face because his back was to me, but I could see *their* faces clearly. I knew Adam was talking because they were all looking at him. After about five seconds, Tank Top's face broke into a grin, but I could tell something was wrong. Even from my vantage point, I could see the smile wasn't genuine. He stepped toward Adam, and Adam took a small step back. He didn't raise the bat, but I got the feeling he was about to. Thurman put his hand on Tank Top's chest, stopping him. He then turned toward Adam and said, "You need to get out of here." I couldn't hear him, but I could read his lips. As Adam walked away, Tank Top continued staring at him with that same mindless grin. Thankfully, he didn't follow.

When Adam reached the truck, he tossed the bat through the open back window and climbed into the cab. He closed the door and started the truck, the roar of the eight-cylinder engine filling the mostly empty parking lot.

"What'd you say to him?" I asked.

"Just told him the truth," Adam replied without emotion. "I told him he was a fucking dick."

I absorbed that for a second, stunned but not surprised. "Why'd you take the bat?" I suspected I already knew the answer, but I couldn't think. I was totally spent.

We reached the edge of the parking lot and stopped. Adam looked past me to check for oncoming cars. "I could tell he was a hothead," Adam said, as he pulled out onto the road, "and I wanted him to know he was gonna have his hands full if he came at me."

I stared at him for a while, but Adam didn't look at me. I think I knew what he did was wrong, at least the way he went about it. But I can tell you one thing, and it still holds true even thirty-nine years later. I never loved him more.

10

One Year Later, Saturday

National Board Company, known in the electronics manufacturing industry as NBC, has been making printed circuit boards in Everton, NY, for the last forty-two years. The next time you use your smart phone, your TV remote, your computer, or almost anything electronic, you can rest assured there's at least one printed circuit board inside it. Doubtful it's one of ours, as these particular items are usually either high volume or hi-tech, neither of which is NBC's specialty. But if you stop to get gas in the Northeast United States — or certain sections of the Midwest or Southwest — there's a good chance one of NBC's circuit boards is operating quietly inside the pump to help you do it.

I joined the company in 1994 as an associate engineer and eventually made my way into the front office where I handled more of the sales-related tasks. I found working directly with customers to be much more interesting work. Because of my engineering background, I was able to communicate with buyers and engineers on a more technical level — something we'd never had before, or so I was told.

I never thought working in a printed circuit board shop would be my calling when I was navigating the halls of high school or earning my engineering degree from the University of Buffalo. For that matter, it never dawned on me even after a few years working there. *I'll eventually find what I really want to do*, I told myself, as do millions of other people who aren't wise enough or perhaps lucky enough to discover their calling early on. Of course, time marches on whether you're one of the lucky ones or not, and once you immerse yourself in your work, the years really begin to roll by. Then you decide to get married and have a child or two, and before you even know what happened, your twenties are in the rear-view mirror. And after a decade of diapers, play dates, birthday parties, soccer practices, homework, and coaching Little League — all on top of fifty-hour work weeks — you discover your thirties packed up and went looking for your twenties. Suddenly, you wake up one morning on a floor mattress within shouting distance of fifty, and it dawns on you that this *was* your calling whether you like it or not. What were the lyrics from that great Pink Floyd tune? *And then one day you find, ten years have got behind you, no one told you when to run, you missed the starting gun.* Sums it up perfectly, really, except the lads from London could have just as easily said twenty years instead of ten.

I walked through NBC's front door at 9:35 am and started down the hall. Connor had a game at 11:00, so the plan was to grab a few folders and then run back to Laura's to pick him up. I passed by the main work area, which housed several cubicles, a couple of which belonged to the two women who worked for me. Neither was in at the moment, which wasn't unusual for a Saturday. Actually, it didn't look like *anyone* was here. I considered this to be a lucky break. If no one was around, I couldn't get dragged into a prolonged work discussion. It wouldn't take much to make us late for the game.

I was almost to my office when my boss, Carolyn, came bounding out of hers. She was dressed in a gray Armani suit, which fit her five-foot-five-inch frame perfectly. She looked like she'd just stepped off the pages of *Fortune* magazine. This was her normal attire during the week, but it was a bit unusual for a Saturday. Weekends were when she could often be found on the shop floor wearing blue jeans and a long-sleeved tee-shirt. She saw me and smiled, but I got the feeling she wasn't exactly thrilled to see me.

"Hey, Dan, I didn't think you were coming in today. Doesn't Connor have a game?"

"Yeah, but not until 11:00. I just stopped in quick to grab a couple things. Why all dressed up?"

"Oh, Bob asked me to give a plant tour."

Bob Obrien and his brother, James, had owned NBC for the last fifteen years. I was about to ask her who the tour was for, but right then her phone rang. I got the funny feeling she was relieved. "Hold on a sec," she said, before slipping back into her office.

I walked into my office and grabbed the papers I needed. When I came out, Carolyn was waiting for me, but she seemed anxious. "I have to run, but tell Connor to hit a couple home runs for me."

"You should come and watch the game." Carolyn hated baseball, even Little League.

"Yeah, good idea," she said, laughing. "Then after that we can watch the grass grow. Hey, before I forget, remember I'm meeting with Bob and James next week."

"Oh, that's right."

"Think you can hold down the fort while I'm gone?"

"Probably not, but we'll do our best." I headed toward the door. "Listen, have fun up there, and don't drink too much good wine."

"I'll try not to." She smiled and headed for the production floor.

In my opinion Carolyn was the single biggest reason why NBC was still in existence. She was hired as the General Manager nine years ago and came in—like a lot of GM's do—like her Armani suit was on fire. She inherited a company with a lot of so-called skilled employees, but what she really had was a lot of high paid men hoping to coast out the remainder of their careers without leaving too much of their own skin behind. Men who weren't thrilled with an attractive, driven female in her early thirties suddenly calling the shots in what had always been a male-dominated industry. Those feelings evaporated quickly, however, during her first couple months on the job. She was bombarded with reasons why we couldn't do various things. *We don't have the right equipment. We don't have the manpower. We don't have the expertise.* Instead of arguing and threatening like a lot of GMs would have done, including her predecessor, she calmly and systematically took away everyone's excuses. At a time when other shops were scaling back, she purchased new equipment, including new photo imaging technology and a new plating line. Then she worked harder than anyone else in the shop. She led by example and never deflected blame if she screwed up. "You want to earn the respect of your employees?" she said to me one time. "Be accountable for your own mistakes."

It was safe to say in the last five or six years, Carolyn was the glue holding the entire place together. There was no question in my mind she could have headed up a Fortune 500 Company if she really wanted to, but then again maybe not. She was far too honest.

11

Connor and I arrived at Saxon Field around 10:30. We didn't usually have games on Saturdays, but there were so many rainouts in the beginning of the year we had to play some makeup dates. I drove down the narrow road to the parking lot, thinking about Adam. Yesterday was a year to the day since his funeral, except funeral wasn't really the right word for it. Party was probably more accurate. The last thing Adam wanted was a bunch of people getting together at a church or a funeral home (or God forbid, a cemetery) to mourn his death. He told Jen if people were going to get together to reminisce or to bitch about him, it was going to be a party somewhere, or it wasn't going to happen at all. So that's exactly what Jen did. She opened up her home to his closest friends and family, and we had a celebration of his life…and got completely hammered. We played his favorite music—mostly Cream, Led Zeppelin, and Pink Floyd—drank, laughed, and told stories to each other into the wee hours of the morning. I got to meet some of his local friends who helped fill in the gaps formed when we almost lost touch with one another.

Unfortunately, Billy wasn't able to make it. He explained to Jen that his wife was having a major surgery and she needed him there. He sent a letter, though, that talked a lot about Adam and the crazy stuff they did together as kids. I read it aloud just after dinner. Everyone was feeling comfortable, but no one was drunk yet. I thought it was important to do it before the night became a blur. Billy's letter had everyone laughing through most of it, and then it turned sentimental. When I was done reading, which included a few pauses to regain my composure, there wasn't a dry eye in the house.

Billy was the only childhood friend Adam had kept in touch with. I hadn't seen him in ten years, but he would always hold a special place in my family. When Jess died in that horrible accident, he was the first one to make it to our mother's house. It seemed like he was there for a week straight, doing everything he could to keep the three of us from falling apart. He went with our mom to identify Jess's body because neither Adam nor I could do it. He fielded the phone calls and helped us plan the funeral. He didn't have to do any of that, and in fact, most men probably wouldn't have.

I'm sure there's something Billy could do to make me turn against him, but the list is damn short.

That weekend at Jen's was also a turning point for me and Laura. I broke down at the last minute and invited her to come. It was going to be just me and Connor, but Jen had mentioned Laura a few times when she was giving me the details on the party. She didn't come right out and ask me to bring her, but I got the feeling she wanted Laura there, and that, of course, trumped everything. So the three of us headed out for West Chester, just like we would have in the old days. Since we were going to be stuck in the car for over six hours, round trip, I vowed to keep things civil, if not downright upbeat. With Adam being front and center in my mind, I was able to focus on that instead of what Laura had done. It was still there, of course, but it was on the back burner instead of barking in my face like some feral dog. The trip actually ended up being fun. There were a couple times at the party when I almost forgot what had happened. Certainly, the booze had a lot to do with that, but it was eerie just the same. Connor was thrilled we were talking again instead of arguing all the time. When I saw how happy this made him, I vowed things were going to change — that *I* was going to change even if it killed me. And for the most part, I was able to do it.

I pulled into the parking lot and found an empty spot. So far, this season had been going a lot better than last. Tremon Little League did a redraft each year, so basically every team started from scratch. For me and Connor that was a good thing. Our team struggled last year, and this season probably wouldn't have been much better. Individually, Connor was also having a much better year. He still wasn't hitting as well as he would have liked, but he had emerged as one of the better eleven-year-old infielders. And since the team was doing okay, Connor was happy. For me that was what mattered most. After all, he wasn't going pro in baseball or any other sport.

Connor hopped out of the Saturn and jogged toward the batting cages where our head coach was warming up the team. I climbed out a little more slowly and followed him. After a few strategic back stretches, I headed toward the equipment shed, hoping someone had already started on the field.

12

The game didn't go exactly as planned. A controversial play at home plate ultimately determined the outcome. According to Connor, our coaches (namely me) had let the other coaches steal the game. I couldn't argue with him. That's one of youth baseball's dirty little secrets, at least in the leagues that use teenage umpires. If you're not actively trying to manipulate outcomes — especially on an unusual play — you'll end up getting the short end of the stick more often than not. We took the high road today and paid for it with a loss. Of course, taking the high road has its advantages, but after the game I would've been hard pressed to name one. It didn't help that the men in the other dugout were the poster boys for overly competitive youth coaches.

Laura was on the side of the house planting flowers when we arrived. It was one of her new hobbies, along with reading. Connor told me she held a book club meeting every other month. We smiled and waved to each other, but she didn't come out to the car. Even though we got along now, most of our communications came by text or email.

The divorce had been final for six months. We both used the same lawyer, a friend of ours from the early days of our marriage. Everyone told me it was a mistake to have the same lawyer, but Laura and I both trusted her, and the last thing we wanted to do was fight. We'd caused Connor enough anguish. We vowed to make the divorce as painless and inexpensive as possible. Basically, we just split everything we had right down the middle. There wasn't much in the way of paper assets, but there was the house and the two cars. The trickiest part was working out child support, but we managed that, too.

For me, things starting getting a lot better once Connor accepted the situation. My anger, which for quite a while bordered on flat-out hatred, faded dramatically. I still had my moments, mostly when I saw other families doing the things the three of us should have been doing, but for the most part I kept my emotions under control. I still blamed myself for not being strong enough to forgive Laura. I had desperately wanted to for Connor's sake, but it just wasn't going to happen. For a while we kicked around the idea of staying married until he went off to college. Apparently, that wasn't all that uncommon, but ultimately I felt like that would be worse than getting the divorce. What kind of an example of a healthy marriage could that have been? We decided we'd be the best parents we could be to Connor. It's just that we'd be doing it separately. Of course, Laura would handle all the school functions…at least until middle school.

I waved goodbye and started for my apartment, also known as *The Palace* to me and Connor. I'd dubbed it that after Connor declared "it wasn't very nice" about a month after I moved in. He laughed so hard he almost choked on his turkey sandwich. After that it sort of became our inside joke. Our Mom always taught us to have a sense of humor about life. She said it made things easier. When I got close, I passed by the field where Connor and I sometimes came to practice. I glanced out at the train tracks running along the back side of the field when the idea came to me. *I wonder if they're ready yet?* On the other side of the tracks was a second field that led to a dense wooded area. In the brush near the tree line were tons of wild berries. My mom used to call them black caps. They were smaller than both raspberries and blackberries, but they tasted like a combination of the two, only a little more tart. We used to pick them near our old house on Marcell Street when we were kids. Connor and I had stumbled upon this particular patch three years ago. There were so many ripe berries that year, I decided I'd try to gather enough to make jam. I liked picking them because it reminded me of Adam and Jess, but I also found it relaxing as hell, especially after a bad day at work…or a stressful baseball game. By the end of that July, we had what I hoped was enough berries. Three months later Laura and I split a bottle of wine and took a crack at making the jam. Neither one of us had ever done it before, but we found directions online. We ended up with sixteen eight-ounce jars. The jam didn't set properly, but we didn't care. It tasted awesome. When we were done, we made love on the couch in the living room. The dishes never got done until the next morning.

Even though I wanted to work out, I pulled into the field and headed toward the train tracks. I thought about going back to the house and grabbing Connor, but I was pretty sure he wouldn't feel like helping me today. He was probably already in the basement, playing video games and killing people online. I grabbed a plastic bag from the back seat and hopped out of the Saturn. A few seconds later I was crossing the railroad tracks and walking alongside an abandoned shoe factory. I reached the edge of the building and headed out across the second field, avoiding gopher holes as I made my way through the long grass. As I approached the tree line, I could already feel my blood pressure dropping. It wasn't exactly the Alaskan wilderness, but it still felt pretty remote. If I ignored the bike paths and the occasional beer can, left behind by partying teenagers, it wasn't hard to imagine this little strip looking much like this a thousand years ago. The best thing about it was there were no idiots arguing over balls and strikes or controversial calls at home plate.

The black cap bushes grew where the field ended and the trees began. There were several varieties of plants and bushes growing in among the black cap vines, and all of them seemed to be fighting for the same space. The end result was like an impenetrable barbed-wire fence preventing you from advancing into the trees. Everything looked to be in full bloom and at the peak of its lush greenness. The sun had shifted far enough west, so the tallest trees provided a refreshing wall of shade. I could see some of the ripe, black-colored berries standing out among clusters of red. I used the bat to push aside a long prickly branch and waded in. I started plucking the ripest berries from the clusters and dropping them into the plastic bag. With shorts on, I couldn't get too far into the brush, but there were still plenty of black ones to pick.

I worked my way slowly along the tree line and tried to let my mind wander. Unfortunately, it kept returning to the boring waters of my love life. While I'd had a few dates since the divorce, and one brief relationship, I just hadn't fully connected with anyone. The relationship was with a saleswoman from a local radio station. After a handful of dates in just over three weeks, including a weekend getaway in Vermont, she ended up going back to her longtime boyfriend. It was just as well. She didn't seem all that interested in Connor, and that would have been a deal breaker.

Forty minutes later, I'd gathered all the berries I could reach. There were plenty more further in, but it wasn't worth tearing up my legs to get them. They'd still be here in a couple days, along with a lot more. I'd come back with jeans on and make a killing. Maybe I could convince Connor to come with me, but I sort of doubted it. I thought the days of him helping me pick black caps might be over. The thought made me sad, but I pushed it away. Connor had come a long way in the last six or seven months, and for that I was truly grateful. If he didn't want to pick berries anymore, that was okay with me.

I walked back across the field toward the railroad tracks. The site of the abandoned factory made the return trip considerably less scenic. A minute later I was in my car and heading for The Palace.

13

I had just pulled into the bike shop parking lot when I noticed a couple college-age women unloading a couch out of the back of a blue pickup. They were parked in front of a small apartment complex next door. The renters were mostly young families, but there was one elderly woman living in the building, too. There were no college students that I knew of, but it looked like these women were moving into one of the units on the ground floor. *Or maybe they're just delivering the couch,* I thought. At any rate, they were struggling to get the couch off the truck. I had no desire to unload a couch right now, but I felt a gnawing obligation to help them.

I slipped out of the Saturn and headed across the lawn toward the apartments. One of the women was standing on the truck bed and the other was standing on the ground directly behind it. I could see the couch was pretty big. It was sitting at an angle, with the back end resting on the closed tailgate. As I approached, they started laughing. The woman on the ground turned toward me.

"Hi there," I said.

"Are you our knight in shining armor?" she asked, still chuckling. "I think we overestimated our capabilities."

I saw right away I was wrong about their age. They were both in their mid-twenties, maybe even a touch older. The one who'd spoken was wearing a gray tee-shirt and a snug pair of running shorts. Even at first glance, I could see she had ample curves in all the right places. Her dark brown hair was pulled back into a tight ball. Flushed cheeks and a line of sweat glistening on her forehead told me they'd been at this a while. "I don't know about a knight in shining armor," I said, smiling, "but I'll definitely give you a hand."

"A couple guys loaded it up for us, and we didn't realize how heavy it was."

"*You* didn't realize how heavy it was," the woman in the truck said. "I tried to tell you." She was dressed in a tank top and an equally snug pair of black spandex.

"It was her uncle's couch," the woman beside me said, rolling her eyes. She extended her hand. "I'm Ally. Nice to meet you."

I shook it, noticing it was warm and a little sweaty. I also noticed there wasn't a ring on it. "I'm Dan. Nice to meet you, too." I glanced back toward The Palace. "I live above the bike shop, there."

"Oh, so we're going to be neighbors," Ally said, smiling.

"Are you both moving in?"

"Nope, just me."

When I first saw her, I thought she was a little plain-looking. Not unattractive, certainly, but a little plain, nonetheless. The more I saw her smile, the less I thought this was true.

Ally pointed up to the woman standing on the truck bed. "That's Katie, my know-it-all friend."

"That's me," Katie said, smiling. She gave me a wave and I returned it. I thought they looked enough alike to be sisters.

"Well," I said, "for starters, why don't we get the tailgate down, and then we can drag it off the back."

"Sounds good," Ally said.

"I'll hold up the couch, and you can get the tailgate."

"Okay."

I reached up and put both hands under the couch. It was hanging over the edge of the truck by about four feet. I lifted the couch and found it to be heavier than I expected. "Okay, I got it."

Ally lifted the handle and dropped the tailgate with a metallic thud. She reached up and grabbed onto the couch, helping me lower it to the bed. I could feel the warm moisture from her body through my shirt. When you've had as little physical contact with the opposite sex as I've had in the last year, this counts as a significant interaction. Ally didn't seem to notice. I was just a neighbor trying to lend a helping hand, and if that meant getting a little close, then so be it.

"Okay," I said, "why don't we drag it off? I'll carry this end, and you two can carry the other end." I turned back and spotted an open apartment door on the first floor. "I'm guessing you're moving into that one?" I pointed even though there wasn't much question as to which one I meant.

"Smart and handsome," Katie said from above.

Ally laughed, and again it struck me how wrong my initial impression of her looks had been. She was growing more attractive with every sound she made.

"I apologize for her," Ally said. "There's no filter."

I chuckled. "No apology necessary."

I dragged the couch out while Katie pushed. We almost went too far before I could change my grip, and the back end of the couch headed toward the ground. I recovered and lifted it back to level. Katie jumped out of the truck and grabbed the other end with Ally. Once they got it off the truck, we started toward the open door. I could tell by its weight it was going to be a tough job. Ten minutes later, and after two failed attempts at getting the couch through the front door, we finally got the behemoth into the living room. It was hot outside, but the apartment was sweltering. I could feel sweat running freely down my back.

"Sorry, we haven't put in the air conditioner yet," Ally said.

"No problem." I looked around the apartment and saw furniture and boxes scattered about. It was obvious the couch was just the tail end of a long day of moving. "Do you guys have anything else to move?"

"No, but I wish you'd stopped over earlier," Katie said, shaking my hand. "We could've used your help." She waved her hand around the room as if I needed to be convinced.

"Well, do you have more? I can help you tomorrow, and I can probably get my son to help, too."

"No, just small stuff from here on out," Ally said. "How old's your son?"

"Connor's eleven."

"Oh, nice. Does he live in the apartment, too?"

"Sometimes." I laughed at the confused look on her face. "We're—me and Connor's mother, I mean—are divorced. They live nearby and he stays with me two or three nights a week, but we don't have any set schedule." I noticed Katie had slipped into another room.

"So, you guys get along then? You and your ex-wife, I mean."

"Yeah, it wasn't always that way, but we finally realized it wasn't doing Connor any good to be at each other's throats. You know what I mean?"

"I do, unfortunately. My older sister divorced her husband last year, but they haven't figured that out yet. My two nephews are caught right in the middle of it." She wiped more sweat off her brow. "I have to go outside. It's too hot in here."

"Yeah, good idea." We headed out the door and onto the driveway. It suddenly hit me I was overstaying my welcome. "Well, I can see you have a lot to do, so—"

"My God, I'm so sorry. Would you like a bottle of water? I'd offer you a cold soda or a beer, but there's nothing in the fridge."

"No, thanks, Ally. I'd better get heading back." I smiled and turned to go.

"So, how long have you lived above the bike shop?"

"Oh, I guess it's been a little over a year now. I sort of lucked out. My landlord owns the shop and used to live in the apartment. He was getting married and moving out just when Laura and I were separating. My old house is only a mile or so down the road." I pointed in the general direction, and she nodded as if she knew the neighborhood. By now I was starting to wonder if my overall exhaustion was conspiring with my imagination to make me think this attractive twenty-something was finding me interesting. "What about you? Are you from around here?"

"Syracuse. I'm going to grad school at Binghamton University. It's a pretty intense program, and I didn't feel like making the commute every day. I've been doing it for two weeks, and I'm already sick of it."

"I don't blame you. It's like wasting over two hours a day. What are you studying?"

"Business Administration."

"Good for you. I've heard they have a great program."

She still wasn't hinting that she wanted the conversation to end, but I sensed it could go from just two people talking to *creepy old guy who won't leave* in a matter of seconds. "It was great meeting you, Ally." I extended my hand toward hers. "I'm sorry I didn't get home earlier."

She smiled and shook my hand again. "Oh, God, you were a huge help. Thank you so much. I'm sure we'll run into each other soon."

"I hope so." Before I started back toward my apartment, I got another good look at her face, and the number twenty-six popped into my head. She was around twenty-six-years-old and a very nice woman. I suspected she had already spent two or three years in the working world. Sales was my guess. She seemed comfortable in her own skin and quite mature.

I'd just stepped into my apartment when I remembered I'd left the black caps in the Saturn. I turned around and walked back down the steps. I glanced toward Ally's apartment, but she'd already gone back inside and closed the door. I retrieved the large cup of berries from the front seat and headed back up. I was filling the cup with water when I heard a knock at the door. I turned and saw Ally standing on the landing. Her gray shirt and black running shorts were visible through the glass. I stepped quickly to the door and opened it.

"Hi there," I said. "What'd you forget?" Just then I noticed she was holding something in her hand. It looked like a can of Labatt Blue Light.

"Hi," Ally said, smiling. "My friend finally got here and she brought us some beer." She extended the beer toward me and I took it. It felt icy cold in the warm, muggy air.

"Wow. Thank you, Ally. That's very nice of you, but you didn't have to do that."

"Yes, I did. We'd still be trying to get that couch off the truck if you hadn't come over."

I sort of felt like I should invite her in, but the apartment was a complete mess. There were dirty dishes on the counter and the living room was a disaster. I opened my mouth to say something, but Ally spoke first.

"Okay, I'll let you go," she said. "Thanks again for your help."

"Ally, it was no problem at all. Really. And thanks for the beer."

"Okay, see you later."

She headed down the stairs, and it took every ounce of strength I had not to step onto the landing and watch her go. If someone had told me then how much time we'd spend together over the next week, I would have never believed it.

Jackson & Franklin

14

That afternoon I was watching television with Jess when our mom got home from work. It was a *Brady Bunch* episode we'd already seen five times—the one where Marsha gets hit in the nose with a football right before her big date. I'd been wallowing in a post tryout funk for most of the afternoon. By the time 3:30 rolled around, I'd convinced myself I was the worst player on the field.

The only thing that seemed to take my mind off my horrible tryout was Ms. Becker. I remember praying that Mom was going to come home with good news. Maybe Ms. Becker had awoken from her coma and was in the midst of an amazing recovery. I knew it wasn't likely, but like Mark had said, maybe God might get involved and make something happen. He said it had happened before, and I believed him. I just prayed it would happen for Ms. Becker.

Mom walked through the front door in her nurse's uniform, her matching white cap covering up most of her dark brown hair. She took one look at us—Jess on one side of the couch and me on the other—and said, "It's such a beautiful day outside. Don't tell me you two have been sitting here watching television all afternoon." Mom never said TV for some reason. It was always *television*.

She walked over to the mirror and began removing her cap. When she was done, she walked back toward us, smiling. I thought she looked a little like Kate Jackson, one of Charlie's Angels, *especially* when she smiled. Kate wasn't my favorite Angel. That spot, of course, went to Farrah, but I thought they were all beautiful. Adam just shook his head whenever I told our mom she looked like Kate, but Jess agreed with me. I don't know if Jess really thought that or just said it because she knew our mom liked hearing it.

Jess hopped up from the couch and gave Mom a hug. "I was just outside playing with Allison, but she had to go home."

"What about you, mister?" Mom said, turning to me with a look of disapproval. I had nothing in the way of a defense and we both knew it. I'd been in the exact same spot for almost two hours. I prepared myself for a lecture when I saw her face change. "Oh, how did the tryout go?"

"Not very good."

"What do you mean not very good? What happened?"

"Nothing. I just didn't play good." I wasn't about to get into specifics. I almost told her about Tank Top, but that would've made her angry and led to a million questions I didn't want to answer. "There's no way I'm making the Majors. There were too many good kids."

"You did all right," Adam yelled from upstairs. He walked down the hallway and then came down the stairwell, dragging his hands along the ceiling as he went. He stopped on the final step, his hands still raised above his head. "He didn't play his best, but he did okay. I'd say middle of the pack."

I figured Mom would jump on that, and she didn't disappoint. "See, you always think you did worse than you really did. I bet you did fine."

Fine. God, I hated that word as a kid, as does every other who's ever heard it. You did *fine* meant one thing. You didn't do *good.* "I don't know. I felt like I played terrible."

"I think you're gonna get picked," Adam said.

That ended it as far as Mom was concerned. Adam had played baseball and he'd witnessed the tryouts first hand. If Adam thought I was going to make it, then I was going to make it. "Me, too," she said emphatically.

"Did you see Mr. Baxter at work?" I asked.

"No, he wasn't in today, but I'll see him Monday. I'm pretty sure he went to the tryout."

I didn't want to talk about baseball anymore. "What about Ms. Becker, Mom?"

Mom looked at me and smiled. I could tell she knew the question was coming. "Well, I do have some news about her, honey." She came over and sat on the couch between me and Jess. "There hasn't been a change in her condition as far as I know, but they transferred her to Wilson Hospital in Binghamton. They have better facilities to handle someone in her situation. She was already gone when I got in to work."

I scanned Mom's face for clues she might be lying, but I didn't see anything. If she knew I was doing that at ten-years-old, it would have broken her heart. "What do you think is gonna happen to her, Mom?"

"Well, honey, I honestly don't know, but I'm praying for a miracle. I think that's all we can do."

We talked about Ms. Becker for a while longer. Jess and I both agreed that praying for her was probably the best thing we could do. Even Adam, who'd come down from the stairwell and into the living room, nodded his head in agreement. I don't know if I realized it then, but I'd already taken the first small step toward acceptance. Mom promised to call into work later that night to see if she could get an update on her condition. That way I'd have some idea what was happening when I headed into school on the following Monday, and I wouldn't have to rely on Mr. Holt for information.

If that previous Friday was any indication, and I was pretty sure it was, Mr. Holt wasn't going to be providing daily updates.

Right then I heard a car door slam. Jess ran to the window and looked out. "Mark's here!" she said, her voice thick with excitement, "and he's got a pizza!"

I ran to the window, joining her. "It's a Nate's pizza!" As far as I was concerned, Nate's made the best sheet pizzas around.

Mom laughed. "So, that's what it takes to get you off the couch, huh?"

I glanced up at Adam. He smiled and shook his head before heading back up the stairs. I thought for sure he hadn't heard us. "Adam, Mark brought a pizza!"

"I know, Danny. I'll be right down. I just have to change."

Jess opened the door and Mark carried the pizza into the house. He could have brought in five tickets to Disneyland and we wouldn't have been more excited. He carried the pizza into the dining room, and Jess and I trailed behind him like we hadn't eaten in days.

15

I spent Sunday morning watching my favorite show, *This Week in Baseball*. The show played highlights from the previous week of Major League Baseball. It aired each Sunday at 11:00 am, and I never missed it. And more often than not, Adam and Jess watched it with me. Adam pretended he didn't like it, but I know he did. As we watched it, he liked to get me going by saying stuff like, "That was nothing" or "That guy's overrated." It took me a while to catch on—much longer than it probably should have—but I finally did. After I stopped reacting, he stopped doing it, and the show became something we all enjoyed together.

The festivities always began with Mel Allen narrating brief and often spectacular highlights over a cool-sounding intro. If there were better voices for the job, I had never heard them. And while I loved the entire show, my favorite part was the ending credits. That's when they played the best theme song of all-time: Deh, nu-neh neh, nu-neh nu-neh nu-neh neh. If that music didn't get your adrenaline flowing, you were dead. Simple as that. It played over a select group of iconic players and fantastic plays, all running in perfectly timed slow motion. It was the same plays every week, but they never got old. And there were two that really stood out. Freddy Lynn climbing the outfield wall and making a ridiculous catch to rob someone of a home run. God, I hated Boston back then, but it was hard to hate Freddy Lynn, especially when you saw that play every week. The other play was of the Montreal Expos' Ellis Valentine gunning down someone at home plate from right field. That was probably my favorite play because as a ten-year-old right field was usually where I found myself. In Little League, rightly or wrongly, coaches often put one of their weaker players in right field. But like so many other things in my young life, I was blissfully unaware of that fact at the time.

I heard somewhere that the theme song had been used other places, but it found its home on *This Week in Baseball*. Maybe it would have had the same effect showing slow-motion football or basketball highlights, but I doubt it. There was something about a slow-motion baseball play that just seemed to synchronize with the notes.

I think the other reason I loved the show was because it put a fun spin on professional baseball, especially the individual players, at a time in my life when I believed I might someday be one of them. Truth be told, the feeling was probably stronger than *might*. After all, I was playing Little League in the baseball factory known as Everton, NY; was a huge fan of the New York Yankees—who had just recently fought their way back to the top; and watched *This Week in Baseball* religiously. I mean, how many other kids were doing that at ten-years-old? If I had known the answer was hundreds of thousands in the U.S. alone (aside from the Everton part, of course), it probably wouldn't have dissuaded me. Nor did the fact that I wasn't that good in the first place—an average ten-year-old, at best. And naturally, the specific details of how I was going to rise to the ranks of a professional player in the span of the next decade or so, besting the millions of other kids around the world who also played and loved baseball, never occurred to me. If someone had told me then that I wouldn't even make the high school team, I would have told them they were crazy.

When the show ended, I went up to my room to do my homework. I had three chapters to read from our social studies text, but I had zero desire to do it. I opened my math book instead. I was halfway through the first problem when the phone rang. That didn't happen often, especially on a Sunday, so it got my attention. It crossed my mind it might be a call from my new coach, but that possibility seemed remote. After all, tryouts had just been held the day before.

"Hello?" Mom said, as she answered the phone. With the door open, it sounded like she was right outside my room. "Oh, hello, Vic. How are you?" I heard surprise in her voice, but I could tell it wasn't genuine. It had too much mustard on it.

My heart kicked into a higher gear. Even if Mom knew another guy named Vic, what were the chances he'd be calling her on a Sunday afternoon, the very day after tryouts?

"He is home," she said. "Hold on a second, and I'll get him."

I heard her set the phone down on the kitchen table, then start walking toward the stairs. She had no idea I could hear every word she was saying. I opened my door all the way and saw Jess standing in her doorway just a few feet away. She was smiling at me with a broad grin, still missing its two front teeth.

"Danny, you have a phone call," Mom yelled.

I walked down the hall, rounded the corner and started down the stairs. "Who is it, Mom?"

"I'm not sure." She turned away, doing her best to hold in a smile.

That was the final nail. Vic Baxter was on the phone, and I'd made the Majors. My heart raced even faster. I walked into the kitchen and picked up the phone. I turned back and caught Mom nodding her head at Jess who'd followed me down the stairs. Mom looked at me and our eyes locked. I couldn't hold it in any longer. A wide grin surfaced on my face as I raised the phone to my ear. "Hello?"

"Hello, Danny, this is Vic Baxter. I'm the coach of Jackson and Franklin."

"Hi," was all I could manage.

"I just wanted to let you know that we selected you in the draft yesterday. You're now a member of J&F. Congratulations, Danny."

"Wow, thank you, Mr. Baxter." I looked up at Mom and Jess and smiled. I gave them the thumbs up even though I don't think I'd ever actually done that before. I watched them hug each other and start jumping up and down silently in front of the television. I couldn't wait to get off the phone, so I could join them in the celebration.

"You're welcome, Danny," Coach Baxter said. "We're going to start pretty quick. Our first practice is next Saturday at Archer Field on Dickinson Street at one o'clock. Do you know where that is?"

"Yeah, it's close to my school."

"Okay great, we'll see you there. Make sure you tell your mom about practice."

"I will."

As soon as I hung up the phone, the screaming started. Anyone walking by the house right then would have thought my mom and sister were being attacked by a maniac. I knew with Mom, some of the excitement had to do with Ms. Becker. She knew I needed some good news, and she also knew how badly I wanted to make the Majors. I ran into the living room and hugged them both. And then it was the three of us acting like lunatics, screaming and jumping around. Mom was crying a little, and I think Jess was, too. I was glad that Adam and Mark weren't there. Jess and Mom would have still gone crazy, but I don't think I would have. I think I would have been more reserved, trying to follow the lead of the older males. Mark and Adam would have been happy for me, but they wouldn't have shown it in the same way. There would have been a heavy pat on the back from Mark and maybe a quick hug from Adam but certainly not the other stuff. We would have taken the news like men.

So, yes, I was glad they weren't around when that call came in, and I'm even more grateful for it today. Mom and Jess have both been gone now for over twenty years. I think of them often, of course, and every once in a while, that's the memory I replay in my mind. The three of us screaming and jumping around like fools in that small living room on Marcell Street.

16

The walk to school with Jess on that Monday morning was probably the best of the year. Hell, it was probably the best of *any* year at West Everton Elementary. While I was still upset about Ms. Becker, the realization I'd made the Majors was dominating my thoughts. One of the things that made that particular walk so great was the fact that word had already gotten around on who'd been drafted. A couple kids passed by us and offered me their congratulations. My guess was someone must have heard about it at church the day before, and then it spread like a good rumor from there. Suffice it say I was on cloud nine. My days toiling in the Minors were in the past, as was my poor showing at the tryouts. I was now a proud member of J&F, one of the best teams in the league. Practice was the following Saturday, and until then, at least, the sky was the limit. I wondered how many home runs I would hit that year. Maybe I'd set the league record for ten-year-olds. And maybe one of the coaches would discover I had a knack for pitching. I wouldn't be the ace — not at ten — but maybe I'd be able to work my way into the starting rotation. Eighteen games was a long season. Practically anything could happen. Maybe I'd even picked up some wheels over the winter without even realizing it. Perhaps I'd lead the league in stolen bases. I could be Everton Little League's version of Lou Brock.

By the time I walked up the school steps, the euphoric feeling was starting to crumble. The reality that the wonderful Ms. Becker had been replaced by the unpredictable Mr. Holt was easy to ignore while away from the actual school, but considerably more difficult when you were just about to enter his classroom for more than six hours. A classroom where, for all intents and purposes, he was dictator.

Luckily, Monday mornings held something to soften the blow. Dodgeball. It was a tradition started a few years earlier by our gym teacher, Mr. Landry. All the fifth and sixth-grade boys (and a few of the girls) loved it because it was something fun to look forward to coming off the weekend. So every Monday from 8:20 to 8:50, we all headed down to the gym to try to kill each other with red dodgeballs. I dropped my books off at my desk, then walked Jess to her classroom and headed down to play. I was only a few steps from the gym doors when I heard someone call my name. I turned to see Jason Billings approaching. Like me, I didn't think he'd done very well at the tryout, and I wondered if he'd been drafted.

"Hey, Danny," Jason said, "I heard you're on J&F?"

"Yeah, how 'bout you?"

He smiled at me. "Rotary Club."

It's funny how players in the Minors didn't know much about the other teams in their own league, but they knew who was good in the Majors. I was no exception. Rotary Club had made the playoffs the previous year and lost to J&F. And I was pretty sure they had some good players coming back. "That's cool. You guys should be pretty good."

Jason's smile grew. It was a smile that said *There's more to come.* "Yeah, and we picked up Zach Hardy and his brother, David."

David wasn't the pitcher Zach was, but he was a big kid and an all-around good player — an All-Star for sure. I had been reaching for the door handle, but I pulled my hand back and looked at him. Using my recently acquired lie-detecting abilities, I studied Jason's face, thinking he must just be messing with me. It wasn't possible that the Hardy brothers could be on Rotary Club because they played for Nationwide the year before. "No, they can't be on your team," I said, my voice totally void of confidence. "They're already on Nationwide."

"I guess their dad decided to coach with Mr. Russo this year or something. I don't know how it happened, but they're *definitely* on my team."

"And you still have Russo and Blake?" Will Russo was the best pitcher in the league after Hardy. He didn't throw it quite as hard, but he was damn good, and he was a lefty, which made him even harder to hit. Jojo Blake was tall and fast and one of the best shortstops in the entire league.

"Yep, everyone's back from last year. We're gonna be good." Jason's smile grew even wider.

I ran his words through my head. *We're gonna be good.* That was a massive understatement. If Rotary Club had both Hardy and Russo, they could pretty much just rotate them as their pitcher game after game. And if they needed someone else to throw a spare inning here or there, they could use guys like Jojo Blake and David Hardy. No other team had four pitchers like that. No other team even had *two* pitchers like that, and that wasn't all. There were a few other skilled players on their team — I just didn't know their names. In short, if what Jason was saying was true and Rotary Club had added the Hardy brothers, they would not only be the best team in the league, they would dominate.

I knew the rules, though, at least the basic ones, and once you were on a team you couldn't just switch because you wanted to. I tried sounding more sure of myself. "No, that can't be right, Jason. You can't just switch teams like that."

"I don't know. Maybe they changed the rules this year or something." He was still smiling, but it seemed to have taken on a bit of a sneer.

Jason walked past me and slipped into the gymnasium. As the door closed, I heard echoing voices, squeaking sneakers, and the ricochet of dodgeballs. I remember standing there in the hallway in a state of mild shock. I couldn't say I knew Jason well, but he never struck me as one to make up stories just to get a reaction. For that reason I didn't think he was lying, but I thought he had to be mistaken. In my mind there was no way the other coaches or the board, which I figured was made up mostly of those same coaches, would ever allow them to do that. There was a reason for the draft, and it was the same reason kids stayed on one team once they *got* drafted: So powerhouse teams couldn't be easily assembled. Even at ten I understood that much.

The dodgeball games were pretty intense, so there wasn't any time to check the accuracy of Jason's story with anyone else. When I got back to my classroom, I asked another kid who played baseball, but he hadn't heard anything about it. That meant one of two things. Either Jason was just messing with me — again, not likely — or I had been on the very front end of some incredible breaking news. The kid I really needed to hear from was Matt Baxter. His uncles were our two main coaches, and surely he would have heard about such an important development if it were true. Unbelievably, at 8:55 he still wasn't in class. The most important scandal of my young life was unfolding, and the one person who could confirm or deny its authenticity looked like he might not even be in school.

At 8:58 on the nose, Matt finally came hustling into class, but Mr. Holt decided to get started early that day. He was already stepping around his desk, math book in hand, heading toward the blackboard. I didn't want to wait until lunch, but I wasn't keen on getting yelled at, either. Matt's desk was one row ahead of mine and one spot to the left. Just as he sat down, Mr. Holt stopped to say something to a girl in the front row. I decided to chance it. "Matt, is Zach Hardy on Rotary Club?" I whispered. At first Matt just stared ahead, motionless. I didn't think he heard me and was contemplating whether to ask him again when I saw his head jerk up and down. It was so quick it took me a second to realize he'd actually nodded.

My God, it's true, I thought. Getting a head nod from Matt Baxter was all the verification I needed. It carried more weight than a thousand words from anyone else. My mind raced like an out-of-control slot machine. There were ten teams in the Majors that year, and the coaches — not one of whom could I name other than Vic Baxter — had let a couple dads determine who was going to win the league before anyone had held their first practice. Once my shock level began its descent, another line of thinking started to develop, this one much more personal. We were going to face Rotary Club twice during the regular season and maybe a third time if we were unlucky enough to meet in the playoffs. I knew we'd face Russo at least once, but I figured the other time, we'd more than likely get a break. It was just how these things usually went, or so I'd been told. Now we'd face Zach Hardy in that second game and maybe again in the playoffs. The excitement of being selected for the Majors, especially on what I thought might well be the best team in the league, seemed like a hazy memory from another lifetime.

17

That evening I was in the backyard throwing pop-ups to myself when Mom yelled out that it was time for dinner. I played that game a lot when there was no one else around. Before Adam met Julia, he was always available to play catch, but that spring it seemed like he was never there to do anything because he was always at her house. Jess told me one time she didn't think Julia liked Mark all that much. I remember thinking that was weird. I figured it was because he sometimes acted like our father and Adam resented that. I made one final toss, imagining I was making the final out to win the championship for J&F. I threw it a little higher than usual and the ball veered off course. I knew right away it was going to be a tough catch. I tracked the ball as it reached its apex, then stumbled into the middle of the yard to where I thought it would come down. When the ball approached to within fifteen feet or so, I fell backward and made a snow-cone catch. I leapt to my feet, raising my hands above my head in celebration.

"Hey, nice catch," Mark said from the doorway.

"Thanks," I said, embarrassed. I knew Mark was helping Mom with dinner, but I didn't think he'd be watching me.

"Come on in, Danny. I have to leave pretty soon, and your mom and I want to talk to you guys about something."

"Okay." I ran across the patio, then bounded up the steps and into the house.

"Wash your hands," Mom said, as she carried a bowl of steaming pasta into the dining room.

I did as I was told and then sat next to Jess. Mark and Mom were directly across from us. I saw there was a bowl of corn and a smaller container of peas on the dining room table. There was also a medium-sized pot of spaghetti sauce with what looked like meatballs in it. In those days Mom often made homemade sauce, but this looked (and smelled) like she'd just added some meatballs to a jar of red sauce. That was fine with me. I liked the jar sauce just as much.

"So, how was school?" Mom asked.

"Good," Jess said. "Boring."

Mom smiled and looked at Mark before turning back to me. "How about you, Danny? How was your day?"

"It was okay, I guess. Everyone was talking about tryouts — oh, listen to this. Jason Billings told me Zach Hardy and David Hardy are on his team this year. And they already have Will Russo and Jojo Blake."

"I take it they're all good players?" Mark asked.

"You know Zach Hardy," I said, probably a little too emphatically. "We watched him that one time, remember?"

"Oh, is he the kid that throws pretty hard?"

"Yeah, he throws *really* hard, and so does Will Russo. And now they're both on the same team."

"Okay, now why is that such a big deal?"

Are you kidding me? "Because they were on different teams last year, and now they're on the *same* team. They're gonna kill everyone."

Mark inserted a fork-full of rolled spaghetti into his mouth. He looked at me and nodded his head as he chewed. "I got it now. Hardy wasn't drafted by this team. He just got put on it this year."

"Yeah, that's right."

"Sounds like some of the dads are making up their own rules," Mom said.

Mom was always quick to spot an injustice, and she was usually just as quick at pinpointing the source. I think people who typically abide by the rules usually are, but that wasn't the only reason. Mom was just smart and knew the sneaky games people liked to play.

"Well, how did they do it if they weren't supposed to?" Mark asked.

"No one knows," I said.

"It doesn't sound right to me," Mom said. "I'll ask Vic about it. Maybe he knows what happened."

"You guys just have to beat them anyway," Mark said. I was about to say how unlikely that was, but Mark moved on to another topic. "Well, your mom and I have some exciting news." He was smiling.

I looked at Mom, and she was smiling, too. "That's right," she said. "As you know, Mark's been a big part of our family for the last year." Jess and I looked at each other. "We decided that next spring we're going to make it official and get married. We haven't picked a date yet, but it will be right around this same time."

I looked at Jess again, and her face was about as happy as I'd ever seen it. Her eyes were sparkling and her grin spanned the entire width of her face. She bounded out of her chair and ran around the table to our mom. I wasn't quite as thrilled as Jess — I don't think that would've been possible — but I was pretty happy, too. I think my relative calmness was because I already suspected it was coming. I followed Jess around the table to embrace our mom, and then we both hugged Mark. I knew Adam would have been happy, too, but I don't think he would've hugged anyone.

"Can I be your maid of honor?" Jess asked.

"Of course," Mom said, laughing. She hugged Jess again.

I got the sense Mom was nervous about telling us, although I don't know why. I think both Jess and I already thought of Mark as our stepdad.

Mark gave me a light slap on the back. "And you and Adam can be ushers."

"Will I get to wear a tux?"

Mark laughed and then looked at Mom. "Maybe. We're not sure yet how formal it's going to be."

"You can definitely wear a suit," Mom added, "but we'll probably have to get you one. I don't think your old one fits you anymore."

She grinned, and a thought came to me out of nowhere. *I've never seen her happier.*

18

Wednesday

I said goodnight to our new production supervisor and headed through the solid glass door connecting NBC's production floor to the front offices. The old super left three months ago after taking a job at another board shop in Pennsylvania. Based on the rumors floating around the front office, it was a much better offer. I didn't blame him for leaving. In fact, I'd been wondering if I should start testing the waters myself to see if anyone might be willing to do the same for me. I loved working for and with Carolyn, and I also respected NBC's owners — the one I knew anyway — but I wasn't getting any younger, and it had been quite a while since my last raise. At the very least, I might be able to use another company's offer to improve my situation.

I grabbed my keys out of my desk and headed for the door. It was 6:05, and I'd had enough for one day. I slipped out the front door and had almost made it to my Saturn when I heard Carolyn's voice behind me.

"Dan, wait up," she said.

I turned back to see her standing in the doorway. She'd been out of the office all week, meeting with the owners. We'd spoken on the phone several times, but I hadn't seen her in the flesh since I'd stopped by the office on Saturday. "Hey, I thought you weren't coming back until tomorrow?"

"Yeah, I got back early. What are you doing right now? Does Connor have a game tonight?"

"No, not tonight. I was just thinking about grabbing some Chinese food before heading home."

"I need to talk to you. Can I buy you a drink? I'll make it quick. I promise."

"Sure." I didn't feel like going anywhere, but I was already getting the sense this was going to be important. I thought about the strange feeling I had when I stopped in on Saturday and found Carolyn getting ready for a plant tour.

"Okay, I'll meet you at Friday's."

"Sounds good."

I hopped in my Saturn and headed out of the parking lot. I got to TGI Friday's first, so I waited for her outside. Carolyn arrived a minute later and walked toward the entrance. As usual, she looked both stylish and professional, but I thought she looked pretty stressed-out, as well. We made our way into the restaurant and found two empty stools at the bar. It seemed crowded for a Wednesday, but a quick scan told me I didn't know anyone.

"What can I get you?" asked the young woman behind the bar. Her smile made me think of the woman I'd met over the weekend. *Ally.*

Carolyn looked at me. "Feel like a martini?"

I was planning on ordering a rum and coke, but a martini didn't seem like a bad idea. "Sure, why not?"

"Two Bombay Sapphire martinis," Carolyn said. "Straight up, extremely dry with olives."

"Okay, coming right up," the bartender said, before disappearing to the other side of the bar.

I looked at Carolyn. She looked tired and a little worn out, like maybe she hadn't been sleeping well. "So, how are you?" I asked. "I feel like I haven't seen you in weeks."

"I know," she said with a quick smile.

"How did the meetings go?"

"Well, James isn't doing very well, so I only met with Bob this time. They haven't officially diagnosed him, but Bob thinks it's Parkinson's. Apparently, their mother suffered from the same thing before she died."

"Oh, that's awful." We typically saw Bob only three or four times a year, but everyone liked and respected him. And as far as I knew, no one had ever met James, aside from Carolyn. We were still discussing it when the bartender came back and placed the martinis in front of us. I picked up my glass and touched Carolyn's. "Cheers."

Carolyn smiled, broader this time, but still lacking her usual warmth. "Cheers."

I took my first sip, a big one, even more confident something was up. I could tell she was hesitating, so I helped her get the ball rolling. "So what's going on?"

"Look, Dan, I wanted to meet with you. There's something important I need to talk to you about."

"Okay. Shoot."

"There's no easy way to say this."

Jesus. "Carolyn, what is it?"

"I'm leaving NBC."

Even with advance warning, I felt like someone had kicked me in the back of the head. If I'd made a list of all the possible things I would have expected her to say at that moment, *I'm leaving NBC* wouldn't have been on it. Carolyn *was* NBC. There were definitely some good people there—I hoped most would consider me among that group—but Carolyn was the driving force that kept everything clicking along. And that was just on the work end. Personally, the thought of her leaving was both shocking and intensely depressing. She was by far and away the best friend I had at NBC.

"Take another sip," Carolyn said. "It will make this easier to talk about."

I followed her suggestion and swallowed an even larger gulp. The gin was really hitting me now. When I looked back at her, the rest of the bar had already slipped into the background. I could hear distant conversations around us, but all I could see was Carolyn. "What do you mean you're leaving NBC? Are you leaving the area?"

Carolyn stared at her drink. "We are. Jeff got offered a position with a company in Houston. It's essentially a startup and they offered him a stake in ownership. It's an incredible opportunity. We're going down next week to look for a house."

"Next week!" I said it louder than I meant to. "Carolyn, I can't believe this. Who's going to run NBC?"

"I don't know."

Those words hit me almost as hard as the news she was leaving. "You don't know? They haven't found your replacement yet? Does Bob even know you're leaving?"

"He knows. Actually, Dan, there's something else I need to tell you."

"Jesus, there's more?"

"I'm telling you this because I trust you. But you have to promise me it stays between us. There's going to be an announcement tomorrow, but I don't want anyone to hear it before then."

"Of course."

"Bob and James are selling NBC."

"Christ." I picked up my drink and finished it before turning back to Carolyn. "The hits just keep on coming."

"It's been in the works for a couple months now, but it just became official this week."

"And you're just telling me now?"

"The first time I heard about it was two weeks ago, and it just became official on Monday. If Bob knew I was telling you, he'd flip."

"Who are they selling to?"

"It's a family-owned group out of Ohio. They own a handful of contract manufacturing plants and also a small circuit board shop. They wanted something with more capacity."

"What's their name?"

"I can't tell you that yet, but we've never done anything for them before. I don't think we've even done any quotes for them."

I flagged the bartender down and had just ordered a second martini when another thought hit me. "What's going to happen to all of us?"

"That was one of the final sticking points. Bob was trying to ensure everyone would be kept on for at least six months, but they wouldn't guarantee anything. Obviously, they'll have some of their own people, but I think they'll want to keep most of our team in place. And they already know about you. I spoke to one of the new owners personally about the job you've done. I took them on a couple private tours last week."

Again, I thought about seeing Carolyn on Saturday. That had to be when she'd given at least one of those plant tours. "I appreciate that, Carolyn," I said, knowing it meant next to nothing. Without an agreement in place, anyone could get axed, regardless of what might have been said during a clandestine plant tour. I was growing increasingly numb by the second.

"Bob's not in a strong financial position. Several of his investments have done poorly in recent years. He was basically forced to sell. Unfortunately, the buyers figured this out and knew he wasn't in a position to dictate anything. Frankly, Bob and James were lucky they stuck with the agreed-upon price. They could have negotiated lower. Bottom line, they had to accept the family's offer with no conditions."

"I don't know what to say, Carolyn. I think I'm in shock right now."

Carolyn put her hand on my forearm. "Everyone is going to learn about this tomorrow, but I wanted you to know beforehand."

"When do they come in?"

"It's their shop Friday morning. Technically, it's their shop tomorrow at midnight. I don't know if they're planning on coming in on Friday or if they'll wait until Monday."

"My God." I knew something like this could happen, and in fact, it happened all the time with private companies, but usually something got leaked and people knew about it in advance. As far as I knew, no one at NBC had heard about this. Everyone would be blindsided. And even though she was leaving, I also felt bad for Carolyn. I hoped Bob O'Brien was coming in himself to tell everyone. This wasn't Carolyn's doing, and it wasn't fair to ask her to deliver the news. Just then the woman returned with my second martini. "What about you, Carolyn? When's your last day?"

"Tomorrow."

"Are you kidding me?" Again, I said it louder than I meant to. Carolyn didn't seem to notice.

"I wish I was. I'm holding a meeting with the front office in the morning and then production and shipping in the afternoon. I'll probably come in tomorrow night to get my things and clean out my office."

"Jesus. I can't believe this."

"I know. I'm sorry. This happened so fast. I knew Bob was talking with some different groups, but I didn't know how far it had progressed until

late last week. He called me at home and told me about the final deal on
Monday. And while all this was happening, Jeff got the offer. He'd been
speaking with these guys for a few weeks, but the ownership part surprised
us. It was too good to pass up. My initial plan was to stay here until Bob
found a replacement...but that's not going to be necessary."

"I wonder how many of us they'll keep. The fact they wouldn't agree to
anything doesn't leave me with a good feeling. A lot of people have invested
a hell of a lot in this company." For emphasis, I picked up my fresh martini
and took a long sip.

Carolyn turned to me. "Who do you think you're talking to, Dan? You
think I don't know that? You think I don't realize what everyone has done?"

Her tone caught me completely off guard. Later it would occur to me she
was feeling guilty over leaving NBC, especially given what was happening,
but in the midst of my gin-fueled shock and disappointment, her harsh tone
acted like a switch inside my head. I was suddenly as mad as I'd been in a
long time, and it was rooted in my belief that she'd known about this for
longer than two weeks. I opened my mouth to say something to that effect
and then closed it again. Even in my current state, I knew staying here
would be a huge mistake. Carolyn was a good friend, but she was still my
boss.

"I'm sorry, Carolyn. I have to go." I slid off the bar stool and practically
ran for the door before I could say anything else.

19

I drove home with a touch of nostalgia for my old life. I still felt it from time to time, and tonight it was carrying a lot more bite than usual. It occurred to me, yet again, that I needed to make some changes. I'd pretty much been on cruise control since the divorce. This certainly wasn't new information, but tonight was a stern reminder that I needed to start acting. Not only was Carolyn leaving, but the entire future of the company was uncertain. *My future* was uncertain.

My thoughts drifted to Adam, a place they often went when I was feeling overwhelmed. He always had a knack for getting me pointed in the right direction. Out of nowhere, our last phone conversation popped into my head and I could suddenly smell the stale odor of sweat mixing with Old Spice aftershave. Frightening images began flooding my thoughts — images that I'd been battling to subdue since Adam had resurrected them in that final call. I thought about Connor, purposely focusing on his face and his voice until the images faded. It was the same trick I'd used in the aftermath of catching Laura with Alan McBride. It wasn't like the mental pictures went away completely, but the technique provided just enough of a buffer for my brain to start functioning again.

When I rounded the corner to my apartment, there was something else to drive my thoughts. Several cars were parked in the bike shop parking lot. The shop always closed by 6:00, so I knew they weren't customers. I also noticed more cars than usual parked along the street in front of the apartment complex. As soon as I turned into the lot, I saw why. Ally's door opened and two people came out, joining a small group of four or five others already standing in the driveway. They were all holding what looked like cans of beer, and a couple were smoking, as well. *Ally's having a party*, I thought.

I parked my Saturn in the one available space and hopped out. I kept checking my phone to see if Carolyn had texted me, but so far she hadn't. I still couldn't believe she was leaving. I don't think too many of us had worked with a stronger leader, and for that reason alone, the news would floor everyone. And just as they'd be picking themselves back up, they'd be hit with the revelation that NBC had been sold.

I walked toward the stairs and got a better look at the group standing outside Ally's apartment. From here I could see she wasn't among them. I'd just started up the stairs when I heard my name. I turned around and saw the other woman from Saturday. She was dressed in a pair of white shorts and a blue tee-shirt. Her name came to me just as she reached the bottom of the stairs. "Oh, hey, Katie, how are you?"

"I'm doing great, thanks. Listen, Ally's having a party and wondered if you wanted to come. It's just a bunch of business-school friends."

I looked up at the group again, thinking I must have just missed her the first time.

"Oh, she's inside," Katie said. "She told me to be on the lookout for you. She wanted to thank you for helping us out the other day."

My plan was to have a glass of wine, call Connor to say goodnight, and then try to get some sleep. I decided to keep that to myself, however. I already felt old enough. "Katie, helping you guys was my pleasure. Unfortunately, I have to work on a presentation for tomorrow." It was a lie, but I thought a good one.

Katie smiled. "Oh, come on. You can have one beer, and then you can go home and create your masterpiece."

I couldn't help but laugh at that, and as foolish as it was, the thought of seeing Ally again excited me, especially in this kind of setting. "Okay, you've convinced me. Let me run up and change out of my work clothes. I'll be right over."

"Okay. We're coming up to get you if you don't show up."

I thought of several responses, but none that could be said aloud. I opted for something safe. "I'll be there. I promise."

"All right," Katie said, before turning back toward the apartment.

I went inside and changed into a pair of khaki shorts and a golf shirt. I picked royal blue because Laura used to tell me it brought out the color in my eyes. I slipped into a pair of loafers, brushed my teeth, and was out the door. I was moving as fast as possible, so I couldn't find a way to talk myself out of it. I was halfway down the stairs when I remembered I hadn't called Connor yet. It was already almost 8:00, and he was usually in bed by 8:30 on school nights. If I didn't call him now, I wouldn't talk to him tonight. I took a seat on the third step from the bottom and found his number on my cell phone. I didn't want him to have a phone yet, but Laura convinced me it was a good idea. She reasoned we could keep in closer communication when he was out with his friends or touring the neighborhood on his bike. It was hard to argue with that logic, so I didn't, and he ended up getting a smart phone for Christmas.

As I waited, I listened to the relaxed banter of the grad students. I guessed they were all somewhere in their early to mid-twenties. I couldn't hear specific words, but I could make out some light ribbing and plenty of laughter. When Connor answered I could tell right away he was already half asleep. We spoke for a couple minutes, and I told him I loved him. I had just ended the call when a text came in from Carolyn.

Dan, sorry about tonight. Tough situation for everyone. We'll talk tomorrow.

I decided to text back right away even though I was still pissed at her. *Sorry about running out. I guess I got overwhelmed with everything. Will be tough around here without you. See you tomorrow.*

I dropped my phone into my pocket and headed over to Ally's. I passed by the group of students, which had grown to seven strong. I didn't see Ally or Katie among them. My long-range age estimates appeared to be spot on. Everyone looked to be right around Ally's age, maybe a year or two younger. A couple glanced at me when I walked by, I'm sure wondering whose father was crashing the party.

I pushed the thought away and was about to knock on the door when it opened up and a young woman stepped out. She smiled at me and I smiled back. I stepped inside the apartment, absorbing the cooler air and the sound of a band I knew but couldn't quite place. I took a quick look around, thinking Ally had done an impressive job of unpacking and organizing. Gone were the boxes stacked everywhere on Saturday. She'd also managed to hang a few pictures and bring in additional furniture. And all of that was accomplished with a full course load. I thought about how long it had taken me to get The Palace in order. I still had boxes on the kitchen floor two months after moving in.

A few people were sitting on the same couch the three of us had carried in on Saturday, and a couple others were lounging on a loveseat. There were probably an additional ten or eleven people standing around the room, talking. I did a quick inventory, noting everyone was around the same age as the others with the exception of one couple who looked to be in their late thirties. I guessed they were a young professor and his wife. As I made my way toward the kitchen, Katie came into view.

"Dan!" she yelled, coming toward me. "I was just about to come and get you."

"I know, I was afraid of that, so I tried to hurry."

Katie laughed and grabbed my arm. "There's beer and wine in the kitchen, and I think some rum." She began leading me in that direction. "Ally's in there, too. She'll be happy to see you."

We rounded the corner, and I spotted Ally across the kitchen, talking with another woman. There were roughly half a dozen other people scattered about the room, but I still had a clear view. Ally looked incredible. Her brown hair hung down around her shoulders, and her cheeks had that same natural rosiness I noticed on Saturday. She was wearing a pair of khaki shorts—snug enough to show off her great figure—and a white button-down blouse. She was absolutely beautiful, and the best part was she didn't seem to know it.

Two large coolers stood open near the women's feet, and behind them on the counter were five or six bottles of red wine. Ally saw Katie dragging me along and she smiled. I couldn't help but notice it was unforced and immediate. I walked toward her, trying to keep *my* smile from taking over my face. I'd never been great at hiding my emotions, especially when I saw something I liked.

"Hi, Dan," she said, still smiling.

"Hi, Ally, thanks for inviting me." I turned to look at Katie, but she was already walking away. The other woman had disappeared, too. It was just the two of us. *Beauty and the old guy.*

"I stopped over to your apartment earlier, but you weren't home."

"Yeah, I went out for a drink with some coworkers."

"Well, I'm so glad you could make it. I wanted to thank you for helping us out the other day."

"Ally, I carried one thing, and you two did all the work...and you brought me a beer."

Ally laughed. "I did, but that wasn't enough. That couch was soooo heavy, and we would have been in trouble had you not shown up."

"I doubt it. Hey, nice job getting the apartment ready. That was quick. I think I still have a box or two I haven't unpacked yet."

Ally laughed again. "Oh, don't worry. I had some help. Katie was here, and my mom and sister came down, too."

"From Syracuse?"

"Yep, Clay, actually. Oh, I'm sorry. What would you like to drink?"

I looked down and saw she was drinking a Corona. "How about one of those," I said, pointing. "That looks good."

"One Corona, coming up." She turned and bent over toward one of the coolers.

Without thinking, I found myself following the curve of her back down toward her hips. I caught myself and turned away quickly. I was already feeling out of place. The last thing I needed was to get caught ogling the host.

We talked about school for a while, and it turned out I was right. The couple in their late thirties was a professor and his wife. I'm sure everyone at the party suspected I was just a professor they hadn't met yet. I decided it was better than being someone's father. After about twenty minutes or so, Katie came back and introduced me to a couple of her male friends while Ally got pulled here and there. Their friends seemed like good guys, but one of them bore a striking resemblance to my favorite elementary school guidance counselor, Alan McBride. He was the same height as McBride, and his mannerisms were frighteningly similar. He even had that cocky *I'm going to bang your wife when you're not home* kind of vibe going. And not for the first time, thinking about McBride made me think about Mark, which led to memories of Adam and Jess and the things that happened when we were kids. When all that started bouncing around in my head, I knew it was time to go. I'd had three Coronas in about forty minutes, and that was on top of the gin. I was definitely going to be feeling it tomorrow. If I didn't leave now, I was bound to have a couple more and would in all likelihood end the night by saying something foolish to Ally—something along the lines of how beautiful she was. That would probably put a quick end to our friendship just as it was getting started.

I said goodbye to Katie who tried hard to get me to do a beer funnel before I left. I figured they must all have a light class load tomorrow, but I still had to make it to work. I escaped Katie and found Ally in the living room. She was talking to the professor's wife. After quick introductions, the woman excused herself.

"I have to head back," I said. "I need to work on a presentation for tomorrow." I was proud I'd remembered the same white lie I told Katie earlier.

"Are you sure you can't stay? I'm sorry I left you with Katie. She tried to make you do a funnel, didn't she?"

"She did," I said, laughing. "I had a lot of fun tonight, but I do have to go." Even drunk, that sense I was overstaying my welcome was coming on fast. I thought about giving her a quick kiss on the cheek but thankfully came to my senses. I grabbed her hand instead. "Thanks again, Ally. I'll see you later."

Before she could say anything else, I slipped out the door.

The Majors

20

The first full week in Mr. Holt's class had been pretty uneventful. There were no additional tears even though everyone had heard about Ms. Becker's condition. A call had gone out that Monday night to all the parents. Mr. Holt made a brief mention of it but didn't open up the floor to questions like he'd been forced to do on his first day. He avoided that hardship by saying, "Now you guys know as much about it as I do." Even the girls that had broken down the previous Friday handled the news okay. We all loved Ms. Becker, but the major shock had been dealt with. She was gone for the rest of the year, and Mr. Holt would be our teacher. Because she didn't die in the accident, I think most of us thought she'd be back eventually.

I didn't see the new girl when I first walked into the classroom on that Friday morning. I was thinking about our upcoming practice and feeling some of the same nerves I'd felt before tryouts. This time, though, it was mostly just the good kind. I was already in the Majors, and that wasn't going to change. Plus, no one expected a lot out of the ten-year-olds, or so I hoped. I walked past Mr. Holt's empty chair (he'd brought in his own by that point) and made my way toward my seat. My desk was in the back row, second from the window and three removed from Mr. Holt's desk. I preferred it over the front of the class, mainly because there was too much pressure up there. I was a firm believer that a direct correlation existed between proximity to the teacher and the likelihood of being called upon.

Our desks had a hinged Formica top that lifted up to reveal a good-sized storage area. The seat itself was attached to the desk, making it a mobile unit. For the disorganized kids, a category to which I definitely belonged, the storage areas were like a garbage dump where anything and everything could become lost. I opened the top of my desk and threw my books onto a scattered pile of notebooks and miscellaneous papers. As soon as I sat in my seat, I noticed Amy McLaughlin was sitting right beside me. Normally, there was an empty desk to my right, but on that day Amy was there instead. *Why* Amy was there was suddenly the burning question. My eyes, following some unspoken orders, traveled up Amy's column until it reached the front of the class. And there I discovered the answer. Sitting in the front row was a girl I'd never seen before.

I could only see the back of her white sweater and the curls of her short brown hair, but my initial thought was she looked scared. She was crouched down in her seat, shoulders slumped, with her hands on her lap. By the position of her head, I could tell she was staring either at her desktop or the ground directly in front of it. She was completely motionless. It was as if she was thinking *No one will notice me as long as I don't move.* Right then there was a loud clap as Mike Walters (aka Big Mike) dropped his math book on the floor. The new girl whipped her head to the left in reaction to the noise before whipping it back almost as fast. Two of my assumptions were confirmed. She was, in fact, new—I had definitely never seen her before— and she was, in fact, terrified. Her eyes looked like they were about to leap out of her head and make a mad dash for the door.

A few minutes before 9:00, Mr. Holt walked into the room and headed toward the front of the class. When he got there, he turned to face us. "Okay," he began, "since everyone is here already, we're going to get started early." There was a light groan from someone, Big Mike, I think, but he ignored it. "We have a new student this morning." He gestured toward the new girl with his hand, and I saw her shoulders slump even further. "Her name is Lisa Bonner. Let's all say hello to Lisa." Almost everyone offered a quiet but polite hello. "Lisa, why don't you tell us something about yourself?" Mr. Holt said.

There was a quick almost indiscernible shake of her head. I immediately felt bad for her. It was her first day in a new school, and she was obviously a little shy—maybe even a *lot* shy. Anyone could see that except for Mr. Holt. Or maybe he saw it and didn't care.

Mr. Holt chuckled. "Okay, do you mind if *I* tell the class a little bit about you, then?" She returned a quick nod. It was obvious she didn't want to be the focus of anyone's attention, but what choice did she have? "Lisa just moved here from a town called Scranton, Pennsylvania, which is about an hour south of here. She went to Emerson Elementary School, and her teacher was Mrs. Smith. I got a note from Mrs. Smith yesterday, and it said Lisa was a wonderful girl and a joy to have in class. Well, we're very glad to have her join us."

I knew Mr. Holt was just trying to be nice, but his awkward delivery made the whole thing uncomfortable. Mercifully, he let it drop soon after and moved on to his normal daily lesson, which so far had been math followed by more math with the occasional discussion of social studies or science mixed in. The first full week with Mr. Holt was almost over, and English had yet to make an appearance.

That Friday's lunch period was a lot like all the prior lunches that week. Mostly, I sat with Matt and peppered him with questions about our team and the upcoming season. He'd already spent one full year with J&F and knew all the returning players and coaches. Matt wasn't a huge talker, but by the end of that week, I had a pretty good idea of the team makeup. We were no Rotary Club, but we'd be good. Matt said we'd lost only three players from a team that had won the championship. Two of those players were really good, he said, but he added that the heart of last year's team were the three eleven-year-olds. And now they were back for their final season as twelves. He told me their names, but the only one I'd heard of was Truck Macavoy. I figured Truck wasn't his real name, but Matt assured me that's what everyone called him. Truck was one of the best catchers in the league and was also a great hitter. He'd hit twelve homers as an eleven-year-old, which was almost unheard of. There were also five returning elevens, including Matt, and then the four drafted tens. Matt said his dad felt like they had the best draft of any team in the league. He also said his two uncles — the actual coaches — were excited about the upcoming season. We needed to find a couple pitchers, but we were going to have a solid team.

When lunch was over, we headed out to the playground where anywhere from six to ten kids would typically assemble near the basketball court. Normally, we'd play a pick-up game or two, but that week we just shot around and talked baseball. The most common topic was Rotary Club and the fast one they'd pulled to assemble their team. Jason Billings came down with the flu, and since he was the only kid in our school actually on Rotary Club, there was no firsthand knowledge of anything. That was fine with us. Nothing comes more naturally to ten-year-olds than rampant speculation. Among the more popular theories of the week was that Mr. Hardy got into a fistfight with another coach, so he had to take his sons to another team. Another was that Mr. Russo hated the J&F coaches and wanted to beat them so badly that he "bent" a few rules to build a stronger team.

By the end of that week, a kid named Cam Bender had emerged as someone who knew more than anyone else about the inner workings of the Everton Little League. He was a sixth-grade eleven-year-old and not a strong player, but he seemed to know what he was talking about. Someone said his dad used to be a board member in another baseball league, but no one could say which one. It wasn't exactly top-of-the-line credentials, but it was the best we had. Plus, he sounded confident, which goes a long way, whether you're a kid on a playground or a fifty-year-old in a boardroom. He started us out with some basic rules. Each head coach is able to name one assistant, and if that assistant has a son who hasn't been drafted yet, they can add him to the team as a coach's pick. Bender said if Hardy had been named as Russo's assistant coach, he could, in theory, bring his two sons along with him. There were two problems with that idea. One was that the assistant coach was supposed to be able to bring only one kid along with him, not two. The other problem (and I remember it being the much bigger of the two) was that once a player has been drafted, he has to stay on that team for the duration of his Little League career. So even if they found a way around the first rule, they wouldn't have been able to sidestep the other without board approval. Bender explained that the second rule was the only way the league could keep the teams more or less even. Otherwise, certain dads would get together to form two or three powerhouse teams, while the other eight—filled with younger, less-talented kids—would be served up as the sacrificial lambs. Survival of the fittest at its finest.

That was where our knowledge, limited as it may have been from the onset, dipped even further. Not one of us, and on that particular day the count was eight, had any direct connection to a current board member. That made Bender's opinion even more valuable, and by that Friday afternoon his words were traveling around our little circle mostly uncontested. Once the season was underway, he would slip quickly and anonymously into the background again, but that week he was *The Man*. Bender was adamant the whole thing went down something like this: Hardy and Russo proposed the idea to the board with Hardy citing some kind of issue with his old team, perhaps that he didn't get along with the other coaches. (The fistfight angle had been dropped by that point.) After both sides debated the topic, probably in heated fashion, the board put the matter up for a vote. There were no cell phones or emails for members to weigh in, so the only votes cast were from those in attendance. If a few key members weren't there for the meeting, then Hardy and Russo would have had an easier time getting it pushed through. That happened all the time, according to Bender's father. None of us were in a position to argue with him, so we didn't. Plus, it had really happened, so his theory couldn't have been too far off.

Like Bender, most of us had discussed the issue with our parents. The general consensus was that everyone recognized the incident for what it was. *Complete bullshit.* But while everyone was pissed off about it, no one was close enough to the situation to know what had happened or to do anything about it. It was one of those injustices, while minor in the whole scheme of things, was a pretty big deal at the time and had a way of getting under your skin and festering like a bad infection. An infection that would suddenly flare up each time you had to play them.

When the bell rang, I walked in from the playground with Matt, and we headed down the hall together toward our classroom. As I walked into the room, I glanced over toward the new girl, Lisa. She was sitting at her desk. I thought she still looked a little scared but no longer terrified. She looked back at me and Matt before turning around again.

On Mr. Holt's first day, he'd taken about ten minutes to talk about what he called *his rules*. They were of the standard variety and included such staples as *no talking during class, no cheating, no trespassing in someone else's desk*—he spent a lot of time on that one—and, of course, *no passing notes.* I don't think they were all that different from any other teacher's rules, except he'd taken the time to talk about them up front, whereas most teachers addressed them on an as-needed basis. By the time we'd reached fifth-grade, everyone knew these rules cold, and they either followed them or had become adept at breaking them. So when Mr. Holt laid them out to us that day, no one raised an eyebrow.

I didn't know it then, but Mr. Holt had also briefed Lisa Bonner on *his rules.* Her dad had dropped her off early so she could get settled in. Mr. Holt had taken some of that extra time to bring her up to speed. I don't know if Lisa wasn't listening closely enough, or if she didn't realize how seriously Mr. Holt took them, but either way she would understand soon enough.

It was about 2:00, a time of day that would prove to be quite dangerous in Mr. Holt's class. Lunch had been over for about an hour, and it was a natural time for people—adults and kids alike—to lose their focus. Just four years earlier, we would have all been napping on soft mats, dreaming about cookies and recess. At the urging of a girl named Jackie Neal, Lisa had been playing Russian roulette for the past fifteen minutes by passing notes back and forth. I'd seen them talking together at lunch, and I'd made the reasonable assumption Jackie was her very first friend at our school. Unfortunately, Lisa couldn't have known that Jackie had been a seasoned note passer since the nap-filled days of first-grade. Typically, if someone in the front of the class was passing notes, the people behind them knew it. I had no idea it was going on, which meant the two of them had been doing a pretty discreet job of it. Mr. Holt was up at the board, giving us yet another lesson on the joys of fifth-grade mathematics, when Lisa got a little overconfident. Or maybe she was just tired, but either way, she lost her edge. She made the rookie mistake of reaching her arm out toward Jackie as Mr. Holt was turning around. She whipped her arm back—and that I did notice—but she was too late. Mr. Holt saw her. He charged forward with an eerie quickness and grabbed the note from her already-trembling hand.

"Passing notes in my class?" he bellowed. Lisa was too stunned to say anything. The intensity of his voice and his unexpectedly quick movements had startled everyone. "Are you going to answer me?" His tone had grown even angrier. "I asked if you were passing notes in my class."

"No," she said, her voice sounding like that of a cornered mouse. She was too scared to admit it. That was a mistake, but I don't think there was much she could have done right at that point.

"Oh, really," he continued on. "Let's see what we have here." In theatrical fashion, he unfolded the paper and then held the note up for all of us to see. He then held it in front of his eyes and began reading. "This is boring. I can't wait to go home." He pointed to the note as if we didn't know that had been the source, and then he looked back at Lisa. "Oh, so you're bored, huh? It's your first day in a new school, and you're bored? You're so bored that you're passing notes with your new friend, Jackie, even though I specifically told you not to."

Lisa's head shook in fluttery movements, but she didn't speak. I don't think she *could* speak. I could only see the back of her head, but I sensed she was about to cry. With Lisa all but broken, he turned his attention to Jackie. "Miss Neal, you've been in this school for a long time, and you should know better than to do something like this." Jackie was sitting one seat to the right of Lisa, and I could see the side of her face. There were no tears, nor were they coming anytime soon. Jackie was a tough girl, and I think Mr. Holt knew it. He was about to say something else when something made him turn back. Lisa's shoulders were shaking by that point, and I realized she'd started to cry. Mr. Holt was still angry, but I saw something else clawing its way through the furious exterior. It took me a few seconds to recognize it, but it finally came into focus. He was excited. He actually seemed to be enjoying the moment. Whether he was truly enjoying it, or if it just appeared that way, I don't know, but one thing is for certain. His tenuous grip on civility snapped when he saw her crying.

"Oh, so you're going to cry now? Is that it? You pass notes in my class, when I specifically ask you not to, and then you cry when you get caught?" He wasn't as loud as he'd been a few seconds earlier, but he was still yelling. I thought that was a good sign. Again, I was mistaken. He took a step toward her and bent down, his hulking frame hovering over her. His face contorted in a grotesque expression of mock sympathy. And then in a childlike, sarcastic voice I'll never forget, he said, "What's the matter, Lisa, do you want to go back to Mrs. Smith's class? Does Mrs. Smith let you pass notes to your friends?"

At that moment I knew we'd gone down the rabbit hole. The words were awful enough, but his tone was worse and seemed impossible given his appearance. In a matter of seconds, he'd transformed from an angry fifth-grade teacher into a playground bully, taunting tears out of a hapless victim. He'd created a crack in her armor, and he was going to tear at it until her insides spilled out onto the floor for all to see. It didn't matter that she was just a little girl, nor did it matter that it was her first day in a new school. She had fucked with him and then lied about it, and for those unspeakable crimes she had to pay the price.

"I didn't hear you, Lisa," he continued in that same awful voice. "Do you want to go back to Mrs. Smith's class?"

She was sobbing by that point, just shaking her head back and forth, no doubt praying for him to stop. But there was no one to stop it, only a classroom full of scared and confused children. He continued asking her those terrible questions until something finally triggered him to stop. I think it was the sight of her falling completely apart. All that remained on his face was a look of what I can only describe as satisfaction. And then even that was gone. As soon as the monster had made its appearance, it had vanished.

"Okay, so we're not going to do that again, right?" he said in his normal voice. By then he'd backed up and was no longer leaning over her. Through the sobs, which wouldn't stop until he excused her to go to the bathroom a minute later, Lisa nodded her head eagerly. By the time she'd left the room, Mr. Holt was already back at the chalkboard, resuming his lesson as if nothing at all had happened.

21

I woke up that Saturday morning thinking about baseball. My first practice with J&F was at 1:00 pm, and to say I was looking forward to it would have been a massive understatement. Unlike tryouts, where I had a healthy dose of anxiety mixed in, I remember feeling almost pure excitement. I was officially on the team, and our first practice was the start of my Major League career.

As the morning wore on, my thoughts kept wandering to Mr. Holt and the insanity of what happened in class with Lisa Bonner. I told my mom about it, but I found it difficult to describe what had actually occurred. I just couldn't find the right words for what he'd done. I must have come pretty close, though, because when I finished telling her the story, she looked concerned. It was a look she got once in a while when she was upset about something. She said it sounded like Mr. Holt had been cruel. As soon as the word left her mouth, it sounded right. It was the one word that had been escaping me. In addition to being extremely angry, Mr. Holt had also been *cruel*.

I ate a late breakfast of waffles and sausage and then watched TV with Jess before heading outside to play catch with Adam. Julia had to work, so for once he was home. It wasn't quite as warm as it had been the previous Saturday for tryouts, but it was still pretty nice, and there were only a few white clouds dotting the sky. Before I knew it, it was time to leave for practice. I had my stuff together in plenty of time, and Archer Field was only five minutes away, but we were still in a rush to get out of the house. That always seemed to be the case whenever we went anywhere. It didn't matter if our destination was two minutes away or two hours. We were always leaving with barely enough time to get there. I think that tendency was just built into my mother's DNA. By the time we pulled up to the field, it was almost exactly 1:00. I looked out the window and saw two men standing off to the side, talking, while the kids had already paired off to play catch. I didn't do a head count, but it seemed like the entire team was already there.

"I told you we were gonna be late, Mom."

"We're not late, Danny. We're right on time."

That comment perfectly summed up my mom's thoughts on punctuality. "Okay, can we just try to get here early next time? Everyone's warming up already."

"Okay, honey." I looked over at my mom to say goodbye and saw she was looking out at the two men. "The taller guy is Vic. I'll come over and say hi."

"No, Mom, don't do that. I'll go by myself."

My mom looked at me, and I thought for sure she was going to object, but she didn't. "Okay, have fun, honey."

I hopped out of the car and ran over toward the two coaches. The two men stopped talking and turned toward me as I approached.

"Danny?" Vic asked. He had dark brown hair and equally dark, intense eyes. He looked like he was pissed off about something, but I sensed he wasn't.

"Yes," I said.

"Welcome to J&F, Danny. I'm Vic and this is Ted." He pointed toward the other man who looked younger and a lot less intense. I realized then it was Vic's eyes that made him seem angry. They looked like they could burn a hole right through you.

"Hi," I said. I thought about extending my hand like Mark had taught me, but I didn't.

"Danny, tell your mom to get you here about ten minutes early," Vic said. "That way you can warm your arm up before practice starts." I was about to tell him I'd already warmed up with my brother, but he spoke too fast. "Go with those guys over there."

He pointed toward three kids standing a little ways off to the side from the rest of the team. They were playing catch in a triangle formation. I slipped my hand into my glove and walked over toward them. When I got close, I noticed how big they were. I realized these were probably the three twelve-year-olds. I watched a couple of their throws and then I was certain. All three seemed to throw the ball hard and accurate with little effort. Their catching technique was equally as smooth and effortless.

One of the kids was stocky and had broad shoulders. He wasn't the tallest of the three, but he was the most solid. I figured that had to be Truck. He threw the ball to another kid who was about the same height but much thinner. He had thick, curly brown hair that seemed to be bursting out from underneath his J&F hat. Matt had told me his name, too, but I couldn't remember it. The kid looked at me and smiled, but I could tell the smile wasn't meant for me. It was something Truck had said to him. The third kid was a little taller than Truck and maybe even heavier, but he didn't have as muscular a build. His straight, dirty-blond hair hung well below the edge of his hat. He looked at me as I approached the group with an expression that was a long way from friendly.

"Go over there," he said, pointing. "I'll play catch with you,"

Truck looked at the thin kid with the curly brown hair and said, "You go over there and *I'll* play catch with *you*."

The three of them laughed at that comment, and I joined them awkwardly even though I wasn't sure what was funny about it. Right then the thin kid's name came back to me. *Eric*. And then like a series of levers falling into place, the other twelve-year-old's name back to me, too. *Justin*. I walked over to the spot where Justin had pointed and turned to face him.

"You ready?" he asked.

I nodded, and as soon as I did that, he rifled the ball toward me. I got my glove up just in time. I don't think it would have hit me in the face, but it would have zoomed right past my head. I looked back at him, and he just stared at me. I wanted to say *What the hell are you doing?* but something inside told me to keep my mouth shut. Justin was one of the twelve-year-olds, and I was pretty sure he was testing me. I'd been through similar experiences before with Adam and his friends. If I bitched about it, I'd be labeled a whiner, and that wasn't something I wanted to be. Without thinking much about it, I fired the ball back at him as hard as I could. Luckily, I'd already warmed up with Adam, or I probably would have thrown my arm out on the first toss of the year. Justin caught the ball and looked at me. I thought he was going to start bitching at me when a broad smile creased his face. I tried not to smile back and held most of it, but a small one escaped anyway. He nodded at me and threw it back again. It was another hard throw, but nowhere near like the first one. We played catch for a few minutes when Vic called for us to bring it in.

The team gathered around the two coaches in a haphazard circle. I scanned the group and saw Matt about ten feet away. He gave me a quick nod and I did the same. I looked at the other kids and was pretty sure I could tell who everyone was, or at least how old they were. I was confident I'd just met the three twelves, and I already knew who the other three tens were because I recognized them from the Minors. That meant everyone else had to be an eleven.

"Okay, guys," Vic said, "welcome to J&F. As most of you know already, I'm Coach Baxter. You can call me Coach or Vic. I don't care which. This is my brother, Ted, and it's the same deal with him. We've got four new kids this year. Why don't we go around the group and everyone can say their name. Truck, you can start."

By the time we got around the circle, I'd learned that I was right about the three twelves, and I'd gotten their names right, too. I also remembered what Matt had told me about their positions. Truck was our catcher, Eric played shortstop, and Justin was our best pitcher.

"For you new guys, we won the championship last year, and I fully expect us to compete for it again. Isn't that right, Justin?" Vic looked directly at the kid who'd almost beheaded me a few minutes earlier.

"Absolutely, Coach," Justin said, a serious expression on his face. Vic stared at him until he smiled.

Vic then looked around the group, burning each of us with his intense gaze. I kept thinking he was going to smile, but he didn't. His face was almost comical in its intensity, but it was then I realized *his eyes* were smiling even when his mouth wasn't. "Okay, everyone head out onto the field, except Truck and Eric. We're going to have batting practice." There was no real baseball field, but Vic and Ted had already set up bases, so we had the basic gist of where to go. The eleven-year-olds ran out and took over the infield positions while the rest of us—the ten-year-olds—stood around looking at each other.

"You guys head out to the outfield," Ted said.

Vic grabbed a bucket of baseballs and headed out to where the pitcher's mound would normally be. I passed by Justin at first base and ended up in right field. Throughout batting practice I made a couple good plays, but I also made my share of mistakes. I came charging in on two fly balls only to have them go sailing over my head. Both times, Justin looked out at me and said, "The first thing you should do on a fly ball is take two steps back." When I did it a third time, he yelled, "Are ya gonna do that all year?" Luckily, there were no more fly balls hit to me because I probably would have done it again.

Finally, it was my turn to be on deck. I came running in from the outfield, found a helmet that fit, and began taking warm-up swings. A couple minutes later, I stepped up to the makeshift home plate.

"Do you know how to bunt?" Vic asked.

"I think so." I vaguely recalled a coach showing me the basics in the Minors, but it was only once.

"You think so, huh?" This time both Vic's eyes and mouth were smiling. "Okay, why don't you show me?"

I squared around into a half-assed bunting stance, and he knew immediately I had no idea what I was doing. He walked in and gave me a quick lesson on how to square around and where to hold my hands on the bat. When he thought I had it, he walked back out and said, "Okay, lay a bunt down." He wound up and threw the pitch. I promptly squared around and bunted the baseball directly into my right eye. When it swelled up to the size of a golf ball, Vic immediately sent me home for the day. I didn't think twice about it, and I made it home just fine, but I remember my mom almost having multiple heart attacks when I walked into the house. The first one was when she saw my face, and the second was when she learned Vic had let me walk home alone after taking a baseball to the head. Back then most people didn't even think about concussions. I guess my mom was just ahead of the curve.

22

After our first practice, I sat on the couch watching *Tom and Jerry* with an ice pack on my eye. It was still swelled shut, and my mom said it would probably stay like that for two or three days. It was a little sore when I moved my eye, but other than that it didn't really hurt.

At around 4:00, Jess came downstairs and asked me if I wanted to ride bikes. At first I said no because I was watching TV, but I changed my mind quickly. I told her I wanted to walk, though. The truth was I didn't feel comfortable riding my bike around with only one good eye, and Mom wouldn't have let me anyway.

"Where do you wanna go?" I asked. By that point we were already heading out of the driveway—me on foot, Jess on her bike.

"Let's go down near the golf course."

"Okay." It didn't make much of a difference to me where we went as long as it wasn't too far. The golf course fit that bill, and it was all downhill.

Jess coasted slowly down Marcell Street while I walked alongside her. It was still sunny, but it had started to cool down, so we both had jackets on. We made our way across Griffen Avenue and headed toward Valley View Golf Course. As we approached the fence bordering the course, we watched a guy tee off on the twelfth hole. There were some bushes growing along the fence, but we still had a clear view of the fairway, about sixty yards away.

"I think golf courses are pretty," Jess said.

"I don't think they all are, but this one is."

"What hole is this?"

"The twelfth. That's the fairway right there, and that's the green over there." I pointed to each as I said it.

Right then a utility cart buzzed along the fence directly in front of us. I could tell the two men riding in it were workers because they were heading in the wrong direction. The cart had been blocked out by the brush growing along the fence, so we didn't see it until it was already on top of us.

"That's Billy!" Jess yelled. "Billy!"

I watched as the driver looked back at us, his long brown hair flopping in the wind. Suddenly, the cart slowed and then came to a stop. He looked back again, and even with only one good eye, I could see Jess was right. It was Adam's friend Billy. He began backing the cart up toward us.

"Hi, Billy!" Jess said, unable to hide her excitement.

"Quarter-Pint!" Billy yelled when he got close. He stopped the utility cart and turned it off. "How ya doing?"

"Good, Billy. What are you doing?"

Billy looked at her, an easy smile spreading across his face. "What's it look like, Quarter-Pint? I'm working." Jess just stared at him, smiling. I didn't realize until that moment that she had a crush on him. Billy turned to me. "Hey, Danny — Whoa! What the hell happened to your eye?"

"I bunted a baseball into it."

Billy laughed. "You gotta be more careful, man!"

"I know, I —"

"Hey, I heard you made the Majors."

"He did," Jess said, beaming.

"Congratulations, man! What's your brother doing today? Sleeping?"

"Yeah, I think he *is* sleeping right now," I said.

Billy laughed even harder. Everything was funny. "Figures. Well, hey, I better get back to work. I don't wanna get fired. Take it easy, Danny." He started up the cart again. "See ya later, Quarter-Pint!"

Jess was still smiling when Billy's cart turned behind a row of pine trees and disappeared from sight.

23

I missed our second practice due to my swollen eye, which by that point wasn't all that swollen anymore, and our third practice got canceled twice due to rain. By the time we finally got together again, it was a full two weeks since the bunting incident. The swelling was long gone and my vision had returned to normal. The only hard evidence it had happened at all was a fading black-and-blue patch under my eye.

Miraculously, my mom managed to get me to practice by 12:45. I remember I was one of the first kids there. Based on how she'd reacted after the first practice, I was more than a little worried she'd want to talk to Vic about letting me walk home alone. I climbed out of the truck, fully expecting her to follow. When she stayed in her seat, it dawned on me she'd probably already said something to him at work.

As I walked toward our two coaches, the sun slipped out from behind a cloud, and I felt its rays warming my face. There was no breeze, and that day was pretty mild to begin with, so I removed my jacket, leaving me in just a tee-shirt and jeans. Back then most of the kids wore jeans to practice unless it was hot enough for shorts. I saw Matt digging a baseball out of a bucket and headed toward him. There were two other kids already playing catch, both of them elevens. One was named Chris, and the other was Paul.

"Hey, Danny," Vic said, "let me see that eye." I stopped and walked over to him. He put a hand on my chin and tilted my head back. "Looks pretty good. No problems with your vision, right?"

"No, it's fine."

"Okay, no bunting today," he said, smiling.

I laughed. "Okay." I started to walk away when his voice stopped me again.

"And, Danny, no more walking home alone." He shot me one of his intense stares.

I smiled and turned away, wondering what method I should use to kill my mother when I got home. I walked over to Matt. "Hey, Matt, do you wanna play catch?"

"Sure."

We headed out to where Paul and Chris were already warming up. I was dying to talk to some of my new teammates about the Rotary Club scandal. I'd expected it to be a hot topic at the first practice, but I never got the chance to talk about it. It was still being kicked around at school, but not like that first week. I walked up beside Chris. "Chris, what do you think about Rotary Club?"

"What about 'em?"

"You know...that Zach and David Hardy are on their team now."

"Oh, yeah, I heard that, but I don't know too much about it."

"Doesn't it piss you off?"

"I guess so."

I started playing catch with Matt who by that point had made his way next to Paul. Two other kids arrived and walked up beside me. One of them was another ten-year-old named Peter.

"Are you guys talking about Rotary Club?" Peter asked.

I could tell by his voice that he and I were on the same page. "Yeah, it's bullshit, isn't it?"

"Yeah, I can't believe they let them do that. How did that happen?"

"It doesn't matter," Truck said. Peter and I wheeled around, startled. Truck had come up behind us, and he didn't sound happy. "We have to play 'em anyway, so it doesn't matter how it happened."

"That's right," Chris said.

I noticed a hint of indignation in Chris's voice that wasn't there a minute earlier. It was like he'd picked up on Truck's tone and tried to copy it. I didn't necessarily agree with Truck's logic, but I wasn't about to say so. One look at Peter told me he wasn't going to say anything, either. Truck had come in and shut the conversation down before it ever really got started. He was a twelve-year-old, and if he didn't think we should be talking about it, then we wouldn't. That's just the way it was.

As far as I was concerned — and I think the other three tens felt the same way — the twelve-year-olds were a little like gods. Not only were they the strongest players on our team, they were also the elder statesmen. They were the kids who'd been around forever, which at that point in my life meant two whole years. They had fought the wars against the powerful teams and the great players like Zach Hardy and Will Russo. They weren't afraid to play against those two or anyone else. And if they *were* afraid, they sure as hell didn't show it. Truck, Eric, and Justin knew everything there was to know about playing in the Majors, and they would lead the rest of us fearlessly into battle.

Peter and I would talk more about Rotary Club at our next practice (once we were sure no one else was around), but we would never bring it up in front of the team again. Truck had spoken, and that meant the issue was dead. Still, I knew it wouldn't be forgotten...by anyone.

About ten minutes later, after everyone had arrived and warmed up, Vic sent us out to take fielding practice. As expected, I was sent to right field again. When I saw Justin head over to first base, I remembered what he'd said to me at our first practice when I kept charging in on fly balls. *Are ya gonna do that all year?* I didn't want to hear that again, and the look of disgust on his face was even worse. I reminded myself for the hundredth time to take two steps back as soon as I saw the ball in flight.

As it turned out, I had a few minutes to think it over because Vic wanted to work out the infield. He was standing at home plate with a bat in his hand, much like Thurman had done at the tryouts just three weeks prior. "Nobody on," Vic yelled, and fired off a shot toward Paul at third base. Paul used his chest to knock down a tough hop, then snatched the ball off the grass with his bare hand and made a perfect throw to first. Vic raised the bat again and hammered an equally hard shot toward Eric at shortstop. He plucked it out of the air with seemingly no effort at all and threw a strike to Justin. From what I'd seen of Eric up to that point, he was smooth, confident, and efficient. Mom would later say he was graceful. The next ball went to Matt at second base. He didn't field it cleanly, mainly because it took a bad hop, but he jumped on it and made the play. Then Vic turned toward Justin at first base who promptly bent down and got ready. A moment later the ball was bounding toward him. His movements were clunky compared to Matt and Paul, and downright clumsy compared to Eric, but he knocked it down, grabbed the ball, and touched the bag. I thought it was going to be my turn, but instead Vic laid a bunt down. Truck scrambled out with surprising agility and threw an absolute bullet to first. Truck's arm was what Adam would have called *a cannon.*

"Let's go again," Vic yelled, and hit another hard grounder to third. As I watched our starting infield make play after play, I began to get a sense of why J&F had won the championship the previous year...and why Vic thought we could do it again. It occurred to me that what I was watching was a lot closer to how the Yankees played than anything I'd seen in the Minors. And everyone seemed to be having fun, especially Eric. He was always smiling and there was an ease about him that I'd never seen before, especially from someone as talented as he was. But instead of being cocky, he gave off a vibe that said *Yeah, I'm good, but who gives a shit?* I think that was the day the *man-crush* started. I looked up to all the twelves, and even most of the elevens, but I wanted to be *like* Eric. To me, he was the personification of cool.

I stood in right field thinking about where I was going to put the championship trophy when I heard Vic yell in my direction. "Abbot hit your cutoff man." Before I could even think about what was happening, I heard the crack of the bat, and I saw the ball sailing toward me. Instinctively, I stepped toward the infield. You'd think it would be the other way around—

that you would feel the urge to go back—but you don't. After a moment, I realized the ball was carrying over my head, and I began to back pedal. I almost got back far enough, but as I reached for it, I fell backward. The ball skidded off the tip of my glove and rolled toward the fence. I got up and retrieved it as fast as I could, and then threw it in to Matt. As I walked back to my original position, I saw Justin turn away from me, shaking his head. I could tell he wanted to say something, but he managed to hold it in.

"Try another one," Vic yelled. "And remember to take a couple steps back first. You can always run in and catch it if you have to."

I nodded and tried to prepare for the next play. *Step back first,* I told myself as I watched Vic toss another ball into the air. He swung the bat and skied one in my direction. Despite what I'd just said in my head, I took a step in, but it was a small one. I recovered quickly and took three big steps back. I had the ball clearly in my sights, but it was still climbing. Finally, it reached its peak and started its descent. I almost lost it in the graying clouds, but I picked it up again. As the ball approached, I only had to take three or four small steps in before I caught it. An enormous sense of relief washed over me. I threw the ball in to Matt, and that was when I noticed Justin moving toward me. When I looked at him, he stopped walking. In theatrical fashion, he bent his knees and leaned his upper body back, spreading his open hands to the side. As he did that, a huge grin stretched across his face.

"Abbot, you did it!" he yelled.

I remember him holding that pose for a second or two before standing up again. He was still smiling when he turned back toward first base. I just stared at him. I wasn't at all sure what to make of what he'd just done, but I *was* sure of one thing. I'd officially arrived in the Majors.

24

Thursday

Thursday was one of the worst days I ever had at NBC or anywhere else as an adult, save the unexpected evening I spent with Laura and Alan McBride. Bob O'Brien did end up coming in to break the news to everyone. He was visibly distraught as he explained why he was selling the company. He was much more candid than I expected, especially concerning his financial situation, and I think his obvious distress helped the situation some. As I suspected, everyone was blindsided by the news. There was some yelling and a couple people were crying. A lot of us had been here the last time the shop was sold, but we'd known it was coming for over a month. This time there'd been no warning at all. One minute we all had jobs, and the next minute *Who the hell knew?*

Bob relayed what he knew about the new owners, which was surprisingly little. It was a family-run operation headquartered in Ohio. The father was retired and his three sons now ran the business. If Bob knew much more than that, he wasn't sharing it with us. In the end, everyone accepted there wasn't a whole lot Bob could do. His brother was ill and he had to sell the shop, and this was the only solid offer he had. The truth was if it wasn't for the O'Briens, NBC would have probably closed over a decade ago.

As the afternoon wore on, we gathered in small groups, trying to guess what the new owners would do. The general consensus was they would bring in three or four of their own key people and retain everyone else, at least until they could determine if they wanted to keep them long-term.

Carolyn spent the afternoon saying goodbye to everyone. Unlike any other general manager I'd ever had, people actually cared she was leaving. When she came into my office, it was almost 4:00. She closed the door behind her.

"Hi, Dan."

"Hi, Carolyn. Fun day so far?"

Carolyn chuckled. "Yeah, it's been great. Hey, sorry I reacted like that last night. I guess I'm just feeling guilty over everything."

I was still confident she'd known about the potential of a sale longer than two weeks, but my anger was losing steam. Even if I'd known a few weeks ago, I probably wouldn't have done anything about it, other than worry. "This isn't your fault, Carolyn. And I'm sorry I sort of ran out. I guess I didn't handle the news all that well." I didn't feel the need to tell her I was on the verge of calling her a liar.

"Don't worry about it. Listen, when Jacob, the new owner, was here last week, I told him how important you were to the shop."

"Well, thank you for doing that, but do you think it'll matter?"

She looked at me for a few seconds. "I don't know. I hope so."

A few minutes later Carolyn told me she had to run out for something and would be back by 5:00. When I left NBC at 5:50, she still wasn't back. I probably should have known I would never see her again, but it didn't occur to me then.

When I got home, I stepped out of the Saturn and glanced toward Ally's apartment. I thought about her smile when Katie brought me into the kitchen. All day I'd been wondering if Ally was really as happy as she seemed or if it was simply my imagination. I was still wondering when I headed up the stairs to my apartment. I was almost to the top when I heard a woman's voice behind me.

"Hi, Dan."

I knew it was Katie even before I turned around. She was walking away from Ally's, heading toward the road. "Hi, Katie."

She gave me a sly smile. "Did you have fun at the party?"

"I did."

"How did that presentation go today?"

"Not so good. You guys got me drunk last night."

Katie laughed. "See, I told you that you should have done that funnel."

"I don't think I would've made it into work today."

"Ally said next time she's going to *make* you do it."

My first thought was that Ally could probably make me do a lot of things, but that was soon overridden by the realization she'd been talking about me and also that there might actually *be* a next time. "I'll think about it," I said, chuckling.

"See you later, Dan." Katie waved and then slipped behind the building.

I turned back and continued up the stairs, praying that Ally would throw another party soon.

25

Friday morning I decided to go in early. I figured it couldn't hurt on what might be my first day with my new bosses. I walked through the front door at 7:40. I was nervous, but I also knew there wasn't anything I could do to prepare. Carolyn wasn't sure if they would come in today or just start fresh on Monday. There were several new cars in the lot, so apparently today was the day. I knew it was going to be strange and even depressing for a while without Carolyn around, but I'd had new bosses before. I was confident I could do it again. I did think it was strange Bob didn't introduce any of the new owners to the staff, but it wasn't unheard of, either. Sometimes the new guys wanted to come in without any preconceived notions.

Our receptionist told me the new ownership group had set up their temporary offices in the conference room. According to her, they were already in there when she arrived at 7:00 am. Apparently, Jacob had come out to introduce himself to a few of the engineers, but that was all she'd seen of him or anyone else. She wasn't even sure how many people were actually in there.

The front section of NBC held only seven true offices, and I had one of them. Three of the offices were shared by more than one person, and all the other employees worked in open areas or cubicles. I did some quick math and realized the chances of me holding onto my office were pretty slim. After working in a cubicle for over thirteen years, I'd grown to love the privacy of my office. The thought of losing it was a depressing way to end an already depressing week.

I made a call to the production supervisor to check on the status of a couple jobs and then began writing up a proposal due next week. It was 8:29 when Amy Carlisle knocked once and stepped into my office. Amy was one of two employees who reported directly to me. She handled customer service duties while Karen Glascow handled Requests for Quote. Both were pretty self-sufficient, but they each came to see me whenever there was an issue, or if there was an important decision to be made.

"Hi, Dan," Amy said. "I'm glad you're here."

Amy was one of the employees who'd shed a few nervous tears yesterday. It was obvious she was still anxious. "Hi, Amy. What's going on?"

"I just came out of the conference room. They called me in a few minutes ago and told me they'd be keeping me on through an evaluation period. They called Karen in just before me and told her the same thing."

I was immediately ticked-off. Obviously, they had an organizational chart. They should've started with me and then worked their way to Amy and Karen. *Unless they don't plan on keeping me around,* I thought. I pushed that idea away and reminded myself not to get paranoid. This was their first day in the building, and they simply wanted to meet everyone. Just then there was another knock on my door — this one much more forceful. As the door opened, a man with blond hair and piercing blue eyes stuck his head inside the room. He looked like he was in his mid-fifties.

"Dan Abbot?" the man asked.

"That's me," I said, trying to sound as casual as possible. I stood and stepped around my desk before extending my hand. The man continued into my office and shook it.

"I'm Jacob Dayton. I'm one of the new owners of NBC." He looked at me with an expression that was more grimace than smile. "Amy, would you mind excusing us?"

"Of course." She glanced at me before slipping out the door.

Dayton turned back and closed the door behind him. I think I sensed — mostly from his initial mannerisms — that I was about to be let go, but I still had to stick around for the official word. It was a little like a dream. It had the same surrealistic feel, but unlike most of my dreams, things were moving with incredible speed instead of plodding along in slow-motion.

"It's nice to meet you," I managed. I knew I had to play this thing out even though every instinct was telling me my career at NBC was entering its final minutes. "Would you like a seat?" I pointed to one of the two chairs in front of my desk.

"No, thank you. Listen, Dan, I'm not going to delay this. It wouldn't be fair to either of us. Both Carolyn and Bob made a point to tell me what an excellent employee you are, and I have no doubt that's true, but the fact of the matter is we already have someone from one of our own facilities who's going to fulfill that role here." He looked me in the eye. "I'm sorry, but we don't have a need for your services."

You have to be fucking kidding me. It was a full two seconds before I realized I hadn't said it aloud.

"I'm sorry, Dan. I really am." Dayton was still standing right in front of me, but it sounded like he was speaking from the end of a long hallway. "Mr. Burgen will help you get your things together."

A security guard I'd never seen before stepped into my office and handed me a medium-sized box. It was one of our own shipping boxes. I could see our logo stamped on the side. Without saying another word, Dayton stepped out, leaving me and my new friend, Mr. Burgen, alone in the room. He seemed extremely interested in what I was doing. In fact, he couldn't take his eyes off me.

I sat at my desk, staring blankly ahead for a solid minute or so. I started thinking about Adam. He would have been my first phone call. A strange and almost terrifying thought hit me. *Who can I call now?* It's funny how fast you can reach a point in your life when that list gets frighteningly short. I knew I could call Carolyn, but I didn't want to talk to her. And, of course, there was Laura, but I didn't want to talk to her, either. Adam was who I wanted right now—who I needed—but that wasn't going to happen. I opened my desk drawer when it hit me. I could call Jen. She'd not only be sympathetic, she'd also give me some solid advice on what my next move should be. And Lord knows I owed her a call. It had been months since we'd last spoken.

With Adam and Jen on my mind, I began slowly packing up the remnants of my twenty-three-year career at NBC. I think a part of me wanted to cry...and if I wasn't so stunned, I probably would have.

26

Watching someone get fired is a strange event at a small company like NBC. Most of the time people know it's coming or *should* know it's coming. There's usually been a bad performance review (or several), and rumors are already circulating. Occasionally, it hits people by surprise, like it did me today. When this happens there's a sense of stunned guilt among the survivors — guilt that they're still there while you got axed. That's why so many people try to hide when the execution goes down. I think of movie scenes like the one in *Jerry Maguire* when Tom Cruise's character addresses his officemates after being fired. Everyone is in attendance and riveted as Cruise makes his speech. It makes for a great movie scene, but in real life, two-thirds of that office would've found a reason not to be there. And most of those who couldn't escape would've been on the phone or hiding under their desk.

When Mr. Bergen escorted me out of the building, the front office area was all but deserted. Two notable exceptions were Amy and Karen. They each stood beside their desk, staring in disbelief. I smiled at them as best I could. Amy followed me into the parking lot and gave me a tearful hug. I could tell she didn't want to let go, but I told her to get back inside before she got herself into trouble. You never want to make a spectacle of yourself in a situation like that. Show your emotions later at the bar, but never do it at the workplace. Never make the new boss look bad.

I suppose I should've known it was coming when Bob O'Brien didn't introduce any of us to the new ownership group. It just made it that much easier for Dayton to pull the plug when the time came. I had hoped my close ties with our customers would keep me there long enough for them to get the chance to know me, but that just wasn't the case. I knew much of it came down to money. I was one of the higher-paid front office employees, so if they could bring in one of their own at a lower salary, then why wouldn't they? And I suspected *that* part of it wasn't even true. My guess was there wouldn't be anyone brought in. I'm sure they felt Amy and Karen could handle everything at a fraction of the cost. In the end there were five of us from the front office who were either let go or simply left — Carolyn among them. The new owners kept everyone else, at least for the time being. Amy had sent me a text update once the carnage was over.

As I drove home, I reminded myself that all good things must come to an end. I quickly modified it to *All good things (and even a lot of things that weren't that great to begin with) must come to an end.* I thought that second one was a more accurate description of my life at NBC. I thought about my old therapist, Eileen, and what she would tell me if I were to call her. She'd tell me to use this as an opportunity to make my life better, although she wouldn't word it quite like that. She'd say something like *make my life more meaningful.*

I entered The Palace feeling better but still unsure about what to do next. I'd already left one message on Jen's cell phone, and there wasn't anyone else I wanted to talk to right now. Carolyn had texted me several times, but I ignored them. The fact she'd given me only one day of warning had fought its way back to the forefront of my mind. I thought about calling my dad, but with him I never knew what I'd get. I might find the understanding father, looking to dole out helpful advice, or I could just as easily get Mr. Doom & Gloom, wondering how I managed to lose such a good job as I approached the dangerous age of fifty. The uncertainty was enough to prevent me from making the call.

I turned on the television and flipped aimlessly through the channels. It was 9:25, and for the first time in forever, I had absolutely nothing to do for the rest of the day. As I watched SportsCenter run through the highlights of last night's games, I vowed to give myself the weekend to get over the shock. I would relax with Connor and keep my mind on anything that wasn't related to NBC. I would probably go out for drinks later with some of my coworkers, *or former coworkers,* but other than that obligation, I vowed to leave it alone. Dwelling on what happened and panicking about what to do next would only raise my blood pressure.

By the time 11:00 rolled around, I realized saying I wouldn't dwell on it and truly accomplishing the feat were two different things. I kept coming back to the fact Carolyn hadn't given me more notice. I realized the others didn't have any warning at all, but the others didn't have the relationship we did. I found it impossible to believe she didn't know the sale was coming much earlier. Official word might not have come down until Monday, but she had to have a pretty good idea at least two or three weeks ago. Even learning about it on Monday would've been a hell of a lot better than just thirty-six hours before. I was also starting to feel like she knew my fate, which is why she decided that yesterday would be her last day. And I'm sure the new owners asked her opinion on Amy and Karen. I would have never expected her to lie just to save me, but she could have at least given me a heads-up. I felt like I deserved better. I would've had a lot more respect for her if she just told me the new owners weren't going to keep me around.

I almost texted her exactly that, but I decided to hold off. I'd gotten myself all worked up, and I didn't want to accuse her of something just because I was pissed off.

I went into the kitchen wondering how I was going to get through my first day unemployed when the idea hit me. *The baseball field.* There were always a million things that needed to be done. There was a hole in right field — dug by an endless supply of bored right fielders — a pitcher's mound in need of more clay, an entire infield in need of more dirt, and that was only the beginning. I could kill an afternoon without even thinking about it. It would be hot, but it was just what I needed.

I ate a bowl of Frosted Mini Wheats — my second of the morning — and then headed into the bedroom to change.

The Evil
Empire

27

The night of our first game arrived a week and a half later. Jess helped me get ready by throwing me grounders in the backyard. When we finished, we ran in through the back door of our house and into the kitchen. The clock read 4:30. "Mom, we have to leave in ten minutes!" I yelled. We were supposed to be at the field by 5:00 for warm-ups. It only took about ten minutes to get to Barnell Field, but knowing our mom and her habit of pushing everything to the last second, I didn't want to chance it.

Right then Mom came rushing into the kitchen, looking more or less ready to go. She was wearing a pair of blue jeans and a light blue tee shirt. "Honey, what do you want to eat?" she asked, sounding out of breath. "You have to eat before your game." I could tell by her voice she was excited about our first game, too.

I hadn't eaten anything since lunch, but I wasn't the least bit hungry. I was so nervous, I almost felt queasy. Still, I knew from past experience that she would make me eat something. "Okay, how about a peanut butter-and-jelly. I only want half, though."

"Okay, and you can wash it down with a glass of milk. That will coat your stomach and make it feel better."

"Can you make it right now? I don't wanna be late to my first game."

"I'll take one, too, Mom," Jess said cheerfully, "but make mine a whole one please." Clearly, Jess's stomach was just fine.

"Yep, that's what I came down to do." Mom scrambled to make the sandwiches while Jess and I got the milk.

"Is Mark coming to my game, Mom?"

"He's going to try if he gets home in time."

I knew his house was close to Barnell Field. Jess and I had walked there one time after a Minors game, and it only took us about five minutes.

"Who do you play tonight?" Jess asked.

"Everton Plumbing."

"Are they good?"

According to Peter, Everton Plumbing was terrible. Again, Truck had put an end to the conversation when he announced that "Anyone can beat anyone" with the obvious implication it was pointless to talk about it. It had become clear Truck didn't like any kind of speculation or analysis. If it wasn't right there in front of you, it wasn't something you should be talking about. And most of the time, even if it *was* right there in front of you, you still didn't need to talk about it. "No, I don't think they're very good."

"Who is Jackson and Franklin anyway?"

I looked at Jess, confused. "What do you mean?"

"I mean who are they? Is it a store or something?"

"It's a…" It was then I realized I had absolutely no idea. I played for a team called Jackson & Franklin, but I had no idea who Jackson & Franklin actually were. I didn't want Jess to know that, though, so I decided to take a guess. "I think—"

"It's an accounting firm in Everton," Mom said.

"Yeah," I said.

Jess looked at me, and I thought she was going to call me on it, but she didn't. "Is Eric playing tonight?"

I chuckled. She'd seen him at one of our practices and thought he was cute. Of course, I also knew if he ever talked to her, she wouldn't be able to utter a sound. "No, he actually quit the team. He doesn't like baseball anymore."

Jess's eyes darted to me, but she quickly realized I was kidding. "Shut up, Danny."

"I had you."

"No, you didn't!"

Even if I hadn't seen her expression, the yelling told me I was right. You'd think I would have let it slide, given that I didn't even know who sponsored our team. "Yes, I did, Jess, and you know it."

"You did not!"

"Okay, that's enough, you two," Mom said, placing our sandwiches in front of us. "And, Jess, I don't want to hear that kind of language out of you again."

"Sorry, Mom."

"Okay, now eat up. I'm going to fix my makeup and we'll head out."

We got to the field about five minutes before 5:00. While Mom found a parking spot, I looked out and saw about half my team already warming up. My stomach rumbled, and for an instant I thought I might get another look at my peanut butter-and-jelly sandwich. Thankfully, the feeling passed. I grabbed my glove and bat off the seat and opened the truck door.

"Good luck, Danny," Jess said.

"Thanks, Jess." I jumped out and walked over to Mom's window. Normally, I wouldn't have done that, but I was really nervous. She sensed that and grabbed my shoulder.

"Good luck, honey. You're going to do great."

"Thanks, Mom."

"Remember to watch for cars. This is a parking lot."

"Okay, Mom."

I took a quick look around, lowered my hat against the sun's rays, and headed toward the field. It was another beautiful spring day, low seventies and clear skies. As I neared the first base dugout, I smelled freshly cut grass and it reminded me of tryouts. I hadn't been to Barnell Field since that day, over a month earlier by then. Given how poorly I'd played, it seemed almost impossible to believe I was back there and about to play in my first game.

I could see my teammates playing catch out beyond second base while Everton Plumbing used the infield. Our jerseys were dark blue with red sleeves lined with white pinstripes. The words Jackson & Franklin were printed on the front in white letters. Our hats were the same combination of blue and red, only with the initials J&F instead of the words printed out. Everton Plumbing's jerseys were the exact same design, except they had a combination of light blue and dark blue instead of blue and red. I didn't think they were even close to as sharp as ours. Rounding out our uniforms were white pants per Vic's instructions. My mom had just picked up my pair earlier that afternoon.

I entered the dugout and left my bat along the fence before joining my teammates in the outfield to warm up. There was plenty of talk about who the opposing pitcher might be, especially among the tens. Of course, by then we were careful not to let Truck hear us. According to Chris their starting pitcher was a kid named Tommy Wagner. Chris said he wasn't super-fast, but he wasn't slow, either. He said he had average speed, whatever that meant.

Before I knew it, we were lined up along the first baseline for the national anthem. I did my best to stay focused and tried to prepare myself for the game. We were the home team, which meant we'd be taking the field first. Vic rattled off our positions, and I discovered I'd be starting my Majors career on the bench. I also learned I was hitting near the bottom of the batting order. Only Peter was after me. Everyone batted in the Everton Little League, and with Paul not there for some reason, it meant I was hitting tenth. I found a spot on the bench next to Peter and watched our team warm up.

Justin was on the mound for us that night. Because he was our ace, I expected Vic to use him that night and then maybe one other time before our sixth game of the season against Rotary Club. Justin's motion wasn't pretty to look at, but he had a great arm, and according to Matt, he usually found a way to get the job done. Once the game was underway, he struck out the first two hitters on six straight pitches and got the third to pop up to Eric at shortstop.

When Tommy Wagner came out to warm up, I got a crash course in what "average speed" meant in the Majors. As far as I was concerned, he threw heat. He wasn't as fast as Justin, but he still threw it pretty hard. There wasn't a single pitcher in the Minors that even came close, but I would soon learn our team wasn't the least bit phased. Eric and Matt started our half of the inning with hard hit singles, and then Truck pounded his first home run of the season over the center field fence. It looked like we might get more when Wagner walked the next two batters, but he settled down and got three straight outs. We didn't add to our lead, but we did well enough to ensure I'd bat in the next inning.

After another one-two-three inning for Justin, it was our turn again at the plate. A kid named Dave, another one of our ten-year-olds, started off the inning by striking out. Ready or not — and I was most definitely not — it was my turn to make the lonely walk to home plate. As I left the dugout, I glanced into the stands and saw Mom, Jess, and Mark. Adam was standing alone near the fence. A surge of confidence flowed through me, but it died soon after when I realized that at that moment, it was just me against the entire opposing team. It wasn't the first time I'd walked toward home plate, but it *was* the first time that thought had occurred to me. Baseball and softball are the only team sports where that happens. Sure, your teammates are right there supporting you, and your coaches are there to offer encouragement, but when you're standing in that batter's box, it's just you against nine other guys. And unlike batting practice, where Vic's goal was to get me to *hit* the ball, Tommy Wagner's goal was the exact opposite. And if I looked silly in the process, all the better.

"Take good cuts," Ted yelled from the first base coach's box. "Just like in practice."

I walked toward home plate where the catcher and umpire waited. I stepped into the batter's box, then remembered I was supposed to look at Vic who was coaching third.

"C'mon, Danny," Vic said, "wait for your pitch."

He clapped his hands, and I turned back toward the pitcher. I raised my bat and lowered myself into my stance. I immediately noticed muffled voices coming from the concession stand directly behind me. I couldn't make out exactly what was being said, but I could tell it was more than one person. There were other voices nearby, but these I *could* make out.

"No stick up there," a kid said behind me. The fence protecting the opposing dugout was only about twelve feet away. I could tell the kid was leaning against it to get as close as possible.

"Let's go, Tommy," said another voice. "He can't hit you."

Words of support flowed from my dugout.

"Let's go, Danny," Peter said.

"Start us off," Chris added.

All of these voices — the kids in the dugouts, my coaches, the muffled drone of the concession stand, the distant buzz of the bleachers — all blended together into a chorus of sounds echoing off the walls behind home plate. I did my best to block it all out and focused on Wagner's windup. He released the ball, and I tried to locate it in the late afternoon light. Just as I picked it up, it passed by me, and I heard a loud pop in the catcher's mitt.

"Strike!" The umpire yelled.

"Okay, Danny, you saw one," Vic said.

Barely. The next pitch seemed like a carbon copy of the first. I picked it up a bit earlier, but I couldn't bring myself to swing. I think I did flinch, though, which I considered a step in the right direction.

"One more just like that, Tommy," yelled the kid behind me. "No stick up there," he said again for good measure.

"Step out of the box," Vic said. I did as instructed and looked down the line. He was walking slowly toward me. "Relax. Okay? You have two strikes on you, so protect the plate."

I knew that meant I had to swing at anything close. I nodded and stepped back into the box. The last thing I wanted to do was strike out looking — on three straight pitches, no less. Unfortunately for me, Tommy Wagner knew that, as well. I dug my feet into the dirt, hoping it would make a difference.

"C'mon, Danny!" Adam yelled from what sounded like a mile away.

I watched as the baseball left Tommy Wagner's hand. At first the ball seemed to be in roughly the same location as the two previous pitches, but as I stepped toward Wagner and began the lumbering motion that was my ten-year-old swing, I realized the pitch was high. I don't think I ever considered trying to check my swing. I think my brain knew it wasn't even remotely possible, but I did try to raise the level of my bat as the ball approached. I actually did a decent job of it, and had I not been so late on my swing, I might have been able to generate a foul tip and survive until the next pitch. It wasn't meant to be. The catcher caught the fastball, crossing the plate somewhere around neck high.

"Strike three!" the umpire yelled, and just like that, my first at-bat in the Majors was over.

28

The next morning I spent most of the walk to school thinking about our first game. Sadly, my second and third at-bat looked a lot like my first. I struck out both times without making contact. It wasn't exactly how I envisioned starting off my Majors career.

I said goodbye to Jess and watched her walk down the hall and into her classroom. I entered my room and made my way to my desk. As soon as I sat down, Matt turned around.

"Hey, Danny, what'd you think?"

"It was great, but I struck out three times."

"Don't worry, you'll get used to the pitching. It takes a few games."

I prayed he was right. I could live with striking out as long as I hit the ball hard every once in a while. I was about to ask him about our next game when Mr. Holt walked into the room. What had been the healthy sound of chatting ten-year-olds quieted immediately. Matt whispered something about talking more at lunch and turned around.

In the ten days that had passed since Mr. Holt taunted Lisa Bonner into tears, things had been pretty quiet. There'd been a couple mild outbursts, but nothing that came close to that first incident. I think it was mostly because we were all scared of him. But as the days passed, there were a couple kids who grew more comfortable. One of those was Big Mike who sat just to the left of Lisa in the front row. Big Mike had earned his nickname by being literally twice the size of most of the kids in our class. And once the name was out there, it stuck, and he didn't seem to mind. Big Mike liked to fool around, mostly just talking and making faces at his friends, trying to get them to laugh. On that particular morning, Big Mike was talking to Lisa. I could tell she didn't want to talk to him, and other than one-word responses every so often, she didn't. Instead, she seemed to merely tolerate him. Mr. Holt also tolerated Big Mike as long as his antics occurred before the opening bell. It was now five minutes past, and he was still whispering in Lisa's direction.

"Okay, class," Mr. Holt said from behind his desk. "Let's open our math books to page 276. And, Mike, if you keep talking, you and I are going to have a problem. Do you understand me?" Big Mike looked down at the top of his desk and nodded his head. He slouched in his chair, looking more like a poor-postured adult than a fifth-grader. "And sit up straight."

There was something in his voice that told me he was in a bad mood. That wasn't always easy to detect in Mr. Holt, but I sensed it wouldn't take much to set him off—even less than usual. I'd also noticed he'd been growing increasingly impatient with Big Mike in the preceding days. None of these things boded well for Big Mike, although I don't think he realized it. He straightened up in his seat and then promptly slid back to his original position.

"Okay, Mike, what did you get for number...Why don't I see a math book on your desk?"

Big Mike's head was hanging down, his chin resting on his chest. "I forgot it at home."

"You forgot it at home. Well, that's just great, Mike." There was a hint of the same mocking tone he'd used on Lisa, but it hadn't been fully unleashed yet. "You talk in my class; you forget your homework—not that you even did it in the first place; you slouch in your chair like a slob; your desk is an absolute mess. What do you have to say about that?" Big Mike offered no reply. "Well, I'll tell you what, Mike. You can sit right here during lunch and do your homework while everyone else is running around outside. How does that sound?" Mike muttered something unintelligible. I looked over again at Mr. Holt and saw his face had turned a dark red. "What did you say to me?" His voice had already risen to a yell.

"I said that sucks." It was loud enough for everyone to hear.

A light gasp echoed throughout the classroom. I locked eyes again with Kathy Anderson, my co-conspirator the day we discovered Ms. Becker wasn't coming back. We both knew Hurricane Holt was about to make landfall, and I think everyone else knew it, too. I turned back again to Mr. Holt and found him just staring at Big Mike, mouth agape. The expression wasn't unusual, but I think this time he really was stunned. Without warning, he picked up his plastic apple pencil holder and whipped it across the room, pens and pencils scattering everywhere. The apple skidded off the top of Big Mike's desk with a loud knock and then ricocheted onto the radiator where it rattled between the wall and the glass window before falling to the floor. The pencil holder was hard and heavy. How it didn't crack the window, I have no idea. Mike bolted upright in his seat and spun his head back toward his teacher. Mr. Holt had finally closed his mouth, but now he looked like an angry bull ready to charge. I, like everyone else, was dumbfounded by what I'd just witnessed, but even in my shock, it struck me how accurate the throw had been. Mike's desk was the second one in from the window and probably twenty feet from Mr. Holt. If the throw had been off by a foot in either direction, the apple could have easily hit Big Mike or a number of other students.

By that point everyone's eyes were on Mr. Holt, and I'm pretty sure we were all thinking the same thing. If he was willing to throw a hard object across a crowded classroom, then anything was possible. As I stared at his seething face, it wasn't hard to read his thoughts. *This kid still doesn't understand I'm the fucking boss.* Mr. Holt climbed out of his chair and stepped around his desk. He was moving with that eerie quickness again that not only belied his usual sloth-like movements but didn't seem natural for a man of his age and physical stature. He darted up the aisle toward the front of the room, his eyes fixed on Big Mike. "What did you say to me?" he bellowed. As soon as he passed Lisa's desk, he pivoted left toward Big Mike and lunged at him. He fell forward, planting his enormous hands on the desktop. From my vantage point, his head looked perilously close to Big Mike's. I had a brief vision of Mr. Holt lurching forward into a vicious head butt. Big Mike was leaning back, terrified. "I asked you a question!" The class had slipped into another stunned silence. The only audible sounds were Mr. Holt's sandpaper-like voice and his strained breathing. "You think you're a big man, don't you, Mike? But you're not so big with me right here in front of you, are you?" Big Mike just stared at his desktop, probably unable to speak.

Right then Mr. Holt looked down and saw some crinkled papers sticking out of the desk. It turned out to be the last bit of fuel he needed. He dragged the desk forward with Big Mike still planted in the attached chair. Given his size and weight, it couldn't have been an easy task, but Mr. Holt was in a rage. He lifted the top of the desk—tilting it open—then gripped both sides with his huge hands. Grimacing, Mr. Holt wrenched the desktop sideways, and the high-pitched whine of grinding metal filled the air. He twisted it back the other way, the sound growing even sharper. The top of Big Mike's desk stood erect at an odd, unnatural angle. He continued working the desktop, back and forth, the grinding metal sounding like tortured screams. His face, now flushed and shining with sweat, had contorted into that of a madman. After the fourth or fifth twist, the right side broke free with the metal hinge hanging off the edge. After another violent twist, the left side broke free, as well. He stood there staring at Big Mike, panting. He was like a silverback gorilla who'd just uprooted a good-sized tree in a dramatic display of dominance.

I don't think Mr. Holt would have been able to accomplish the feat had it been anyone else sitting at the desk. Big Mike was the only kid heavy enough to counteract the force he'd needed. I expected him to toss the desktop against the wall or at the very least drop it onto the floor, but he did neither. Instead, he walked calmly to the blackboard and leaned the desktop against the wall beneath it. He then returned to Big Mike's desk and stared down into the messy pit. Even from the back of the room, it looked like a haphazard pile of books, papers, and garbage. If not for the garbage, it could have been my desk. I noticed several items had fallen onto the floor, including a textbook, several loose sheets of paper, and a crumpled brown lunch bag.

"This is disgusting," Mr. Holt said. He was no longer yelling, but he was out of breath. "You're a complete slob, but that ends today. Get up." Big Mike scrambled out of his seat. When he turned toward us, I saw he was on the verge of tears. As soon as Mike was clear of the desk, Mr. Holt grabbed it and turned it on its side, dumping its contents onto the floor. When everything was out, he turned the desk and chair right side up again. "Now go get the garbage can and clean this mess up."

Big Mike walked over to the garbage can, doing his best to hold in the tears. It was a battle he couldn't win. As he headed back toward his battered desk, they broke free and began their descent down his puffy red cheeks. Mr. Holt took no notice as he made his way — now sloth-like again — back to his desk. Much to my relief, and probably everyone else's, as well, Big Mike held it together pretty well. There were a few tears, but not much else. I don't know if any of us could have handled Big Mike sobbing in front of the entire class. He was easily the biggest and toughest kid among us, and I think for that reason alone it would have been too much.

Mr. Holt must have thought he was handling it pretty well, too, because with Big Mike on his hands and knees cleaning up the mess, he resumed our math lesson.

29

That afternoon I was sitting on the couch watching *Gilligan's Island* when I heard my mom pull into the driveway. I glanced at the clock and saw it was just after 3:45. Through the side window, I watched her climb down from Big Red and walk across the yard toward the front steps. I found my seat on the couch just as she entered the house.

"Hey, mister, how are you?"

"Hi, Mom."

"What's the matter?"

"Nothing. I guess I'm just thinking about the game last night and how bad I played." The truth was I was thinking more about what had happened in class with Big Mike, but I wasn't sure I wanted to talk about it. I didn't want to upset my mom.

She walked over to the couch and sat beside me. "Even the stars make mistakes, Danny." I knew by stars she meant professional baseball players. I smiled at her choice of words and she smiled back. "There are a lot more games to play this year, and you're only going to get better. Trust me on that, okay?" I nodded. She stood and walked over to the mirror to remove her nurse's cap. "Where's your sister?"

"She's upstairs doing her homework, I think. Mom, can I talk to you about something?"

She looked at me and I think knew right away it was something serious. She walked across the room and joined me on the couch. "You know you can talk to me about anything, Danny. Is it Mr. Holt again?"

I wondered how she always seemed to know what I was thinking. "Yeah, but it's nothing big, Mom."

"Was it Lisa again?"

"No, it was a kid named Mike. We call him Big Mike."

"Okay, I think I know who you're talking about."

"He was talking in class today, and Mr. Holt got really mad at him. Then he made a wisecrack, and Mr. Holt lost it."

"What do you mean he lost it?"

"Well, first he threw an apple pencil holder across the room —"

Her eyes grew wide. "You mean one of those hard ones, like the one on my desk at work?"

"Yeah, that exact same kind."

"Jesus," Mom said, then caught herself. "I'm sorry I swore, Danny. How far did he throw it?"

"All the way across the room. It had to be twenty feet. He whipped it, Mom. It was actually a great throw because it hit the top of Mike's desk and flew into the wall."

"Were there other kids around when he threw it?"

"Yeah, everyone was sitting at their desks."

My mom thought about that for a second and then checked her watch. "Okay, what happened next?"

I thought about leaving it at that, but I knew I had to tell her everything. "Then Mr. Holt went over to Big Mike and started yelling at him. Then he lifted the top of his desk and ripped it off."

Her mouth dropped open. "He did what?"

"He ripped the top of the desk off. He had to work it back and forth, and it took him a while, but he finally got it off."

"Are you sure, Danny? It came completely off?"

"I'm positive, Mom. He was holding it in his hands after he did it."

"My God." She checked her watch again, and I figured she was wondering when Mark would be home. She looked back at me with that concerned expression I didn't like. We sat in silence for a few seconds until she thought of something to say. "And Mike has the same kind of desk you do, right? The kind where the chair's connected?"

"Yeah, we all have the same desks."

Her face grew even more serious. "He didn't hit Mike, did he?"

"No, he didn't touch him, but he dumped his desk on the floor."

She shook her head, but I could tell that didn't faze her as much as the other things had. She checked her watch one more time. "Mark gets home around five o'clock. He's coming over for dinner, so we can talk more about this." She gave me a quick kiss on the forehead and walked into the kitchen.

When Adam got home at 5:30, I was upstairs doing homework. I could already smell green beans cooking on the stove, but when Adam opened our bedroom door, the mouthwatering aroma invaded our room. Once a month, Mom would empty a bag of green beans into a large frying pan with olive oil and then add what she called her *secret spices*. Jess and I loved them. Even Adam, who wasn't much of a vegetable eater back then, made an exception for those.

Adam walked over and slapped me on the back. "Hey, Danny, Mom said your teacher ripped the top off some kid's desk?"

"Yeah, he kept twisting it back and forth, and it finally came off."

"Are they the same desks we had?"

I described the desks to him, and he was convinced they were the same ones he'd had six years earlier. He made me run through the entire story, asking questions along the way. He was still digging for details when I heard Mark come through the front door.

"Who wants some pizza?" Mark yelled up the stairs.

I heard Jess's door open, and a second later she was in our room.

"Hey, Jess," Adam said, smiling.

"Hi, Adam," she said, giving him a quick hug. "Mark's here with pizza!" Without her front teeth, there were plenty of extra hissing sounds.

"We heard him. We'll be right down, okay?"

"Okay," she said, and was gone. I heard her run down the hall and start down the stairs.

"She really is cute when she's not being a pain in the ass."

I hated it when Adam said stuff like that. He sounded too much like an adult. I knew he was several years older, but when he made those kinds of comments, I felt like I was still a kid and he was becoming a man. I felt like he was leaving me behind.

"Let's get something to eat," he said, "and then we'll sit down with Mom and Mark to talk about it."

Another one of those comments. We headed out of the room together and followed the smell of pizza and green beans down the stairs and into the dining room. Mark had placed the sheet pizza, half plain and half sausage, on the dining room table. I grabbed one piece of each and put them on a paper plate. I sat at the table next to Jess, and Mom slid a second plate full of green beans in front of me, along with a napkin. A second later, Adam handed me a glass of milk.

While we ate, there was no mention of Mr. Holt, and Mom finally started to relax. She had a glass of red wine with dinner, which I think helped. We talked about baseball, my first game, in particular. Adam and Mark both agreed I needed to swing at more pitches. When we were done eating and talking, over half the sheet pizza was gone. Mom picked up the box and carried it into the kitchen. Jess grabbed the milk and followed her in. Once they were out of the room, Mark looked directly at me.

"Your mom says you've been having trouble with Mr. Holt." He said it quietly, and I could tell he didn't want Jess to hear him, although I wasn't sure why. She knew all about Mr. Holt.

"Yeah, I guess so." I liked Mark a lot, but it still felt awkward discussing something like that without our mom in the room.

"Why don't you tell me what you told your mom?"

"I wanna hear it again, too," Adam said.

I ran through the story a third time, including as many details as I could remember. By the time I got to the part about Mr. Holt dumping Big Mike's desk onto the floor, Jess was upstairs and Mom was back at the table.

"Wow, he sounds like a real piece of work," Mark said. Mom nodded her head in agreement.

"He sounds like an asshole to me," Adam said.

Both Mark and Mom shot Adam a look. "Adam, I've asked you not to swear in the house," Mom said.

"Sorry, Mom. My mistake." He sounded sincere. She nodded, and Mark looked back at me. I got the feeling Mark didn't want to let it go. I wondered what he would do when he and our mom were married.

"Well," Mark said, "I'll agree with Adam so far as to say that Mr. Holt sure sounds like a jerk. He clearly has trouble controlling his temper." Back on common ground, we all nodded in agreement. "I've actually had teachers like him, Danny."

Mom looked at Mark doubtfully. "You've had teachers that ripped off the top of a desk?"

"Well, I'm not sure about that, but they did other things. I had a teacher, a woman, who used to slap kids across the face if they got mouthy. They'd never let you do that now, but they did when I was in school. Times have certainly changed." He said it like he almost missed the old days where teachers could rough up kids with impunity.

"What about throwing pencil holders across the room?" Mom clearly didn't like the direction Mark was heading.

"Don't get me wrong. I'm not saying it's acceptable. I'm just saying it's better than it used to be. Obviously, it was foolish to throw that pencil holder, but I'll bet you it wasn't as risky as it seems. Danny, I'll bet if you stand at Mr. Holt's desk and look at Mike's desk, it's probably a pretty clear path. Still stupid to do, I agree, but if Mr. Holt played baseball growing up, like you do, I'll bet it was pretty easy for him to do."

"I don't care if you play shortstop for the New York Yankees," Mom said. "It was an incredibly dangerous thing to do."

"I agree," Mark added quickly.

"Mark, do you think that desktop could have been defective?" Adam asked.

"I've actually been thinking about that since your mom called me." Mark turned to me again. "I know exactly what kind of desks you guys have because I went to the open house a few months ago. Those desks are pretty solid. I'm not saying it's impossible to do, but it would be really hard to rip off the top without doing something to it first."

Adam leaned forward in his chair. "You mean he doctored the top before he ripped it off?" I could tell by his voice the idea seemed plausible to him.

Again, our mom was on the other side. "I'm having a hard time believing a teacher would *doctor* a desk or whatever just so he can rip the top off of it."

"I'm not saying he did that for sure," Mark said, "but it's possible. And believe me, there are people who do things like that. He's trying to scare the class so they don't give him any more problems. That's why he humiliated that girl for passing notes. And, Danny, you said this Mike kid had been a problem, right?" I nodded. "I don't think it's that far-fetched to believe Mr. Holt knew he'd have to deal with this kid at some point, so he messed with his desk and waited for the kid to screw up again."

"It sounds crazy," Adam said, "but I have to agree with Mark. It wouldn't be easy to rip off the top of one of those desks. I don't think I could do it."

"It wasn't easy," I said. "It took him a while, and Mr. Holt is a lot bigger than you, Adam."

"And maybe he did do it without altering the desk," Mark said. "I'm just saying there are people who think ahead and do things like that. There's all sorts of stories about coaches who rip up jackets or bags or whatever in front of their teams, but they actually took out the stitches beforehand." He smiled like the stories were all on the same level.

"I'm not sure what's worse," Mom said, "a lunatic who rips off the top of a desk, or a psychopath who sets it all up beforehand to terrify a bunch of fifth-graders."

Mark opened his mouth, but he closed it again quickly. It was pretty hard to disagree with Mom's logic. He looked at Adam, knowing he'd been defeated, and they smiled at one another. It wasn't the first time they'd been outsmarted by Mom, and it wouldn't be the last. Mark took another route. "I guess the question now is what do we do about it?"

"I could pay him a visit," Adam said, no trace of a smile remaining.

"Don't even think about it," Mom said sharply. She didn't have to ask him if he was serious. I would learn later our dad had a pretty bad temper when he was young, and I already knew that Adam had one. Apparently, the apple hadn't fallen far from the tree.

"That would be very foolish, Adam," Mark said.

Adam looked at him, clearly not appreciating his tone. Whatever small bond that might have existed a second earlier was long gone. "Okay, Mark, you can figure it out then."

Adam walked out of the room over our mom's objections and headed upstairs. She looked at Mark, but I couldn't tell if it was in anger or frustration. After a few seconds, Mark said, "How about this? I'll call the school and talk to the principal tomorrow. I'll tell him we heard about what happened with Big Mike. I'm sure it won't be the only call he gets. Then Mr. Holt will know he's being watched, and I'll bet it won't happen again."

"I don't want Mr. Holt to know it was me," I said.

"Don't worry, I'll make sure the principal doesn't mention any names. Mr. Holt won't know you said anything. And like I said, I'll bet there'll be a *bunch* of calls."

Mom put her hand on my wrist. "Sounds like a good idea to me," she said, smiling.

"I think the Yankees are about to start," Mark said. "Why don't you put them on, and I'll help your mom finish cleaning up."

30

It was a full two weeks later when we played Rotary Club for the first time. Peter was a huge *Star Wars* fan and had been calling them The Galactic Empire that entire week. Justin picked up on the nickname and modified it to The Evil Empire, which spread quickly throughout the team. Peter wasn't happy to have his nickname first stolen and then modified, but he reluctantly fell in line. What else could he do? Justin was a twelve. Given how good Rotary Club was, and the fact they had a certain evil-ish swagger about them, the name really did fit. Even Truck seemed to approve, although I never heard him use it. And, of course, once they became The Evil Empire, it wasn't long before Peter rebounded and dubbed Zach Hardy, Darth Vader. Given the huge reflective sunglasses Hardy wore, that name fit perfectly, as well.

At our final practice before the game, Vic seemed especially intense, and it wasn't just the fake kind he showed sometimes when he was fooling around. He wanted to win the game. You could see it on his face. I also saw it on the faces of my teammates, at least the older ones. The tens were primarily concerned with who'd be pitching as if there was some huge difference between Will Russo and Zach Hardy. But the older kids, especially Truck, Eric, and Justin, had a look about them I hadn't seen before. They'd been playing against the kids from Rotary Club for three years, albeit not on the same team. They went to school with those guys, and they didn't want to lose to them. I suspected there'd be humiliations to suffer, both real and imagined, if we lost the game. And, of course, there was the unspoken situation, hanging in the air like an upstate New York fog. *They cheated.* They assembled a powerhouse team that should have never existed in the first place. It made everyone—coaches, players, and especially parents—want to beat them that much more.

For me it was about finally coming face to face with the two best pitchers in the league. I knew either Zach Hardy or Will Russo would pitch, and it hardly mattered which. They were both monsters as far as I was concerned. The talk at school that week, fueled mostly by Jason Billings, was that Hardy would be on the mound. He also said Hardy was wild during his last outing. "Batters were hit," he said gravely, although he was vague on the exact number. I think his plan was to terrify us, and with me at least, it worked. I'd been taking small steps, trying to prepare for that day, but I wasn't ready yet and I knew it. I feared they'd know it, too, as soon as I headed out to home plate.

Mom was out somewhere with Mark, and they were late picking me up. By the time we arrived at Barnell Field it was 7:20, and the game was supposed to start at 7:30. Our team was already in the outfield, warming up under the lights, so I ran through the gate and headed out. I glanced over at Rotary Club, but they were already sitting in their dugout. A few minutes later Vic called us in. As I ran toward our dugout, I looked up at the sky and saw the last bits of dusk slipping away. The gray sky had all but given way to a menacing blackness, looming above the lights. Everyone found a seat on the wooden bench except Justin who was leaning against the wall. He was pitching, and he looked far too amped up to sit down.

"Okay, listen up," Vic said. Everyone's eyes were on him, and the dugout was silent. Usually, he had to say something a couple times to get our collective attention, but not that night. You could feel the extra tension hanging in the cooling air. "Russo is starting tonight. He likes to throw fastballs until he gets two strikes, and then he throws the curveball in the dirt, so try to lay off it. And some of you younger guys," —he looked right at me—"we need some production out of you. Don't be intimidated. Russo's a big kid, but he doesn't throw any harder than Tommy Wagner." I knew what Vic was trying to do, but I doubted that was true.

"Let's get started, coach," the umpire said.

"Okay, hands in," Vic said. We all crowded around him and stuck in a free hand. I smelled laundry detergent and bubble gum, but it was impossible to tell the source of either. "J&F on three. Justin, count us off."

"One, two, three!" Justin yelled in my ear, and the mystery of the bubble gum was solved. I could tell by his voice he was one hundred percent jacked. As the mob separated, I turned around and got a look at his face. It was beet-red and his expression was almost angry. He was an intense kid, but I remember it being a couple levels beyond anything I'd seen before.

We headed out onto the field and lined up on the third baseline for the national anthem. Just as the song started, I removed my hat and got my first good look at Rotary Club. They were enormous. They seemed more like a JV baseball team than a group of ten-to-twelve year-olds. Hardy and Russo were standing side by side near home plate. Both were larger than any of our players and seemed as big as half the coaches in the league. I continued down the line, looking at each player. There were some average-size kids, but on the whole they were huge—easily the biggest and heaviest team in the league. And if their body language was any indicator, they were also the most confident. You might think a group of kids that age couldn't have a true swagger about them, but you'd be wrong. These guys looked like they were on their way to the championship celebration party and just happened to stop by the field to get a few photos. They fooled around with one another, laughing about some anonymous joke while they jostled for position along the baseline. As I finished my slow scan through their lineup, my eyes settled on Jason. He was staring at me…and smiling. I looked away as fast as I could.

We finished the national anthem and headed back to our dugout. Even though we had Justin going for us, I had a bad feeling we were about to become The Evil Empire's sixth victim. I scanned the faces of my teammates for signs of what I was feeling but didn't see anything. Then I got to Peter.

"Jesus, did you see how big those guys are?" he whispered.

"Yeah, I did. They're huge."

We sat on the bench and watched Will Russo saunter out to the mound to take his warm-up pitches. Someone, I think it was his dad, said something to him and he laughed, loud and deep. He sounded like a man. I watched him step onto the pitcher's mound and begin surveying his work space. It must have been satisfactory because he placed one foot on top of the rubber and looked in toward his catcher, Alex Monroe. Russo leaned forward and then began his windup. After a series of awkward movements, mostly just flying arms and legs to my inexperienced eyes, he released the pitch. An instant later there was a loud popping sound in Monroe's mitt. I think I saw the ball at one point, but I wasn't sure. I wondered where exactly I would find the nerve to walk out there. I knew much of Russo's peculiarity was simply the result of him being a lefty, but strange motion or not, he had crazy velocity. He was every bit as fast as Justin and probably even a little faster. We'd faced a couple good pitchers, but no one in the same league as Russo, regardless of what Vic said.

Russo was on from the start and got through the first three innings without a single base runner. In the process, he managed to make Matt, Eric, and Paul look like inexperienced hitters. Only Truck put a ball into play, and that was a sky-high pop up to the shortstop. And despite the pre-game warning from Vic, Russo got a few of our hitters to chase curveballs in the dirt. One of those was Justin who promptly slammed his bat onto the ground, drawing a stern warning from the umpire.

Justin, on the other hand, struggled to find the strike zone, which — according to Vic — had suddenly shrunk. After giving up two runs in the second inning, he started the third by walking three straight batters. Zach Hardy then promptly cleared the bases with a triple. Then, after yet another walk, Alex Monroe hit a three run homer over the left field fence. When the inning was finally over, the score was 8-0, and everyone was hanging their heads.

I was up first, so I walked into the dugout and grabbed a helmet. After a few warm up swings, the umpire yelled, "Batter up!" I started toward home plate when I heard another voice behind me.

"C'mon, Danny," Adam said. I turned to face him. He was standing on the other side of the fence, about ten feet away. "You can do it. Just pretend it's me pitching."

I nodded, thinking *You can't throw it that hard, bro* before continuing toward home. By that point the sky was completely dark and the bright infield looked both beautiful and strangely artificial. As I neared the batter's box, I glanced out at Russo and found him staring at me. I'm not sure why that surprised me, but it did. I got the immediate sense he was sizing up the threat, and since I was the number ten hitter, I'm guessing he wasn't worried. It was the top of the fourth, and we had yet to have our first base runner. That meant Russo was halfway to a perfect game.

I looked down at Vic before stepping into the box. He offered his usual words of encouragement, trying to build my confidence. When he was done, I stepped into the batter's box and put my hand up to ask for time. I dug my feet in as best I could while Russo glared at me from the mound. I felt like it was my first at-bat in the Majors all over again. Russo went into his wind up, and I did my best to ignore his high leg kick. I remember hoping I'd be able to pick up the ball when I heard the familiar popping sound behind me. I knew what that sound meant — that the ball was already in the catcher's mitt — but it didn't seem possible. There may have been a brief flash of white just before the pop, but I wasn't sure.

"Strike!" the umpire yelled. It seemed to me like he was getting louder as the game went on. I wondered if it had anything to do with the possibility of a perfect game.

The next two pitches were indecipherable from the first and both were strikes. I saw each a touch better than the one prior, but I still couldn't bring myself to swing. Three pitches and I was already headed back to the dugout. Russo hadn't bothered messing around with the curveball, nor did he worry about location. He threw three straight fastballs right down the middle, knowing I couldn't do anything with them.

When I got back to the dugout, I dropped my helmet on the ground and headed for the bench. I no sooner sat down when Paul walked up to me. He didn't usually say much to me or any of the other tens, so I knew it wasn't going to be a friendly pat on the back. I leaned back against the cinder block wall and looked up at him.

"You gotta swing the bat, man," he said. "You can't just look at three straight strikes." I nodded, but he wasn't done yet. There was a lot of frustration in the air, and the older kids had to let it out on someone. "You looked like shit up there, man. You looked scared." After the second *man*, I realized he didn't know my name. "We can't beat these guys if you're scared." He walked away towards the bats and helmets.

He was right, of course. I *was* scared, and admitting it to myself didn't make me feel any better. I watched Justin get up from the end of the bench and walk toward me. I thought for sure he was going to pile on, but he continued past me and walked out of the dugout. I looked down the bench and found Eric and Truck sitting side by side. They both looked dejected, but there was something else festering behind their blank stares. They were pissed off. I looked at Matt and Chris and saw the same thing. They didn't like losing, but it wasn't just losing, I realized. It was losing to *these guys*. And not only were we losing, we were getting embarrassed.

Vic put Peter in to pitch the fifth inning. He was so much slower than Justin, Rotary Club had trouble hitting him. Eric and Truck both got base hits, so Russo finished with a two hitter. The final score was 9-0, only one run away from being mercied. If we could have gotten a couple base runners in the sixth, I would have batted again, but Russo struck out the side to end the game. I was scared to go out there again, but I wanted another chance so I could prove to Paul and everyone else that I had the courage to do it. And I wasn't going to just stand there. I was going to take some hard swings. That was the plan anyway, but as my mom was fond of saying in those days, it wasn't meant to be.

31

The following day, Matt and I headed out to the basketball courts after lunch. Just after we walked outside, we ran into Jason. Matt saw him approaching and took off running. I wasn't as smart. Like I said, Jason and I were never really friends, but I didn't dislike him, either. I found that changing as the school year progressed. Because of Rotary Club's success, he'd been growing increasingly cocky. From what I could tell, he had nothing to do with it, but that didn't seem to matter. Like me, he batted near the bottom of their order and also played a lot of outfield. He wasn't exactly a crucial cog in The Empire. The broad smile on his face that day told me he wanted to rehash the game and in all likelihood rub it in, as well. I struggled to remember what he'd done at the plate. I remembered one strike out against Justin, although he did go down swinging. I couldn't recall if he'd batted against Peter or not.

"Hey, Danny," Jason said. His smile was gone, replaced by the same smirk he'd worn the day he told me about the Hardy brothers joining his team. As soon as I saw it, I knew it would be painful.

"Hey, Jason."

"Wow, I thought you guys were better than that. You did win the championship last year, right?"

What a jerk. "We played a bad game, that's all."

Jason snorted. "You guys only have a couple good players, and Justin is *not* a good pitcher. We crushed him."

I wasn't sure which insult to address first. I decided to defend Justin. "He had a bad game and the ump wasn't giving him any calls, either." That was a bad line to take, but I couldn't think of anything else to say.

"Wow, you're blaming the ump because Justin sucked?"

"Shut up, Jason. Next time will be different."

"I hope so. It'd be nice to have some competition. Russo's not even our best pitcher." He added a laugh I'd never heard before. Find some success (or stumble into it) and suddenly you're a different person.

"The season's not over. We'll see what happens next game."

"Yeah, and maybe you'll actually swing next time."

He took off running before I could respond. I wanted to chase after him and punch him in the face. That's what Adam would have done, but I wasn't Adam. At times like that, though, I wish I was.

I headed down to the basketball court where the gang was just starting to assemble. I was grateful Jason hadn't been playing with us lately. The last thing I wanted to do was rehash the previous night's drubbing with the basketball crew — with Jason's commentary as an added bonus. Turns out we didn't need him. Two other kids had stuck around after their early game to watch ours, and it was the only thing they wanted to talk about.

32

Friday Evening

All told, I put in about five and a half hours down at Saxon Field, including a ninety-minute lunch break. After that the heat got to be too much. I never heard the official temperature, but it had to be pushing ninety degrees. It turned out to be exactly what I needed. I hardly even thought about getting fired, and by the time I left the field, I was physically exhausted.

After a long shower, I headed over to Laura's to grab Connor around 5:30. The plan for tonight was pizza, an on-demand movie, and some heavily buttered popcorn—all while remaining within about five feet of the air conditioner.

I pulled up next to Laura's house, and Connor came running out the back door, duffel bag in hand. He looked up at me and smiled. A second later the door was open and he was inside the Saturn. I felt the momentary wave of hot, humid air before he closed the door again.

"Hi, Dad. Why are you wearing that?"

I glanced down at my tee-shirt and basketball shorts, realizing he was expecting to see me in work clothes. Sunday night I would stop over to Laura's and explain to them that I'd lost my job. Until then, it would just be a normal weekend. "I took the afternoon off and went over to the baseball fields."

"Oh, cool."

Right then an idea hit me, and I decided to run it by him just for the hell of it. "Hey, bud, there's a ton of berries ready, and I haven't picked any since last weekend. What do you say you and I pick some before we get the pizza? It's too early to order it anyway."

"No way, Dad. It's too hot."

"Actually, the bushes are in the shade right now, so it won't be too bad. We'll just go for a half hour. I want to get them before the bugs do."

"I'm sorry, Dad. I know I you like to make jam, but—"

"And last time I checked, you liked to eat it."

"I do like it, but I don't feel like doing that tonight."

I'd expected him to say that, but I had one more trick to throw at him. "Okay. Gosh, I hope I can make the jam this year."

"I have faith in you, Dad." He looked at me and smiled.

I smiled back as we pulled into the bike shop parking lot. Just then I saw Ally come out of her apartment and walk toward the back of the building. She was carrying some sort of plant in a ceramic pot. By the size and shape of it, I was thinking tomato plant. Behind the apartments was a fenced off section of yard that someone had used as a garden last summer. I never saw anyone tending it, but I remember seeing a few tomato plants and maybe some cucumbers.

We climbed out of the SUV and headed toward the stairs. I watched Ally set the plant near the fence and turn back toward her apartment. Just like the day we met, she was wearing running shorts and a tucked in tee-shirt. Even from here, I could see the curves beneath her clothing. Any human male still breathing would have noticed, but it seemed like I could almost feel them somehow. It had been a long time since the weekend in Vermont. It occurred to me, and not for the first time, if I didn't have sex soon, I would officially lose my mind.

Ally noticed us and waved. "Hi, there," she said, smiling.

"Hi, Ally," I said, "planting a garden?" Of course, it was obvious, but I couldn't think of anything else to say.

"I am." She took a step or two toward us. "Is this your son?"

"Yeah, this is Connor."

I started walking toward her and Connor followed. She met us halfway. She looked a lot like she did on the day we met—hair up, little or no makeup. And also like that day, I noticed her hairline was wet with sweat. Out of nowhere, I had a brief but intense vision of making love with her in a sweltering room. The air conditioner worked fine, but we didn't want it on. The hotter the better. I could almost taste the salt on her skin.

"Dad?"

Connor was looking at me funny, and I could tell I'd missed something. "I'm sorry, what was that?"

"I asked what you guys were doing today," Ally said.

At first I thought she was inviting us to do something, but then I realized she was just being nice. "Oh, we're going to grab a pizza and order a movie."

"That sounds fun."

"I think we're gonna pick some berries first," Connor said. "Do you wanna come with us?"

That little shit. I looked at Connor, embarrassed. It was then I realized he was trying to set me up. I hadn't said a single word about Ally, and I don't think he could have already picked up on my attraction to her. I think it was simply that *he* liked her and was making the assumption I would, too. "Connor, I'm sure Ally has other —"

"My dad makes this awesome blackberry jam," Connor continued.

"Well, they're actually wild black raspberries," I said, as if that mattered. "We call them black caps. We used to pick them as kids."

Ally's eyes lit up. "Oh, I know what you're talking about. We used to pick them, too. They used to grow along our road, probably still do. I'd love to go with you guys." She looked at me, and I realized in that inexplicable way that happens when you like someone's personality that she seemed even more attractive. "If that's okay," she added.

"Yeah, of course you can come with us. We'd love to have you, but you'll have to change." I looked down at her legs, grateful to actually have a reason to do it. Like every other part of her body, they were shapely and muscular. "There are a lot of prickers in the bushes, so you'll need to wear jeans or sweats."

"Oh, that's right. I remember that now. I used to cut my hands when we were kids."

"It's a little buggy, too, but I have some bug spray."

"No problem. So is gardening."

I looked at Connor, and he had a huge grin on his face. I couldn't help but give it back to him.

"Okay," Ally said, "I'll go change into a pair of jeans, and then I'll meet you back here?"

If she could have read my thoughts right then, she probably would've had me arrested. "Sounds like a plan," I said. As we walked up the stairs, a thought came to me. It was the same one I'd been having since the day we'd met. *There is no way she's not with someone.*

33

We walked past the empty shoe factory on our way to the black cap bushes. Ally told me the same thing had been happening to manufacturing companies in Syracuse for the last thirty-some years. Little by little, larger companies had been moving operations overseas, leaving abandoned buildings behind to taunt the populace with what had once been. She told me her father had lost his job about fifteen years ago and described how they struggled for a while because of it. I wanted to tell her I could relate, but I wasn't going to talk about it in front of Connor. Eventually, the conversation shifted to more pleasant topics.

"So, what position do you play?" Ally asked, turning to Connor.

"Mostly shortstop and second base. Sometimes I pitch, too."

"A coach's kid playing shortstop? That's a little unusual, isn't it?"

The joke went over Connor's head. "I don't know. I guess so."

"He deserves it, though," I said. "He's a good infielder." As soon as I said it, I wished I hadn't. I knew she was just joking around, but I'd heard from enough parents to know it was a common sentiment. *The coach's kid gets the preferential treatment.* And the funny thing is, while shortstop may be the glory position, in Little League it ranks far behind both the pitcher and catcher in terms of importance. And half the time, depending on the speed of your pitcher and the accuracy of your infielders' throws, it can even slip behind your first and second baseman. But those subtleties are lost on the average parent who thinks their kid might just be the next Derek Jeter.

Ally just looked at me and smiled before turning back to Connor. "How's your team doing this year?"

"We're eight and seven, so not great. But much better than last year."

I figured we were somewhere around .500, but I couldn't have told you our record. I thought about my Little League days, musing over how things change. Back then I could've told you our exact record on any given day, along with who was pitching our next game and who we were likely to face.

About three-quarters of the way there, we all stopped talking. It was simply too hot, especially in jeans. It was almost 6:00, but it still felt just as hot as when I was working at the field. We were all wearing baseball caps, which helped some, but it was still brutal. I grabbed an extra one for Ally, and she put it on without hesitation. Not surprisingly, I thought it looked cute on her. Just before we reached the black caps, we hit the shade. When a light breeze picked up, it almost felt like a completely different day.

Connor and I were carrying long, sturdy sticks. I handed mine to Ally and found another one in the tree-line.

"What are these for?" she asked.

"They hold the prickers back when you're picking berries."

"I didn't realize I was working with a professional."

I laughed. "Listen, I don't show my secrets to everyone."

"I feel honored." Right then we reached the black cap bushes. "My God," Ally said, when she saw the berries. Plum, ripe black raspberries dotted the green landscape. "How much jam do you make?"

"Not as much as you might think. It takes a lot of berries to make one jar."

"I can't believe how many there are. We only had a couple small bushes near our house."

"Yeah, this is a lot. We had a few bushes behind our house, too, but nothing like this."

"Where did you grow up?"

"Just across the river near Valley View Golf Course."

"Oh, I know where that is. I played there in a tournament once with my dad."

My God, she golfs, too? "So, you're a big golfer, huh?"

"I used to be. I don't have the time anymore." Ally looked at me. "A second ago you said *we*. Do you have siblings?"

"Yeah, one sister and one brother. Both deceased, I'm afraid."

"I'm sorry to hear that."

I looked over at Connor. He'd moved away from us and was picking furiously. He would've been doing much better if he wasn't eating two or three berries for every one that made it into his cup. "No worries. We're doing fine. Right, bud?"

Connor looked over at us. "What's that, Dad?"

I figured he'd heard us but wanted to make it look like he didn't. "Nothing, bud, but let's try to get one in your cup for every one you eat." Ally laughed and ate one herself. "And remember, only pick the black ones." Connor was infamous for picking anything that wasn't green.

"Beggars can't be choosers," he said.

Ally laughed hard and looked at me. "I think he got you there, Dad."

"Yep, he did. What about you, Ally? I'm guessing you have some younger brothers?"

"I do. Just one. He's twenty-three now. I also have an older brother who's twenty-eight. And then my sister's thirty-one."

I almost asked her how old she was, but decided not to. She'd pretty much narrowed it down for me anyway.

The three of us worked our way down the row of bushes, talking baseball and plenty of other topics. She was also a big Yankees fan and did, in fact, work for a couple years in retail sales. Eventually, she decided that wasn't for her and went back to school to get her bachelor's degree. Now she was just one year away from earning her MBA. She planned to test the waters in upstate New York but fully expected to have to leave the area to find the work she wanted. With her outgoing personality, there was no question she'd find success wherever she ended up.

After a while, Ally drifted toward Connor, and he had her laughing right away. If Connor didn't like you, he didn't say much. He wasn't rude, but he wouldn't open up, either. Clearly, the opposite was true with Ally. He was babbling away like they were old friends. I followed behind them, working my way deeper into the bushes and picking the ripe berries they missed. Even though I'd come here many times, I was amazed at how many berries there were. It was more than I'd remembered from past years. After just forty minutes, my large cup was already two-thirds full.

A few minutes later Connor started looking over at me. Having picked berries with him before, I could tell he was getting antsy to leave. If it was just the two of us, he would have just started complaining, but with Ally here he didn't want to be rude. So instead, he moved directly to phase two and started killing bugs with his stick. I couldn't blame him. It was still awfully hot, and berry picking did get tedious after a while. I knew Ally was the only reason he'd even lasted this long.

"Dad, can we can go soon? I'm hot and I'm hungry."

"I think that about covers it," Ally said, smiling.

"Yeah, he's pretty good at stating his wants and needs."

Ally laughed. "Kids usually are."

"Yeah, let's get out of here, bud. You did great today." I almost mentioned the reason why, but I knew that would embarrass him.

We worked our way out of the bushes and headed back toward the car. I started it and we climbed inside. It took a few minutes for the air conditioning to fully kick in, but once it did, it felt great. I looked at Connor in the rearview mirror and had a crisp flashback of driving home after an afternoon of hiking. That old feeling of nostalgia, also known as missing my old life, started coming back, but I fought it off. Now wasn't the time to get caught up with old memories and past lives. That's how I'd started to think about it now. My life with Laura was like a past life. I think if Connor hadn't made it through to my new one, I might have even convinced myself it had happened to a different person.

Ally was riding shotgun and holding the three cups. I saw she had almost as many berries as I did, and Connor had picked more than he ever had before. Combined with what I'd already picked, I was pretty sure we had enough to make at least one batch of jam. We pulled into the bike shop parking lot and rolled to a stop.

"Do we have to get out?" Ally asked. "The air conditioning feels too good."

"You can come up to The Palace," Connor said. "Our air conditioner works pretty good."

Ally looked at me, and at first I wasn't sure why. I was stunned Connor had invited her over like that. I probably shouldn't have been, given how much he liked her, but I was. It finally hit me why Ally looked confused. "Oh, The Palace—that's what we call my apartment because it's not very nice."

Ally laughed hard. "I like that. I might have to use it."

I tried to make a smooth transition back to the invitation, but I butchered it. "Yeah, you can come up to our place if you want." There wasn't anything I wanted more, but it just didn't come out that way. It sounded more like Connor had put me on the spot, and I was just being polite.

"Actually, I have a report to write, but I want to go with you guys again. That was really relaxing."

"You have to be kidding me," Connor said.

We laughed, but I was already kicking myself for choking. I only hoped I'd get another chance. "Yes, definitely. I'll come and get you the next time we go."

"Okay, sounds good."

We got out of the car, and Ally handed me the cups. She'd combined hers and Connor's, so there were only two. We walked to the stairs together and said goodbye. When Connor and I reached the landing, I turned back and watched her enter her apartment.

It was two and a half hours later, and halfway through the movie, before I stopped debating whether or not to invite her over for popcorn.

Eddie

34

Saturday games were an oddity, but we had a couple on the schedule. Our first came in our ninth game of the season. We were 7 and 1, our only loss the drubbing by Rotary Club. Things started out pretty uneventful that Saturday, boring even, but by the end of the game, it would go down as one of the more memorable of the entire season.

Jess and I got to the field at 2:00 for my 3:00 game. Mom let us ride our bikes there for the first time without Adam. It was a big deal and she wasn't real comfortable about it. It ended up being Mark who talked her into it. I remember he kept telling her she was being overprotective, and they almost got into an argument. Finally, she agreed, provided she could drive by the field later to make sure we made it okay. It worked out great because she brought my bat and glove with her, which meant I didn't have to carry them. We locked up our bikes near the concession stand and then sat in the bleachers until it was time for our game.

Up to that point of the season, I hadn't exactly been setting the world on fire with my bat. I'd only had one base hit, a dribbler down the first baseline that I managed to beat out somehow. I say somehow, because despite some of my preseason fantasies, I hadn't picked up any "wheels" over the winter. I'd hit a few balls hard, but they always seemed to go directly to someone for an out. Vic told me that's how baseball goes sometimes.

Unfortunately, my play in the field hadn't been much better. I'd made a couple of catches (along with two or three errors), but I hadn't done anything to set myself apart from all the other rookies. And other than a couple brief stints in practice, I still hadn't made an appearance in the infield. So when Vic sent me to first base to start the fifth inning—of a tie game, no less—I was terrified. On the first live pitch of the inning, a big kid with a clumsy swing hit a line drive right at me. I barely had time to react, and I certainly didn't have time to think. When it was over and the ball was still in my glove, I couldn't believe it. I heard Mom yell "Wahoo!" from the stands, and then both Matt and Eric said, "Nice play, Danny," at the same time. God, it felt good to make a play, to actually help the team, instead of being dragged along on its coattails like a bag of helmets.

The next batter was a kid named Bobby Fullerton. He was only ten, but he was one of the best pure hitters in our league. On top of that, and very much a source of great concern to me that day, he was a lefty who liked to pull the ball. Vic told me to back up a few steps. I gladly did as instructed and prepared myself as best I could. Chris delivered a pitch that was way outside. Fullerton chased it and hit a ground ball toward Eric at short. He fielded it effortlessly, as usual, and came up ready to throw. I'd been playing so deep, I had to run hard to get to the bag. When I looked up, Eric had his arm cocked, waiting for me. It must have screwed him up because his throw was low. I could hear Fullerton chugging down the line as I stretched my left leg out toward the approaching ball. I realized if I was going to make the play, I would have to scoop it out of the dirt. The ball approached and I fielded it cleanly off a short hop. When the umpire yelled, "He's out!" half my team erupted like I'd made the play of the season. I think everyone was honestly shocked I'd pulled it off.

As I approached the dugout, I glanced up at the bleachers and saw Mom holding her fist in the air. She had a huge grin on her face, as did Jess. Just as I was heading into the dugout, I felt a slap on my back. I turned to see Eric's smiling face.

"Danny," he said, his grin growing wider, "nice play, man." He ran past me and into the dugout. I think if the season (and perhaps even my life) had ended right then, it would've been deemed a success.

Our bats exploded in the next inning, and we won the game 8-3. To my great relief, and I'm sure Vic's, as well, I made it through my debut at first base without committing a single error. I also got my first *real* hit of the season, a hard grounder up the middle. As great as it felt, the hit took a backseat to what I'd done in the field.

Lying in bed that night, I kept thinking about my play and the reaction of my teammates, especially Eric. Despite the fact that it was my first decent game of the season, I allowed myself to wonder if Vic might be considering me for an All-Star team.

35

I spent most of that Sunday watching TV and doing homework. It was almost 6:00 pm when I heard the phone ring. Mom answered, and I could tell it was Mark. When she hung up, she yelled upstairs to me and Jess and asked us to come down. I was working on a difficult math problem, so I was more than happy to take a break. When we reached the living room, Adam was still sitting in front of the TV, watching golf with Billy. Mom turned it off and told us she wanted to talk to us for a minute.

"We were watching that," Adam said, not even trying to hide his frustration.

"I know," Mom said. "I'll turn it back on. I just want everyone's undivided attention for a minute."

"I agree with you, Mrs. Abbot," Billy said. "I think Adam watches too much TV."

Mom smiled at him but didn't say anything.

Adam punched Billy on the leg. "Okay, you got our attention. What's up?"

"Mark's stopping over in a little while with his son, Edward."

"Mark has a son?" Jess asked.

"My God, Jess," Adam said, "where have you been?" Most of the time Adam was sweet to Jess, but he could also be short with her, especially if he wasn't in a good mood.

"Adam, please," Mom said. "Yes, Jess, Mark has a son from his first marriage. He's twenty-two-years-old, and he's in his first year of law school at Vanderbilt University. He's going to be a lawyer someday."

"Oh, my God," Adam said. "Is that what happens when people go to law school?"

Jess and I laughed, but Mom seemed less amused. "Okay, Mr. Wisenheimer, that's enough out of you for one night."

"Do you want me to take care of him, Mrs. Abbot?" Billy grabbed Adam's arm and the two of them began tussling. Billy was stronger and before long had Adam's arm pinned against the couch. Adam just started laughing and gave up the struggle.

Jess gazed at Billy, smiling, and then turned toward Mom. "Are lawyers rich, Mom?"

"Well, that's a hard one to answer, Jess, because there are all kinds of lawyers. Take Edward, for example. Mark said he wants to work for the government, but that's just one option. You can be a lawyer in whatever field you want. Some lawyers make a lot of money, but others work for average or even low wages. It just depends."

"When are they coming, Mom?" I asked.

"They're leaving Mark's house right now. They'll be here in less than ten minutes." She turned toward Adam. "Adam, I'd like you to talk to Edward. Maybe law school is something you should consider."

Adam chuckled. "I don't think I'm the lawyer type, Mom."

"Yeah, Mrs. Abbot," Billy said, "I hate to side with Adam over you, but I think the man has a point." Adam hit him again, a little harder this time, and the tussling started up again.

"You might be right, William," Mom said, smiling, "but keep in mind, there *is* no lawyer type. You can't believe what you see on television. For that matter, there's *nothing* on television that's anything like the real world."

"Maybe so," Adam said, "but I still can't see myself becoming a lawyer."

"Okay, fine. Then Jess and Danny...and William, maybe one of you would like to become a lawyer someday, so don't be shy. Ask Edward anything you like."

"What's he like, Mom?" Jess asked.

"I actually haven't met him yet. He lives with his mom in Pennsylvania."

"Can I put the golf back on now?" Adam asked.

Mom shook her head. "Go ahead, but I want the television off before they walk in the house. Got it?"

"Got it."

Billy shook off Adam's hand and stood from the couch. "Thanks for the offer, Mrs. Abbot, but I gotta get going."

"Oh, yeah?" Adam said, smiling. "What *exactly* do you have to do?"

Billy fought to hold a straight face. "I gotta get something for my dad at the store."

"What do you have to get?" Jess asked, stepping toward Billy. She'd sniffed out the game and wanted to be a part of it.

"It's confidential, Quarter-Pint." Billy placed his hand on the top of Jess's head and sat her down next to Adam. He said goodbye to each of us and slipped out the front door.

Ten minutes later we heard Mark's car pull into the driveway. I was sitting next to Adam, watching Lee Trevino battle Andy Bean through the final holes of the Danny Thomas Memphis Classic.

Adam kicked me in the leg. "Turn this off," he said. "Mark's here."

Normally, that would've led to an argument, but Mom entered the room and turned it off for us.

There was a knock at the door, and Mark poked his head into the house. "Hello-hello," he said.

"Hello-hello," Mom answered. I got the distinct impression she was nervous.

Mom looked over, and with her right hand she motioned for us to stand. Jess and I complied immediately. Adam was notably slower.

"Hi, guys," Mark said, smiling. "I'd like you all to meet my son, Eddie."

Mark turned around to look behind him as Eddie followed him into the house. When I looked at Eddie's face, my first thought was that he'd rather be anywhere else in the world. My second thought was that he didn't look anything like Mark. Eddie was almost as tall as his dad, but he was skinny and gangly, awkward-looking. His shoulders were hunched over, and he shifted his weight silently from one foot to the other. A thick patch of brown hair hung down over his forehead, covering most of his left eye.

Mom walked forward and hugged him. If I didn't know better — and, of course, at the time I really didn't — I would have said it was the first hug he'd ever received. As far as I could tell, Eddie didn't hug her back. Mom stepped back, pretending like it was a normal interaction, and then turned to Adam. I was nervous Adam was just going to burst out laughing, but thank God he didn't. "This is my oldest son, Adam," she said.

Adam leaned forward and they shook hands. "Nice to meet you," Adam said. Eddie nodded but didn't say anything.

"And this is my younger son, Danny, and my daughter, Jess."

Eddie stepped forward, almost reluctantly I thought, and shook my hand. It was then I got a better look at his face and the expression he was wearing. Today I would recognize it as basic arrogance, but back then I just thought he was nervous. He didn't want to be there and was obviously uncomfortable, but it was more than that. I got the sense he didn't like our mother, or any of us, really. The fact he didn't know us at all didn't seem to matter. When he shook Jess's hand, he seemed to linger a bit. *Maybe he doesn't mind having a new sister,* I thought.

"Eddie, c'mon in and sit down," Mom said cheerfully. She sounded like the mother on some 1950s sitcom. I began to wonder if maybe I'd just imagined the uncomfortable introductions.

We all took a seat around the dining room table. In the better light, I could see Eddie's complexion wasn't very good. If it wasn't for the scowl on his face, I might have even felt sorry for him. The three of us tried to make small talk with Eddie while Mom and Mark went into the kitchen to get some lemonade. It was mostly just one-word answers and frowns from

Eddie. I could tell Adam had already had enough of *Mr. Law School*. I just hoped he wouldn't make it obvious to Mom or Mark.

"So, Eddie," Mom said, as she poured the lemonade, "Mark tells me you're studying to be a lawyer."

"Yeah, that's right," Eddie said. It wasn't what I would have called friendly, but it was downright jovial compared to most of the responses I'd heard up until that point.

"Yeah, he's doing well," Mark said. "He really likes it. Don't you, Eddie?"

"It's great."

Adam glanced at me, and we came extremely close to losing it. I think if either one of us had cracked even the tiniest smile, it would've been over.

"I was talking to Adam about looking into law school," Mom said, still desperately trying to get some kind of dialogue flowing.

"You need to have good grades," Eddie said smugly.

"Oh, I do," Adam said, looking right at him. "Straight A's." Eddie stared back at Adam but didn't say anything.

Mark looked at me, clearly sensing the need to change the subject. "Danny made the Majors this year, and he's only ten."

"Don't all the ten-year-olds make it?" Eddie asked. "I mean as long as they're not terrible, that is."

Mark ignored the comment. "Eddie, do you remember when I coached your Little League team?"

"Barely. That was a long time ago."

Mark turned back to me. "Maybe I'll help coach your team next season, Danny."

Eddie rolled his eyes. "Don't you think your coaching days are over, Mark?" He stared at his father who seemed to be growing more and more uncomfortable with his behavior.

I was shocked to hear Eddie address his father by his first name. Sure, Adam called our mom Ann once in a while, but it was always done in jest, and he'd never do it in front of people he'd just met. Mom told me later it wasn't all that uncommon for older kids to do that, especially when the parents were divorced.

For the next twenty minutes, we sat there listening to Mom and Mark pretend like we were carrying on a normal conversation while Eddie acted like an idiot. He was like a spoiled nine-year-old trapped inside the body of a twenty-two-year-old man. I couldn't get over how different he was from Mark. Mark was confident, outgoing, and friendly, even warm. It didn't seem like Eddie had picked up any of these qualities. Clearly, he didn't want us to become a part of his family, and he certainly didn't want to become a part of ours. Mom and Mark were wise enough to leave that topic out of the evening's discussion. And for his part, Mark whisked Eddie out of there after a pretty short visit.

Later, after Jess had gone to bed and we were alone in our room, Adam told me he thought Eddie was the biggest douche bag he'd ever met in his life. I was in no position to argue with him. Of course, we would never say anything like that to our mother, although Adam did tell her he didn't think Eddie was all that nice. My mother didn't agree with him, but she didn't scold him for saying it, either.

One of the great moments of our young lives came the following night when Adam and I overheard a phone conversation Mom was having with a friend from work. She was talking about their visit and how Mark had brought his son to the house. Then she said quietly that "Eddie was an arrogant little prick." We started laughing and couldn't stop. It was the kind of laughter that's fun at first, but then you really do want to stop but you can't. It was a long time before I was finally able to get a hold of myself…and my stomach still ached the next morning.

36

By the time we played The Evil Empire again, almost three weeks had passed and our record was 14-2. Our second loss came courtesy of Maine's Formalwear. We'd been cruising since losing to Rotary Club, and truth be told, had probably been getting a little cocky. Maine's Formalwear was a definite wake-up call and proved Truck's theory that "Anyone can beat anyone" on a given night.

Vic was treating that second game a lot differently than he did the first. We all knew it was an important game, but Vic was acting like it was anything but. "It doesn't matter if we win or lose," he said at one point. "Our playoff seeding won't change either way." That may have been true, but most of our players felt differently. We wanted to win the game. There were the same reasons as before, but there was also the confidence factor. If everything went as planned, we'd play them a third time in the championship game. If we could beat them, or at least give them a competitive game, then there was no reason we couldn't do it again with everything on the line.

When I got to the field around 5:00 and saw Paul warming up to pitch, I was pretty surprised. It kind of fit with the "it doesn't matter if we win or lose" attitude Vic had had all that week, but I was still wondering why we weren't using Justin. He was our best pitcher and he was available. Why not put him out there? I looked over at Rotary Club and saw Darth Vader warming up with their catcher, Alex Monroe. Clearly, they had a different strategy.

After the national anthem, we gathered in the dugout. "Okay, guys," Vic began, "like I told you at practice, we're looking at this game like a scrimmage. If we win, great. If we don't, great. We're just getting ready for the playoffs, and we're getting a chance to see Hardy — who we'll probably see again in the championship game."

Two things hit me at that moment. The first was that Vic was simply trying to take the pressure off of us. He wanted to win that game as much as ever. The second thing I realized was the true reason why Justin wasn't pitching. Vic didn't want Rotary Club to see the *real* Justin before the championship game. He hadn't been himself the first time we played them, and that wasn't likely to happen again.

"Okay, bring it in," Vic said. "J&F on three."

"One, two, three, J&F!" we all yelled in unison.

Right from Paul's first pitch, you could tell this game would be different. Paul was an intense kid to begin with, but the look he carried out to the mound that night told me this was personal. He didn't throw as hard as Justin, but he changed speeds well, and he had better control. With Truck calling the pitches, Paul cruised through the first three innings. Predictably, Zach Hardy did the same. He was his usual dominant self, delivering one ridiculous fastball after another. I was one of his hapless casualties.

The fourth inning brought two-run home runs by both Zach Hardy and Truck, so the score was tied at 2-2. And that's when things got interesting. I don't know if something happened when Hardy hit his home run, but when Paul stepped to the plate in the bottom of the fifth inning, he looked like a man possessed. His eyes were bulging out of his head, and his lips had drawn into a tight line. Maybe Paul didn't like the slow-motion way Hardy rounded the bases after his home run, or maybe there was some off the field issue we didn't know about. Whatever it was, Paul was as jacked up as I'd ever seen him.

Hardy's first pitch missed high. Paul never even stepped out of the batter's box. It was as if he couldn't wait to get to the next pitch. Hardy stared in at home plate, nodded at his catcher, and began his relaxed windup. He released the ball with a flick of his wrist, and it rocketed toward the plate. Paul stepped toward the mound and unleashed a ferocious swing. The ball clipped the top of the bat and shot straight back, nearly beheading the umpire, before crashing into the backstop. The trajectory of the foul ball told Hardy (and everyone else) that Paul was right on his fastball. Hardy had a good changeup, but he didn't throw it often, mostly because he didn't need to. He gambled Paul wouldn't expect him to use it, but he gambled wrong. Paul waited on the pitch and then pounded a line drive over the left-center field fence for a home run. The ball never got higher than thirty feet off the ground.

Paul was a damn good hitter, but I never expected that. What he did next, though, was straight out of the *Twilight Zone*. Initially, Paul had bolted out of the box, unsure if the ball would clear the fence. Once it was gone, though, he slowed and turned his body toward Hardy. Paul began hopping down the first baseline, pointing and screaming at him. He continued yelling until he reached first base where Ted grabbed onto him. Hardy just stood there, staring straight back. Peter and I sat in the dugout, stunned into silence, our mouths hanging open. We knew Paul would have to bat against Hardy again—if not that night, then certainly in the near future. Whatever Ted said to Paul worked because he didn't say anything else or even look at Hardy the rest of the way around the bases. Hardy recovered and struck out the next three batters.

The way Hardy kept his cool during Paul's antics, it was almost like he knew what was coming next. When Eric started off the sixth inning by booting a grounder he could've fielded in his sleep, we should've packed it in and called it a day. Paul walked the next two batters, and then Will Russo cleared the bases with a grand slam. Unfortunately, things went even further downhill from there. By the end of their at-bat, Peter was pitching and the score was 11-4. We weren't able to mount any kind of comeback, so that's how the game ended. Vic kept us in the dugout for a few minutes after the game. He knew we were down, but he was about as upbeat as he could be. He congratulated Paul on a fine outing, which it really was up until the sixth inning. When he finished the pep talk, he pulled us into a tight group and lowered his voice. "What I'm about to say I don't want you telling anyone else. Not your friends. Not your girlfriends." That brought a few smiles. "Not even your parents. Do you understand me?" Only a few kids responded, and that sparked an immediate change in Vic's demeanor. The easy-going coach was gone. His eyes were suddenly blazing, and his words sounded more like a hiss. "Do you understand me," he asked again, and that time everyone responded. "What you're feeling right now is how they're going to be feeling all summer. Justin's going to shut them down, and we're going to win the championship next week. Is that clear?" Vic didn't wait for an answer. He started nodding his head, and it sparked a chain reaction that swept through the entire team. "J&F on three!"

It was our loudest chant of the year.

37

When the following Monday rolled around, I wasn't looking forward to dodgeball like I usually did, mainly because I knew Jason would be there. No doubt he'd be looking to rub in their victory. Two straight wins, two straight games that ended up being routs. Making matters worse, he got a hit in the final inning. Granted, it wasn't much of a hit, and he got it off Peter when the game was essentially over, but it was still a hit in the scorebook. I only hoped Jason wouldn't end up on my dodgeball team. If he did, he could torture me for the entire session.

As I entered the gymnasium, finding my way onto the opposing team became my primary focus. There were about twenty kids standing in the middle of the gym floor, all waiting for Mr. Landry to unlock the storage room. I did a quick scan for Jason and didn't see him. For a second I considered the possibility he might not be in school. *Maybe he's sick,* I thought. Just then I heard a voice behind me, and close.

"Danny, there you are," Jason said. "I was thinking maybe you wouldn't show up today."

I knew it was going to be bad, but his tone told me I'd underestimated just *how* bad. "Hey, Jason."

"Well, surprisingly, you guys put up a good fight for a while, but then it got ugly again."

"Yeah, it was a good game."

"I didn't say *that*. I mean 11-4 isn't exactly close."

I'd already had enough and could feel myself growing angry. "It was close until the end, Jason."

"Okay, Danny, if that's how you wanna look at it."

"That's how —"

"Did you see my hit? We were just too much for you guys in that last inning."

He said it like he had something to do with their rally. He didn't. I wanted to come back with something, but I couldn't think of anything to say. The truth was he'd gotten a hit and I didn't. Finally, something came to me. "Yeah, you got a hit off Peter. He's our worst pitcher." I wasn't proud of throwing Peter under the bus, but I didn't have much of a choice.

Jason continued on as if I hadn't said a word. "Good thing Justin didn't pitch, or it would have been even worse."

I was about to jump in with both feet to defend Justin, but I realized that's exactly what he wanted me to do. I'd made that mistake after the first time we played. "Well, the only games that matter are the playoffs. We'll see what happens then."

"Got some bad news for you, Danny. That game isn't going to be any different, and that's if you even make the championship. Maybe you'll get knocked off before that."

Jason was right about one thing. If we met in the playoffs, it would have to be in the championship game. Our teams were destined for the top two seeds, no matter what happened the rest of the season. "We'll see, Jason."

Right then Mr. Landry unlocked the storage closet and began throwing out dodgeballs. They were scarfed up by the waiting crowd, and teams were hastily established. Much to my relief, Jason and I ended up on opposing sides. I was safe from his harassment for the next thirty minutes, and if I slipped out early I could avoid him until lunch.

I did end up leaving dodgeball early but not because of Jason. There was a math homework question I didn't understand, and I was hoping to get with Mr. Holt before class started. When I entered the room, he was sitting at his desk, reading the sports section of the local newspaper. His face was completely buried, so I didn't bother to say good morning.

I hurried to my desk and dumped my lunch and textbooks inside. It was still a mess, despite what had happened to Big Mike. You'd think that incident would've been enough to get me to clean up my act, but it wasn't. Since that day, however, I always made sure there were no papers sticking out of the sides.

I grabbed my math book and headed back to Mr. Holt's desk. I glanced at the clock and saw it read 8:52. We still had a full eight minutes before class was supposed to start. I walked up to the side of his desk and stood where I thought he could see me. I expected him to lower the paper, but he didn't. After a few awkward seconds, I said, "Mr. Holt?"

He folded the paper down and looked at me. "Yes, Danny, what is it?" He said it without even a hint of friendliness.

I remember wishing that I hadn't come for help, but it was too late then. "I wanted to ask you about number four on the math homework. I couldn't figure that one out."

He lowered the paper, and I thought he was going to fold it up and set it aside. Instead, he raised it up again. Initially, I didn't think he was going to say anything else. I started to get nervous and was about to turn away when he finally spoke. "I don't have time right now. You should've come in earlier."

I know I should have said something like *Okay, Mr. Holt,* but I couldn't bring myself to do it. I'd seen him help other kids right up to 9:00 and even later. Plus, he was reading the newspaper, for God's sake. He just didn't feel like helping me. I turned and started back toward my desk.

"Hey, Danny," he said.

I looked back at him. "Yes?"

"You have a short fuse, you know that?" I noticed his eyes never left the paper.

At first I didn't know what he meant. Then I realized either Mark or my mom must have called the principal about Big Mike's desktop, and then the principal either recently told Mr. Holt who'd called or he finally figured it out himself. I didn't know what to say because there was no acceptable response. Up until that moment, it had never occurred to me I had a short fuse. And even if he was right, I wasn't going to admit it to *him.* Sometime later, I realized it was the most blatant example of the pot calling the kettle black in the history of mankind, but of course, I couldn't have said that even if I thought of it.

When he turned the page and kept reading, I took that as my cue to head back to my desk.

38

On the way home from school that Wednesday, I couldn't stop thinking about baseball. We had our final regular season game at 5:30, but I wasn't looking forward to it. The problem was I hadn't helped my team since the night I played first base. That game, as it turned out, was both a blessing and a curse. I don't think I ever fully understood I hadn't been a producing member of the team until I actually produced. Once that happened, the fact I was dead weight most of the time became painfully obvious. And being a *producer* is kind of addictive. You're suddenly a member of the team, whereas before, you were just one of the tens. Now the older kids take the time to talk to you, and even the coaches treat you differently. Everyone looks at you like you belong. It had been quite a few games since I'd felt like that, and to be perfectly honest, I missed it.

When Jess and I reached our house, I noticed the front door was unlocked. Usually, there wasn't anyone home yet, and we had to use my key to get in. I figured Adam must have decided to come right home after school instead of going to Julia's. We slipped inside and set our book bags on the floor.

"Adam?" I yelled up the stairs.

I heard rushed footsteps coming from what sounded like Jess's room, but there was no response. I stepped to the bottom of the stairs, looked up, and yelled again. It wasn't like Adam not to answer me, and I started to get nervous. Right then I saw a man round the corner and start down the stairs. Adrenaline flooded my bloodstream. I was about to turn and run when I recognized him. It was Mark's son, Eddie. A wave of relief washed over me.

"Oh, hey," Eddie said, looking down at me.

He was trying to sound surprised, like he didn't know anyone was in the house, but I knew he'd heard us. I stepped off the landing and back into the foyer. I wondered how he got in, then figured he must have used Mark's key. I wanted to ask him why he was in our house with no one home, but I opted for something safer. "How did you get in?"

He looked at me with some of the same contempt he'd displayed on the night we met, but then his expression changed and he sort of smiled. It was hard to tell with Eddie because his smile looked so unnatural. "My dad gave me a key. I figured someone would be home."

I was thinking that didn't make a lot of sense, given that the house was all locked up. He should have realized no one was there, but I didn't dare say so. By that point Eddie had stepped into the foyer, and Jess and I had backed up into the living room. I remember praying that Adam or Mom would get home soon. Eddie shouldn't have gone upstairs, and they would've told him so.

"Hi, Jess," Eddie said.

"Hi," Jess replied nervously.

Eddie smiled, more normally this time, but it still seemed awkward. He wasn't angry like he'd been that first night, but there was something about him I didn't like. I couldn't have told you what it was, but there was something a little off about him.

"So, you guys made the playoffs, huh?" Eddie asked.

He was still looking at Jess, so it took me a second to realize he was talking to me. "Oh, yeah, we're gonna make it. Our last regular season game is tonight, but it doesn't really matter if we win or not."

Eddie turned back to me and nodded. "Well, I better get going."

I got the feeling he was even more nervous than we were. "See ya later," I said.

We watched Eddie slip out the front door and then cross the road before climbing into a small orange car. He started it up and drove down the hill without looking back.

Chris started the game for us and at first was doing well. By the bottom half of the fourth, we were up 5-2. With Justin at first base, I spent that entire game in right field. Since my stellar debut in the infield, I'd been back there only once, and that was just for one inning. I did get some time at first base in practice, however, especially when Justin wasn't there.

That particular night, right field had been pretty uneventful. I fielded one grounder, but that was it. My mind was wandering quite a bit, but by the time the bottom of the fifth came around, I wasn't thinking about anything except trying to stop a furious comeback by Everton Plumbing. Chris started off the inning by getting a strike out, but then everything fell apart. Three walks and a couple hits later, the score stood at 5-4 with one out and runners on first and third. When the next batter stepped to the plate, I heard Vic yell, "Be ready, Danny!" It was the same kid who'd hit the ground ball to me earlier in the game. He proceeded to foul off five straight pitches, and I found myself losing focus. I was slipping into a daze when I heard the *tink* of the aluminum bat and saw the ball flying toward me. I took my usual errant step toward home plate, but I'd been playing too deep to begin with, so for once it paid off. As the ball began its rapid descent, I realized I was still too deep. I began stepping awkwardly toward the infield. Right about then it occurred to me the runner on third would likely be tagging up and coming home as soon as I caught it. *If I caught it.* As the ball continued downward, my walk turned into a run. With my glove turned upside down, I caught the ball at about knee level. Right then I heard Vic scream "Home!" I took three quick steps and unleashed everything I had toward home plate. I didn't get my feet right, but there wasn't anything I could do about it then. The ball was gone, and it looked like it was going to sail high. I watched Truck flip his mask off while the runner trudged down the third baseline. Truck looked like he was about to jump when suddenly he turned sideways, straddling home plate. He raised his mitt and caught the ball at eye level before dropping down to block the plate. The kid slid into home but found Truck's glove instead.

"He's out!" The umpire screamed.

My team erupted, and I ran toward the infield where Matt and Justin converged on me. I remember Matt rubbed his hand on my head, knocking my hat off. Then Justin delivered a hard noogie. It hurt, but the pain faded as the three of us ran toward the dugout and my waiting teammates. I ran into the mob, and we celebrated like we'd won the game.

The actual win came an inning later. I ran out of the dugout and got a hug from Mom. Adam gave me a high five. He'd shown up at some point, but I wasn't sure when. Jess smiled at me, but she didn't say anything. *No big deal,* I thought. Maybe she was just getting sick of baseball. I didn't blame her.

I ran to use the bathroom and then headed back toward the parking lot where I saw Big Red slowly approaching. Adam was driving and the windows were down. Jess was hanging her head out the back window, her dirty-blond hair flowing everywhere. I walked toward the truck when I saw Justin coming toward us. He was wheeling a bike that looked a couple sizes too small. I was hoping he didn't want to give me another noogie. When he got to within about ten feet, he dropped his bike and fell into that same stance he'd used the day I caught the fly ball in practice: upper body leaning back, knees bent, hands to the side.

"Abbot, you did it!" he yelled. "You saved the game!"

I hadn't thought of it that way, but I guess I sort of did. I could hear Mom and Adam laughing. Jess just stared at him like he was some strange animal that had crawled up from a nearby creek.

"Great game, Justin," Mom said. "And great season. What are you guys, 15 and 3?"

"Thanks, Mrs. Abbot." He stood up and walked past me toward the front of the truck. "That's right. We're 15 and 3. Should be 18 and 0 (he pronounced zero as 'oh'), but we had a couple bad games."

A funny thought hit me then. Baseball meant a lot to me—a heck of a lot, in fact—but standing there watching Justin talk to our mom, I could see it meant *everything* to him.

"Justin, throw your bike in the back, and we'll give you a ride home," Mom said.

"No, that's okay, Mrs. Abbot." He was already heading back toward his bike. "I like riding home at night."

"Are you sure? It's no problem."

"Absolutely. See ya later." In a flash, he mounted his too-small bike and started pedaling away across the parking lot.

I climbed into the back seat and watched Jess slide over to the other side. She still hadn't said a word about my play. I didn't care, but it wasn't like her. She was always a selfless kid and didn't mind celebrating someone else's good fortune. I hung my arm out the window and waved to a few of my remaining teammates as we drove through the parking lot. We pulled out onto the road, and I felt the cool night air blowing in my face. I knew in a minute or two it would be too much, but right then it felt awesome. I was dreaming about my play when I heard Jess's voice beside me.

"Deh, nu-neh neh, nu-neh nu-neh nu-neh neh."

I looked at her, knowing exactly what she was humming. It was the theme song from *This Week in Baseball*. That was why she hadn't congratulated me. She knew I'd made a play like the one in the ending credits and wanted to spring it on me during the ride home. Adam picked up on it immediately and joined her. I could see his smiling face in the rearview mirror. Mom looked at her three children, a little bewildered, and then started laughing. They continued humming as Adam drove through the Everton night toward our house. I just sat there, listening and smiling.

I think there's a part of me that still is.

39

Much to my dismay, Jason decided to join up with the basketball crew the next day at school, and the topic of conversation was the following week's playoffs. Even worse, he knew all the seedings and exactly how the tournament would be set up. He got challenged early on by Cam Bender—the sixth-grader who rose to fame during the initial days of the Rotary Club scandal—but Jason weathered the storm and emerged as the more knowledgeable. Matt knew just as much, if not more, but he was too soft-spoken to force his opinions on anyone. He quietly, and I think begrudgingly, confirmed everything Jason was saying.

There were ten teams in the league, and each one had played every other twice. At 18-0, including fourteen mercies, Rotary Club was the number one seed. We were next with 15 wins and 3 losses. According to Jason, we were decent but quite a ways down the totem pole from them. Only the top six teams made the playoffs, which meant us and Rotary Club would get a bye in the opening round and then only have to win one game to make the championship. If the higher seeds won out in the first round, we'd end up playing The Lions Club, and Rotary Club would play Mason's Auto. I thought both those teams were pretty good at the end of the year, so it didn't make much difference who we played. Jason was adamant Rotary Club would crush Mason's Auto, and he was equally confident our game was a pick 'em even though The Lions Club had seven losses and we'd already beaten them twice. He went on to say it didn't matter if we won or not because we didn't have what it takes to beat them. No one did. When Cam Bender mentioned how competitive our second game was until the very end, Jason laughed it off as a bad night. Their only bad night of the season. By the time he was done talking, I think everyone in the group would have given their left arm to see them lose. And it didn't matter which game it was, as long as Rotary Club wasn't holding the championship trophy when it was over.

40

Saturday Morning

I woke up around 5:30 am (my usual workday wake-up time), remembered it was Saturday—and that I no longer had a job—and fell back to sleep until around 7:00. Connor was already up and I assumed playing on his phone in the other room. I should have gotten up then, but I made the mistake of closing my eyes again. The next time they opened it was 8:36. I rarely slept that late, but the funny thing was I could have slept longer. I'd gone past the point of feeling refreshed and slipped into a deeper sleep. It felt like a really good drug, and all I wanted was more of it. If I closed my eyes again, it might have been noon before I resurfaced.

"Connor?" I said, and got no response. "Connor!" Still no response. I figured he'd gone outside to ride his bike or to see his friend Josh who lived right down the street.

I climbed out of bed and shuffled to the kitchen to make coffee. I was scooping a Columbian blend into the filter when Ally's face popped into my head. Meeting her was like a small gift from God because it took my mind off getting fired. There wasn't anything to our relationship other than a budding friendship, but that was enough. I don't think I'd ever met someone with whom I seemed to click so quickly. Even Laura took a little while before we felt fully comfortable with one another. With Ally, it seemed that way right out of the chute. As I waited for the coffee to finish brewing, it hit me why. I wasn't even on her radar as someone she might be interested in, and likewise—in her mind—I wouldn't be interested in her. She simply saw me as a nice, middle-aged guy who has a son and lives in the next building over. It was a sobering, depressing thought.

I was just taking my first sip of coffee when Connor came through the door. "Morning, bud. Were you at Josh's?" I took two more quick sips. The fog was lifting but very slowly.

"No," he said, hugging me.

I smelled bug repellent, still on his skin from last night. "Where'd you go then?"

"I went over to the mini mart and got a donut, and then I was talking to Ally for a while." He smiled at me. "She was in her garden."

Oh, God. He probably shared our life story. "What did you two talk about?"

"A lot of stuff. The Yankees mostly, but she was showing me how to plant vegetables, too. She's really smart."

"Yeah, I think she is."

"She goes to Binghamton University."

"I know."

"Do you like her, Dad?"

"Yeah, she's nice."

Connor smiled. "You know what I mean, Dad."

"You mean, do I like her like a girlfriend?" Connor nodded. "I really don't know her very well. I only met her a week ago."

"Well, I like her. I think she'd be a good girlfriend for you."

I chuckled. "Oh, yeah?"

"Sure, why not?"

"I'm too old for her, don't you think?"

"She's twenty-seven. That's not that young."

"You asked her?"

"Yeah."

"You're not supposed to ask people that."

"Why not?"

"Because it's considered rude." Even as the words left my mouth, I was thinking that a lot of times it wasn't rude at all, especially when an eleven-year-old was the one doing the asking. It was just one of those rules we collectively followed, like saying *God bless you* when someone sneezed.

"She didn't seem mad."

"It's no big deal. Don't worry about it."

"Oh, I almost forgot. She asked me about making the jam. She wanted to know when we were gonna do it."

"Oh, yeah?"

"Yeah. I said maybe we could do it before my game. We play at three, right?"

"Connor, we can't do it today. I have to get tops for the jars. Plus, the jars are in your mom's basement."

"Yeah, I saw them the other day. Can't you just get more tops at the store?"

I knew I could get more tops, along with everything else we needed, but I wasn't sure I wanted to. Nor was I convinced Ally wanted to spend her morning with me and Connor making jam. Sometimes Connor got carried away when he wanted something to happen. "Yeah, I can get that stuff at the store, but I thought we were going to do something today. Maybe we can go fishing."

"I'd rather make jam."

"Did Ally say she wanted to?"

"Yeah, she said she doesn't have any classes today. And she said she always wanted to learn how to make it."

"And you're sure she said *today*?"

"Yeah, Dad, she really said that. Maybe she likes you."

"I doubt that, but if you want to do this, we need to get moving and get the stuff together. We have to leave for your game by two o'clock." A huge smile spread across his face. "I think you want her to be *your* girlfriend," I said.

Connor thought about it for a second. "I might be up for that."

41

We didn't see Ally on our way out, but she was just pulling back into the apartment complex when we got back. I got out and grabbed the jars out of the backseat. We'd stopped over to Laura's and grabbed them out of the basement. We also borrowed a couple large pots. Connor was carrying those, along with the sugar and jar tops from the grocery store. Laura seemed pretty interested in what we were up to, sensing there was more in the air than just making jam, but she didn't say anything. It felt pretty good to see her curiosity piqued. I only wished I could be a fly on the wall when Connor described Ally. Hopefully, he wouldn't leave out how attractive she was. I had no doubt Laura would pull out the *He's old enough to be her father* line.

Ally came walking across the lawn as we neared the stairs. "Good morning," she said, smiling. It was a wide, easy smile that pushed her cheeks toward her large brown eyes. It reminded me of the smile she gave me in her kitchen the night of the party. The butterflies in my stomach suddenly stirred.

"Good morning," I said. "I heard you wanted to learn how to make jam."

"I do, but are you sure you can do it today? Connor and I were talking, and I kind of feel like I might've rushed you guys into it."

"Not at all. I usually do a batch in the summer and then another one in the fall." That was a lie, but I wasn't about to make my new friend feel bad. Plus, there was no one here to call me on it. Connor had never helped make the jam, so he had no idea.

"Okay, that's great. I've always wanted to learn. My mom used to make jam when I was a little girl, but I never learned how to do it."

It struck me then that something may have happened to her mom. "It's pretty easy," I said. "The instructions are right on the pectin box."

"What's pectin?"

"It helps make the jam set."

"Oh, okay."

"If my dad can do it, it must be pretty easy," Connor said.

I laughed. "Thanks, Connor."

"I don't know," Ally said, trying to hold in a smile, "he seems pretty sharp."

Connor smiled, clearly pleased with himself. Ally told us she needed to unload some groceries, and then she'd be right over. We made our way up the stairs and into our apartment. Thankfully, a front had moved in overnight, bringing cooler temperatures along with it. It was still hot, but nowhere near the brutal temperatures of yesterday. With the air conditioner running, it would be pretty comfortable inside the apartment.

Connor and I set everything up while we waited for Ally. I filled the larger of the two pots with water and set it on the electric stove to boil. I'd use that pot to sterilize the jars. I also filled the smaller pot to sterilize the lids and screw tops. Before we left, I grabbed the bag of frozen berries out of the freezer and put them in a container of warm water to thaw. They were ready, so I dumped them into a ceramic bowl. Next, I took the berries we picked yesterday, drained the water they were soaking in, and dumped them onto a flat baking sheet.

Just then Ally knocked on the door, and Connor let her in. She walked over and I pointed to the baking sheet. "These are the berries we picked last night. They've been soaking overnight, which should clean them off and kill any bugs."

"Yum," Ally said.

"Now we just need to remove any leaves or stems or spiders we might happen to find."

"Gosh, I hope I find a spider," Ally said.

Connor laughed. "Me, too."

Once we were done picking through the berries, I dumped them into the ceramic bowl with the others. "Now we crush the berries until it's like a milkshake."

"Can I do that, Dad?"

"I was hoping you'd want to."

"Can I use my hands?"

"You can if you wash them really good with soap." Connor washed his hands a second time and began crushing the berries. "We only need five cups to make a full batch, and I think we'll have that easy."

"Looks like it," Ally said.

"When Connor finishes, we'll bring them to a boil and then start adding the sugar."

"How much sugar?" Ally asked.

"I think six or seven cups, believe it or not."

"That's a lot of sugar."

"Yep, that's why it tastes so good. You can get away with less. I think I did five one time and it tasted fine."

"Okay, so what's next?"

"Then you add the pectin, which makes it set, and then you pour it into the jars. It's not the end of the world if it doesn't set. It's still pretty thick stuff, and it tastes just as good."

I checked the large pot of water and saw it was almost to a boil. The smaller pot, which we'd use to sterilize the lids and screw tops, was almost boiling, as well. I picked up one of the eight-ounce jars. "Then you put one of these jars into the hot water for a few seconds to sterilize it. Pull it out with the tongs and let it cool a bit, then fill it with berries and put a lid on it. Then you screw on the top and wrap the jar in a towel so it cools slowly. You want to be wearing an oven mitt or using a towel when you do all of that, of course."

"Of course," Ally said, and smiled.

Our eyes held for just a second. "Are you making fun of me?"

"A little bit."

"Just checking. Okay, as long as the top doesn't pop up, you can store them for up to a year. If it does pop up, you just need to put it in the fridge and eat it like you would any other jam."

"Sounds pretty easy."

"Yeah, it's not too bad."

"What's freezer jam? Is that a different process?"

"Yeah, I think it is. I've heard it's even easier, but I don't know how to do it. I don't think you boil the berries, though, so I'd rather do it this way. Makes me feel like I'm killing off anything dangerous."

"Like spiders."

"Yeah, like spiders," I said laughing. "You wouldn't want to open one and have a spider jump out at you."

Ally hit me in the arm. "Thanks, Dan. Now I'll never be able to open one!"

I noticed Connor was still absorbed in the berry-crushing process. I decided to take a small chance. "Don't worry, you can just call me, and I'll come over and open it for you."

She smiled and her eyes caught mine for another instant before looking away. "Okay, I might have to hold you to that."

Not bad, I thought. It was about the best I could have hoped for. At the very least, it put her on notice she was on my radar even if I wasn't on hers. That didn't mean we couldn't be friends, but it did mean I didn't want her stopping by to show me the new dress she'd bought for her hot date. Maybe I was overthinking things, but that's what happens when you've had as little contact with the opposite sex as I've had in the last year. Overthinking things is all you've got.

Connor finished crushing the berries, and a minute later we had them heating on the stove. It turned out we had just over ten cups, so we could make a double batch. When the berries started to boil, Ally added the sugar while I stirred. We used about twelve cups, which was less than the recipe called for. Once we got the berry-sugar mixture boiling again, we added two boxes of pectin. By this point Connor had grown bored of the operation and had slipped into the living room with his phone. After we brought it back to a rolling boil, I set the timer for one minute. Then I dropped the first jar into the hot water, and a few seconds later Ally pulled it out using the tongs. When the minute was up, I filled the jar with the berry-sugar-pectin mixture, doing my best not to spill any on the rim of the jar. Ally placed one of the lids on it, and I used a hand towel to screw the top on. I moved the jar onto another towel and covered it up.

"One down, thirty-six more to go," I said. Ally looked at me, unsure if I was joking or not. "Just kidding. It will probably make about sixteen jars this size."

"Perfect. Eight for you, eight for me."

I smiled. "Sounds good to me."

We continued the same process, one jar at a time, until the berries were gone. Working side by side, we were constantly bumping into one another. At first it was a little awkward, but after a while it was just nice. When the last jar was safely under the towels, I lifted the empty pot and set it on a hot pad. "Okay, Ally, you get the first taste."

"Should I use a spoon?"

"Just use your finger. Do it near the top, though, so it's not too hot."

She ran her finger along the edge of the pot where the jam had cooled into a thick film, then put it in her mouth. "Oh, my God, that is so good."

I tasted it next. "Yeah, that is pretty good, isn't it?"

"I can't believe more people don't make this."

"No one wants to pick the berries."

"I thought it was fun."

"Okay, I'm taking that as a commitment to go again."

"Absolutely. I'm in."

I looked at her and our eyes locked. In any other universe, I would've leaned in and kissed her right away. Everything felt right, and I was pretty sure she was thinking the same thing. But in my particular universe, there were quite a few speed bumps, and they slowed me down just enough. Right then Connor came bounding back into the room.

"Oh, it's done," he said, "Why didn't you tell me?"

We both started laughing. "Go ahead," I said. "You can eat what's left in the pot. Excuse me for a second."

"Sure. I'll fight Connor for the rest of the jam."

I ran into the bathroom and looked in the mirror. *Nice job, Dan. That was smooth.* I took a few deep breaths and washed my face in the sink. When I came out, I saw that Ally had moved the large pot into the sink and was filling it with water. "Oh, thanks, Ally."

"Sure, no problem. Listen, I have to get going, but I wanted to say thanks for including me. That was really fun, and I learned a lot."

"No problem at all. You were a huge help. I wouldn't have wanted to do that with just Connor. There'd be about seven broken jars."

Ally laughed. "Okay, well I'm sure I'll see you soon."

"Okay. Thanks again, Ally."

Ally said goodbye to Connor and then headed for the door.

"Ally, wait a second." I grabbed another towel and wrapped up four of the finished jars. I handed them to her. "There you go. Make sure the tops don't pop up."

"Really? Are you sure?"

"Absolutely. Actually, I should probably give you more." I started to grab another two jars.

"No way. This is plenty. Really. Thank you so much. I'll talk to you later."

And with that, she was out the door.

The
Championship

42

We practiced that Saturday and then again on the following Monday. At the second practice, Vic told us we'd be playing The Lions Club on Wednesday. He delivered the news like we couldn't wait to hear it even though most of us already knew. He thought they would throw Bobby Fullerton who we'd already faced earlier in the season. Vic maintained the relaxed attitude he'd had going into our second game against Rotary Club. He kept preaching his recent mantra of taking things "one game at a time." There was no sign of the intense coach who'd boldly predicted a championship after that tough loss. It was probably just as well. Because he'd made the prediction only that one time, I think it carried more weight.

By the time that Wednesday night rolled around, we were more than ready. The pitching rules reset for the playoffs, so Paul was available to pitch again. That meant we could save Justin for the championship game on Friday night. The Lions Club didn't stand a chance. Paul picked up where he left off against Rotary Club, sixth inning excluded, of course. It took until the top of the fourth before they even had their first base runner. Conversely, our hitters jumped all over Fullerton and chased him in the second inning. We did the same thing to the next pitcher and ended up mercying them by a score of 12-2. I picked up my fourth single of the year on a soft liner over the second baseman's head, and more important, I picked up just my second RBI of the season.

When the game was over, we gathered our equipment and exited our dugout. Rotary Club had the late game, so they were lined up outside the fence. As usual, they looked like a good-sized Teener League team. A few congratulatory words were exchanged by a couple kids who knew each other, but for the most part, neither team said much to the other. We all knew, barring an absolute miracle, we'd be playing that Friday night for all the marbles.

I passed by some of their bigger kids on my way to where I'd seen my mother and Mark waiting for me in the bleachers. With a notable feeling of relief, I realized I was going to avoid Jason. Maybe he was late or maybe he'd eaten a bad taco for dinner. I didn't much care as long as he wasn't there. Seeing him in school every day was more than enough for me. I had just made eye contact with my mom when I heard a ratty-sounding voice beside me.

"Hey, Danny," Jason said. I turned and saw him emerge from behind the hulking body of Will Russo.

I should've kept walking, but I was curious to see how he would try to spin what we'd just done. "Hey, Jason."

"Looks like we'll be playing one more time."

"Yeah, if you guys win." By that point, I'd started giving it back to him. Jason smiled. "Wanna put some money on it?"

I decided not to take the bait and started walking again. He reached his arm out and stopped me. "I watched a lot of your game. Didn't look like Fullerton had his good stuff."

"I don't think it would have mattered even if he did. We're hitting too good right now."

"You better be able to score more than you did last time against us because we're gonna get a lot more than four runs against Justin."

I thought about what Vic had said after our second loss to Rotary Club. I wanted to repeat it to Jason, but I knew I couldn't. "We'll see," I said, and started walking again.

"Hey, Danny, I saw your hit. Congratulations. You finally made it out of the infield." He turned and started walking into the dugout.

What an asshole, I thought. Of course, I didn't say it.

43

The final hour of class on that Friday was pretty tense. At around 2:00, Mr. Holt left the room for a little while. We were all talking quietly, enjoying the break, when we heard him yelling at someone in the hallway. Our door was closed, so we couldn't hear exactly what he was saying, but he sounded really angry. No one was the least bit fazed, but when he got back to the classroom, I think we all expected him to unleash his fury on us. Instead, he seemed pretty relaxed, like he'd blown a gasket and now he could coast out the remainder of the day. It always amazed me how Mr. Holt could do that. He was ape-shit crazy one second and calm as a spring daffodil the next.

When the bell rang, I walked out into the hallway, filled with its usual Friday afternoon craziness. I gave a quick glance down the hall for Jess — didn't see her — then scanned the crowd for Jason. He was one classroom closer to the exit, but I thought for sure he'd be waiting for me, so he could make a few predictions about the championship game. To no one's surprise, Rotary Club rolled over Mason's Auto 16-3. I headed out of the school and made my way down the stairs to our usual meeting spot. All the way there, I kept expecting Jason to pop out from somewhere, but he never did. I didn't know if that was a good omen or a bad one. A few kids said "Good luck," but that was the extent of the championship talk.

When the stream of kids began to slow, there was still no Jess. I waited for a few more minutes, thinking she was just running late again. When the buses pulled away, and I was alone on the street, I started to worry. Then I saw Big Red trundling down the road, and I knew something was up. As it got close, I saw our mom behind the wheel. She saw me and pulled over to the curb.

"Hi, honey," she said, rolling her window down. "Hop in."

One look at Mom's face told me that whatever was happening wasn't good. I looked back at the school. "What about Jess? She hasn't come out yet."

"Jess is home. Mark picked her up a while ago. Hop in. I'll tell you on the way home."

I walked around to the other side of the truck, trying to think of why Mark would have picked her up early. The only thing I could think of was she'd gotten hurt in gym class. Just going home sick wasn't enough to cause the stress I saw on our mother's face. I opened the truck door and climbed into the cab. "What happened?" I asked, not at all sure I wanted to know.

"Supposedly, your sister and Susan Neely were fooling around in the girls' bathroom and Mr. Holt heard them. He came into the bathroom and Susan made some kind of disrespectful remark. He spoke to them, which, of course, means he was screaming at them, and then he took them down to the main office."

"Oh, my God. I heard him yelling from our classroom, but I couldn't tell what he was saying."

Mom turned to me. "Are you sure you couldn't make anything out?"

"No. We could tell he was mad, but that was all."

"How far is your room from the girls' bathroom?"

"It's across the hall from our room and three doors down. It's right across from Jess's room." I watched our mom ponder that for a second. "What did Susan say to him?"

"I don't know, but I doubt it was anything serious. It doesn't take much to set that asshole off." I could tell there'd be no apology coming this time. "I haven't spoken to Jess yet. The principal relayed this to me at the hospital about fifteen minutes ago."

I didn't know what to say. I knew Jess was terrified of Mr. Holt, and I'm sure him coming into the bathroom like that must have really frightened her. At that moment I hated him more than I could put into words. When we walked into the house a few minutes later, Mark was sitting with Jess at the dining room table. She wasn't crying, but I could tell she had been. When she saw our mom, she immediately burst into tears.

"I'm sorry, Mom," Jess said. "I couldn't stop crying at school, so they called you."

Mom went over to the table and sat next to her. "It's okay, honey. It's no problem at all, so don't worry about it." She kissed the top of Jess's head and hugged her. "Why don't you tell me what happened, honey?"

"I'll grab you a glass of water, Jess," Mark said, before heading into the kitchen.

At first Jess was having trouble talking, but with Mom sitting beside her, she calmed down. Before Jess got too far into the story, Adam got home and took a seat at the table. Mark returned with the waters while Mom brought Adam up to speed. Then it was Jess's turn again.

"Me and Susan had to go to the bathroom, and our substitute, Mrs. Jacobs, said we could. We're always helping her with stuff in class, so she's really nice to us. After we went, we were washing our hands and Susan splashed me with water. I started laughing and splashed her back. Then we both started giggling and I guess screaming a little. All of a sudden we heard Mr. Holt yelling from behind us. He screamed, 'What's going on in here!' It scared me so much that I started crying." Jess began to cry again. It was almost like she was reliving it right there at the dining room table. Mom wrapped her arm around her again to calm her down. I glanced at Adam, and it wasn't hard to read his thoughts. He'd had enough of Mr. Holt. I remember thinking that the two of them would be meeting soon. I half expected Adam to run out the door at any second.

"At first Susan was scared, too, but when she saw me crying she got mad. She told him to get out of the girls' bathroom. She told him he shouldn't have gone in there. He just looked at her like he wasn't sure what to do, but then he started screaming at her, asking her who she thought she was to talk to him like that. He grabbed her arm and then he grabbed me, too, even though I wasn't saying anything. He pulled us out into the hall, really hard." She held up her left arm. "My arm still hurts."

"You didn't tell me that, Jess," Mark said, suddenly looking a lot more concerned.

"I'm sorry," Jess said, "I forgot."

"It's okay, honey," Mark said. "I just didn't realize he put a hand on you. That's totally unacceptable."

"So is all the rest of it," Mom said.

"I agree," Mark said, "but yanking a kid's arm is on an entirely different level."

"What happened next, Jess?" Adam asked. There was no emotion in his voice, and I knew that meant he'd already made up his mind to do something. Everything from that point on was simply information gathering. I glanced at our mom, and the look in her eyes told me she understood it, too. I looked at Mark, but he didn't seem to have picked up on it.

"He pulled us down the hallway and told us we were gonna go to the principal's office. Then he let go of my arm, but he kept ahold of Susan's until we got close to the main office. She kept telling him it hurt, but he wouldn't let her go. She was crying, too, by the time we got there."

Mom looked at Mark. "I'm going down to the school."

"No, Mom," Jess said, on the verge of tears again. "Can you go on Monday? I just wanna be with you right now."

"And it's Friday afternoon," Mark said. "By the time you get down there, it'll be a ghost town. You'll probably have a better chance of getting the principal tomorrow morning. We'll go down together."

"Yeah, Mom, please don't go down right now," Jess pleaded again.

Mom kissed her forehead a second time. "Okay, honey, I'm not going anywhere."

Adam stood and walked around the table to Jess. He rubbed her back and kissed the top of her head. Then he looked at me. "Go get dressed. I wanna warm you up for your game."

44

I was in my room getting changed for the game when I heard Mark and Mom talking at the bottom of the stairs.

"Good luck tonight, Danny!" Mark yelled.

"Thanks!" I stepped toward the door. "Are ya coming?"

"Absolutely. I'll be there, and I think my son, Eddie, will be there, too. He's supposed to come back into town tonight."

I forgot all about Eddie letting himself into our house. I wondered if Jess had told Mom.

"Get me a base hit, okay?"

Given I had four hits all year, with only two leaving the infield, we both knew that would be a minor miracle. I played along anyway. "Okay, Mark, I'll try."

I heard the front door close, and then I heard Jess's soft footsteps climbing the stairs. I slipped my jersey over my head and met her at the door. "Are you okay, Jess?"

"Yeah, I'm okay." Her face was still blotchy, but the tears had stopped for good. "Are you excited about tonight?"

I was glad she'd changed the subject. I'd reached the point I didn't even want to think about Mr. Holt, let alone talk about him. "I'm pretty nervous, to tell you the truth. I just hope we win."

"I think you will. You guys are gonna win the championship tonight, and then the Yankees are gonna win the World Series again. It's gonna be perfect." She looked at me and smiled. "And you're gonna get the game-winning hit."

"Okay, I don't know about that. I'll be happy if we win."

"Me, too, but I think you're gonna do something special. Oh, I forgot to tell you. Adam said to hurry up. He wants to leave now."

"Okay."

"Mom's gonna take me shopping before your game." She smiled again, and I felt like the old Jess was back.

"Okay, I'll see you tonight then," I said. Jess went into her bedroom, and I headed for the stairs. Halfway down, I heard Mom and Adam talking in the dining room. They were using hushed voices, so I sat on the steps and listened.

"Adam, don't you dare go to that school. Do you understand me? Mark and I will handle it tomorrow morning."

"You give me five minutes with that dick, and I'll —"

"Adam! You know I don't like that language."

"Okay, give me five minutes with Mr. Holt, and he'll never bother Jess or Danny again."

"Violence is not the answer, Adam."

"Sometimes it is, Mom. There's a reason that guy is teaching in elementary school. If he tried that shit...sorry. If he tried that stuff in high school, he'd get the crap beat out of him."

"Well, I think you're right about that, but you're not going to be the one who does it. Is that clear?" Adam didn't answer right away. "Is that clear?"

"Yes, Mom, it's clear."

"So, you're not going down to the school when you take Danny to warm up, right?"

"Right."

"Or any other time."

"Or any other time, Mom."

They say mothers know their children better than anyone, and up to a certain age that's undoubtedly true. But there's a time in most people's lives when no one knows them better than a sibling. A sibling can often see through the lies even when a mother no longer can or, more likely, no longer wants to. Adam would warm me up, but there would be a stop or two along the way. I was all but certain of it.

I came the rest of the way down the stairs, jumping off the bottom step to make sure they heard me. I grabbed my glove, my bat, and a couple baseballs, then started for the door. Just before I made it out of the house, Mom kissed me and wished me luck. The plan was for Adam to take me to the field, and then Mark would drop her and Jess off later after they went shopping.

Adam had told Mom we were going to Archer Field to warm up, but I knew we were heading to the school. Normally, Adam would've been talking about the upcoming game on the drive over, but this time he was mostly silent. His expression reminded me of that day at tryouts when he strolled out to chat with Tank Top. I wondered if he had any intention of warming me up at all. We passed by the golf course and crossed over Main Street. When we reached Dickinson Street, he took a left toward the school.

"I thought we were gonna go to Archer Field," I said. I tried to say it seriously, but Adam must've heard something in my voice — that sibling thing again. He never even looked at me. He just smiled and kept driving.

"What kind of car does Holt drive?" Adam asked.

I didn't really want to tell him. It was almost 4:30, and there was a good chance Mr. Holt had already left for the day, but if he was still there, Adam would confront him. I would've loved for someone to give Mr. Holt some of his own medicine, but I didn't want it to be Adam. I didn't want him to get in trouble. "He drives a gray car," I said finally. "I don't know what kind it is, but it's pretty big."

Adam started driving through the side lot. "Let me know if you see it."

The lot was mostly empty, and I could already tell it wasn't there. "I don't see it, Adam."

"Okay, let's check the other lot, too."

We drove to the larger parking lot in front of the school, but Mr. Holt's car wasn't there, either. "Are we gonna warm up," I asked, "or did you just come down here to find Mr. Holt?"

Adam looked at me. "Of course we're gonna warm you up. You're in the championship, Danny. I just wanted to see if he was here, that's all."

I didn't believe that for a second, but I let it slide. A minute later Adam pulled up to the curb where the buses picked up kids after school. I grabbed my glove and the baseballs off the back seat while Adam grabbed his glove and the bat. As soon as I got out of the truck, I watched Billy pull up behind us and get out of his car. "Adam, Billy's here! How'd he know we were gonna be here?"

Adam gave me the look he saved for when I said something especially stupid. "Because I called him, Danny, and told him to meet us here. He's gonna help you warm up."

"Oh, cool."

"Hey, Danny," Billy said. He was wearing black basketball shorts and a light colored tee-shirt. "You made the championship game! Congrats, man!"

"Thanks, Billy. You coming to the game?"

"Wouldn't miss it. Think you guys have a chance?"

"Of course they do," Adam said.

"I don't know. I hear that Hardy kid's pretty good." Billy was smiling at me, and I could tell he was just messing around.

"He's no better than Jimmy Romano was," Adam said, sounding almost angry.

Billy winked at me. "Yeah, Jimmy must have struck you out twenty times in Little League. I think it's still some sort of record."

"Screw you," Adam said, laughing. He turned toward me. "Every time you bat against these guys, you look like you're scared. And they know that, believe me."

"I am scared. You never had to bat against them. You'd be scared, too."

Billy chuckled. "Oh, he was definitely scared of Jimmy."

"Would you please shut the hell up? I'm trying to help my brother."

Billy laughed. "Don't worry about it, Danny. I was scared, too, when I was ten. Just try to stay in there and swing hard. The fear goes away after a while."

I wanted to say *Unless you get hit.*

We slipped inside the fence and headed toward the baseball field. Adam looked over at the school. "Which one is your room?"

I pointed to the windows of our classroom. "That one," I said, without thinking.

"Go over to the field. We'll be right there." He tossed his glove toward me. I noticed he kept the bat as he started for the school. I also noticed Billy went with him.

"Adam, he's not here!" I looked at the windows again. To my great relief, the lights were off.

"Don't worry, Danny. I just wanna look."

I stood there watching while Adam and Billy ran to the window. I think I know what would've happened that day had Mr. Holt been in the room. I just wonder if it would have changed anything.

45

I scarfed down the last few bites of my peanut butter-and-jelly sandwich on the way to Barnell Field. Mom had made the sandwiches and left them covered on the kitchen table, so they would stay fresh. I ate the first half right there, along with a glass of milk, and then I had the other half on the way to the game. Peanut butter-and-jelly sandwiches had kind of become my unofficial pregame meal. I wasn't the superstitious type, but it had worked for me all season—at least in terms of wins and losses—so why change it?

By the time we made it to Barnell Field, the third place game was already halfway over. Bad pitching and poor defense led to a score that looked more like a football game. It was an entertaining matchup to watch, but it ran late. When we finally started our warm-ups, the lights were on and the cloud-filled sky was almost full dark.

Vic was smiling a lot, trying his best to keep things light, but it was obvious everyone was feeling the pressure. There was usually some joking around as we waited our turn to field grounders or pop-ups, but that night there was none of that. I caught my first pop-up, no problem, but Vic didn't hit it very high. I lost the second one in the lights, and it fell to the ground in front of me. I remember wishing it was a day game. It wouldn't be the only time that thought would cross my mind.

After my third time through the line, I glanced toward the bleachers and was shocked by the number of people I saw. The stands were completely filled, and there were people lined up along the fence all the way into the outfield. I figured a lot of it had to do with it being the championship game, and I also knew there was some extra interest because Rotary Club was 18-0. Sure, it was just Little League, but it had been a long time since a team went undefeated and maybe even longer since one team had two pitchers like Hardy and Russo. Everyone wanted to see if Rotary Club could finish the job, and of course, there was the issue of how the team had been assembled. No one was talking about it anymore, but no one had forgotten it, either. Aside from the Rotary Club families, no one wanted to see them win. You could see it in the faces of the random people and hear it in their words of encouragement. Rotary Club had messed with that fundamental sense of fair play. If you break the rules or manipulate them too much, folks turn against you—at least the honest ones do.

Vic had just sent us into the dugout when I found my family sitting in the bleachers. Mark was talking to someone, but Mom and Jess both waved. I looked along the fence and found Adam standing in his preferred spot near the utility pole. Billy was right beside him. Adam gave me the thumbs up, I'm sure thinking whatever success I might have in the game could be linked directly to their warm-up session.

I headed into the dugout and saw Justin sitting alone at the far end of the bench. He was wearing one sleeve of what looked like a varsity football jacket over his pitching arm. He was just staring at the ground, clearly in another world. No one was talking to him, and I sure as hell wasn't going to be the first. Vic called us together for a quick speech, but Justin just stayed where he was, staring ahead in a fog.

"Okay, guys," Vic started, "let's remember the things we worked on all year. They're the home team, so we're up first. Hardy is starting for them. We hit him last game, and we're going to hit him again tonight." I thought about Paul dancing down the first baseline, taunting him. "Listen to your base coaches. If we tell you to go, then don't hesitate. If you hesitate, you'll get gunned down. These guys are too good. Infielders stay down on the ball and make good solid throws to first. Outfielders make sure you backup your infielders. You have to be ready out there. Always know what you're going to do with the ball *before* it's hit to you. Does everyone understand that?"

We all either answered yes or nodded. I could tell Vic had more, but we got called out for the national anthem. Rotary Club was lined up along the first baseline. There was no fooling around like there had been before the first two times we'd played. That night they looked deadly serious. Russo was staring directly ahead, and Hardy was staring at the ground. It was strange to see him without sunglasses on because you could actually see his eyes. He was still huge but not as menacing as usual. He almost looked mortal. I knew where Jason was, but I was determined not to look at him. When the national anthem was over, we ran back into the dugout to check the batting order. As usual, Matt, Eric, and Truck were our first three batters. I had moved up over the prior few games into the ninth position. It wasn't like I was hitting the ball well, but I was making contact a lot more. I sat next to Peter and looked down at the end of the bench. Justin had reclaimed his spot, alone and as far away from everyone as he could get. I just stared at him, utterly fascinated by how different he could be depending on when you saw him. One minute he was insanely intense, like he was then, but after the game (or with the game in hand) he was crazy loose. His mood and even his personality fluctuated more than anyone else on the team.

"Don't be afraid up there," I heard a voice say directly in front of me. I turned to see Paul about a foot away. "You guys gotta be confident when you go out there." I was relieved to see he was talking to both me and Peter. "You know what he's got now. You can hit him. Just get your bat out there, and let his pitch do the work."

We both nodded eagerly, knowing anything else would have been unwise. Paul moved on, offering words of encouragement to everyone on the bench. He even spoke to Justin, which surprised me. It surprised me even more when Justin responded. I couldn't quite hear what he said, but it struck me that Paul was the only kid who could have talked to Justin right then, aside from Truck and Eric. Anyone else would've been told to get lost.

Once the game was underway, Hardy started off hot, striking out both Matt and Eric. Truck hit the ball hard, but it went directly to the left fielder, and he caught it for an out. I headed out to right field to start the bottom of the first. I almost offered a word of encouragement to Justin, but I chickened out. I tried to sneak a few peeks at him while he was warming up. It looked like he was throwing well, but it was hard to tell. I also thought he was throwing well the first time we played Rotary Club, and things didn't exactly work out. Finally, Justin delivered his last warm-up pitch, and Truck threw a bullet to Eric covering the bag at second base. We were ready to go, or so I hoped. Because of how I'd fielded while warming up with Adam and Billy, I felt pretty good about my chances of making a play. I didn't like playing in the outfield at night, but I told myself it didn't matter. I was ready.

Justin got the leadoff hitter to hit a weak grounder to Chris at first base, but the next batter, Jojo Blake, hit a single right up the middle. Next up was the lefty, Will Russo. Vic had me back up, along with all the other outfielders. Justin delivered a first pitch fastball, but it was outside for ball one. I tried to think about what I would do if he hit the ball toward me, but Justin worked so fast I didn't have much time. The second pitch looked inside, but Russo pulled it and hit a towering fly ball right toward me. Earlier, at the park, I'd stepped back first, but there under the lights and the pressure, I took two small steps forward. I caught my mistake right away and began backpedaling hard. I lost the ball momentarily in the clouds and the endless blackness beyond, but I managed to pick it up again. Unfortunately, I couldn't tell depth. I only knew that it was sailing in my direction, and according to Newton, it had to come down at some point. I stumbled around for what seemed like forever, waiting for the ball to begin its descent. Finally, it was earthbound, and my brain gave me the first report on my position. It wasn't good. I was way too deep and the ball was dropping fast. I staggered forward, and it quickly morphed into a run. At the last instant I dove forward, reaching out for the ball. I felt it glance off the edge of my glove, and then I was on the ground, rolling. I scrambled to my feet, but Peter was already there and had the ball in his hand. Blake had gambled I was going to drop it and scored easily. Russo ended up at third. It would go down in the books as a triple, but there was no denying I'd misplayed it. I looked in at Justin, and he was just staring at me. I'm pretty sure he would have strangled me if given the chance.

The rest of the inning played like a horrible nightmare. My mistake started a chain reaction of errors, walks, and base hits that threatened to end the game before it ever really got started. With the bases loaded and the score 5-0, Justin settled down enough to strike out the last two hitters, although "settled down" probably wasn't an accurate description. From my vantage point in right field, it looked like his head might actually explode. His face was a wild shade of red that somehow got overshadowed by insane, bulging eyes. Not only was he throwing harder than I'd ever seen him throw, but he was horrifying to look at. I'm pretty sure he simply scared those last two guys into striking out.

I got to the dugout just in time to see Justin whip his glove against the wall. I don't think I've ever seen another human being closer to coming apart. He was making these crazy wheezing sounds and talking to himself in short, choppy rants. I tried to stay as far away from him as possible and slid onto the bench behind Chris and Matt. If Justin spotted me, he was going to go off, and that's if I was lucky. No one dared come near him for fear of being attacked. Just as I was wondering how long it would go on, Vic came into the dugout and grabbed onto him. He pulled him back to the bench and began talking to him in hushed tones. Vic had his arm around him and was trying to bring him back from whatever dark place he'd slipped away to. At one point I heard Vic say, "It's not over," but I couldn't make out the rest of it. Whatever Vic said to him worked because when he left, Justin was leaning back against the wall and staring at the ground. Just before Vic exited the dugout, he turned back suddenly. "Justin, you're up first. Get us going."

A minute later Justin was at the plate, looking out at Zach Hardy. On the first pitch, he fought off an inside fastball and hit a bloop-single over the second baseman's head. Justin stood on first base and turned back to the dugout. He looked enormous, like some kind of mythical giant. "C'mon you guys!" he screamed. "Let's go!"

Paul was up next. He walked slowly toward home plate. Just before stepping into the batter's box, he stopped and looked down the third baseline at Vic. It was obvious he was much calmer than the last time he faced Hardy.

"Let's go, Paul," Vic said. "Be patient up there."

Paul nodded and stepped into the box. I wondered if Hardy would bean him for what he did in the previous game. But with Justin on first base and no outs, it wasn't likely. One thing was for sure, though. Paul wasn't going to see another changeup. The first pitch was way inside, backing Paul off the plate. Paul smiled but didn't look at Hardy. He just stepped out, looked at Vic, and then stepped right back into the box. The second pitch was high and tight. Paul lunged backward to avoid being hit and ended up on his back.

"That's two!" Vic yelled at the umpire. Mr. Hardy said something from the other dugout, but I couldn't make it out.

Paul stepped back in, still smiling, and looked at Hardy. I'm sure in hindsight Hardy would've thrown inside again or even hit him because Paul hammered the next pitch over the center field wall. It was a towering shot that left no doubt. Paul cleared the bases without incident this time, and we mobbed him at home plate.

The next three batters were no match for Hardy, and he struck them out without a single foul tip. I was standing in the dugout waiting to bat when the top of the inning ended. The score was 5-2. Right then I saw Vic approaching out of the corner of my eye.

"Danny, you're playing first base this inning," he said.

I thought about my error, knowing it was why Vic was making the move. I was actually relieved. Playing in the outfield at night was far from easy, and I just hadn't done it enough. I grabbed my glove and a ball and headed out to first base. Justin took only three warmup pitches before telling the umpire he was ready. With Rotary Club's huge first inning, they had batted through their entire ten-player lineup, plus the first two hitters. That meant Will Russo was starting off the inning. Justin seemed to have fully regained his composure and struck him out on a third strike foul tip.

Zach Hardy was up next. He stepped to the plate and jumped on the first pitch. He hit a hard grounder into the gap between short and third. Eric, who was playing deep in the hole, ran to his right and lunged for the ball, but when he stood up he didn't have it. Hardy rounded first base, and I felt the ground shake. He was like a Clydesdale. I noticed all that, but I couldn't take my eyes off our left fielder. I remember wondering why he wasn't throwing the ball in. I heard the first base coach tell Hardy to take a big turn. Eric was walking slowly back to his normal position. Something wasn't right, but I didn't know what. *Keep watching Eric,* I told myself. Hardy took an extra step or two toward second when Eric suddenly raised the ball in his hand and started running toward me. The first base coach screamed for Hardy to come back. Eric threw the ball toward my outstretched glove, and I tagged Hardy's hand as he dove headfirst into the bag.

"He's out!" the umpire screamed.

I leapt into the air, arms raised above my head, feet bent up behind me. Eric continued jogging toward me as Hardy climbed slowly to his feet and walked back toward the dugout. Eric put his free hand on my glove. I saw he was trying to hold in a smile, but he was having a hard time doing so.

"Danny, calm down," he said. "It's only the second inning."

I nodded, immediately realizing I'd gotten carried away. Eric ran back to shortstop, and I gathered myself for the next play. Justin struck out the next batter, and the inning was over.

46

Saturday Afternoon

Connor had his best game of the season and we won 8-4. Throughout the game, I stuck to my vow of not thinking about NBC. After getting four texts from Carolyn yesterday, I finally responded and told her I needed a couple days to cool off. I hadn't heard from her since. Ally, on the other hand, was a welcome distraction. I kept going back and forth between *We almost kissed in the kitchen* and *Maybe I just imagined it.* Somewhere around the third inning, I finally stopped debating it. We almost kissed, and there was no doubt about it. It was probably better we didn't because Connor would've walked in and seen us, and that isn't something I would've wanted to deal with. If there really was potential for more than a simple friendship, I wanted to do it the right way. Connor walking in on us kissing just a few days after meeting wasn't the example I was looking to set.

As I pulled into the bike shop parking lot, I decided it was time to get some answers. If I invited her over for dinner, I'd find out pretty quick if she was involved with someone or not. Connor was spending the evening with Laura, so I figured tonight was as good a night as any. I'd stop over and invite her in person. If she said yes, I could run out to the grocery store to get what I needed. I could also make a stop at the liquor store to grab a couple bottles of wine.

I walked toward the stairs and glanced over at Ally's apartment building, surprised at the nervous tingle in my stomach. I didn't see Ally's car in the lot, nor did I see it on the street. I decided that maybe I'd slide a note under her door if she wasn't home. The idea seemed romantic, and it would save her from having to stumble through an embarrassing explanation if she didn't want to come.

I decided to grab a much-needed shower before walking over. I entered The Palace and glanced at the counter where we'd stacked the jars of black cap jam. I pulled the towel back and saw the lids were still intact. None of them had popped up, which meant our efforts had been a success.

Just then my cell phone vibrated, and I saw I had missed three calls from Jen. I was about to call her back when a call came in. I didn't recognize the number but decided to answer it anyway. "Hello?"

"Hi, Dan. It's Ally."

The nervous feeling was suddenly back in full force. "Hi, Ally." I wondered how she got my number, then realized it must have been Connor.

"I'm sorry to bother you—"

"Not at all." I could've added the concept of her bothering me wasn't even possible, but I let it pass.

"Do you have the local news on by any chance?"

"No, I just walked in the door, as a matter of fact."

"You know how we were talking about Valley View Golf Course yesterday?"

"Yeah, I remember."

"Well, you're not going to believe this. They found a body there this morning, next to one of the greens. It's on Channel 2 right now."

"A body?" I felt like she had to be mistaken. Someone was playing a joke on her or maybe on someone at the golf course. The fact it was on the news all but ensured it wasn't a joke, but that didn't occur to me then. By now I was in the living room, trying to find the remote. I'd just turned on the television when I heard a voice in my head say *My God, is it possible?* The voice seemed young, like that of a child around Connor's age. I thought I recognized it, but I wasn't sure.

I found Channel 2, and just like Ally said, the screen showed what appeared to be a live image of Valley View Golf Course. It was the twelfth green from about fifty yards away. Once the leaves were off the trees, we could see that same green from the backyard of our childhood home on Marcell Street. Across the bottom of the screen ran a red news ticker with the words *Breaking News* in white letters. Clearly, there'd been some excavation to the left side of the green. Two large mounds of freshly turned dirt stood beside what appeared to be a fairly deep hole. It looked to be about eight or nine feet long and four or five feet across. It was then I noticed a few objects out of place on a golf course, four of them in black uniforms to be exact. The Everton Police Officers were standing around the perimeter of the twelfth green just inside a line of yellow police tape. I grabbed the remote again and turned up the volume.

"Again, we're reporting live from Valley View Golf Course," an anonymous female voice said. The camera panned to a young reporter who looked to be in her late twenties. "About three hours ago, the skeletal remains of a human male were found alongside the twelfth green. There was no identification found with the body, but according to police there were items discovered leading them to believe he may have been buried there nearly forty years ago. They aren't yet disclosing what those items are, but the police—"

Oh, my God, that internal voice said again. *Billy helped him. Billy helped him bury the body.* I suddenly felt like I was slipping into a vast hole, a massive vortex with smooth, slippery sides—dragging me to a place I hadn't visited in decades. I'd never felt anything remotely like it in my entire life, but even amidst this sensation, I realized I knew that voice. It was me as a child.

I could hear someone else talking through the cell phone, but I had no idea who it was. "Dan, are you okay?" a female voice asked. I looked back at the television and discovered I could no longer hear the woman on the phone, nor could I hear the reporter. If there had been a camera on me at that moment, it would have recorded me hitting end on my cell phone before slowly placing it on the table. It would have also recorded me staring at the television for over twenty seconds before picking the phone back up. The camera would have shown this, but I would've had no recollection of it. My mind was focused on calling Adam, and *only* on calling Adam. It would take hearing Jen's recorded message on voicemail before I remembered my older brother had died just over a year ago. That may be hard to believe, and in fact, I probably wouldn't have believed something like that was possible before it actually happened to me, but it's the truth. Given enough of a shock, the human brain is capable of just about anything.

Of course, even then I realized people are killed and buried every single day, and sometimes their bodies are driven for hours or even days before reaching their final resting point—or not so final, as the case may be. This could have been just about *any* body from just about *any* where, but I knew it wasn't. I knew exactly who it was, and I also knew exactly who'd put him there, although before that moment I never would've suspected Adam would have chosen Valley View Golf Course. Part of my knowing was the reporter's statement that the body had been there for nearly forty years, but that had only been the final nail. Sometimes things fall into place and you just know. Sometimes the truth stumbles down that mental staircase in your brain and rolls right into the fucking living room.

There could have been and probably *should* have been a million questions floating around in my mind, like how in the hell did they carry his body that far? Or how did they get it onto the golf course without being seen? Or how come no one noticed the freshly filled hole next to the green? There should have been all of those questions and more, but instead there was only one. *What am I going to do now?* And even that one question was dwarfed by a single thought.

Adam's gone and I'm all alone.

The
Championship
Part 2

47

I was on deck when our last at-bat ended, so that meant I was up first. I was convinced Hardy was about to make me pay for tagging him out at first base. And if the tag didn't piss him off, surely my excessive celebration did. I made the lonely walk to the batter's box, wishing I hadn't gotten so carried away.

"Let's go, Danny!" Adam yelled from the stands.

I stepped into the box, dug my feet in, and looked out at Hardy. He was looking in toward home plate, waiting patiently. When the umpire squatted into position, Hardy began his trance-inducing windup. And just like the previous time I'd faced him, he delivered a pitch I barely saw. I heard it, though—felt it even—and it scared the hell out of me. The umpire declared it a strike, and I was already behind in the count.

"Let's go, Danny," Vic said, clapping his hands. "If you see a strike, I want you to swing the bat!" Obviously, he was sensing my fear from the third base coach's box. At that point he probably could've sensed it from another continent.

I thought about what Vic said, realizing that *seeing* the strike was ninety-nine percent of the problem. I told myself I was going to swing at the next pitch no matter what. I knew Hardy wasn't worried I'd actually hit the ball, which meant I'd likely see a strike. After all, the scouting report on Danny Abbot was *no stick up there*. Hardy finished his windup and released the ball with that maddeningly simple flick of his wrist. I thought I saw something coming toward me, but I wasn't sure. I stepped toward Hardy and swung as hard as I could. I'd like to say I saw the ball at the last instant and guided my bat toward it, but that's not what happened. I managed to make contact, but it was one hundred percent luck. I heard the *tink* of my aluminum bat and felt a faint vibration on the handle. I was so shocked I'd actually hit it, it took me a second to realize I'd hit a slow roller down the third baseline.

"Run!" Vic screamed.

I lumbered out of the box and chugged down the first baseline as fast as my stunned legs would carry me. No one in attendance that night would have described it as quick.

"Dig it, Danny!" Ted yelled from the first base coach's box.

I felt like the base was moving back two feet for every one I gained. Finally, I reached the bag and realized the first baseman's foot wasn't even on it. For whatever reason there had been no throw. Adam told me later the third baseman dropped the ball and then kicked it. It was an error, but at the time, I thought I had an infield single. I heard our fans cheering, my mother sounding like I'd just hit an inside the park home run.

Peter stepped to the plate next. He was the only lefty in our lineup, and I wonder if that bothered Hardy. Or maybe it was the third baseman's error. Whatever it was, Hardy threw inside and hit Peter in the thigh. Thankfully, it was a glancing blow because Peter was a skinny kid, and the pitch probably would've killed him. As it was, Peter stayed on the canvas for a couple minutes before staggering up to a loud ovation.

As expected, Hardy buckled down and regained his focus. It wasn't something you could see on his face because he always looked focused, but you could see it in his pitches. He struck out Matt on three straight fastballs and then got Eric on a curveball in the dirt.

Truck walked slowly to the plate with two outs and runners on first and second. After catching for just two innings, he looked totally spent, like he'd run a couple miles in the hot sun. As I stood on second base, it occurred to me I wasn't usually in that position. First of all I wasn't on base all that much, at least not when it mattered. I looked over at Vic, and he reminded me there were two outs, which was code for *Run on contact*.

"Come on, Truck!" Justin yelled from the dugout.

"Wait for your pitch, now," Vic said.

Truck must've liked what he saw because he swung at Hardy's first pitch and hit one of his patented sky-high fly balls to deep center. I took off for third, knowing Vic would send me all the way home. The center fielder started backing up as the ball soared toward him, a white projectile against a pitch-black sky. He reached the fence and prepared to jump but then dropped his shoulders and hung his head as the ball sailed over him. I waited at home plate for Peter, and then our entire team was suddenly there to mob Truck. Unbelievably, the score was now tied at five apiece. Just two innings earlier it had seemed like the game might already be over.

Hardy struck out Justin to end the inning. I watched Justin as he walked back to the dugout, expecting some type of blowup. He wasn't happy, but his look had definitely changed. After that first inning, he was about to implode, but right then he simply looked determined. He'd been given a second chance, and he knew it.

For the next couple innings, it was like a pitching clinic for both Justin and Zach Hardy. Not a single player reached base for either team. I was one of Hardy's casualties. That second time he sent me back to the dugout on three straight fastballs. I swung hard at the last two, but I wasn't able to make contact again. By the top of the sixth inning, the pressure was intense.

The entire season had come down to one inning between the best two teams in the league.

In baseball, home runs usually get the headlines, but it's often the small hits that make the difference. Matt stepped to the plate against the best Little League pitcher any of us had ever seen. Hardy had found his groove again and looked poised to shut us down for a third straight inning. His first pitch was a fastball for a strike. On the second pitch, Matt made one of the key decisions of the game. He took it upon himself to lay a bunt down the third baseline. Hardy got to it first and made a good throw, but Matt was quick, and he beat it out. When I pressed Matt at school on the following Monday, he told me he noticed the third baseman was playing too deep.

I don't know if it was the pressure of a tie late in the championship game or if it was simply bad luck, but Hardy picked a bad time to get wild. He made two errant pitches to Eric, both of which made it past the catcher, Monroe, and all the way to the backstop. The second one was more Monroe's fault, but either way, Matt was suddenly standing on third base with no outs. In typical Hardy fashion, he pulled it together and struck out both Eric and Truck. Justin walked to the plate with a chance to knock in what might be the winning run. Unfortunately, it wasn't meant to be. Hardy threw a low fastball that got past Monroe again. The ball could have done a lot of things when it hit the backstop, including bouncing straight back to Monroe—as it often did at Barnell Field—but that time it scooted left toward the Rotary Club dugout.

"Go!" Vic said, and Matt took off running for home.

Hardy was already on his way to cover the plate, and Monroe was moving quicker than I'd ever seen him. He got to the ball and flipped it back toward Hardy in one fluid motion. Even before Hardy caught the ball, I could tell it was going to be close. The ball, Hardy, and Matt converged upon home plate at exactly the same time. Hardy caught the ball and applied the tag to Matt's thigh just as his feet were crossing the plate. The umpire — who'd already shed his mask — loomed over the play. With bodies and dust flying everywhere, he stepped forward for an even closer look. A deafening silence fell over the entire park as we waited for the call.

"He's safe!" the umpire screamed.

Both Rotary Club coaches came bolting out of the dugout to argue the call, but there was nothing they could do. It was a bang-bang play, and as Peter pointed out, ties always go to the runner. Matt came trotting back, smiling, and we mauled him as he reached the dugout. Hardy ended up walking Justin, but he got Paul to pop up to the second baseman to end the inning.

We took the field for the bottom of the sixth, and I was more nervous than I'd ever been in my life. We were just three outs from beating the best team in the league; three outs from the championship; three outs from immortality, or so it felt like to me at the time.

Justin had shut them down since the first inning, and almost as if fate were rewarding him, only the back half of their batting order was standing between him and the championship. There was only one problem. The back half of Rotary Club's lineup was better than most teams' front half. First up was their number six hitter, Alex Monroe. Monroe was more than capable of tying the score with one swing. Justin seemed almost overly aware of that fact and walked him on five pitches. I immediately got a sinking feeling in my stomach because both their number seven and eight hitters were more than capable. On any other team besides Rotary Club (and maybe ours), they'd both bat near the top of the lineup. Their number nine hitter, none other than Jason Billings, was a big step down, but even he could put the ball in play. The only truly weak-link in their entire lineup was their number ten hitter, a kid named Carmen Mills.

As Monroe reached first base, I stole a glance at Justin. What I saw scared me, but it also made me feel better. Something had come over him in the last few innings. He stared in at Truck, his face almost comically serious. His cheeks were a glowing red and his eyes were blazing like Vic's did sometimes, but unlike Vic's gaze, there wasn't even a trace of humor. Justin looked possessed, and I got the feeling whatever was inside him wasn't the least bit benevolent.

Justin threw three straight fastballs to the number seven hitter, each a little higher than the one prior, and struck him out for out number one. He tried using the same strategy on the next batter, but the kid had other plans. On the second pitch, he chased a high fastball and hit a shot up the middle. Eric took two quick steps and dove, knocking the ball out of the air. It rolled into shallow center field. Eric scrambled to his feet, retrieved the ball, and backhanded it to Matt at second base for the second out. Monroe wasn't a fast runner, but it was still a close play. There wasn't another shortstop in the league who could've pulled it off. That brought Jason to the plate, and the magnitude of the situation hit me like a punch to the gut. We were just one out from the championship, but we (and me, in particular) were also just one play from disaster. If Jason got a hit or did anything that could be construed as positive, and then they went on to win the game, I would never hear the end of it. It would be far worse than anything I'd endured from Jason up to that point. My worst nightmare almost came true when he hit a hard line drive down the first baseline. I lunged for it, but the ball landed about six inches foul. Justin went inside on the next pitch, but it got away from him, and he hit Jason in the shoulder. Five minutes later, after milking the incident for all it was worth, Jason finally got up from the ground and made his way to first base. I should've been ready for what came next, but the game was too intense.

"He didn't wanna pitch to me," Jason said, "so he had to hit me."

I decided my best move was to just ignore him, so that's what I did. Carmen Mills stepped to the plate with runners on first and second and two outs in the bottom of the sixth. If Justin didn't get him out, Rotary Club would have the top of their order coming to the plate. After Justin's last pitch, I was worried he was getting tired. He still had that crazy, possessed look in his eyes, but he'd thrown a ton of pitches. He put my fears at ease with a hard fastball right down the middle. Carmen just watched it, a look of sheer terror on his face. I felt for him because I understood. I look back now and wonder why fate would do that to a kid like that, but it so often does. Justin followed the first pitch up with a high fastball. Carmen swung, but I'm pretty sure the ball was already in Truck's glove.

"One more, Justin," Vic said.

"Come on, Justin," Paul said from third.

"Let's go, Justin!" I heard a woman scream from the stands. Somewhere in the back of my mind, the voice registered as my mother's. Her words seemed to unleash a plethora of other voices, calling encouragement to both Justin and Carmen—so many, it soon became impossible to distinguish one from another.

Finally, Justin was ready, and he began his windup. I bent my knees and told myself to be ready, just in case. The pitch was low, almost bouncing in the dirt, but Carmen swung anyway. To his credit, he timed the pitch pretty well, but his bat flew right over the top, missing the ball by only an inch or two. I watched Truck tag Carmen, and the umpire raised his hand into a fist. The game was over. I turned back to look at Justin. He was stepping toward Truck, screaming, his arm extending out in a phantom punch. Everything seemed to slow down then. Justin dropped into his favorite stance—upper body leaning back, knees bent, hands to the side, somehow smiling at Truck and screaming at the same time. Truck threw his mask off and sprinted out toward him. Vic had been standing at the edge of the dugout. I watched him leap into the air, both fists extended toward the sky, before charging out toward the mound. I saw Eric and Paul look at each other in disbelief and then turn and run toward Justin. Out of the corner of my eye, I caught Matt sprinting toward the mound and realized I was doing the same. Truck reached Justin first and jumped into his arms, wrapping his legs around his waist. I think Justin was the only kid on the team strong enough to hold him. And then we were all there, first mobbing Justin and Truck, and then turning to each other, jumping around, hugging and screaming at one another. Then Peter and Chris reached us from the outfield and joined us in the celebration. Someone stumbled to the ground—I think it was Justin, still holding Truck—and then we all tumbled beside them and on top of them into a screaming, laughing pile.

I didn't have to ask anyone, nor did anyone have to tell me. I just knew. It was the best moment of my life.

48

Mom always used to say she didn't like dark shades on the windows because it would encourage us to sleep in too late. I think that was true, but looking back now, I also think we didn't have the money for those kinds of things. So when the bright sunlight fought its way through the clouds and streamed through the curtains on that Saturday morning, it woke me up right away. I turned away from the windows and stared at the wall. For a few seconds, there was nothing. Just me in my bed, relaxing on a carefree Saturday morning. I wondered if we had practice that day, and that was when everything came flooding back. *We're the champions!* We took down The Evil Empire—The 19-0 Evil Empire—and we were the 1978 champions of the Everton Little League. I wasn't sure how we did it, but we did. Justin had pitched the game of his life, and we beat the most talented team in the league. For an instant I was back at the field. Carmen Mills swung over the top of the low fastball and the umpire yelled, "Strike three!" I saw Justin standing on the mound, leaning back and screaming. Truck had already shed his mask and was sprinting toward him. It was a brief vision, but I was filled with a sense of euphoria that approached what I felt after the game. It didn't get all the way there, but it got pretty close. We were the champs, and we'd done the impossible. It mattered not at all that no one in the world, save about 150 people—maybe twice that if you counted all the other players in the league and their parents—even gave a shit. Of course, the reason it didn't matter was because I didn't know that. Right then, the morning after, it seemed like it had to be one of the biggest sports stories in the country.

I rolled over and looked down at Adam's bed from the top bunk. It was empty. His blanket was all askew, and I got the feeling he'd woken up a while earlier. I also sensed he wasn't downstairs, and at first this seemed perfectly normal. It wasn't unusual for Adam to hop on his ten speed and disappear, especially on a Saturday morning. Then it hit me that he'd gone to find Mr. Holt, and all thoughts of the championship evaporated.

I rolled over and slid down off the top bunk. Part of me, a big part actually, wanted to see someone get in Mr. Holt's face, and maybe even push his mean, ugly head up against the wall. But I didn't want it to be Adam.

Mr. Holt was a big man and strong enough to rip the top of a desk off its metal hinges. If Adam challenged him, there would be a fight, and I wasn't sure Adam would win. The thought Adam might get arrested didn't even cross my mind…not then it didn't.

I noticed Jess's door was closed, so I decided not to call out for Mom. Jess liked to sleep in on Saturdays, dark shades or not. I passed by Mom's room and saw her bed was already made. Right then I remembered what Mark had said the night before and immediately felt better. He said he would go with Mom to speak with the principal. I figured Mom and Mark must have headed out early and went down to the school, and although it didn't seem likely, maybe Adam had gone with them.

When I got to the kitchen, I saw a note from Mom on the table.

> Jess and Danny,
>
> I got called into work this morning. Hope to get out around noon. I'll call when I can. Love you tons,
>
> Mom
>
> P. S.   J&F are the champs! Wahoo! We'll celebrate tonight with pizza! So proud of you!!!
>
> P. S. S.   Start your homework.

I ran to the back door and looked out onto the patio where Adam kept his ten speed. It was gone. I knew where he was — where he had to be. Adam had gone to find Mr. Holt. I was furious with myself for not telling Mom that Adam had been looking for him the night before. I'd been so absorbed with the game, and so happy we won the championship, I hardly even thought about it. It crossed my mind once after I got into bed, but I was so tired and so drunk on our win that it slipped away easily.

Adam wouldn't bother with the principal. He'd go right to the source, and there wouldn't be an ounce of subtlety about it. That word wasn't in Adam's vocabulary yet if, in fact, it ever was. I stared at the empty spot where he normally kept his bike, wondering what I should do. I could call

Mom at work, but that would send her into a panic. I could call Mark. I was pretty sure he was off on Saturdays. I could also ride over to the school myself. If I saw Adam's bike there, I could call Mom from the main office. I'd been to the playground a couple times on a Saturday, so I knew there was usually someone there. I tried to remember if I'd ever seen Mr. Holt's car there but couldn't. I decided the best option would be to ride my bike over to the school. That way I wouldn't panic Mom for what might turn out to be no reason at all.

I headed back upstairs to get dressed. I was almost to the top of the stairwell when it hit me that Adam might just be at Julia's. I couldn't believe I hadn't thought of that earlier. Her number was written on a sheet of paper next to the phone, along with a host of other numbers. I spun around and was just about to head back down when I heard Jess's door open.

"Danny, is that you?"

Her voice sounded scratchy, and as I turned to her, I thought she looked a little groggy. Still, I was happy she was up. "Hi, Jess. I'll be right back. I have to call Julia's house to see if Adam's there."

"Isn't he fishing with Billy?"

That's when it all came flooding back. Adam was talking to Mom about their plans to go fishing when we first got home from the game. A huge sense of relief crashed down on me. I climbed the last two steps and started down the hall. Jess was standing in her doorway, staring at me.

"Where's Mom?" she asked.

"She got called into work."

"No one else is here?"

"No, it's just us."

"Can I talk to you for a minute, Danny?"

"Sure, Jess. What's wrong?" I asked the question, but I already knew what was wrong. She'd been thinking about Mr. Holt. I knew from past experience that it was easy to keep replaying his actions over and over in your mind. She stepped back from the door, and I followed her into her room. She walked across the floor and sat on her bed. When she looked up at me, I could tell she was about to cry. I walked over and sat next to her. "It's okay, Jess. Mr. Holt scared me, too, but Mom and Mark are gonna take care of it." Jess opened her mouth to talk, but she didn't say anything. It occurred to me she might not have told us everything. "It's okay, Jess, you can tell me. What's wrong?"

"You have to promise me, Danny, that you won't tell anyone."

"I won't, Jess. I promise." I said it without even thinking. I had no idea what Mr. Holt had done, but I was starting to get nervous.

"Swear to God, Danny?"

"I swear to God, Jess."

Jess hesitated again and then started to cry. I put my hand on her arm. "Jess, it's okay, just tell —"

"Mark came into my room last night."

The words were sandwiched between short, choppy breaths and heaving sobs. Once she got it out, she seemed to relax. The sobs slowed, and she was breathing more normally again. I waited for a few seconds. "To talk about Mr. Holt?"

"Well, at first he said he wanted to talk about Mr. Holt. I was sleeping, but he woke me up when he sat on my bed. His breath smelled bad and he sounded funny. He was kind of mumbling. I think he was drunk." Jess looked like she might start crying again, but she didn't. "He put his hand on my stomach. He told me he wanted to do something to make me feel good. He said he wanted to make me feel better after what happened with Mr. Holt. I said okay because I thought he was gonna give me another neck massage."

It suddenly dawned on me she was upset over something Mark had done, and a strange feeling came over me. Jess looked like she was in some kind of trance, like she was telling me something that happened a long time ago. I'd never seen her look like that, and I didn't like it.

"He started touching me down there. She looked down at her legs. He asked me if it felt good and I said no. I felt like he shouldn't be doing that, but I didn't know what to do. Then he pulled my underwear down and started touching me again. He kept asking me if it felt good, and I kept telling him no. I wanted to tell him to stop, but I didn't know what to do. He started breathing really heavy and looking at me. Then he left really fast."

I just sat there, slipping into a kind-of-daze myself. I couldn't imagine why Mark would want to touch Jess like that, but I think I also realized it was wrong. I remember wishing that Jess was telling this to Mom or Adam instead of me.

"After a little while, he came back. He said it was something that men did for girls to help them feel better. Then he said I must be too young still. He told me I shouldn't tell anyone about it. Even Mom. He said it was a normal thing to do, but no one ever talks about it. Then he said we never had to do it again if I didn't like it. And then he left."

When she was done, she just stared at me. I got the feeling she wanted me to say something, but I had no idea what to say. I don't think I had ever been more confused in my entire life.

"Do you know about that, Danny? Is that what men do to girls?"

At that moment I would've given almost anything to be talking about Mr. Holt again. The following week in school, all the girls in our class were getting a booklet and watching a movie about their bodies. Mr. Holt told us about it a few days earlier. Most of the boys were curious, and some of the girls were teasing us and acting like it was a big deal. I stood there beside

Jess, wondering if they were going to learn about stuff like that in the class. If so, I no longer wanted to know anything about it. "I don't know, Jess," I said finally, "I really don't. I think you should ask Mom."

"No! And you can't tell her, either. You promised! You swore to God!"

"I know, don't worry. I won't tell her." I said it, but I didn't know if I would or not. I didn't know what to do. What Mark had done didn't sound right to me, and I didn't like how Jess was acting. It really bothered her. I also didn't like her reaction when I suggested she tell Mom. She always told our mom everything. Something wasn't right.

We talked for a few more minutes until Jess was confident I would keep her secret, and then we headed downstairs to have breakfast. I barely thought about the baseball game for the rest of the morning.

When Adam and Billy got back at 10:40, I was in my room trying to get some homework done. The truth was I was trying to distract myself from thinking about what Jess had told me. It all seemed so incredibly strange. Why would Mark do that? Why would Mark *want* to do that? I thought about it off and on for over two hours, and I couldn't come up with a single reason.

As soon as Adam walked in the front door, Jess popped her head into my room. "Remember, Danny, you promised not to say anything."

"I won't, Jess." I realized then she was embarrassed by what Mark had done. She had to tell someone, and that someone turned out to be me. But once she'd done that, she didn't want anyone else to know, especially Mom or Adam.

"Hello?" Adam yelled up the stairs. "Do you guys wanna see what I caught?"

Billy laughed hard. "*He* didn't catch anything!"

Jess looked at me and smiled. She was excited to see what they'd brought home and so was I. For the first time since Jess told me about Mark, I thought maybe it wasn't such a big deal after all. Maybe everything would be fine. She ran out of the room toward the stairs, and I rushed to keep up.

49

I remember that day going by in kind of an anxious blur. Everyone was coming and going, doing a million different things. The only person I didn't see was Mark. When I heard Adam ride his bike onto the back patio, it was almost dark. Mom had left about an hour earlier to take Jess to her friend Allison's for a sleepover. She said she'd be right back, but then she called to say she was going to have a glass of wine with Allison's mom and would be home in a little while.

Earlier, I decided I'd do exactly what Jess had asked and keep my mouth shut. If it wasn't bothering her, and it really didn't seem to be as the day went on, then maybe it wasn't that serious. But after Jess and Mom left, and I was forced to face my thoughts alone, I began to second guess myself. I couldn't get past the way Jess had sounded when she first told me. And then there was how she was making sure I wouldn't tell anyone. She was so scared someone would find out. The whole thing just wasn't right even though I couldn't have told you exactly why. It was a little like that day Mr. Holt had been so cruel to Lisa. I knew it wasn't right, but I couldn't find the words when I tried to explain it to my mother.

Adam came in the back door and found me sitting on the couch, watching TV. "What are ya watching, bro?"

"Nothing." It was the truth. I'd been flipping around the channels, but I couldn't seem to focus on any one show.

"Hey, I forgot to ask you earlier. How's it feel to be the champs?"

Actually, it had felt great until Jess and I had our little sit-down. "Yeah, it feels pretty good."

Adam had been on his way to the stairs, but he stopped and looked at me. "Pretty good? It should feel great. I played five years of football and probably even more baseball, and we never even came close to winning a championship."

I knew Adam could sense something was wrong, so I had to be careful. Despite my concerns, I had no intention of betraying Jess's confidence. "No, it does feel great." I looked at him and smiled.

"Everything okay, Danny?" Adam asked. It wasn't like him to notice our moods, or to care even if he did.

"Yeah, everything's fine." I needed to change the subject. "What are ya doing tonight?"

"I'm heading over to Julia's—after I take a shower, of course. I don't wanna smell bad when things get hot and heavy." He looked at me and smiled and then disappeared up the stairs.

Just as I heard the shower come on, I got that feeling again where my brain was trying to solve something without any direct input from me. Adam's words were running through my mind, like some kind of mental tape recorder. *When things get hot and heavy.* He had said things like that to me before, just joking around, and I didn't usually think too much about it. When I did think about it, I envisioned them kissing or tickling each other or something. I had no idea what sex was, and I would have been horrified if I did.

I could hear Adam upstairs. As he stepped into the shower and pulled the curtain closed, an idea came to me so frightening and clear that I got up off the couch and turned off the television. *Adam is touching Julia.* Adam's touching her in the same way Mark was touching Jess. And then it occurred to me that she's probably touching him, too. At the time, I couldn't even imagine why they would want to do that, but even so, it seemed different from Mark touching Jess. A lot different. Julia was Adam's girlfriend, and they were the same age. Mark was an adult and Jess was just a kid, even younger than I was. I suddenly knew I had to tell Adam. He would know what to do. And while I truly doubted it, maybe he would say what Mark had done was okay. Either way, the responsibility wouldn't be all mine anymore.

I listened as Adam got out of the shower and got dressed. He was super-fast when he wanted to be. In a matter of just a few minutes, he was back downstairs again, dressed in black shorts and an orange tank top. He looked at the blank television screen and then back at me, but he didn't say anything.

"Danny, when's Mom coming home?"

"She should be back soon. She took Jess to Allison's house for a sleepover."

Adam nodded and then sat in a chair to put his sneakers on. He looked at me like he'd just thought of something. "Aren't the Yanks playing Detroit tonight?"

"They were supposed to. They got rained out."

"Maybe you and Mom can play a game or something. Or get Mark to take you out to celebrate your win."

Right then Mom's note came back to me. She talked about going out for pizza to celebrate. She hadn't brought it up when she got home, and I forgot all about it.

As Adam sat there tying his sneakers, I began to lose confidence. Suddenly, I wasn't so sure telling him was the right thing to do. I promised Jess I wouldn't, and she didn't seem *that* upset. If I told Adam, I'd be going against what Jess wanted, and wasn't that the most important thing? I sat there in a near stupor as Adam finished getting ready and headed toward the back door. My brain had locked down. If Adam had looked at my face at that moment, he would've known something was very wrong, but he didn't. He was already at Julia's house, probably down in the basement doing whatever it was they did together. Actually, that's what I used to think before that day. After my new revelations, I had a pretty good idea what they were doing.

"Okay, Danny, we'll see ya tomorrow."

The back door was open. I knew in a few seconds he'd be gone.

"Adam?" The door slammed shut and panic swept over me. I wanted to jump off the couch and go after him, but I couldn't move. My legs felt like silly putty, but that wasn't the worst of it. There was a voice inside my head, the same one that told me a few months earlier Ms. Becker wasn't coming back to school. The voice sounded distant and scared, but it was *screaming*. It was screaming that if I didn't tell Adam right then, I would never tell him. I didn't know why that was true, but I was certain of it. "Adam!" I yelled as loud as I could. My voice echoed throughout the quiet living room, startling me.

At first I didn't hear anything. I thought I was too late. Adam was already pedaling away toward Julia's house. Then I heard him bound up the back steps. I could tell by the way his feet hit the landing that he'd jumped all the way to the top. He pulled the back door open and darted into the kitchen, scrambling to where he could see me. I was still sitting on the couch.

"Jesus, Danny! What the hell? I thought you were dying in here or something."

"I have to talk to you, Adam."

"Isn't that what we were just doing?" He took a few cautious steps toward me, I think realizing what he'd sensed earlier must've been true. Something was bothering me, and it wasn't little. "What is it, Danny?" By then he was almost to the living room.

I took a deep breath and began telling him everything Jess had told me. I'm pretty sure it was word for word.

50

Adam interrupted me once early on, but then he just stared at me silently until I finished. He had that same look he had when Jess was telling the story about Mr. Holt, but I could tell it was worse this time. With Adam things sort of went in reverse. The angrier he was, the less emotion he showed — up to a point anyway.

As soon as I was done talking, Adam started in. "Jess said this happened last night?"

"Yeah."

"Why didn't you tell me this earlier?"

"Because I promised her I wouldn't tell anyone."

Adam stood up and began pacing around. "Okay, you're sure she said he pulled her underwear down?"

"Yeah, Adam, that's what she said."

He continued pacing and was opening his hands and then closing them into fists. I think by that point I knew the answer to this question, but I still had to ask it. "Is that normal, Adam, what Mark did? Is that what men do?"

Adam stopped moving and turned sharply toward me. I thought he was going to yell, but instead he exhaled and his shoulders relaxed. "No, Danny, it's not normal at all." For a few seconds Adam looked deep in thought and then he looked up at me. "Where's Jess?"

That was another sign Adam was starting to lose it. I told him where she was not even five minutes earlier. "She's at Allison's house...and Mom's with her."

"How long have they been there?"

"I don't know. About an hour."

"Is Mark with them?"

"No, I don't think so. Mom called to say she was gonna have a glass of wine with Allison's mom." I knew Adam was about to do something, and I had a pretty good idea what it was. "Adam, you need to wait for Mom before you do anything. Why don't you call her? I wrote the number down near the phone."

Adam looked at the phone like he was debating what to do. For a second it seemed like he might actually call her. I should've known better.

"I'll talk to Mom, but I'm gonna get some answers first." Adam took off for the back door.

"Adam wait! You need to wait for Mom!"

He stopped and turned back. His face reminded me of Justin during the championship game...totally possessed. "Don't tell Mom anything until I come back. Do you understand me?" He took several small steps toward me as he spoke. "Danny, did you hear me?" He was almost on top of me.

"Okay, Adam. I won't tell her."

"If she comes home, tell her I went to Julia's. I'm not fucking around here, Danny. Don't you dare tell her." And then he added, almost as an afterthought, "Don't call her, either."

"I won't," I said, unsure if I would or not.

Adam looked at me and then turned and ran for the back door. I followed him, but he slammed it shut before I could get to it. I flung the door open just in time to see him rolling off the patio on his ten speed. The patio light wasn't on, so I couldn't see too well, but it looked like he was holding something against his leg. As he rolled around the corner and disappeared into the night, it dawned on me what it was. My baseball bat.

"Adam, wait!" I yelled, but he didn't respond.

I ran back into the living room and over to the phone. I found the paper with Allison's phone number. I reached for the receiver when Adam's words reentered my head. *Don't call her, either.* Then my mind jumped ahead. What would I even say to Mom if I reached her? I didn't know, but I had to do something. Adam had taken the baseball bat, and unlike the day he confronted Tank Top, I didn't think it was for show. My hand was shaking as I picked up the receiver. I ran my fingers clockwise over the rotary dial, one number at a time. It seemed like everything was happening in slow motion, but I finally got to the last number. I was thinking about what to say when I heard the repetitive drone of a busy signal. Panic swept through me. I dialed the number a second time and got a busy signal again. That noise had never sounded so menacing.

I stared at the phone, knowing what I had to do. Adam had a head start and he rode faster than me, but maybe I could still get there before anything bad happened. I'd never ridden to Mark's house at night, but I knew the way. I had to try. I scrambled out to the back patio and grabbed my bike. It was a Schwinn five speed I'd gotten for Christmas. I sped away from the house, hoping the bat would slow Adam down. I figured he had a three-minute head start and would probably double that lead on the way over. There were a couple different routes to Mark's, but I decided to use the same one Jess and I took on our bike trip to Barnell Field.

The ride was a blur. I saw a few cars, and I passed by a heavy set man walking his two dogs, but that was about all. What I remember more than anything was the cool night air whipping against my face as I sped along. I was going as fast as I could, probably as fast as I'd ever ridden. Finally, I started getting close. Normally, I would've been able to see the lights of Barnell Field, but with the season having just ended, there were no games going on. I turned left off Abaleen Drive, trying to keep as much speed as possible as I started up Powers Avenue. It was a steep hill, and I knew from past experience I'd struggle to reach the top. Jess and I had only made it about halfway up, but I felt like I could do better. I stood and pedaled as hard as I could. Just when I thought I wasn't going to make it, I reached the crest, and the road leveled out. I looked to my right, between the houses, and caught a glimpse of a dark and empty Barnell Field about a hundred yards away. Just twenty-four hours earlier, I was down there playing the most exciting game of my life.

It struck me I had no idea what I would do once I got to Mark's. I was hoping I wouldn't have to do anything. Maybe he wasn't even home. I prayed for that possibility as I turned left onto Amherst Street and started up yet another hill. The adrenaline that had carried me to that point was fading fast. I was exhausted, and the hills were sapping what little strength I had left. Finally, I reached Mark's street and turned right. I saw taillights in the distance, but otherwise the road seemed deserted. A few porch lights were on, and there were periodic streetlights shining down, but there was no one milling about.

Mark's house was the sixth one on the right. As I got closer, I noticed his porch light wasn't on. *Please be gone,* I thought. Then I saw Adam's ten-speed lying on the side lawn, and my heart all but stopped. I rode up to the driveway and hopped off my bike, trying to catch my breath. I laid my five-speed next to Adam's bike and looked up at the side of the two-story house. There was only one light on inside, and it was near the back. *The kitchen.* I listened for voices but couldn't hear anything except for the countless crickets and a dog barking in the distance. I also heard a car door close, but it sounded like it was a few streets over.

I knew there was a back entrance off the kitchen, so I headed in that direction. I was almost past the side door when I noticed it was open. The screen door was closed, but the inside door was ajar. I leaned my head against the screen and listened for voices. There was nothing. Even the crickets had gone silent. I started growing even more nervous. Adam was definitely in there, so why couldn't I hear him? Right then I realized I didn't see Mark's car. It could have been in the garage, but it wasn't in the driveway, nor was it in the road. I knew that could mean only one thing: Adam was inside, waiting for Mark to get home.

I opened the screen door and stepped into the house. To my left was a wooden stairwell, leading down to the basement. Straight ahead was a shorter stairwell, which led up to a closed wooden door. I knew on the other side of that door was a narrow hallway, which took you into the heart of the house. If you went right, you entered the kitchen — left, you found the living room. I was about to call out for Adam when I heard a strange sound coming from the kitchen. It reminded me of when Mom used a mallet to tenderize a chicken breast. The sound repeated itself three or four times. Then I heard a heavier sound, like something banging against the wall. I felt the vibration through the wooden floorboards.

I stepped forward and started cautiously up the stairs, my heart beating out of my chest. My throat felt like sandpaper, and my mouth was filled with a coppery bitterness. I knew something was terribly wrong, but I didn't know what. Just as I was opening the inner door, I heard the banging sound again. Every instinct in my body told me to run away as fast and as far as I could, but I fought them off and turned my head around the corner. With the kitchen light on, I could see everything clearly, but my brain was unable to register the scene before me. Mark and Adam were on the floor. That much was clear. Mark was on top of him, straddling him. The rest of it, though, was like catching a glimpse of two strange creatures on some alien landscape. You know what they are, but you can't even begin to comprehend what's happening.

The first thing that came into focus was the mallet sound. It was Adam's fist striking Mark's shoulder. It occurred to me he was trying for Mark's face, but his arms weren't quite long enough. I watched Adam's leg kick out suddenly and saw his sneaker strike a cabinet under the sink. Somewhere under the thick blanket of shock that had enveloped me, my brain registered that *that* was the banging noise. At that point another realization came over me. *Mark is strangling Adam.* I think I would have stood there watching the ghastly scene until it was over had I not kicked something. Whatever that something was banged into the island where Jess and I had eaten Jell-O pudding not even two weeks earlier. The noise startled me out of my walking slumber, and I saw it was my baseball bat. Up until that moment, I didn't know I'd been moving toward them. In my mind, I was still at the top of the steps, watching from a distance.

Mark heard the noise and wheeled his head around toward me. I knew it was Mark, but right then I was convinced I was looking at a demon. His face was bright red and covered with a shiny layer of perspiration. His hair, normally so well-kempt, was filled with sweat and hanging down in his eyes. Mark stared at me with seemingly no recognition at all. It was as if he wasn't there, and someone or some *thing* was using his body to kill my brother.

As Mark was turning back to the task at hand, I got a look at Adam's face for the first time. He was staring at me, his terrified eyes bulging from his head. Movies depict what people look like when they're being strangled to death, but they don't usually come close to capturing the awfulness of the real thing. Adam's face, swollen from the pressure of Mark's crushing hands, was a deep, purplish red. His tongue was protruding from his mouth as he tried desperately to suck in a breath. At first I heard an odd gurgling sound, but then Mark closed off the airway completely, and there was only an awful silence. Adam's eyes, which had fixed on me so quickly, had begun to glaze over in just a matter of seconds.

I expected Mark to stop when he saw me standing there. Surely, he wouldn't kill Adam with me watching. But once he turned back, I realized he was going to do just that. Adam continued striking Mark's arm, but I could see it was losing strength. I knew if I didn't do something fast, my brother would die.

I picked up my thirty-inch Adirondack bat and stepped closer. Adam's face had turned a hideous shade of purple, and his eyes had rolled into the top of his head. I could smell Mark's pungent sweat trying to overpower his cologne. It was Old Spice. Mom had bought it for me to give to him for Christmas. I turned sideways into a rudimentary batting stance and swung at the back of Mark's head. It was like connecting with a massive, waterlogged softball. Mark collapsed forward, his chest covering Adam's face, and then they were both motionless. I could hear Mark breathing, or at least I thought it was Mark, but I couldn't hear Adam. I dropped the bat, jumped over Adam's legs, and tried to pull Mark off of him, but I couldn't do it. He was too heavy. I hopped over to the other side and pushed against Mark's arm and shoulder with everything I had. Finally, I got his upper body past the tipping point, and he fell off Adam onto his back.

My brother looked dead. His eyes were open, staring blankly at the ceiling. His face was still that awful shade of purplish-red, and he wasn't moving. Suddenly, I remembered what they'd shown us in gym class at the beginning of the year. The school nurse had been there, and she had a training mannequin. She called it mouth-to-mouth resuscitation. It seemed so strange to be doing that in gym, but for two whole classes, that's all we did. I put my hand under Adam's neck and lifted until his head tilted back. I could see Mark's hands imprinted on his neck like enormous birthmarks. As Adam's head went back, his mouth opened. I strained to listen for breathing, like they'd taught us, but I couldn't hear anything. I plugged his nose and then lowered my mouth over his, covering it as best I could, before blowing into his lungs. I felt like I'd exhaled a huge amount of air into him, but his chest barely moved. I leaned down to do it again when he jerked suddenly, his head tilting back even further as he sucked in a strained breath. It sounded like he had a golf ball lodged in his throat and was trying to pull in air around it. Adam opened his eyes and looked at me briefly before rolling onto his side. He sucked in another strained breath, then another. With each breath his airway opened a bit more, and the awful wheezing sound lessened. Soon it gave way to a ferocious coughing fit, and Adam raised himself to his hands and knees to fight it.

I realized then he was going to be okay, and I collapsed onto my butt. If the side wall of the island hadn't been there to hold me up, I would've gone all the way to the ground. Adam used one of the island's bar stools to pull himself to his feet. The coughing had stopped, but he was still sucking in large gasps of air and spitting them back out. The color had come back to his face, turning from that awful purple to red again.

I looked down at Mark. He was still lying on his back, his eyes closed. If not for the messy hair and the thin film of sweat on his face, he could have simply been napping. Even his breathing seemed almost normal. It was a bit choppy, but nothing that would suggest he'd just been knocked out with a baseball bat.

Adam looked at Mark and then back at me. "You need to go home, Danny. Right now."

I looked up at him, and he extended his hand toward me. I reached for it, and he pulled me to my feet. I tried standing on shaky legs and almost fell down again. Adam grabbed me and held me up until I clutched the countertop for support.

"You need to go home," he said again. "And you can't tell Mom about any of this. I'll be home in a little while, and I'll tell her what happened."

As soon as Adam spoke those words, I knew this wasn't over. "Why don't we just call the police?" I felt tears coming, and I knew once they hit, I wouldn't be able to stop them.

"I will, but I just need to think. You need to go." He started pushing me back toward the stairs.

"Adam, Mom's gonna know something's wrong when she sees me."

By that point we were at the top of the small stairwell. "Okay, listen to me. Tell her you went for a bike ride, and some older kids chased you. She'll believe that."

"But, what—"

"Listen to me, Danny! I need some time to deal with this, and I need to think. If Mom finds out what happened, she'll drive over here and fuck everything up."

At that moment I knew Adam was going to kill Mark. I looked at him and he read my thoughts. What older brother doesn't know what his younger brother is thinking?

"Danny, listen to me. Mark tried to kill me. You saw that for yourself."

A horrifying realization came to me then. It had been gnawing at me ever since Mark turned around and looked at me, but suddenly it was crystal clear. *I was next.* Mark didn't stop when he saw me standing there. He would've killed Adam, and then he would've killed me. He would have had no choice. Adam's voice pulled me back to the present.

"He's an evil person, Danny. He seemed nice because he was nice to Mom, but he really wanted Jess, and he was gonna kill us to keep it a secret."

I didn't want Adam to kill Mark, but I didn't know if that was right or wrong. I was going into shock if I wasn't there already, and I didn't know what to do. All I knew was I wanted to leave. I looked at Adam and nodded before running down the steps and out the back door.

I was almost to the bottom of Powers Avenue when the tears came. To this day, I don't remember much about the ride home until I turned onto my street and saw our house. Mom's truck wasn't in the driveway.

51

I'm not sure how long I'd been sleeping when I heard my mother scream in the living room. The last time I remember checking the clock it read 10:21, and she had just gotten home. I was still awake when she kissed my forehead, although she didn't know it. I wanted to open my eyes and tell her everything, but I knew if Adam was going to do what I suspected, then it was too late anyway. Better to wait like Adam had said and let him handle it. I just laid in bed and cried until I fell asleep.

The sound coming from the living room was more of a wail, but at that point in my life, I'd never heard anything like it before, so I didn't know what to call it. I immediately climbed down off the top bunk and went to the door. I noticed right away Adam wasn't in his bed.

"My God, Adam," Mom said in an awful, crying voice. "Please tell me you're lying. Please tell me you didn't do that."

"I did, Mom. I had to. I didn't have a choice."

Adam sounded different, too. He sounded much younger, and he was pleading with our mom. I'd never heard him sound like that, and it scared me even more than her voice did. My instinct was to crawl back onto the top bunk, pull the blankets over my head, and plug my ears. But I couldn't do that. I had to hear what they were saying.

"Of course you had a choice! You didn't have to go over there in the first place! You could have called me!"

Amidst her screams I wondered if the windows were open downstairs, knowing that someone could easily hear her if they were.

"Mom, I just went over there to get some answers. He tried to kill me. Did you not hear that?"

"You went over there to beat some answers out of him, you mean! You took a bat with you, for Christ's sake! What did you expect him to do?"

"I don't believe you," Adam said, sounding more like himself again. "Mark strangles your son, and you defend him. Are you okay with him fingering your daughter, too?"

I heard a series of quick slapping sounds and knew what it was immediately. Mom had opened up on Adam's face, and many of the blows were landing. "How dare you say that to me, you fucking bastard! You're a fucking asshole. You're just like your father!"

I heard another slap, but this one was much louder and much more solid. It sounded like someone hitting a slab of meat with a 2 x 4. I knew that hadn't come from our mother's hand. I rushed to the end of the hallway and down the stairs. As I rounded the corner, I expected to see our mother in an unconscious heap on the living room floor. Instead, she was sitting on the couch, holding the side of her face. Adam was standing over her. I couldn't see his face, so I didn't know if he was done, or if he was planning to hit her again.

"I'm sorry, Mom," he said, stepping back from her. His voice had returned to the younger Adam I'd heard pleading a few minutes earlier. He sounded like a little boy. "I didn't mean to do that." He raised his hand to his mouth and started to cry.

I watched Mom look up at him and reach her hand out. He clutched it, and she pulled him down to her. He sat on the couch beside her and she wrapped her arms around him. Adam was sobbing by then, his entire body heaving.

"I'm sorry I said that, Adam." She was almost whispering. "You're nothing like him. You're the complete opposite of him." She rubbed his back with one hand.

She looked up and saw me on the stairwell. "Everything's okay, Danny. Go back to sleep."

Adam continued crying. It hurt to see him like that. He'd always been our older brother, so tough and so proud. Our father had abandoned us, and it was his job to protect us. It had *always* been his job to protect us. But at that moment, he was broken. I stared at him, unsure what to do. Then I realized he was trying to keep me out of it. He hadn't mentioned me at all. Part of me *wanted* to stay out of it, to go back to my room and let Mom and Adam figure it out, but that wasn't the real Adam sitting there beside our mother. It was Adam as a child, trying to deal with the aftermath of horror. I think I understood that even then, and there was no way I could do that to him. There was no way I could let him deal with that alone.

"I was there, Mom," I said, already starting to cry. "I followed Adam on my bike, and when I got there Mark was choking him. He looked right at me, but he didn't stop. He was gonna kill Adam, and then he was gonna kill me." I saw Adam's back stiffen as if he was remembering the incident, but he didn't look up. He kept his face buried in our mom's shoulder.

"Is that what happened, Adam?"

Adam nodded. I looked at Mom's face, the left side red and already beginning to swell. I could see whatever lingering doubt or confusion she might have had with Adam's version disappeared completely. I'd been there, too, and that was all she needed. Looking back now, I think Mom knew she'd been fooled by Mark—by what she thought he was and what he could mean to our family. But that was already slipping into the past. Mom was a survivor above all else, and that's exactly what she was going to do moving forward.

She reached her free arm out to me, and I came to her.

52

That next morning I heard Adam climb out of bed and walk across the floor. I rolled over just as he opened the door. Memories of the previous night began flooding my head. "Hi, Adam."

He turned back to me and smiled. "Hey, Danny."

Adam looked terrible. He was wearing a tee-shirt, but I could see his neck and upper chest were still red from the altercation with Mark. There were no visible bruises on his face, but his eyes were puffy and he looked exhausted.

"I'll be right back," he said, and slipped out of the bedroom. I heard him go into the bathroom and close the door.

I was tired but I felt okay. *A lot better than Adam looks,* I thought. I glanced at the clock. It read 10:48 am. I rolled over and slid off the top bunk. As I headed for the door, I smelled sausage and scrambled eggs coming from the hallway.

I passed Adam coming out of the bathroom, and he gave me a pat on the shoulder. "Danny, let's go get some breakfast, and then we'll talk."

"Okay, I just have to go to the bathroom."

More memories flowed from that previous night. The three of us — me, Adam, and Mom — had sat on the couch for a few minutes, hugging, and then Mom had sent me up to bed. Even with my door shut, I could hear the two of them talking quietly. I couldn't make out what they were saying, and at that point I didn't want to. I knew Mark was dead, and I was pretty sure they hadn't called the police. Everything else was a complete mystery.

I came out of the bathroom and headed downstairs. When I entered the kitchen, I saw a large plate of scrambled eggs sitting on the table. Mom was standing at the stove with her back to me. She had a fork in her hand and was fiddling with the sausage. Adam was standing near the coffee maker, holding a blue mug. He turned back toward me and took three large gulps. He made a face like it wasn't particularly good and then smiled again. That little boy I'd seen crying in our mother's arms was long gone. Adam was back and apparently he was a coffee drinker now.

Even though Adam didn't say anything, Mom sensed I was standing there and turned around. I don't know if I actually gasped, but I do remember being shocked. After Adam struck her, her face was red and swollen, but she'd put a bag of frozen peas on it, so I couldn't see it anymore. Standing there in the kitchen that morning, she looked like she'd been in a bar fight. Her entire cheek was swollen and turning a strange shade of purple. I knew from the time Adam rolled his ankle skateboarding, and even from the time I bunted a baseball into my eye, that the bruise would get much darker before it went away. The swelling extended up near her left eye, causing a healthy puffiness beneath it. She saw my expression and forced a smile.

"I'm okay, honey," she said. "It's just some swelling."

She started toward me. I glanced at Adam and he looked away. I knew he felt terrible about what he'd done. I didn't like the idea of him hitting our mom, but after what he'd been through—and I'd only witnessed part of it—it was hard to blame him for anything. Mom reached me and pulled me to her chest. I didn't want to cry, but I felt tears coming anyway. She pulled back and wiped them off my cheeks.

"We're not going to cry today, okay?" She said it gently, and I nodded. "Today, we're going to be strong and start to put all of this behind us." She let go of me and started back toward the stove. "We're going to have breakfast, and then we're going to talk for a while. Okay?"

"Okay, Mom."

I found a seat at the table and watched her finish cooking the sausage. Adam set the table with plates, cups, and silverware. Then he grabbed the milk and juice from the fridge before sitting next to me. Mom moved the sausage links from the frying pan to a separate plate and brought them to the table, along with a plate of toast. Normally, she and Adam would have asked me to help, but that morning they were content to just let me sit there.

I had a million questions, but I knew it was best if I just waited. It soon became clear Mom wanted us to finish eating before we talked about what had happened. So instead of talking about that, we talked about the championship game. At first it was awkward, but once we got going, it was fun to talk about baseball and forget about what had happened, if only for a little while.

As we were finishing up, I could tell Mom was getting antsy. Adam and I were talking about the play where I tagged out Zach Hardy at first base, but Mom just kept checking the clock. She didn't say so, but I think she knew when Jess was coming home and wanted to make sure we had enough time to talk. I cleared the table while Mom and Adam did the dishes. They both filled their mugs with fresh coffee before sitting back down. Adam added three teaspoons of sugar, but Mom was drinking her coffee black.

She took a deep breath and started in. "Danny, we're going to talk about last night, so you know what happened, and then we're not going to talk about it for a long time, okay?"

"I can't ever talk about it?" The idea scared me, although I wasn't exactly sure why.

"I didn't say *ever*, honey, but it would be better if you didn't, and you'll understand why when we're done. If you ever feel like you *have* to talk about it, you can come to me, okay?"

That made me feel better, and I nodded.

"Okay, first I want to say that I'm extremely proud of you. What you did last night was very brave. You saved your brother's life." She reached out and squeezed my hand.

Adam looked at me and nodded. "That's right, bro. I wouldn't be here if you hadn't done what you did."

I didn't know what to say, so I just smiled.

"You saw some of what happened," Mom said, "but Adam's going to tell you what happened when you left."

I think I knew it was going to be a lie even before he started. There was something about the way Mom said it.

Adam leaned forward and looked me in the eye. "After you left, Mark woke up and came at me again. I had the bat in my hand, so I hit him with it. He stopped breathing after that."

I had a lot of questions about how that would've happened, but I knew it was pointless to ask them. I always suspected Adam was going to kill him. I just didn't know how. And as I sat there listening, I realized I didn't want to.

"Mark was an evil person, Danny," Mom said. "I should've seen it coming, but I didn't, and I'm going to be sorry about that for the rest of my life. He did a very bad thing to your sister and then when Adam confronted him, he panicked and tried to kill him. Obviously, he didn't count on you showing up, but he could have stopped when you did. He chose not to. I don't know for sure if he planned to hurt you, but he might have." I looked at Adam. His eyes matched what I was feeling. There was no question what Mark was planning to do to me. "When Mark didn't stop, he showed what he really was inside. He was evil, Danny, and God knows that you and Adam did what you had to do. Never forget that."

"I won't, Mom." The question popped into my head, and I looked at Adam. "Did you call the police?"

Adam almost looked at Mom then, and I think he would've if I wasn't staring at him. "No, I didn't."

Mom grabbed my hand again. "Adam didn't call the police because he didn't think they would believe him, and I think he's right. Mark has friends who are policemen." As soon as she said it, I got that same sensation she was lying. "We think they would've thought Adam got angry over what he did to Jess and went over there to kill him. Normally, I would always say to call the police, but in this case it was too risky."

I knew I shouldn't ask the next question, but I had to. "What did you do with Mark?"

"You don't need to worry about that," Adam said without hesitation. He gave me a look that said *don't push it*. It was a look I knew well.

"It doesn't matter," Mom said, "and you'll find out why in a couple minutes. Just remember what I told you. Mark was a bad person, and God has a way of taking care of people like that sometimes."

I thought it was strange to hear our mom talking about Mark like that. Just one day before he was the man she loved, the man who would become our stepfather. It struck me how fast she'd made the transition. He'd gone from this beloved member of our family to this evil entity, literally overnight.

"Do you have any more questions about last night, Danny?" Mom asked.

I still had a ton, but I didn't think any of them were truly on the table. I was pretty sure Adam had killed Mark while he was unconscious and then disposed of the body. He hadn't called the police because he would have been accused of murder, and our mom didn't call them because she wanted to protect Adam. "No, I guess I don't."

"Okay, remember, this isn't something we can ever talk about. You can never tell Jess or any of your friends…or anyone else. If you ever have to talk about it, wait until we're alone, okay?"

"Okay."

"You did the right thing telling Adam what Mark did to Jess, but you can never tell her you did that. Even if she specifically asks you about it, you can't tell her that you told anyone else. Just tell her that you're there for her if she needs you. If she does bring it up again, just tell her that she needs to tell *me* about it, but try to do it gently. She'll come to me in time, but it has to be *her* time. It has to be her decision to tell me. I can't go to her. Do you understand that?"

"I understand," I said, not really sure if I did.

"Okay, we're going to do something now that's going to seem strange, but there's a reason we're doing it."

I don't think I'd ever been more confused. "Okay."

Mom looked at Adam. "I want you to do this, too."

"Mom, I—"

"Adam, please. Just humor me, okay?" It was the first sign of impatience she'd shown all morning. "Besides, I'm doing this for me as much as I am for you, and I need your help." Adam nodded and stood up. I realized then they'd already discussed this. "I want both of you to walk in and pretend you're seeing me like this for the first time." She pointed to her face.

"I don't understand," I said.

"Follow my lead," Adam said. He walked out of the room and I trailed behind him. "Let's pretend we just woke up and came downstairs." Before

I could say anything, he walked into the kitchen. I followed, more confused than ever. "Jesus," Adam said loudly, "what happened to your face?"

"Sit down, boys."

Adam looked at me, and at first I didn't know why. Then it dawned on me I was supposed to say something. "My God, Mom," I said. "Are you okay?" It sounded like bad acting, but Mom ignored it.

"I'm fine. It looks a lot worse than it is."

"What the hell happened?" Adam asked. His acting, on the other hand, was pretty impressive.

"Well, you kids are going to find out soon enough, so I might as well just tell you. Mark and I got into a huge fight last night. We argued and he slapped me across the face."

The true reason we were doing this came crashing down on me. They had decided not to call the police, but that didn't mean the police wouldn't call them. Mark was gone and he was never coming back, and our mom was his girlfriend. It was only a matter of time before the police came calling, wanting to know what she knew and maybe even us kids, too. And that wasn't the only problem Mom was trying to solve. She had to have an explanation for who hit her and why, and obviously it couldn't be Adam.

I played along as best I could, asking a question every so often, but mostly I just listened in awe to a side of my mother that before that very moment I never would have imagined existed.

53

Saturday Afternoon

I'd never told a single soul what happened that night at Mark's house — not even Laura. I'd come close a couple times early in our marriage, but as the years went by, the urge faded. I think I always suspected if I told someone, it might come back to haunt me when I least expected it. Over the decades the memory got buried, growing colder and colder until eventually I barely noticed it. It was like having a small chest that sits in the living room. Sometimes it's tucked alongside the couch, and other times it's in full view, but it always seems to blend nicely with the décor. You know what's in there, but no one else even seems to notice it. Maybe they think it holds photo albums or maybe a blanket or two. It doesn't bother you, and you hardly ever think about it, but you never forget it's there, either.

Now that they found Mark, that chest was going to be opened for all the world to see, and the one person I could turn to for help was gone. I felt a sudden and burning rage toward my older brother. Why did he have to kill Mark? He could have just tied him up and called the police. Jess and I would have testified, and Mark would've probably gone to prison. Instead, Adam took matters into his own hands, and now Billy and I would have to deal with the repercussions.

I was still staring at Valley View Golf Course on the television when I realized my cell phone was vibrating. I didn't recognize the number, so I wasn't about to answer it. Finally, after the third time they called back, I remembered I'd been talking to Ally. *I must have hung up on her*, I thought. I looked around my apartment, trying to absorb as much present day reality as I could, and picked up the phone. "Hi, Ally. I'm sorry about that. I guess I lost your call." I didn't like lying to her, but the truth wasn't an option.

"Oh, it's okay." I could hear the skepticism in her voice. "I just wasn't sure what happened there."

I knew I couldn't talk to her right now. I had to get off the phone. "Yeah, I'm sorry about that. Then right after I lost your call, I got a call from my ex-wife. I have to go help her out with something."

There was a slight pause, and I had the terrifying feeling Ally was going to ask me what she needed help with.

"Oh, okay, Dan. No problem. I'll talk you later."

"Okay, bye." I hit end and stared at the phone. *There goes any chance of a relationship with Ally.* That should have been the furthest thing from my mind at that moment, but it wasn't, probably because it was easy to envision how everything would play out. Once they identified Mark's body, the police would be hounding me for information on what happened that night. I wouldn't be able to skate by this time without talking to investigators. In 1978 everyone thought Mark had skipped town to avoid a gambling debt and a possible assault charge against my mother. No one bothered to ask me anything because no one thought I knew anything. That wouldn't be the case this time around. This time they'd ask me all sorts of questions, whether they thought I knew anything or not. And it wouldn't be long before my family name got mentioned in the news. It wasn't exactly an ideal atmosphere for starting up a new relationship.

Obviously, I'd be expected to tell the police everything I knew, which was a hell of a lot more than I wanted anyone to know. It would mean Connor had an uncle who killed a man and a father who was directly involved. Connor knowing would be bad enough, but the world knowing would be much worse. Anyone who felt like getting under Connor's skin could do it whenever they wanted to. It might not be on the same level as his mother having sex with his elementary school guidance counselor, but it would be pretty close. If I could tell a lie that would save Connor from having to endure all that, I would. The safest and easiest thing to do, by far, was to stick to the story our mom had laid out for us all those years ago.

Billy, of course, would be of much greater interest. It wouldn't take the police long to figure out he'd worked at Valley View during the summer of '78, nor would it take them long to realize he was a good friend of Adam's. The extent of Billy's involvement would soon be the million-dollar question, the one some young investigator would try to boost his career by answering. Did he simply provide Adam with a key, or did he help him bury the body? Or hell, why stop there? Did he participate in the killing?

That thought had no sooner formed in my brain when the memory of Adam's last phone call came flooding back. Adam had brought up the incident, and that meant only one thing. He'd been thinking about it before he died. Adam must've been worried they'd find the body, and if I knew my brother, he would've put some kind of plan in place to deal with that possibility. And that also meant he would've told Jen. I was almost certain of it.

I focused again on the television and listened to the young reporter repeat what she'd said a few minutes ago. Somehow they knew the body had been there for nearly forty years. I wondered if they'd found a receipt or something else with the date on it. In the end it didn't matter. The point was they knew, which meant they had to already suspect it was Mark. I mean how many people went missing in Everton, NY, in the late 1970s? Certainly not enough to cast much doubt on who this person would be, especially once they connected Billy and Adam. And they might not have even needed that connection. It could have been something as simple as a call going out to one of the old-timers who spits out Mark's name before his next sip of coffee. And if someone did have to pull an old file, there'd be a few around. Mark's disappearance had been a pretty big deal at the time, and his son, Eddie, had raised a big enough stink to ensure records would be properly stored. The only question was how quickly they would piece everything together. My guess was they were probably already searching for Mark's dental records to make it official.

My phone rang again, and I was suddenly sure it was the police. They'd already confirmed it was Mark and were opening the investigation. *Hello, is this Danny Abbot? We'd like you to come down to the Everton Police Station to answer a few questions. Bring your toothbrush and a pillow. You're going to be here a while.* I stared at the caller ID. It was Jen. She couldn't possibly know about this already. "Hi, Jen."

"Hi, Dan. You've already heard, haven't you?"

"Yeah, I just saw it on the news. My neighbor called —" I was about to dive into a full description of Ally but caught myself. I think that was the first outward sign I was starting to lose it.

"Are you okay, Dan?"

"I don't know. It's such a strange feeling. This thing's been buried inside me for most of my life, and now it's going to get ripped out and shown to the world, and I can't do a God damn thing about it."

"Okay, listen to me."

Something was happening to me, but I wasn't sure what it was. It was similar to that feeling of falling into the vortex, but it was even more intense. I felt like I was losing control of myself, like someone else was taking over. I was still here, aware of what was happening, but I wasn't driving anymore. I heard someone on the verge of crying and realized it was me. "I didn't wanna do it, Jen. I didn't wanna hit him, but I had to. He was killing Adam."

"I know, Dan. I know everything. It wasn't your fault."

"He was gonna kill me next. He —" The tears came hard then, and for the next thirty seconds, I couldn't speak.

"It's okay, Dan. It wasn't your fault. I promise you, everything is going to be okay."

As I listened to Jen's soothing voice, another strange thing happened. I stopped crying and started talking. I don't think it was all me, exactly, or at least not all me in the present day. The past that had been buried for so long and my present day reality had come crashing together inside my head. That chest in the corner of the room had finally been opened, and the stagnant air from thirty-nine years ago was mixing freely with the air from today. And I discovered—much to my surprise and certainly to my relief—that I could still breathe it.

After I told Jen everything I could remember about that night, I felt whole again. Other than a handful of short conversations with Mom and Adam, it was the first time I'd talked about it since it happened. I asked a few questions about Billy, but Jen told me Adam said he wasn't involved. I didn't know if I believed that, but I could tell Jen did. She told me Adam made me a DVD that talked a lot about Billy, and that I had to watch it as soon as possible. She also said I had to give it to my lawyer.

"Jesus, Jen. I hadn't even thought about that. I'm definitely going to need a lawyer."

"Don't worry about it. Adam's already retained one for you, and you're going to meet him tonight."

"Tonight? What are you—?" It hit me then that Jen had had me on speaker this entire time. "You're on your way up here, aren't you?"

"I am. I'm already halfway there."

54

It was just before 8:00 when Jen texted that she was getting close. In the ninety minutes since we'd last spoken, I took a shower and inhaled two peanut butter-and-black cap jam sandwiches. While I didn't enjoy them anywhere near as much as I should have, they still tasted damn good. I almost took one over to Ally's apartment, but I figured she was wondering about what had happened earlier, and I wasn't ready to deal with that. I would've had to lie to her again, which would've only made things worse.

Jen had never been to The Palace before, so I decided to go outside and wait for her in the parking lot. When I opened the door, she was standing on the landing. I hadn't seen her in almost six months, but she looked the same as always. *Beautiful.* Tired but beautiful. Her dark hair was pulled back into a long ponytail, revealing her high cheekbones. She smiled at me, and I pulled her into the kitchen. She wrapped her arms around me and we hugged. My thoughts drifted to Adam, and I found myself crying. I'd missed my brother over the last year, but I don't think I ever missed him more than I did right then. He was always our protector. He would know how to deal with this mess. After a couple minutes, we pulled apart, and I saw Jen was crying, too.

"It's going to be okay," she said.

"I know." I grabbed two napkins off the counter and handed one to Jen. "Come on over to the table. I'll get us some coffee."

"That sounds good. I'm a little tired."

"Thanks for coming up here so fast, Jen. You didn't have to do that, but I'm glad you did. I'm sure it's obvious — this thing's really thrown me off."

"Of course it has. How could it not?"

She placed her backpack on the kitchen table and sat in one of the chairs. I dumped six scoops into a filter and filled the coffee maker with water. A moment later the coffee was brewing, and the intense aroma filled the room.

"I've wanted to talk to you about this so many times," Jen said, "but Adam told me not to unless they found the body. I think he always just hoped they wouldn't find it. He used to tell me it was five to one they wouldn't."

"Adam always sucked at math." We both smiled. "How did you find out so fast?" As soon as I asked the question, I realized I already knew the answer. *Billy.*

"Actually, it was your local news. Adam made me get the mobile app for Channel 2. I received a Breaking News Alert about three hours before we talked. When I couldn't reach you, I packed an overnight bag and hopped in the car."

"Yeah, I'm sorry about that. I was at Connor's baseball game. I saw that you'd called when I got home, but then I saw the story on the news."

"Don't worry about it. I called Laura, and she told me you were coaching."

By now the coffee was done, and I poured us each a cup. I grabbed a pint of half-and-half from the fridge and handed it to Jen. She added the cream and took a sip before looking up at me. "Adam recorded a video, describing what happened that night." She placed her hand on her backpack. "He also made a copy for Billy."

"Have you talked to Billy?"

"No, not yet. I tried calling him once, but he hasn't gotten back to me yet. He's in for a pretty big shock."

"I'm sure he's already heard about the body. Even if he wasn't a part of it, it wouldn't surprise me if he's figured out who it is."

"I don't know, Dan. According to Adam, he didn't know anything about it."

I wanted to tell her I doubted that, but for some reason I didn't say it.

Jen continued on. "Adam wants you to give this video to your lawyer, and then he can pass it on to the proper authorities. He hired a man named Maxwell Lewis. He's a criminal defense attorney in Binghamton."

"I've heard of him, but I don't think I'll be able to afford him."

"Don't worry about it. Adam took care of it."

"I can't let him do that."

Jen placed her hand on my wrist. "It's already done. Listen, Dan, we have to move quickly. Adam thinks this disc should get to the police before they figure out that it's Mark's body...or I guess I should say bones."

"I've been thinking about that, Jen. I bet they already know."

"Then we better get moving." Jen unzipped the top of her backpack and removed a CD in a round plastic case. "Dan, remind me. I have a letter from Adam after you watch this."

"Okay."

We walked into the living room, and I turned on the television. Jen opened the case and handed me the disc. I slipped it into the DVD player, and a few seconds later a blue screen appeared. In the center of the screen was a frozen image of Adam sitting at a table. I recognized it as the dining room table at their house in West Chester. I could tell by how strong Adam looked, it was filmed before the cancer had taken hold. Beneath the image was the date. *Just over two years ago,* I thought. I was about to hit play when Jen spoke again.

"He told me the full story about three years ago. He'd read online that Valley View was planning on redesigning the course."

"My God, I'd forgotten that."

"At the time, they were talking mostly about the back nine, and he was worried they might dig up the twelfth green. The funny thing is they finished the redesign, including the twelfth green, and they never found him. So, anyway, Adam made the DVD and then found Max Lewis about a year ago. He wanted to get you someone local. Actually, our lawyer, Al Donovan, knew about him. I guess he comes highly recommended. Al handled most of the initial communications." Jen took another sip of her coffee.

"So, this Max Lewis guy knows that Adam killed Mark?"

"He didn't then, but he does now. I called him before I left to come up here."

"Lucky you got a hold of him so fast."

"I told his secretary it had to do with the body they found at Valley View, and he called me back in less than one minute. I kid you not."

"I believe it. Not much happens around here…not like this anyway."

Jen patted my back and started toward the kitchen. She stopped in the doorway and turned back. "Adam just couldn't shake this feeling they were going to find the body. I'm just glad they didn't find him while Adam was still alive." She paused for a moment. "I'm going outside. I've seen it enough times. I'll come back in when it's done."

I waited until I heard the door close and then hit play. The video started as the last traces of light faded from the day. The camera showed Adam sitting at the table, but then zoomed out to include another man in a suit beside him. I recognized him immediately from Adam's party. Jen had introduced him as a longtime friend and also their attorney.

"My name is Albert Donovan," the man said. "I'm an attorney with Rollins, Donovan, and Houlihan and am registered to practice law in the state of Pennsylvania." It dawned on me these were the preliminaries necessary for the DVD to serve as an official deposition. Donovan turned to Adam. "Please place your right hand on this Bible and state your name."

Adam placed his hand on the Bible. "My name is Adam Abbot," he said. His voice was strong and vibrant. He looked like a man who might live another thirty years or more. It was suddenly clear why Jen had no interest in watching it again.

Donovan walked Adam through a series of basic questions, which established his full identity, his residence, his occupation, and his commitment to telling the truth. When he was finished with the preliminaries, Donovan asked what would prove to be his final question. "Mr. Abbot, can you explain in full detail what happened on the morning of June 18, 1978?"

The morning, I thought. *Don't you mean evening?*

"Me and my brother, Danny, came downstairs around nine or nine-thirty on Sunday morning and found my mother sitting at the kitchen table. She had a huge welt on the side of her face. We asked her what happened, and she told us that she and Mark had gotten into an argument, and then she told us that Mark had hit her. I'm talking about her boyfriend, Mark Dolan."

I realized Adam was sticking to the script my mother had written thirty-nine years ago.

"I think I knew right away that I was going to confront him, but I convinced my mother that I would let her handle it. I recall it wasn't easy, but she believed me. A while later, I told my mom I was heading over to my girlfriend Julia's house, which was what I usually did on Sundays. I headed out around eleven o'clock or so. I took my brother's bat with me, thinking maybe I'd break Mark's leg or his arm or something. As far as I was concerned, he deserved it. After all, that was my mother, and she wouldn't hurt a fly. I didn't think about the consequences of things back then, nor did I think about anything going wrong. I figured I'd hit him a couple times and that would be the end of it. He'd be out of our lives for good. And if he decided to come near my mom again, he'd have a pretty good idea what would be waiting for him...from me at least.

"I rode my bike to Julia's and left it there before walking back to Mark's house. He lived about a half a mile from Julia's parents. When I got there I walked in the house and found him in the kitchen. We started to argue, and at some point he noticed the bat. At first I was trying to hide it from him. He lunged at me and caught me with a pretty good punch to the jaw. It knocked me to the ground, and I dropped the bat. Before I could get up, he was on top of me. Right away he started choking me. I remember this look in his eyes that was absolutely crazy. I want to be crystal clear about something here. Mark was straddling me and was in complete control. This had nothing to do with him trying to subdue me or getting the bat away from me. He was definitely trying to kill me. I think he realized his world was about to be upended. He took pride in the fact everyone thought he was a good guy, and now he was about to be exposed. I think he just panicked. So again, just so everyone understands, he was trying to kill me and would've succeeded had I not been able to get my hands on the bat. It was lying off to the side, and I think Mark forgot about it. Either way, he didn't realize it was within my reach. I was able to raise it up and hit him on the side of the head. It wasn't that hard, but I think I hit him right in the temple. It didn't knock him completely out, but he was definitely out of it. I was able to get him off of me and climb to my feet. He was still on his hands and knees at this point, but he was between me and the door. I was nowhere near full strength, and I wasn't about to take any chances. I swung the bat down and hit him on the back of the head. This time it did knock him out. I leaned over and watched him to see if he was breathing. Obviously, I didn't want to get too close to him. From what I could tell, he wasn't breathing anymore. I waited for several minutes, using that time to recover myself. I remember getting a drink of water from the sink. When I checked him again, he still wasn't breathing. At that point I knew he was dead."

When Adam stopped for a second, I grabbed the remote and hit pause. I started thinking about his story from the perspective of an autopsy. His description of the hit to the back of Mark's head would explain the blow I delivered. The first hit to the temple never actually happened, but the way Adam described it, it probably wouldn't have shown up on an examination of a thirty-nine-year-old skull anyway. The bigger lie was that Mark had stopped breathing after the second hit. He was definitely still breathing when I left the house that night. Adam's words seemed to confirm what I had always suspected. Adam either strangled or suffocated Mark after I left. If he'd hit him with the bat again, it would show up on an examination of the skull. Adam would have known that when he made this video and would have worked it into the story. I hit play again.

"I'm sure there will be questions or opinions on why I didn't call the police. I trust it's obvious why I didn't try to revive him myself. I'll answer my first question by saying that by the time I knocked Mark unconscious, I had absolutely no qualms with him dying. If you want to say that I *wanted* him to die at that point, I wouldn't argue with that, either. I'm sure some will label me a murderer. I'm dead, so I really don't give a shit, but for the record, I'll state that I don't believe it was murder. In fact, I know it wasn't. I hit Mark in the head because I had to in order to save my life, and then I let God or fate or whatever you want to believe handle it from there. My personal opinion is that for a man who beat my mother and then did his absolute best to remove me from this planet, I'd say anything short of me smashing his skull into a pile of dog shit was letting him off easy. But that's just me. You can think whatever you like."

Adam picked up a bottle of spring water, and I hit pause again. I realized I was smiling. This video was vintage Adam. Of course, he was leaving out some important details, like the fact he'd suffocated Mark when he was unconscious. But he left out a few other things, as well. The first being that Mark liked to touch little girls, and the second being that Mark was going to kill a ten-year-old boy when he was done strangling *him*. I hit play again.

"I dragged Mark into the living room and hid his body behind the couch in case anyone came by the house. I went back to my girlfriend's house for several hours before going back home, probably around six-thirty or seven o'clock. I waited until my mom went to bed—I'd say that was around ten forty-five or so—and then I rode my bike back out to Mark's house. I got his car out of the garage and then dragged his body out the back door. It took me a while, but I managed to get him up into the back seat, and then I covered him with blankets. There was a wooded lot behind Mark's house, so there were no neighbors behind him. And once everyone turned off their back porch lights, it got pretty dark back there. That's how it was that night, so no one saw me. Or if they did see me, they never reported it."

Adam paused and looked down at his notes. Finally, he looked back at the camera. "If people are watching this, it means they found Mark's body at Valley View Golf Course. I buried him alongside the twelfth green, and I made the mistake of burying the bat along with him. What I forgot at the time, but remembered a couple days later, was that 'Abbot' was written on the bottom of the handle. I would have been the main suspect, regardless, but the bat ties me to the incident beyond any reasonable doubt. As I've already mentioned, I'm dead and could care less what people think of me or my memory. But there are other considerations here, and that's why I'm making this video.

"One of these considerations is my friend Billy Kent. He worked at Valley View Golf Course in the summer of 1978. I don't think there's any question that the police will suspect Billy was involved that night. I want to state unequivocally that he did not help me, nor did he have any knowledge of what I did that night. He *was* involved indirectly, which I'll explain in a moment, but he had absolutely no knowledge of his involvement. I also want to state that my girlfriend at the time, Julia Richards, had no knowledge of what took place that night, nor did she help me in any way.

"When I left Mark's house, my plan was to dump his body in the Susquehanna River behind the skating rink near my house. I had some ropes, and I figured I could weigh him down with rocks. When I drove by the golf course, I got another idea. I'd played there about a week before, so I knew they were working on the twelfth green. And Billy had said something about it, too. He said they had to dig a pretty deep hole because they were putting in a new irrigation line or something. I decided I would check it out, but I should back up for a minute first.

"I knew Billy had a key that opened the gate along Main Street and also the gate near the skating rink. At some point that spring, I asked Billy if I could make a copy of the key, so Julia and I could sneak out onto the golf course at night, but he said no. He really liked the job and knew he would get fired if we got caught. The breaking point came when Julia's dad hurt his back in early May. He was home in bed for almost three weeks, and that put an end to our sex life. After about a week or so, we were both going crazy, and I had an idea. I told Billy I needed to borrow his car to go to a job interview, but I went out and made a copy of the key instead. Over the next month or so, Julia and I spent quite a few nights on the golf course. A few times we went out there with her friend Betsy Paley and her boyfriend. I'm pretty sure his name was Tom, but I don't remember his last name. Either of them should be able to confirm that I had my own key. So, anyway, that's how I got onto the golf course that night.

"I parked Mark's car in the parking lot of the skating rink and then ran up to the gate, which was only about a hundred yards away. I let myself in the gate, and then I went to check out the twelfth green. The hole was all filled in but it was loose dirt. I ran up to the storage shed and got a wheel barrel and a shovel. I started digging and emptied out the hole in two hours or so. Like I said, they had just filled it in, so it was easy to dig out. I did have to be careful with the new irrigation pipes, though. The original hole was probably five feet deep to begin with, and I took it down another foot or so after that. I didn't know if that was deep enough, but my back was ready to explode by that point, and I was also running out of time.

"I ran back and got Mark's car. I drove it up to the gate and then dragged him out and put him into the wheel barrel. That was by far the riskiest part of the night because anyone could've seen me if they happened to drive by. I was also in plain view of probably four or five houses from a distance of maybe eighty or ninety yards. It was after three in the morning by then, so I'm assuming everyone was asleep. Again, if anyone ever saw me or Mark's car, they never reported it. After I wheeled his body onto the course, I moved his car back into the parking lot and out of view from the road.

"When I got back to the twelfth green, I lowered Mark's body into the hole and worked him under the new irrigation pipes. I was so tired by this point, I was worried about dropping him on the pipes and breaking them, but somehow I managed not to do that. As I already mentioned, I put Danny's bat in there before I filled the hole back in. That was way before DNA, of course, but I knew they could test for blood, and I had no idea if there was any blood on it or not. I just wanted to get rid of it, and I figured that was as good a place as any. Obviously, I knew it wouldn't be found unless Mark was found. In hindsight, there are a lot of other things I would have done with the bat, but you have to remember, I was only seventeen and I was mentally spent. A couple days later, I remembered that Danny had written his name on the bottom of the bat handle with a black marker. It was something our mom made us do on all the things she bought for us, but I just didn't think of it at the time. My testimony here is important because I want everyone to know that Danny was not involved in any way, other than being the victim of my theft."

I hit pause and thought about the bat. I remembered asking Adam about it one time about two or three weeks after everything happened. We were both sitting in our bedroom, and Adam looked at me like he was going to come over and kill me. He put his finger up to his mouth to shush me. By that point I thought all the secrecy was getting a little ridiculous, but I played along. He came over to me and whispered, "It's gone. I'll get you another one."

I picked up the DVD remote and hit play.

"I filled in the hole as fast as I could. There was some extra dirt because Mark's body was in there, so the area around the hole was a mess — a lot messier than it had been. I could tell it was almost daybreak. I was out of time, and I was beyond exhausted. I had no choice but to leave it like it was and just hope no one noticed it. I caught a break there, and that wasn't the only one, but I'll come back to that.

"I left Mark's car in the parking lot and ran back to our house. I snuck inside, took a shower, and changed my clothes. I hid my dirty clothes in my room and ran back to Mark's car. I drove back to his house, got my bike and then rode it back to my girlfriend's house. By this time, her dad had already left for work — his back had healed by then. I snuck in a basement window and fell asleep on the couch. This wasn't unusual because I slept over there sometimes. When Julia woke me up around nine o'clock on Monday morning, I told her I'd gotten into an argument with my mom and rode over there around midnight. I said everyone was asleep, so I just snuck in a basement window and went to sleep on the couch. I also told her I wasn't feeling well, so I needed to sleep some more. I even went into the bathroom and made myself throw up because I needed an excuse to sleep in. I made sure it was loud, so Julia and her mom would hear me. Given what I'd just been through, it wasn't hard to do, believe me. I went back to sleep and slept until almost two o'clock in the afternoon. I didn't have school because final exams had already started.

"I think when the police started asking about Mark a few days later, both Julia and my mom became suspicious. Julia asked a few questions, but she never pushed too hard. I think she knew something had happened between me and Mark, but I don't think she ever suspected I killed him. Julia never liked Mark anyway. She thought he was creepy. She saw things about him that other people couldn't. Bottom line, I don't think she was ever really concerned about him disappearing. My mother was a different story. She'd heard me come home and shower, so she knew my story was bullshit. She kept on me until I finally told her what happened. She was devastated, of course, but she believed me. She thought I should've called the police and an ambulance, but she understood why I didn't. She understood that Mark was a murderer. Just because I was lucky enough to escape doesn't change that fact one bit. I've never understood those who make the distinction between people who *try* to murder someone and those who are actually successful. To me, there's no difference whatsoever. Anyway, when the news broke about his gambling debts and the money he owed to the mafia, a lot of people just assumed he skipped town, and everything sort of just faded away."

Adam looked down at his notes again. I hit pause and tried to process everything he was saying. As far as Adam's performance so far, I thought it was brilliant. Much of it was true or very close to true, but even when Adam was lying, I couldn't tell. He'd practiced the story until he believed every detail. I hit play one last time.

"Okay, I suppose it's time to wrap this up. As I said, my mother knew the truth. She also knew that I probably wouldn't be believed and would be charged with murder, so she covered for me. And again, once the police uncovered Mark's debts, everything just went away. Plus, there was no body and no real signs that anything had happened, so the police had no choice but to let it go. I knew Mark's son was a lawyer somewhere, or studying to be a lawyer, and was pushing for a deeper investigation, but there wasn't anything to investigate. I don't know if the police suspected me or not, but if they did, they never let on.

"I mentioned I caught a couple big breaks that night. I suppose the first one was being able to reach the bat when Mark was trying to choke me to death."

Good for you, I thought. No matter what Adam was talking about, he wasn't going to let anyone forget what Mark did, even for a second.

"Another one came when it started raining around six that morning. It was a typical Broome County thunderstorm—intense and quick. It covered up the mess I made at the twelfth green. Maybe it wouldn't have been noticed anyway, but that storm helped. The last big break, other than Mark's gambling debts popping up out of the blue, came from the golf course itself. I knew the body would begin to stink as it decomposed, but I figured if I buried it deep enough, it wouldn't be detectable. I was wrong. It stunk for over three weeks, and at times it was pretty bad. I remember Billy telling me they must have killed an entire family of gophers when they installed the new irrigation line. But because they were growing so much new grass around the green, they used a temporary green all summer long. It was about seventy yards away, in the middle of the fairway. That meant people got close enough to smell it, but they couldn't tell exactly where it was coming from. And like I said, the grounds crew thought it was just some dead gophers. By early August the smell had virtually disappeared. I played there in a tournament that second weekend and made sure to take a walk all around the green. I didn't smell anything."

I watched Adam's face, afraid he was going to smile. He didn't, but it was close.

"As I said, the only way anyone is watching this video is if Mark's body has already been found. I'm sure certain folks will be trying to poke holes in my story. All I can say is that what I've said here is one hundred percent true. Unfortunately, since *I'm* not available, I suspect the natural human inclination to blame someone will focus on Billy. The conventional wisdom will be that I wouldn't have been able to pull this off on my own. To anyone who may be investigating this case, I ask you to do your best to verify my story. I believe you'll find that it's true. I am solely responsible for defending myself against the murderer Mark Dolan, which led directly to his death and his subsequent burial at Valley View Golf Course."

When the video ended, the screen reset to the original image. I glanced at the clock. The entire video lasted just over twelve minutes. I sat there staring at the screen. I knew Adam had had a long time to prepare for the video, but I was still blown away by how convincing it was. There wasn't a single moment where I thought to myself he was lying. There were a few moments where he seemed overconfident, but none where I actually thought he was lying.

I thought about Adam's last words, wondering how much of the video could be verified. The last I'd heard, Julia had moved to California, but that was probably twenty-five years ago. And I was pretty sure both of her parents were dead. Unless they could find Julia, Billy and I were the only ones left.

55

Ten minutes later Jen and I hopped in my SUV and headed out to see my new lawyer. Jen said she spoke with him again while I was watching the DVD. It seemed crazy that I'd be meeting with a lawyer so quickly, but when I stopped to think about it, there wasn't anything about today that *wasn't* crazy. I pulled out of the bike shop parking lot while Jen punched his address into her phone's GPS. According to her phone, the trip would take about eighteen minutes.

"I can't believe Adam did all this," I said.

"Once he knew he was going to die, he tried to tie up all the possible loose ends — even the ones he didn't think would actually happen."

"What's my lawyer's name again?"

"Maxwell Lewis. His offices are on Ventura Street in Binghamton."

"Does he know what's on Adam's disc?"

"He only knows the basics. Oh, hold on a second. I forgot to give you Adam's letter. He wanted you to read it right after you watched the video." Jen dug through her purse and pulled out an envelope. "Do you want to pull over, or do you want me to read it to you?"

"Have you read it before?"

"Yes, when he first wrote it, but it's been a long time."

"Go ahead and read it to me." I turned onto the exit for Route 17 toward Binghamton.

Jen ripped open the envelope and pulled out a typed letter. "He wrote this the same day he made the video." She cleared her throat and began reading.

"Hey, Danny,

If you're reading this letter, I'm six feet under and they found Mark's body at the golf course. I'm sure that was quite a shock (putting it mildly). While I didn't ask for any of this, I'm still sorry it happened, and I'm sorry that you're left to deal with it.

I'm assuming you already watched the video. If you haven't, please watch it immediately, or this letter won't make much sense. I'm going to say this once now and then again when I'm done. **Destroy this letter after you read it.** And that doesn't mean toss it in the recycling bin! It means put it in the fireplace and burn it.

Okay, that story Mom told us and made us practice all those years ago is still your truth. We came down into the kitchen on Sunday morning and saw her swollen face. Mark hit her and then he disappeared. No one other than you and Jen knows about your involvement, nor do they know anything about Jess. In short, there's no Jess and there's no you. That means everything on this disc after the point where you and I walked into the kitchen that morning and saw Mom is going to be news to you."

I nodded as if Adam were sitting beside me.

"I want you to give this disc to your lawyer. I don't know who that is just yet, but I'm working on it. If you don't like him (or her) you can switch, but you should use him to handle these initial steps. Give him the disc and he can decide the right time to pass it on to investigators. My thinking is the sooner the better. If we give the police a plausible scenario, they'll be less likely to start thinking up their own. But obviously your lawyer will know things that I don't. Hopefully, the police will be eager to close a case this old (almost thirty-seven years as I write this), especially if they have a confession that makes sense. As I said on the disc, my fear is they'll come after Billy. I haven't given this to Billy yet. I'll let you and your lawyer handle that when the time is right. And I know this is against your nature, Danny, but your lawyer doesn't need to know anything beyond what's on this disc. SO DON'T TELL HIM."

An idea hit me for the first time, and I placed my hand on Jen's wrist without even realizing it. I wondered if the bat was the object the police had identified as being nearly forty-years-old. Mom had bought it new for my birthday shortly before the season started. The date of manufacture would probably be pretty easy to trace back once they figured out the model.

Jen looked at me. "Should I keep going?"

"Yeah, please. Sorry. Just lost in thought."

"Don't worry about it."

"Okay, bro, that's about all I have for now. I wish I was there to help, but God had other plans."

I looked at Jen and we both smiled.

"Besides, you've got Jen to help you, and she's a hell of a lot smarter than I am, as I'm sure you've already figured out. Remember, Danny, destroy this letter as soon as you can. I love you, brother. Give my love to Connor and Laura. Make sure you give Connor a punch in the arm for me.

Love, Adam."

Hearing Adam mention Connor was like an unexpected kick to the stomach. It made me feel like he was still here, like he was back at The Palace watching the Yankee game while Jen and I went to get takeout. I didn't have to ask Jen if it struck her the same way. I could tell by the look on her face.

A few minutes later we got off the highway and headed toward downtown Binghamton. The streets were all but dead as the last of the restaurant crowd filtered out and headed home. There were a few early birds hanging outside the college bars, but the real crowds were still a couple hours away. I had the palpable urge to slip into one of those bars, find an open stool, and order an extra dry martini with olives. But I knew if I did that, I wouldn't be able to stop at one. This was the kind of night where three might not be enough. It would be a welcome trip to oblivion for a few hours, but the price of admission would be steep. Dealing with this mess tomorrow, including what might even be a series of police interviews, wouldn't be much fun with a massive hangover.

Just past the bars, we turned right and then took a quick left onto a mostly dark, desolate street. Office buildings lined the narrow road on both sides. A few parked cars, barely outnumbering the working streetlights, were scattered about. Even as recently as a decade ago, this was prime office space. Now it had the feel of a place that wouldn't fill up even if the rent were free. It was a depressing thought that added to an intensely depressing night. We parked the car and hopped out.

"It's the building across the street," Jen said.

Something came to me out of the blue. "Have you talked to Laura again? She called me a little while ago, but I haven't gotten back to her."

"I did—when you were watching Adam's video. I told her something important was going on, and that it's probably going to be a tough time for you. I said you'd let her know what was happening when you were ready."

"Oh, I'll bet she loved that."

Jen smiled. "I think she understood."

"Maybe you should tell her what's going on, Jen. I don't feel like getting into all of that with her." The truth was it would be too painful. It would feel too much like we were married again. My mind made the short leap from

Laura to Connor. I wanted to tell him something before he went back to school on Monday, but I knew there was still the slim chance the police wouldn't be able to definitively connect Mark's body back to Adam. It would mean they didn't find the bat or that our name had worn off the bottom of the handle. I knew both possibilities were remote, but I wasn't going to tell Connor until I knew for sure.

"That's fine," Jen said, "I don't mind telling Laura."

"Just tell her not to talk to Connor yet. I'll do that."

"Okay."

By now we were across the street, standing in front of the double glass doors of a fifteen-story building. There were numerous businesses listed on the door in gold letters, including an engineering firm, a construction company, and two other law firms. The Law Offices of Maxwell Lewis was near the bottom. I peered inside and could see the darkened lobby through the glass. All the lights were off except for one shining at the end of a short hallway. It was bright enough to expose closed doors on each side of the corridor. I tried pulling on the brass bars, but both doors were locked. I glanced down at my phone. "It's ten after nine. He said nine o'clock, right?"

"Yeah, let me text him."

Jen was typing away when a tall, slender man emerged from the darkness. He rounded the corner with a relaxed, athletic gait and headed for the door. He was wearing a dark suit, but the tie had been discarded. He looked like he either worked out often or was one of the lucky few who always appeared to be in good shape. I guessed he was younger than me, but not by much—maybe forty-five or forty-six.

He reached the glass doors and released the locks—the top first, then the bottom—without making eye contact. He opened the door and took a long look at Jen as she walked inside. This wasn't unusual. She seemed to lull most men into a brief trance wherever she went. Jen pretended not to notice, which was also standard behavior. He gave me a considerably shorter glance as I followed her into the lobby.

After relocking the doors, he extended his hand to Jen. "Hi, I'm Maxwell Lewis," he said, with a quick smile. "Please call me Max."

I could see he was back from whatever fantasy he'd slipped away to when he first saw Jen. It was all business from here on out.

Jen shook his hand. "Jen Abbot. Thank you for seeing us at this hour."

"No problem at all."

He turned to me and I looked him in the eye. "Dan Abbot, nice to meet you."

He had me by an inch or two, so I guessed he was about 6'2". I noticed my initial age estimates were off. He was at least my age and maybe even a few years older. The lines creasing his eyes and mouth were clean and deep, and his hair was completely void of grays. I wondered how often he colored it to keep it that dark. It looked jet black in the poor lighting, but I suspected it was somewhat lighter.

"Good to meet you both," he said, in a friendlier voice than I expected, "and I'm sorry about the locked doors. It's pretty deserted around here at night, so I usually keep everything locked up."

"Of course," I said. I hoped he wasn't about to dive into a dissertation about how things had changed in recent years.

He led us down the short hallway, took a right and then guided us into a small conference room. The table was an oak monstrosity, far too large for the available space. A closed manila folder rested at the head of the table. Jen walked around and took a seat on the far side. I slipped into a chair directly opposite her, leaving an open seat between us.

I surveyed the room. Wooden shelves full of old law books lined the walls on three of the four sides. I wondered absently when the last time any of them had been opened. There wasn't any noticeable dust on the shelves, but something made me guess it had been a long time. On the fourth wall hung a large aerial painting of downtown Binghamton, circa somewhere around 1960. *The good old days,* I thought to myself.

"Can I get you something to drink?" Max asked. "Coffee? Water?"

"I'll take a water," Jen said. "Thank you."

"Nothing, thanks," I said.

Max stepped out of the room and returned a minute later with a bottle of spring water and a steaming mug of black coffee. He handed the bottle to Jen, took a seat in front of the manila folder, and turned toward me.

"Okay, first things first, Mr. Abbot."

"Call me Dan."

"Okay, Dan. I've already been paid a retainer to handle the initial proceedings and beyond, so if it's okay with you, we can skip any conversations regarding my fees for now, especially since it's so late. We'll have plenty of time to talk about that over the next few days. I also have a few papers for you to sign, but we can deal with those later, as well. Fair enough?"

I nodded, suddenly feeling very tired. Maybe I'd have that cup of coffee after all. "Sounds good to me."

Max opened the manila folder and looked down at his notes. "Okay, I spoke with Mrs. Abbot earlier today."

"Call me Jen, please."

"Okay, I spoke with Jen earlier, and I just got off the phone with Albert Donovan. They both explained that your brother, Adam, was involved in the killing of Mark Dolan back in the spring of 1978?"

"That's correct," I said.

"And Mark was your mother's boyfriend at the time?"

"That's right." I figured I'd let him tell me what he knew, and then I'd fill in the blanks. I reminded myself what Adam said. *Stick to the script.*

"Okay, I was also told there's a disc your brother made, confessing to the murder—sorry, confessing to being responsible for Mark's death?"

"That's correct."

"I have that right here," Jen said. She slid the disc over to Max.

"Okay, I guess I should probably watch this now." Max rose from his chair and turned behind him where a flat-screen television sat atop a small metal stand. It reminded me of something our teachers would have wheeled into our rooms in elementary school, minus the flat-screen, of course. I could see there was a DVD slot on the edge of the television.

"Excuse me," Jen said, standing from the table. "I'll wait in the hallway. I've already seen it several times."

Max gave her the simple directions to his office. He waited until she left the room and then closed the door and hit play. I watched for a second time as my brother laid out his version of what took place the day Mark died. Max watched the entire video without pausing it once. He did take notes throughout, however. When the video ended, he pressed a button on the remote, causing the screen to go black.

"Okay, I have a few questions for you, Dan. Do you want Jen back in here?"

"No, that's fine." It occurred to me I should probably be taking notes, as well.

"Okay, how old were you when this took place?"

"I was ten."

"How much of it do you remember?"

"I remember all of it, as far as my mother being hit and then Mark disappearing. Obviously, I don't know anything about what was on that video." I felt nervous telling my first lie, but I thought it sounded okay. I noticed Max studying me.

"So, your brother never told you anything about what happened?"

"No. He never wanted me to know."

"Okay, why don't you tell me everything you can remember, starting with when you and Adam came in and saw your mom in the kitchen."

I ran through an abbreviated version of what happened during that first week. Not long after I started, Jen came back in the room and sat down. For the most part, I felt like I was telling the truth. The way my mother handled everything the day after it happened, I really did experience most of the things I was talking about. She'd put on a show, partly for Jess, but mostly so Adam and I would be prepared for dealing with police questioning. I'd always been impressed with my mother, but I was gaining a new and much deeper appreciation for how smart she really was.

When I finished, Max looked down at his notes. "So, once the news broke about the gambling debts, everything sort of just went away?"

"Pretty much. I mean it wasn't overnight, but you could see everyone believed that's what happened."

"Except for your mom and Adam, that is."

"That's right."

"And Billy Kent."

I almost repeated the same answer even though I didn't know for sure one way or the other. "I really have no idea what Billy knew. According to Adam, he's just learning about all of this now."

Max took a long sip of coffee. He looked first at me and then at Jen. "Okay, I'm going to speak freely here."

"Of course," I said.

"Absolutely," Jen said.

"Okay. I watch this video, and I *want* to see a man who's telling the truth about a horrible incident that happened in his life. My gut, however, is telling me he's lying. I think his friend Billy helped him, probably after the fact, and now he's doing all he can to protect him. I can pretty much guarantee that the police will see it the same way."

"I disagree," Jen said without emotion. "I think he's telling the truth, but even if he isn't, won't the police have to prove otherwise?"

"Yes, if they go after Billy, they'll have to prove he was involved, and that's going to come down to whatever evidence they can gather. If they find something to suggest Billy helped him dispose of the body, they could charge him with being an accessory to murder after the fact."

"Should we give this disc to investigators?" I asked.

"At this point I would say no. I think we need to wait and see what happens over the next few days and weeks. Yes, Adam buried the bat with Mark's body, but I think it remains to be seen if they'll be able to definitively link it back to Adam. From what you and your brother are telling me, it sounds like they will, but we just don't know that for sure. I mean if there's no DNA on that bat handle, or better yet another profile that they can't identify, someone could have stolen it from you and then used it to kill Mark. Billy's lawyer isn't going to want this disc handed over to authorities until they have enough evidence to charge him with a crime. Now, if it could be used later to counter an alternate police theory, then I would say to hand it over at that time." Max turned to Jen. "Jen, if I were your lawyer, I would tell you that you need to be concerned with possible civil issues, such as a lawsuit from Mark's immediate family against Adam's estate. Obviously, I have no idea who or how many people that may be, but I wanted to mention it."

I looked at Jen and could tell she hadn't thought of that. I saw Eddie's face in my mind and had a sudden flashback of something my mom had told me a long time ago. She said Eddie was making news as a lawyer in Buffalo or maybe it was Rochester. I didn't know if Eddie would ever try to sue Jen, but it didn't seem out of the question, either. From what I remembered, he was a big enough asshole to do something like that.

Max looked down at his notes again for several seconds and then back at me. "As far as criminal charges, Dan, I don't think you have anything to worry about. Even if they find the bat and your DNA on the handle, I don't think anyone's going to think you were involved. Of course, they'll want to ask you all sorts of questions, but as long as you tell the truth, you shouldn't have anything to worry about."

I hadn't even thought about anyone charging me with a crime, although I guess I probably should have. I was, after all, the one who delivered the knockout blow. I thought about what I was doing—what I'd just told my lawyer. I didn't like lying, but I also didn't like the idea of someone potentially twisting the facts to charge me with a crime, especially when there wasn't anyone to blame here but Mark. I decided to stick with the plan. For everyone's sake, it was better to keep myself out of it if I could.

Fifteen minutes later we were done for the night. Max said he'd be in touch tomorrow morning and sent us on our way.

56

Jen told me she was staying at the Holiday Inn Express, so we took the Tremon Parkway back from Binghamton. I would have offered for her to stay at The Palace, but I only had the one bed, and I hadn't given the place a good cleaning in over a month. I told her I'd drop her off and then come back to pick her up in the morning for breakfast. I knew she had to be exhausted, and this would save her from wasting twenty minutes of extra driving time by going back to get her car. I waited around until she got checked in and then carried her bags to her room on the second floor. I promised to be back at 9:00 am, gave her a hug, and walked back to my car.

I drove home thinking about everything that had happened in the last few days: Carolyn leaves; I lose my job of twenty-three years; I almost kiss my beautiful young neighbor; and, of course, the topper: Mark's bones get found after nearly four decades underground. Any *one* of these things occurring would have been way out of the ordinary. To have all of them happen in the span of just four days was sheer insanity.

When I got close to my apartment, I glanced toward Ally's building, but I didn't see her car. I wondered what her reaction would be when she learned my brother had killed a man and my mother was involved in the subsequent cover-up. I had little doubt that whatever mild interest she might have had in me would evaporate quickly.

I rounded the corner and saw a large blue sedan sitting next to Jen's car in the bike shop parking lot. As I pulled in, I noticed there were two men sitting in the front of the vehicle, and I felt my heart rate quicken. *They identified the body.* I didn't expect it would take them long to confirm Mark's identity. I just didn't think it would be tonight. I had the sudden urge to back out of the lot and keep driving, but I didn't think that would be such a wise idea. Max's words echoed in my head. *"The police probably won't contact you until Monday or Tuesday, but don't talk to them. Just give them my card and have them call me."*

I climbed out of my car, readying myself to relay some facsimile of my lawyer's instructions, when I remembered I wasn't supposed to know anything yet. So why would I have already spoken to an attorney? This was especially true if we weren't going to hand over Adam's disc anytime soon.

I continued on toward the two men. They'd already climbed out of the sedan and were now leaning casually against it.

"Mr. Abbot?" the taller man said.

I noticed both men were dressed in dark gray suits. Everton detectives, I assumed. "Yes, I'm Dan Abbot."

The same man extended his hand toward me, and I shook it. He was a light-skinned African-American who stood about 6'5", which meant I was looking up at him. "I'm Special Agent Andrews, and this is Special Agent Bonolo."

I shook hands with the second agent, who was about my height. We nodded to one another without saying a word.

"Mr. Abbot, we're investigating the discovery of some human bones found this morning at Valley View Golf Course. Did you hear about that?"

Jesus, be careful. "I did hear about that, yes. That's unbelievable."

"Yeah, it really is," Andrews agreed.

"You knew Mark Dolan, didn't you?" Agent Bonolo asked. His voice was unusually deep, and in the shadows of the parking lot, it seemed ominous.

"I did, yeah. He was my mom's girlfriend...I mean boyfriend." I chuckled nervously and was happy to see both men smiling along with me. It was then I noticed both were holding small notebooks.

"Any idea how Mark ended up dead?" Bonolo asked.

"Are you saying it was Mark's body they found today?"

"It was," Andrews said. "Any idea how he died?"

"No, I have no idea."

Bonolo took a small step toward me. "Mr. Abbot, do you mind if we come inside and ask you a few questions? It would be a huge help to us, and we'd really appreciate it."

"Actually, it's not a good time right now. Why don't I have my attorney give you a call?"

"I don't think you'll need an attorney. We just have some basic questions about what you may or may not remember from that time period."

"Honestly, I'm exhausted. I'll just have my attorney call you. Do you happen to have a business card?"

Bonolo studied me for a moment. I thought he was going to keep pressing to come inside, but instead he reached into his pocket and pulled out a business card. He handed it to me and looked back at Andrews. Andrews finished writing in his notebook and pulled a card from his breast pocket.

"Here you go, Mr. Abbot," Andrews said.

I took the two cards and slid them into my pocket. "Okay, thank you."

"We'll be in touch, Mr. Abbot," Andrews said.

"Dan, please."

"Okay, we'll be in touch, Dan."

The two federal agents got into their sedan and started it up. I began climbing the stairs and got about halfway up when I remembered I left Adam's letter in my Saturn. I waited in the darkness until the sedan's taillights disappeared in the distance. They were the only vehicle on the road. I walked back down the stairs and retrieved Adam's letter from the glove box before trudging back up again. By the time I reached the top, my body felt like I'd just run a 5K in work boots.

I unlocked the door and walked directly to the sink. This was a task I needed to do right away or I'd forget. I dug a lighter out of the drawer and lit the edge of Adam's letter. When the flames got to be too much, I dropped the letter into the basin. The smoke set off the fire alarm, and I rushed to remove the battery. After Adam's letter was destroyed, I washed the ashes down the garbage disposal. I felt like I should probably be sad, but I was too tired to feel anything.

I walked straight into the bedroom. As a rule, I never went to bed without brushing my teeth first, but this time I made an exception.

57

That night I had one of the more vivid dreams in recent memory. I was deep in the brush, picking berries with Connor and Ally. They were twenty or thirty feet in front of me, working together to carve the path. We'd gone further in than we'd ever gone before, and the sheer number of ripe black caps was almost hard to believe. They were everywhere, scattered about the prickly landscape like red and black bumble bees. I purposely lagged behind, knowing the rookies would miss the berries hidden beneath the leaves. Besides, they were having a fantastic time together, giggling and laughing like lifelong friends. I was using the semi-alone time to ponder what to make for dinner. I had some chicken cutlets in the freezer and was thinking about whipping up a quick chicken parm, but I felt like that might not be special enough. Ally was coming over. I'd finally worked up the nerve to ask her, and I wanted it to be memorable. It was hard to tell who was more excited, me or Connor.

Suddenly, there was a loud noise in the trees, a distinct, purposeful knocking sound. Both Ally and Connor turned back toward me.

"What the heck is that, Dad?"

I was about to say *I think it's a woodpecker* when I opened my eyes and saw my alarm clock on the bedside table. The large red numerals announced the time as 6:05 am. I felt a powerful sense of disappointment surge through me. I laid there listening to the drone of my air conditioner, wondering if I'd really heard something or if the sound was just in my dream. Then I heard it again, and there was no doubt what it was. Someone was pounding on my door.

"Jesus Christ," I muttered. "Who the hell is this?" As I climbed out of bed, it struck me who it was. *Billy.* He'd watched the news report yesterday and after a long, sleepless night, he'd driven over at the crack of dawn. I certainly didn't mind him coming over, but did it have to be so damn early?

When I reached the kitchen, my heart leapt into my throat. I would have given almost anything at that moment to have Billy standing on the landing. It was still twilight, but I could see the face of Special Agent Andrews looking in through the glass. His broad outline seemed to fill the doorframe.

There was another man beside him, and I could only assume it was Agent Bonolo.

My mind, slow and muddy from not enough sleep, tried to process why they were here. It seemed plausible they'd want to conduct a follow-up interview, but didn't I tell them my lawyer would be in touch? And did they have to do it at 6:00 am? I opened the front door wearing only boxers. Bonolo's sturdy frame came into view, seeming to almost shove Andrews out of the way.

"Mr. Abbot," Bonolo said in that especially deep voice of his, "we have a warrant to search the premises."

Of course you do, I thought. *Why else would you show up here at six o'clock in the morning?* Then it hit me. *They found the bat.* They found the bat, and our name was still on it. Now they were here to search my apartment for more evidence. I thought about Adam's letter, grateful I'd remembered to burn it.

"Is there anyone else in the apartment?" Bonolo asked.

"No, it's just me. Can I see that warrant?"

He handed me a thin stack of papers and entered the apartment. I saw there were others behind him and instinctively stepped aside for fear of being trampled. Two other men and one woman, each dressed in bulletproof vests, entered my kitchen and dispersed to points beyond. I was glad they assessed the threat (or lack thereof) and kept their weapons holstered. I must have looked pretty dangerous standing there in my boxers, wiping sleep from my eyes. As the federal agents began rifling through my apartment, I thanked God Connor wasn't here. He would have been terrified by the invasion, drawn weapons or not.

I glanced down at the papers in my hand. I had no idea what I was looking for, but I saw my name and address. I tried reading further, but my eyes weren't able to focus on the small text. I tossed the packet onto the counter and started for the bedroom. I wasn't crazy about walking around in boxers with my apartment full of strangers. Just then a strong hand clasped my arm and spun me back toward the front door.

"You need to stay right here," Andrews said. "I have a warrant for your arrest. Please turn around, Mr. Abbot."

A million questions flowed through my mind, all fighting for recognition. Finally, the most obvious won out. "What am I being arrested for?"

"A violation of Title 18, United States Code, Section 1001."

"Mind translating that for me?"

Andrews chuckled. "Making a false statement to a federal agent. Turn around please."

As Andrews applied the handcuffs, my mind spun wildly. I felt like I'd just been injected with a shot of adrenaline. The only conversation I'd ever had with a federal agent was last night, and I'd ended it before it even got

going. Right then my lawyer's words rang in my head. I condensed his
instructions down to four words. *Don't say anything else.* Obviously, I'd said
too much last night even though I couldn't fathom how it happened. I tried
running the conversation through my mind, but I couldn't focus. Now fully
cuffed and completely under Andrews's control, I turned back around and
listened as he finished reading me my Miranda Rights.

"Do you have any questions, Mr. Abbot?"

"What happened to Dan?"

Andrews laughed. "Oh, that's right, I forgot. Do you have any questions,
Dan?"

"Yeah, can I get dressed? I don't think anyone wants to see me walking
around in boxers."

"Yeah, I think we can do that."

He put his hand on my arm and led me toward the living room.

Mom

58

Mom took that Monday off from work and drove me and Jess to school. The swelling was mostly gone, but the left side of her face had turned an ugly purplish-black. Again, it reminded me of that first week after bunting the baseball into my eye. I told Mom it was too bad she didn't play baseball because she could tell people she didn't know how to bunt. She smiled at me when I said it, but it was an unhappy smile. I remember thinking it would be a long time before I was able to make her laugh again. Sadly, I was right.

The drive from our house to the school was only a few minutes, five at the most, but I was able to think about what had happened the previous day. It was one of the strangest of my entire life. On second thought, it *was* the strangest of my entire life. The three of us sat at the kitchen table for the better part of an hour, pretending our mom had been struck in the face by her boyfriend. I learned she had suspected he was seeing someone else and when she asked him about it, it led to a fight and he hit her. Things hadn't been good between them for a while, although the arguments had taken place mostly at his house and away from us. After a while she didn't want to talk about it anymore. The bottom line was that she and Mark were broken up, and they would never be getting back together.

When Jess got home around 2:00, we went through the same routine, although it was an abbreviated version. It was interesting to see Jess's reaction. She was truly stunned and began to cry, which was kind of heartbreaking to watch. I knew she would eventually learn the truth, but it would be a long time before that happened. I sort of expected Jess to tell our mom everything right then, but she didn't. As soon as we were alone, though, she did ask me if I told anyone, and I promised her I hadn't. I remembered what Mom said and encouraged Jess to tell her what Mark had done. It took her a couple months, but she finally did.

Later that night, a few hours after Jess got home and about an hour before bed, Jess and I overheard Mom talking to a couple of her girlfriends on the phone. She told them Mark had struck her during an argument and that their relationship was over. We sat together in the doorway of my room, listening. It was no accident Mom made the calls while we were still awake, but of course, Jess didn't know that. All in all, Mom did a superb job of acting. Jess had absolutely no idea that any of it was a lie, and a part of me was almost starting to believe it was true, too—the part that didn't hear the grotesque thud of my thirty-inch Adirondack hitting the back of Mark's head. Mom probably didn't deserve an Academy Award that day—those stellar performances would come a couple weeks later—but it was pretty impressive, nonetheless.

There was one totally unexpected bonus that came out of that awful weekend. Jess had been so shocked by the events surrounding Mark and his breakup with our mom that I think she almost forgot about what had happened with Mr. Holt. Our mom didn't, though, and how I found out about it was one of the more unusual things that ever happened to me at West Everton Elementary.

After making sure Jess got safely to her classroom, I strolled into my room and headed for my desk. I had no sooner unloaded my books and lunch into my desktop when I heard my name.

"Danny," Mr. Holt said. I walked over to his desk, thinking about Jess and how upset she was on Friday afternoon. The memory was still vivid, although it seemed like it had happened months earlier. "Take this down to the main office, would you?" He handed me a manila envelope with what felt like a stack of papers inside. "Just give it to one of the secretaries, and tell them it's from me."

"Okay, sure." I tucked the envelope under my arm and was out the door.

I walked down the hall, thinking about Mr. Holt and the fact that he'd asked *me* to do it. There were plenty of other kids in the room, but he'd waited specifically for me to arrive. I think it was his way of making up with me. He was pissed off the previous week after either Mark or Mom called the principal to complain. Apparently, he'd gotten over it or at least wanted me to think that. I walked past the gym where I could hear the Monday morning crew playing dodgeball. Oddly, I hadn't even thought about it. I turned the corner and looked down the hallway. At the end of the corridor, probably seventy or eighty yards away, was the main entrance to the school. Just then I watched my mother walk through the front doors and turn into the main office. Even from a distance, she looked different, more confident. She was walking with a purpose. It was a walk that said *Don't mess with me.*

I knew immediately why she was there, and I didn't want to walk into the office while she was doing it. I don't think it would've made much of a difference to her, but I just didn't want her to see me. I was looking around for another student to deliver the package when the loudspeaker boomed. It was the principal.

"Mr. Holt, please come to the main office. Mr. Holt, please come to the main office."

Oh shit. I stood frozen in place just outside the gym. I had two options at that point, and they bounced around in my head, threatening to crack my skull wide open. The first was to simply run down the hall and drop the package off quick before heading back. But if I did this, Mr. Holt would assume I'd seen my mother in the office and knew all about the ambush to come. The second option was to hide. I could disappear into the gym until Mr. Holt passed by, and then I could deliver the package while he was meeting with the principal and my mom. I opted for door number two. There was no way I wanted to walk past Mr. Holt as he was on his way for a face to face sit down with my mother — not if I could possibly avoid it. Of course, there was a third option. I could have just headed back toward my classroom, claiming that I heard the loudspeaker announcement. Then I could have handed the package back to Mr. Holt as we crossed paths. That would have been the easiest thing to do, but I didn't think of it then. I was far too panic stricken.

I slipped into the gym and stood next to the door. From that vantage point, I could watch Mr. Holt walk by. In fact, I could watch him walk all the way to the main office if I wanted to. I looked up and observed some of the dodgeball game already in progress. I was standing off to the side, but that didn't mean I couldn't get plunked by an errant throw (or an intentional one). I glanced to the far side of the gym and saw Jason turn away from me and slip into the locker room. I almost laughed out loud. If I didn't have bigger issues to deal with, I would've run in there and rubbed our victory in his face. I almost did it anyway, but after a few seconds the urge passed. With the weekend we'd had, the game didn't seem all that important anymore. There would be times in the near future when I would feel differently, but that day it seemed pretty insignificant.

After what seemed like a long time, Mr. Holt strolled by the gymnasium in his usual sloth-like but somehow cocky gait. It was a walk that said *I'm the king of these here parts, boys and girls, so don't fuck with me.* It occurred to me he was about to be fucked with, whether he liked it or not. It also occurred to me Mr. Holt probably had no idea one of the girls he'd mistreated the other day was my sister. It wouldn't be an angry mom simply complaining about what was happening in the classroom. This was a brand-new offense on a second child, no less, with a mother who'd had one of the worst weekends you could imagine. Suffice it to say, Mr. Holt wouldn't be walking with the same arrogant swagger on his way back to the classroom.

As soon as he entered the main office, I slipped out of the gym and started down the hall. It was still a few minutes before 9:00, but the hallway was mostly empty. There were a couple stragglers — they looked like second graders to me — making their way hurriedly toward their classrooms, but that was all. I was trying to take it slow, but I made it to the office in what seemed like no time at all. In fact, it almost seemed like time had stopped altogether. I had the sudden fear that if I looked back toward those second graders, they would be frozen in place. *Everyone* would be frozen in place except for me, my mom, and Mr. Holt.

I heard my mother's voice even before I entered the main office. She wasn't screaming, which was a huge relief, but she was clearly angry. Principal Keller's office was off the main room to the right, and I could tell by the muted quality of her voice that his door was closed. As I entered through the open glass door, I locked eyes with Mrs. Jacobsen. Her desk was in the far left corner of the room, past the doorway to Principal Keller's office and behind Mrs. Anchor's empty desk. It didn't occur to me until much later that if Mrs. Anchor had been at her desk, I would have never heard anything that day. Both women were very kind from what I remember, but Mrs. Anchor was a little older and much more "old school" in the sense that she would have never allowed me to listen to my mother speaking with a teacher or the principal, let alone both of them at the same time. Mrs. Jacobsen, on the other hand, had the unmistakable look of a deer caught in the headlights of an oncoming tractor trailer, and I'm sure my mother's bruised and swollen face had a lot to do with that. I walked forward and stopped just before Mrs. Anchor's desk. From that vantage point, I could see the back of my mother's upper body through the window as she sat in a chair in front of Principal Keller's desk. Her head was turned to the right, presumably pointed at Mr. Holt who I assumed had to be sitting in the other chair even though I couldn't see him.

Mrs. Jacobsen was still staring at me with startled eyes. "Danny, you—"

In a very serious tone, we both heard my mother say, "That's interesting, Mr. Holt—"

"Lawrence, please," Mr. Holt said, sounding like the most amiable guy in the world.

"That's interesting, Mr. Holt—and please don't interrupt me again—because my daughter said that you grabbed both of them and dragged them out into the hallway. She's also been complaining that her arm hurts, and if it's still bothering her tonight, I'm going to run her up to the emergency room to see if there's something wrong with it. And if I were you, I'd be praying that there isn't."

I knew that was a lie, but I liked the tone my mother was using. She wasn't going to be intimidated.

"That's not what happened," Mr. Holt said, ignoring the threat.

"Well, I'll take the word of my daughter over a man who thinks it's reasonable to rip the top of a desk off in front of a class of ten and eleven-year-olds or to throw a hard pencil holder across a crowded room. Or did those two things not happen, either?"

"Now, Mrs. Abbot," Principal Keller said, sounding as if he was talking to a child, "I think we need—"

"*We* don't need to do anything. *You* need to start doing your job by disciplining a teacher who's clearly out of control."

"Mrs. Abbot, I think you're getting a little hysterical—"

"Hysterical? You call *that* hysterical?" She laughed hard. "What a sheltered life you've led."

I looked back at Mrs. Jacobsen. She opened her mouth to say something. I'm pretty sure it was going to be *Danny, you need to go,* but I turned away quickly.

"I see what's happening here," my mom said, still staring at the principal. "You two are buddies." She let that revelation hang in the air for a long second. "So, when he acts like a damn lunatic, you back *him* up." I remembered what Mr. Holt said about me having a short fuse and knew with certainty that Principal Keller had told him who'd complained. "Well, here's what I'm going to do, gentlemen. I'm going to pay a little visit to the school board to make sure they know about Mr. Holt's teaching style, and I won't be alone. I'll get a couple other *hysterical* parents to come with me. I've already spoken to two or three, and I'm sure I can find a couple others." I watched her stand and turn back toward Mr. Holt. "And if you ever lay so much as a finger on one of my children again, you're going to meet a few of *my buddies,* and I can promise you they aren't nearly as civilized as I am."

My eyes darted back to Mrs. Jacobsen. Her mouth was agape, and her eyes were like silver dollars. She stared at me, and for an instant I think she actually forgot who I was. At the very least, she had forgotten I was standing there. She recovered quickly and shooed me toward the door. I felt the weight of something in my hand and realized I was still holding Mr. Holt's package. I tossed it onto Mrs. Anchor's desk and bolted for the door. Just as I was running into the hallway, I heard Principal Keller's door open. I didn't hear any voices, so I could only assume the men were too shocked to speak. I know I was.

I sprinted down the empty hallway without looking back and rounded the corner toward our classroom. A few seconds later I was outside our door. I stopped there to catch my breath before making my way to my seat. When Mr. Holt got back a couple minutes later, the clock read 9:06. The meeting had been less than ten minutes long, but he looked like a dog that had just been beaten with a very large stick. Mr. Holt didn't look at me the entire day, which became noticeable after a while. With only twenty-four kids in the class, the teacher looks at everyone at some point, even if it's just by accident.

I spent another thirteen days in Mr. Holt's classroom that year, and he spoke to me twice and only because he had to.

As that Monday morning wore on, I started thinking more about the weekend and less about everything else. I kept wondering when the police might come to our house to talk to our mom and maybe even to me or Adam. I worried someone might have seen us on our way to Mark's that night even though we didn't see them. I figured it would take some time, maybe even a few days, before someone reported Mark missing. My mother certainly wasn't going to do it. They'd just broken up, and the bastard hit her, for God's sake. Plus, he was running around with another woman. I don't know how my mother came up with that story on the same night you find out the love of your life molested your daughter and then tried to kill your son, but she did. I think it has something to do with the love a mother feels for her children and the hatred that develops for those who bring them harm.

When I wasn't thinking about our mom or the police, I thought about Adam and what might have happened after I left. I didn't believe the story he told me in the kitchen—not because it wasn't believable, but because I could see the lie in his eyes, and I could hear it in his voice. Nor did I believe what Mom had said about Mark having friends who were policemen. I started worrying Mark had died from my swing and my swing alone. I worried he'd stopped breathing after I left, and then Adam made the rest of it up, so I wouldn't know that I was the one who'd killed him. I tried asking Adam about it twice, but he shot me down both times. He didn't want to talk about it and didn't understand why I didn't feel the same way. The second time, about a week or two after it happened, he dragged me out back near the black cap bushes and told me the police might have bugged our house. By that point the police had already come by and talked to our mom while Jess and I listened in awe from the hallway. After that I didn't bring it up to Adam at all. I did pull Mom out onto the back patio one time and mentioned what Adam had said to me. She smiled at first like the idea was crazy, but after she thought about it, I think she realized it was a possibility. Then I asked her if she thought Mark had died from my swing. Tears filled her eyes and she hugged me. She said, "No, honey, Mark didn't die from that." She admitted they didn't tell me everything, but she said what Adam had told me was pretty close to the truth. I could tell she wasn't lying this time, which made me feel much better. It wasn't that Mark didn't deserve what happened to him, but I still felt a lot better knowing I wasn't the one who killed him. My doubts and fears about that would resurface later, but at the time, my mother's words were comforting.

I don't know how much later it was when the police came again, but this time they were wearing suits instead of police uniforms. I wouldn't realize until years later they were detectives. Jess and I huddled just inside my cracked bedroom door with our hands cupped behind our ears. It probably wasn't necessary because the men had such loud voices anyway. They talked to our mom for a while, and she told them everything she told the other officers. She and Mark had argued late Saturday night after she got home from Jess's friend's house, and then he struck her. They'd been fighting for a couple weeks, and she got the sense Mark was seeing another woman. There was nothing definitive, no hard evidence, but sometimes a woman just knows these things. She hadn't spoken to him since the incident and didn't plan to. Their relationship was over. At some point she would go back and get her things at Mark's house, but there wasn't anything she desperately needed. Some toiletries, a couple outfits — that was about it. She produced a few tears but nothing that sounded overboard. She had loved Mark and planned to marry him someday, but cheating and violence were deal breakers, and he committed both offenses in the very same week. She sounded utterly convincing to me, and by then I had become somewhat of an expert in lie detection.

Adam showed up during the questioning, and the detectives decided to ask him a few questions, too. He told them he'd come home briefly and then spent the evening at his girlfriend's house. He got home late and never saw his mom until the next morning. When it came to acting under pressure, Adam had inherited our mother's nerves. He, too, sounded thoroughly convincing. By then the bruises had faded from his neck, so he didn't have to worry about them drawing attention. I got nervous when one of the detectives asked him if he'd simply gotten "pissed off" when he saw his mom and then stopped by Mark's to settle things "man-to-man." But Adam just chuckled and told him he was really angry at first, but his mom had calmed him down. He handled the questions like a pro, and they moved on quickly. Throughout the questioning, I kept thinking about that first morning in the kitchen after Adam killed Mark. Everything our mom had done — the pretending that had seemed so silly at the time — had all been for that very moment.

Later in the conversation, after Adam had left, they started asking Mom if she knew about Mark's gambling debts. She said she didn't, and I don't think any acting was required. It turned out Mark had a gambling problem he was able to keep hidden from our mom. He owed two local bookies a total of $23,000 and another $10,000 to a loan shark. They asked Mom if they thought he might have skipped town to get away from the debts, and she said she found that hard to believe. But she quickly added that she would've found it hard to believe Mark would've hit her before he actually did. I couldn't see the detective's faces, but I suspected they were nodding. I didn't realize I was smiling until Jess asked me what was so funny. Mom told me later — also out on the back patio — that Mark having such large debts was a very fortunate break for us. It gave him a legitimate reason to leave town. Adam even broke his silence to tell me it was an enormous break. I believe his exact words were, "It's an enormous fucking break."

And that wasn't the only one we caught. As it turned out, no one saw me or Adam on our bike rides to or from Mark's, or I guess I should say no one ever reported it to the police. I know I passed that one guy with his dogs, but I don't know if anyone saw Adam or not. A much larger break came when no one saw Adam carry Mark's body out to the car even though I still had no idea how he'd done it. There was a wooded lot directly behind Mark's house, and I suspected he took full advantage of that, but I didn't dare ask him again.

One big thing that worked against us was Mark's son, Eddie. He was convinced Mark didn't run off to get away from his gambling debts, nor did he believe there was another woman. He pointed to the fact his dad left his car behind and to the fact that he had a good job. And he was adamant his dad had never laid a hand on anyone, let alone a woman. Adam reminded me that Eddie was becoming a lawyer, which he thought made the police take him more seriously. Of course, Eddie didn't know about Mark's debts, and that was the one thing that blew everything else out of the water. If he could keep that hidden from everyone in his life, he could keep anything hidden.

We learned all about Eddie's efforts to keep the investigation alive from a uniformed policeman who came back to our house a couple times. I think his name was Stan. Jess and I thought he liked our mom, but nothing ever came of it that I know of. I think Mom had had enough of men by that point. In the end the police believed our mom and Adam as far as I could tell. The detectives came back to talk to both of them a second time, but that was all. I wasn't there for that one, but Jess heard it all and told me about it. Eventually, the police stopped coming around altogether. Even Stan finally got the hint. And since we hardly ever talked about it, everything began fading into the background. By the time sixth-grade started, the events of the previous spring already seemed like another lifetime.

All of that was waiting weeks and even months into the future, but I still had the rest of that week and the remainder of the school year to make it through. Hell, I still had the rest of that *day*. The talk on the basketball court that Monday was interesting. Matt and I basked in all the attention brought on by winning the championship. Cam Bender had been there to see it and relayed how stunned Rotary Club looked after Justin struck out Carmen Mills to end the game. In the midst of our celebration, I never even looked over at them. According to Cam, they just stood there—players and coaches alike—staring at one another while we danced around on the pitcher's mound. I think they never even considered we might beat them, so when it actually happened, it was just stunned disbelief. I think in a lot of ways

Rotary Club had shown up to collect their trophy, maybe pose for a few pictures, and somehow got beat.

One person notably absent from the conversation was Jason. I didn't expect him to play basketball that day, but I didn't even see him on the playground, and believe me I was looking. No one missed recess unless they were sick or in detention. That told me just how badly he wanted to avoid me, probably even more so than his efforts to duck me during dodgeball. On the way back to class, Matt spotted Jason up ahead and pointed him out to me. Matt usually stayed out of the bullshit, but he knew Jason had been laying into me pretty hard in the weeks leading up to that day. I ran ahead, being careful not to draw the attention of a teacher, and caught him just before he could escape into the safety of his classroom.

"Jason," I said, grabbing his arm, "guess you guys weren't as good as you thought, huh?" It wasn't exactly gracious of me, but I didn't give a shit.

He looked at me, not at all surprised to see me standing there. "You guys got lucky, that's all. We could play ten times, and that's the only game you'd win."

Like a cup of cold water splashed in my face, it dawned on me why Jason had darted into the bathroom earlier. It wasn't just to avoid me. It was because he didn't know what he was going to say. Sometime between the gym and that moment, he'd thought of his response, and judging by the smug look on his face, he was proud of it. Normally, I'm not great at snappy comebacks—as a ten-year-old or now—but that time I think I did okay. "That might be true, Jason, but we won this time, and that's all that matters. We're the champs."

I continued down the hallway, and for the first time ever, Jason Billings was speechless.

59

Sunday Morning

When Maxwell Lewis walked into the Binghamton offices of the Federal Bureau of Investigation, the wall clock above Agent Andrews's desk read 10:15 am. I was still sitting on the same bench to which he'd handcuffed me an hour earlier. When I first got there, I had expected to be taken to a cell somewhere — in the bowels of the building's basement, I feared — but it never happened. Andrews told me Sunday mornings are usually pretty slow in the Federal Building, but the Binghamton Police Department is a different story. "Saturday night brings out the drunks and the lunatics," he said, between bites of his breakfast sandwich.

Just the sight of my lawyer filled me with an enormous sense of relief. *The cavalry is here,* I thought. I'd actually been treated pretty well, but it had been one of the more boring mornings of my entire life. The processing, which consisted of the paperwork, fingerprinting, DNA sampling, and the obligatory photo shoot (also known as the mugshot) was completed by 7:40, which meant I'd been sitting around reading magazines and watching the news on a small television in the corner for the better part of two hours. My hearing was scheduled for 11:00 am, and Andrews told me Judge Tarver liked to be on time. He also told me I was lucky to get a hearing on a Sunday. He hinted there must have been some "pressure from above," but he didn't elaborate. One of the four agents I'd seen this morning, and the only one currently in the office, looked up from her desk when Max walked in. Max pointed at me and she nodded. There was no need for a detailed conversation. This was a routine with which they were both familiar. Max was moving along at a brisk pace, totally unlike the relaxed, athletic gait he had last night. I could tell just by his body language he was pissed off.

"How are you doing?" he asked, as he approached.

"Never been better."

Just then Andrews came walking around the corner, holding what looked like a full cup of coffee. I hadn't seen Agent Bonolo in over two hours.

That was fine with me. I didn't mind Andrews, but I'd already developed a serious dislike for Bonolo.

"Morning, counselor," Andrews said.

"Good morning, Agent Andrews," Max responded. "Think we could remove the handcuffs while I talk to my client?"

I noticed he said *we* as if the two of them were on the same team.

Andrews bent down and removed the handcuff from my left wrist, freeing me from the bench. I was hoping he'd remove the leg shackles, too, but he left them on. He pointed to a closed door in the corner of the office. "No one is using that room, so you can take him in there." He looked at me. "Sorry, so you can take *Dan* in there, I mean."

"Okay, thank you," Max said, looking at me, eyebrow raised.

I stood up and followed Max. When he reached the door, he opened it and turned the light on, stepping aside so I could shuffle past. I could tell right away the room was intended for criminal lawyers and their clients. It seemed too small for more than two people, which would rule out most interrogations, or at least the interrogations I imagined in my mind where two detectives hammered away at some would-be criminal. A small wooden table sat in the center of the cramped room with one chair on each side.

I walked around the table and sat in the chair facing the door. Max opened his briefcase and removed a manila folder. He dropped it on the table, then sat down and looked at me. I was beginning to sense his anger was directed at me.

"What part of don't talk to investigators did you not understand?" His tone was that of an annoyed father talking to his disobedient son.

I'd met this guy about thirteen hours ago, and with the morning I'd had so far, I wasn't even close to being in the mood to deal with his bullshit. "Okay, let's get something straight here. You're not my father or my wife or frankly anyone that has the right to talk to me like that. I've had a tough morning as I think you're aware. (I didn't feel the need to tell him that it had been mostly just boring.) If you don't want to be my lawyer, that's fine, but I don't need *your* shit, too." I regretted it as soon as the words left my mouth. My brother had found this guy, which meant he was good. Adam simply wouldn't have settled for anything less. On top of that, he'd spent a healthy chunk of change to retain him.

Max looked at me, stone-faced, and for a quick second I thought he might just slide the manila file back into the briefcase and head out the door. I was preparing my *please forgive me speech* when he let out a heavy sigh. "Okay, Dan, I suppose this is the moment of truth. I've had clients lie to me before. In fact, clients lie to me all the time. It's probably rule number one in my job description. I think you're probably a good guy, and for that matter, a reasonably honest guy, but the Feds don't give a shit if you're a good guy, or if you're normally honest, or if Adam was defending himself, or even if Mark was the fucking devil himself. They're playing a game here, Dan, and they're playing it to win. Make no mistake about it."

I stared at him, doing everything I could not to laugh in his face. His sincerity coupled with the sheer insanity of what he was saying was almost too much to take. Had I not been awakened at 6:00 am and escorted from my apartment in handcuffs, I would have lost it for sure. As ludicrous as this entire situation had become, Max was one hundred percent right, and I knew it.

"And I don't like losing," Max continued, "but that's exactly where we're heading. If you want me to represent you, you need to tell me the full truth, starting right now."

They can't possibly know I was involved, I thought. "Max, I don't know what you're talking about."

Max opened his briefcase and slipped the manila folder back inside before closing it again. "I'll get you through this initial appearance and prepare the paperwork, but I'm not going to play this game. I can't be your lawyer if you're not going to tell me the truth." He stood up and started for the door before turning back. "We're scheduled for eleven. I'll be back before that." He opened the door and started out.

A wave of moderate panic swept through me. I was in trouble here. I didn't know exactly how or why this was happening, but it most definitely was. And if Max dumped me, things were going to get considerably worse. "Max, wait." I could hear the desperation in my voice, and it made me feel sick. "Come back and sit down. Please. I'll tell you everything I know."

Max closed the door but didn't come back to the table. "Okay, Dan, I'll give you another chance, but this is it. There are some things you don't know about yet. I want to represent you, but I can't do it if you're not telling me everything."

"Okay, I understand. I get it. I was just trying to protect my son, and I honestly didn't think that what I was leaving out would ever come into play—with you or anyone else."

Max came back and sat at the table. "Everything matters, Dan, and everything comes into play, whether you want it to or not. More often than not, I'm behind from the beginning, and when there's shit I don't know about, it's even worse. Now, start at the top, and tell me everything you know."

I looked at my lawyer, maybe as confused as I'd ever been, certainly since childhood. I took a deep breath, thought about where to begin, and started talking.

Just as he'd done during Adam's video, Max took notes and only interrupted me two or three times. I finished my account of what happened with my mother's training session the day after Adam killed Mark.

"So, Adam's the one who hit your mother?"

"That's right."

"And he went over to Mark's that Saturday night because Mark molested your sister?"

"That's right. Does any of that make a difference?"

"Probably not because it has no bearing on the charges against you. We'll come back to that. When you left that night, Mark was breathing. Is that correct?"

"Yes, that's correct."

"What do you know about Billy's involvement? Did he help your brother with the body?"

"I honestly don't know. Since they found the body at Valley View, I'm guessing he did, but I really have no idea." I got the feeling Max was testing me with that question, and I also got the feeling I passed. I had no intention of lying to him again, no matter how small it seemed. "Max, can I ask you a couple questions?"

"Okay, but we don't have a lot of time, and there are still quite a few things I need to go over with you."

"I still don't get how I lied to them. I told them exactly what you told me to say. I took their cards and told them you'd be in touch. The next thing I know they're knocking on my door at six o'clock in the morning."

"It's what you told them before that."

"I don't—"

"You told them you didn't have any idea how Mark was killed."

"That is what I said, but they don't know what I just told you."

"Actually, they do. They bugged your apartment, and that's not even the worst of it."

My mind tried to process both statements but was unsuccessful. Eventually, it wandered back to the first one, I think simply because it was the more tangible of the two. "What do you mean they bugged my apartment?"

"Your friend? I think she went by Annie or Ally? She's a federal agent."

Oh fuck. A horrible wave of embarrassment rolled over me and then settled on my skin like the stench from some rancid pond. I saw myself standing in front of her apartment, the three of us unloading the couch from the truck. I wondered if her friend Katie was also an agent, then realized she had to be. I'd never felt more foolish than I did at that moment. My mind ran through our encounters, searching for something I must have missed, some clue to reality I have should have gleaned but didn't. The surprise of the party invitation, the simple joy of picking berries with her and Connor, the near kiss moment we shared in the kitchen. All of it was fake — contrived moments of complete and utter bullshit. I suddenly felt like an old ghoul — the hapless subject of some sick sorority joke. *Who can bring the oldest, most desperate guy back to the party?* I wondered how many times the two of them had laughed at how easily I'd been conned. *Just strut your ass around, sister, and the dope will come running like the old pervert he is.*

I thought about Connor and felt a fresh wave of hot anger. As embarrassing as it was — and if I'm being totally honest, as crawl into bed depressing as it was — I could live with being tricked. After all, I'd been afraid all along I was the creepy old guy who'd overstayed his welcome, and lo and behold, it turned out to be true. What I couldn't live with was that she'd used Connor to pull it off. He honestly liked her, and she took full advantage of his youth and innocence to get to me. That made her a supreme asshole in my book, and I intended to tell her exactly that if I ever saw her again. And at that moment I felt like I might have to take a few steps to make that happen. "What a fucking bitch," I muttered, without even realizing it.

"Listen, I don't blame you for feeling that way. I really don't. But you have to let it go, and fast. Trust me, it happens all the time. There's a reason they use attractive young women on men our age."

I felt a sudden, almost maddening urge to dive into a deeper explanation — to explain to Max it wasn't as bad as it looked. I wasn't *that* stupid. I truly had been skeptical, almost comically so, but she'd worn me down over a period of days. What man still with a beating heart wouldn't have succumbed to that? I thought about some of the things we talked about: the exodus of manufacturing in Syracuse, the black cap bushes near her childhood home, the detailed discussions about her family. I wondered if any of it were true, and then it hit me. *She'd researched me beforehand.* She knew my life story, boring and uneventful as it was, before she ever stepped foot near my apartment. I wondered what Ally and Katie had said about my life — my divorce, my shitty little apartment. If nothing else, I'm sure it solidified her confidence she'd be able to swoop in and knock me off center without much effort. I had never felt this kind of hatred for someone I barely knew. Then another realization struck, and it embarrassed me all over again. I didn't *barely* know Ally. The truth was I didn't know her at all. Ally wasn't even her real name.

Max continued on. "They found Mark's remains over a week ago, on Friday afternoon, and that set everything in motion."

I thought about meeting Ally and Katie outside their apartment the Saturday before last. "What do you mean they found him over a week ago? I thought they found him yesterday."

"No. They discovered the bones two Fridays ago around four o'clock in the afternoon. The course superintendent and one of his workers were using an excavator to dig up the left side of the twelfth green. He actually pulled up the bones of a hand and forearm in the bucket. It was only the two of them there at the time, and the superintendent wanted to keep it quiet. He made a call to a buddy at the Everton Police Department, and that's what got everything started. A State Police forensics team came in that night after everyone was gone and dug up the rest of Mark's remains. They set up a tent to hide the lights and worked throughout the night. No one else at the golf course even knew about it except for the general manager and the two guys who dug up the bones."

"So, what I watched yesterday on the news was just for show?"

"It seems that way. I'm not sure what kind of deal they worked out with the local news or if they just lied to them, too. I can tell you for sure they found the bones that Friday and then set everything up from there. The usual M.O. is to get the subject out of the house — in this case that was you — and then a team comes in and sets up the surveillance."

Berry picking, I thought. That had to be when they did it. I didn't think I was at Ally's fake party long enough. A memory of Katie trying to get me to stay and do a funnel came back to me. *Those assholes,* I thought again. I wondered if everyone at the party was a federal agent. Suddenly, Ally's phone call from yesterday came back to me. It seemed like good timing when it happened, but in reality it had been cold and calculated. She watched me arrive back home and then called to make sure I put the news on. I'm sure the plan all along was to record my conversations during the initial shock of seeing the story. They executed it perfectly.

"Once they found the bat," Max continued, "they knew it was Mark. They confirmed it the next day through dental records. He went to a guy named Penderton in Everton to get a root canal three or four months before he died. Penderton's son took over the practice in 1992 and still had the records in his office if you can believe it."

After the last twenty-four hours, I'd believe just about anything. "How did they know he went to this guy Penderton?"

"I'm guessing that Mark's son, Eddie, remembered him, but I'll get to all that. I want to bring you up to speed on everything that's happened, so you fully understand what's going on."

My God, they already talked to Eddie. I could only imagine what he said about my family. He'd always thought Adam did it, and now there was proof.

Max continued on. "So, as you probably know, they needed probable cause for the search warrant."

"I figured that was the bat."

"Just finding the bat wasn't enough. They tested the handle and found your DNA. I suppose that was to be expected, but the problem is they didn't find Adam's DNA. Or I guess I should say they didn't find any other male DNA on the handle, other than yours."

Jesus Christ. I wondered how that was possible. Even if Adam never used the bat to hit Mark, he'd used it to hit me grounders and pop-ups at least a dozen times. Surely, his DNA should have been left behind.

"There *was* male DNA on the barrel, which they compared to DNA from one of Mark's bones. It was a match. The main reason they're not charging you in Mark's death is because of the recorded conversation you had with Jen on the phone. It was spontaneous and they know it, and for the most part it matches up with Adam's account on the video. So, in a very real sense, it's a good thing they bugged your apartment. Otherwise, you'd likely be facing more serious charges than simply lying to federal investigators."

I couldn't quite wrap my head around all that, so I stuck with something simple. "That all happened awfully fast, didn't it? And how in the hell did they get my DNA for comparison?"

"You can thank your friend Ally for that, too. She grabbed a used coffee cup and a hair sample from your apartment."

I nodded but managed not to say anything this time. I didn't want Max to see the full depth of how angry I was, and how hurt. It was strange. I was still thinking of Ally as someone I'd connected with as opposed to the federal agent she actually was. She'd tricked me because I was a suspect in a murder case. There was nothing more to our relationship than that.

"They also obtained a warrant for Billy's apartment."

"Did Billy help him bury the body?"

"He did. He wasn't involved in the murder, but he helped him transport Mark's body to Valley View, and then he helped Adam bury him. After the story broke, Billy called his brother and asked him to come over. The two of them talked it over for a couple hours, and Billy incriminated himself."

"Billy didn't say anything about how Adam killed Mark, did he?"

"No. Not that his lawyer told me."

"They didn't bug Jen's house, did they?"

"No. They didn't have probable cause. Even if Adam were alive, they wouldn't have had enough for a warrant, at least initially."

"What was the probable cause for Billy?"

"I don't know specifics, but they tracked down another guy that worked at the golf course that summer. He remembered seeing Billy on the course that night. How he knew it was that specific night, I have no idea, but obviously it was enough to get the warrant. It doesn't sound legit to me, but I'll come back to that."

"Wait a second. Why are the Feds even involved in this case? It seems like this would just be the Everton Police Department."

"Well, the Everton PD is involved, along with the County Sheriff and the State Police, but the Feds are running the investigation. Supposedly, Mark was seen earlier that day at a smoke shop in Pennsylvania. Their working theory is that he may have been killed in Pennsylvania and then transported back to Valley View Golf Course. Again, I have my doubts, but transporting a body across state lines is a federal crime. With the information from the wiretaps and listening devices, that theory will probably be altered or replaced with something else." Max leaned in closer, and I didn't like the look on his face one bit. "Dan, the Feds may end up handing this back to Everton, but they'll still be in charge."

"I'm not sure I'm following you, Max."

"I told you a minute ago the surveillance wasn't the worst of it."

Christ, what else could there be? "This doesn't sound good."

"It's not, but we're lucky to know about it at all—as in extremely lucky. I have a close friend from law school who used to be an Assistant U.S. Attorney here in the Northern District. One of his buddies works for the Feds in the Western District. I don't know what the guy does, and my friend wouldn't even tell me. That's how secretive this thing is and how lucky we are to know it." I didn't like where this was heading, but I still couldn't imagine how it was connected to me or Billy. "The Feds have their official reasons for why they're involved in the case, but they're not the only reasons." Max hesitated and looked me in the eye. It was almost like he didn't want to tell me what was coming next. "I guess he took his mother's last name after his parents' divorce."

"Who's *he*, Max? What the hell are you talking about?"

"Mark's son, Eddie. He goes by Edward Daniels. He's the U.S. Attorney for the Western District of New York State…and according to our source, he's running this whole fucking show."

60

I walked out of the Federal Building at 11:16. Judge Tarver had indeed been on time as Andrews predicted. I had expected a stodgy, no-nonsense older gentlemen, but Judge Tarver was a relaxed, seemingly good-natured human being and might have actually been younger than me. The Assistant U.S. Attorney for the Northern New York District, a man named William McCall, had been tasked with prosecuting my case, and he was *definitely* younger than me. Max, McCall and Judge Tarver were all quite friendly with one another, but that didn't stop McCall from seeking the maximum sentence of five years against me for making a false statement to federal agents. Max pleaded not guilty on my behalf, and after determining that I was neither a flight risk nor a danger to the community, Judge Tarver released me under two conditions. The first was that I could not contact anyone related to the case, namely Billy, and the second was that I could not leave the country. He also added that if I planned on leaving New York State, I had to make an official request with the court. Max informed the judge he didn't believe that would be necessary. The Judge then explained the government had ten days to convene a grand jury, and assuming the jurors concurred with the opinions of the Assistant U.S. Attorney, they would issue an indictment. Max assured me they had enough evidence to do just that. There wasn't a single mention of Eddie in any of the proceedings, which wasn't a surprise based on what Max said. Apparently, only a couple people even knew he was involved.

As soon as I exited the building, I spotted Jen's red Subaru idling at the curb. What had been a cool, clear morning had grown overcast and muggy. I felt like an afternoon thunderstorm was probably in the works. I jogged to her car, hopped into the passenger seat and gave her a quick hug. She smelled great, which reminded me of how badly I needed a shower. I only hoped I didn't smell as bad as I felt. I'd been in the building for only five hours, but it felt like it had been a couple days. Jen flipped her blinker on and pulled away from the curb, merging with the thick late-morning traffic.

I looked at her. "So, how's your day going so far?"

Jen laughed and then pointed out the front windshield. "Do I turn right up here?"

"Yeah, take a right here. That will lead us back to where we were last night. It goes right by Max's office."

"What time are we supposed to meet with him?"

"He said to come by around six. I guess he has some depositions to take on another case, but he thinks he'll be done by then. If it runs late, we'll have to meet tomorrow. He's got something going on later tonight."

Jen waited for a young couple to finish crossing the street and then took a right. "Okay, I talked to Max briefly this morning and found out that both you and Billy got arrested." She was talking fast. "He said the Feds were listening to our conversation last night and that you lied to them later. The news just said that you and Billy had been arrested, but they didn't know anything else. In other words, I have absolutely no idea what's going on, so please fill me in!"

"How much coffee have you had today?"

Jen laughed. "A lot. Now tell me what's happening."

"Okay, but can we get something to eat? I'm starving."

I told Jen everything over hamburgers and fries at A&W. Other than me and Connor grabbing our weekly pizza, I tried to avoid fast food, but this tasted great. The combination of greasy meat and deep-fried potatoes, all buried under thick layers of salt and ketchup, was exactly what I needed. I washed everything down with a large Dr. Pepper. By the time I slurped the last few drops from my twenty-ounce cup, I'd finished bringing her up to speed. Just as Max had done with me, I saved the news about Eddie for last.

"You have to be kidding me," Jen said, staring. She looked like she'd just watched a spaceship land in the parking lot.

I wondered if I'd worn the same expression when Max told me. "It's unbelievable, isn't it?"

"That's the understatement of the century. Thank God Adam isn't here to see this. He couldn't stand that guy, even way back when they were teenagers."

"Yeah, Eddie was pretty arrogant from what I remember. Granted, we only met him two or three times."

"Really? The way Adam talked, it seemed like you guys knew him pretty well."

"Yeah, Eddie left quite an impression. Plus, he did his best to bury Adam back when Mark disappeared."

"It's almost like Mark's pulling the strings from hell or wherever he is."

I chuckled. "That's definitely how it seems."

"I guess it explains why they're going after you and Billy so hard."

"Yeah, and it also explains how they were able to put everything together with Ally so fast."

"Wait," Jen said, "Ally works for Eddie?"

"No, I don't think so. Not directly anyway. She was just one of the federal agents they used in the sting. Max doesn't think many people even know that Eddie's involved."

"Okay, now I'm confused."

"The FBI in the Northern District, which includes Binghamton, are the ones conducting the investigation. They set up all the surveillance and the sting with Ally. And the Assistant U.S. Attorney in the Northern District, a guy named McCall, is the prosecutor."

"I got all that, but Eddie's in the Western District, right?"

"Correct."

"So, Eddie's pushing McCall behind the scenes?"

"We don't know for sure. Max seems to think Eddie's tight with McCall's boss, his equal in the Northern District. I guess our guy — the secret contact in Western NY — reached out to Max's friend to give him the heads up that Eddie's involved, but either he doesn't know the full extent of it, or he isn't willing to talk about it."

"Jesus, my head's spinning."

"Mine, too, believe me."

Jen took another sip of her drink. "Okay, so Eddie hears about the body being found, sits down with the U.S. Attorney in the Northern District, and tells him what? That Mark's his dad and that he always suspected you guys were involved?"

"That's my guess. Something like that anyway."

"And then they hatch the plan with Ally?"

"Yeah, but as Max pointed out, they didn't need Eddie for any of this to happen. Don't get me wrong, I think he's probably behind it, but I *did* lie to the Feds and Billy *did* help Adam bury the body. Max thinks that given Eddie's position, he might have even gotten pulled into it reluctantly. In other words, someone discovers that Mark is his dad and reaches out to him. Now he's involved, but he's probably trying to keep it a secret, especially from the press."

Jen leaned closer. "Or he's covering his butt internally. He hears about the body being found and goes to his counterpart in the Northern District. That way the guy doesn't get blindsided later when the story breaks about it being his father."

I smiled. "Adam was right. You are a lot smarter than him." Jen shrugged and smiled as if to say *What did you expect?* "No, that actually sounds plausible to me. Then if it comes out, Eddie can just say he was trying to protect his family since he knew it was going to be a media circus. As long as he doesn't lie, I don't think anyone will blame him. And it's not like he or anyone else is ever going to admit he's running the investigation. So, in the end, he wouldn't have done anything wrong."

"Do you think McCall knows?"

"Max doesn't think so."

Jen looked out the window like she was deep in thought. "Why doesn't Max leak it? I mean, it could only help you, right? Make it look like some kind of vendetta against you and Billy? I think if people know Mark was Eddie's father, they'll be able to connect the dots that he's influencing the investigation."

"We were actually talking about that. Max isn't so sure it will make a difference. Like I said, it's not like the charges are made up."

"It certainly couldn't hurt, though."

"I agree with you. Max says he thinks it'll come out within a week or two anyway, but he doesn't want to leak it, at least not right away. He didn't say this, but I think his friend is worried about exposing the contact in Western NY. I'm sure we'll talk about it with Max later, but don't discuss it with anyone yet. Max specifically told me not to tell anyone, so please keep it between us for now."

"Of course."

We paused while an elderly man walked past us on his way to the bathroom. "Have you talked to Billy's family yet?" I asked. "I was instructed not to speak with him."

Jen nodded. "I spoke to his wife this afternoon. They're terrified, obviously."

"I'm just glad they didn't arrest *her*, and quite frankly I was worried about you, too."

"Who knows, maybe they still have a few surprises waiting for us."

"Max said they'd probably paint Billy as a flight risk to keep him in custody."

"How nice of them. Listen, I have something else from Adam. He told me not to give it to you unless I absolutely had to, and I think with what's happened it might help us."

I couldn't even begin to imagine what might help us at this point. "What is it?"

"It's a recording of Jess. Your mother taped the conversation when Jess told her about what Mark did to her."

"She what? The original conversation?"

"Yes, I think so. Adam told me she thought it might come in handy someday if they tried to go after him for Mark's murder."

I thought about my mother and how she acted in the aftermath of Mark's death. Everything was about protecting Adam — either reducing the chances of him getting caught or improving his situation if he did. "Why didn't Adam want me to have this?"

"It wasn't that he didn't want you to have it. He just thought it might be too emotional for you."

"Have you heard it yet?"

"I did, once. Again, it was right about the same time Adam made his video. I grabbed that disc yesterday when I grabbed the video. I'm not really sure why. I certainly never thought any of this would happen."

"So, the original had to be a cassette. Adam must have transferred it over to a disc?"

"That's right. I still have the original cassette at my house."

I thought about the old tape recorder we used to have lying around. Jess and I would sometimes tape songs off the radio. I figured that had to be what our mother used when she made the recording. Knowing Mom, she probably thought the tape would not only help Adam but also save Jess from having to be interviewed by a million different people.

"I guess it shouldn't surprise me after everything she did, but I can't believe my mom would think of doing that."

"Adam said when everything happened she just turned into a machine. She swallowed her grief and just started planning on how to protect all of you."

"That's exactly what happened, but I still find it amazing she knew how to do all this. I mean she was a nurse, for Christ's sake, but she was acting like she'd done this kind of thing her whole life."

I was deep in thought when Jen touched my hand. "You need to tell Max about Jess's tape to see if it will help us."

"I already talked to him about it this morning. Not the tape, obviously, but the fact that Mark molested her. He didn't think it would help because it had nothing to do with why Billy and I are being charged. I don't know if the tape changes anything or not, but even if it did, you and I didn't talk about Jess at all in our phone conversation, and Adam didn't say anything about it in his video because he was trying to keep me out of it. The Feds could just say my mother fabricated the tape to protect Adam in case the body was ever found. And with Eddie involved, that's exactly what they *would* say. It wouldn't have been out of the question, especially considering the other stuff my mother did."

Jen looked at me, her eyes blazing again. I could tell she had an idea, and one was forming in my head, as well. "That's a big risk for Eddie. I can't imagine he'd want that kind of information out there, especially since he's hoping to stay in the background. I don't think having a father who molested little girls would do much for his career. And you haven't even heard the tape yet. It sure doesn't sound like a fabrication. It would make the Feds, and ultimately Eddie, look like they're going after two guys who helped get rid of a child molester."

I smiled at her. It was exactly what I was thinking. "Great minds think alike. I wonder if we can somehow leverage this into getting them to drop the charges, or at least into getting them reduced."

"He drops the charges, we don't go to *Dateline*."

"Exactly."

"Sounds like blackmail."

"Jen, here in the U.S. we call that our justice system." Another thought popped into my head. "We do have to be careful, though."

"Why is that?"

"Once the story's out there, our leverage is gone. And this situation is even more difficult because Eddie isn't officially in charge of anything. We can't just request a meeting with him. His influence is happening behind the scenes."

"Maybe your friend Ally can act as a go-between." Jen smiled.

"Wow, Adam was right. You *are* cruel."

She laughed hard. "I'm sorry. I couldn't resist."

"C'mon let's get out of here. I need a shower."

We threw our garbage away and headed back toward the car. Two men in their early thirties walked past us on their way into the restaurant. They looked Jen up and down on their way by. I stared at them, but they couldn't have cared less. "How can you stand that?" I asked.

"What, you mean those guys? I barely even notice. I do notice the ones who don't look, however." She smiled at me, and I couldn't help but think that pool of men had to be awfully small.

Ten minutes later we got back to The Palace and Jen parked her car next to my SUV. I climbed out and glanced toward Ally's apartment building. I wondered how long it would take before I could look at that building without thinking about her. If Eddie got his way, I wouldn't have to worry about it for another five years.

We were almost to the top of the stairs when Jen spoke. "Oh, I forgot to tell you, I have some good news."

I could tell by her tone that that assertion would be extremely debatable. "Oh, yeah, what's that?"

"Your dad's in town. He drove in this morning. I got a text from Laura just before I picked you up. And he brought a lady friend with him."

Jesus, that's all I need right now. I looked at Jen, shook my head, and stepped into my apartment.

61

Normally, I would've used my laptop to listen to Jess's recording, but thanks to NBC's new owners, I no longer had one. I turned on my seldom-used desktop and waited for it to boot up. Jen dug the disc out of her bag and set it on the table beside me. As soon as the computer was ready, I slid the disc into the E drive and selected the only available file. Adam had fittingly named it *momjess*.

My heart was pounding as I double-clicked on the file. A part of me was dreading hearing Jess tell our mom what Mark had done to her, but at the same time I wanted to hear her voice. I hadn't heard it in nearly twenty-five years, and I missed it terribly. Through the speakers I heard a faint hiss followed by our mother's voice.

"I'm sorry, honey," Mom said, "I had to do something quick. What were you saying?"

My God. Our mother's voice was so strong and so beautiful. When I thought of her speaking, it was usually the weak whisperer she'd had in the last months of her life. What I was hearing now was the voice of a woman in her prime. I felt an unexpected jolt of emotion.

"Um," Jess said in her soft voice, "I was asking you if Mark was ever coming back."

At the sound of my sister's voice, the tears broke through and started flowing freely down my face. I was too drained to stop it. My chest heaved, and I felt Jen's hand fall gently on my back. Jess sounded so young. She *was* so young, only nine-years-old.

"No, he won't be coming back, honey."

"How do you know, Mom?"

"I just do, sweetheart. When you're an adult, you just know these things sometimes. He's not coming back."

Mark had been in the ground for almost two months by then, down with the bugs and the worms and the fungi. The thought made me feel better. There was another long pause, and in my mind I could see Jess sitting there, staring ahead, while Mom did the laundry or folded clothes. Jess was thinking about what to do, wondering if she should tell Mom or not.

"There's something I have to tell you, Mom."

"What is it, honey?"

Another long pause. "I told Danny a long time ago, and he told me I should tell you. He didn't tell you, did he?"

Mom chuckled. "I'm not sure what you're talking about, honey. I don't think Danny told me anything. Is it about Mark?"

"Yes. Did Danny tell you?"

"No, honey, he didn't tell me. What is it?"

By now, my tears had stopped. It was heartbreaking to hear Jess struggle, but the overwhelming emotion had passed.

There was another pause, the longest one yet. "This is sort of hard, Mom."

There was a noise that sounded like a door being closed on a washer or dryer. "Jess, you can tell me anything. You know that, don't you?"

"The night Danny won the championship game, Mark came into my room."

I listened as Jess told Mom the same thing she'd told me several weeks earlier. Mom listened patiently to a story she already knew, her calm voice coaxing the information from her little girl. Jess cried at one point, just as she had with me, but Mom's soothing voice had a calming effect on her. She made it through the rest of the story without faltering.

Mom told Jess that Mark shouldn't have done that, and was quick to add that she hadn't done anything wrong. Mom also told Jess she was right to tell her about it. Then Mom told her she loved her more than anything in this world. Shortly after that, there was a clicking sound and the recording ended.

I felt Jen beside me. "Are you okay?"

"I'm okay," I said, looking up at her and smiling. "It was too emotional at first, hearing their voices after so long."

"I can't even imagine."

"That was our little sister." I felt the urge to cry again, but I fought it off.

"She sounds beautiful."

"She was."

"And your mother was amazing. She sounds like an unbelievable woman."

I nodded, but found I couldn't speak. Jen placed her hand on my back again. I did everything I could to fight it, but the tears came again.

I hopped out of the shower and threw on a pair of shorts and a tee-shirt. The last thing I felt like doing right now was talking to my dad. I'm not sure how he heard about all this, but right now I didn't need his involvement. I had to go over to Laura's and say hello to him, maybe catch up for an hour or so, but that was about all I intended to do. I came back into the living room and found Jen sitting on the couch. I grabbed my sneakers and sat in the chair next to her. "I wish my dad would've asked me before driving up here. I would've told him not to come right now."

"He probably heard about it this morning and just hopped in his car."

"Yeah, I think you're probably right."

"I'm sure he just wants to lend his support."

"That's fine. I just don't want him trying to tell me what to do."

"Maybe he'll hand you a blank check for your legal defense."

I laughed. "Yeah, that sounds like him. When I was in the shower, I was thinking what Adam would do if he was in my situation and dad showed up out of the blue."

"That may not have gone over well."

"I think Adam would've told him to get lost." I envisioned the conversation, and for some reason it made me smile.

I stood from the table, pulled a glass from the cupboard and filled it with cold water from the sink. The salt from lunch was working its way through my system and making me thirsty. As I drank the water, I thought about the DNA I was leaving behind. The jars of black cap jam were still sitting on the counter. It was just yesterday morning the three of us had made the jam, but right now it seemed like weeks ago. I wondered if Ally (or whatever the hell her name was) would throw the jars away or end up eating them. In the hours since Max told me, my anger had begun to fade, but the embarrassment was still as strong as ever. I knew Connor would ask me about her at some point, maybe even today, but I still didn't know what to tell him. I supposed the truth would be better than making something up, but I suspected he'd be hurt and probably a little embarrassed himself. I think he'd thought he'd made a new friend, albeit one who was quite a bit older. They'd hit it off, and discovering it wasn't real was definitely going to bother him. *Get the bad guy at all costs, right? Who gives a shit if an innocent eleven-year-old ends up as collateral damage?*

I finished my water and we headed out. As soon as I turned off the stairwell, I saw the reporter. It surprised me even though it shouldn't have. Max told me they'd be calling, and there were already several messages on my phone. It was a young kid from one of the local stations. I recognized him, but I didn't know his name. He was standing in the parking lot, holding a microphone with a cameraman beside him. As I approached, I saw a white van with Channel 2 painted on the side. It occurred to me once they learned about Eddie, there'd be more than one reporter waiting, and they probably wouldn't be local.

"Mr. Abbot," the reporter said, "your mother's ex-boyfriend was found Saturday at Valley View Golf Course, and you've been charged with making a false statement to federal agents. Would you care to comment?" he extended the microphone toward me.

"No, but thank you for asking."

Jen laughed despite herself. The young reporter didn't seem amused. He continued firing questions as we climbed into her car and drove away.

When we got to Laura's house, I saw Connor in the backyard with my father. Connor was in his batting stance, and it looked like my dad was giving him pointers. "Jesus, is he actually giving him batting tips?"

"Sure looks like it," Jen said.

"He makes it up here once every two years, and he's giving my son batting tips."

"His grandson, don't forget." I gave her a look and she smiled. "Sorry. I used to try to soften up Adam, too, but it never went over well."

"Yeah, I didn't have much luck on that front, myself."

Jen parked the car and we climbed into the muggy air. Luckily, the cloud cover was still present, or it would have been unbearably hot. Even without direct sunlight, it was still pretty hazy. I looked up at the lush treetops and they seemed to almost melt into the clouds. I continued into the backyard where my dad was telling Connor how to hold his elbow. I glanced back toward the patio and saw Laura sitting beside a woman I didn't recognize. Just then I remembered Jen telling me he brought a lady friend. I waved to them, and the two women waved back.

"Hey, Dad," I said. "I didn't expect to see you here today."

"Hi, Danny. I heard you ran into some trouble."

"Yeah, I guess you could say that."

Connor ran over and gave me a tight hug. It had been a long time since I'd received an embrace like that. I hugged him back just as hard.

"Hi, Dad," Connor said.

"Hi, bud."

"Mom told me what happened. What's gonna happen to you, Dad?"

I wondered how much Laura had told him. It hurt to hear the concern in his voice. "Nothing, bud. Everything's going to work out fine."

"I think I fixed his swing," Dad said.

"Great, thank you, Dad. He's only batting about .490 this year."

"Yeah, I noticed he's keeping his hands—"

"Okay, Dad, thanks. Why don't we go inside and get a drink, and you can introduce me to your friend." Connor ran deeper into the backyard to grab a few baseballs. I looked at my dad and lowered my voice. "What happened to Jan?"

"We're taking a break. Me and Connie have been dating for a couple weeks now."

"Well, Dad, Jen and I came over here to say hello, but we don't have a lot of time. We have to go back later this afternoon to meet with my lawyer."

"Yeah, Laura filled me in on some of the details. I have to tell you, it's hard to believe this is happening after thirty-some years."

"We're on the same page there, Dad."

"I don't want to take up a lot of your time, Danny. I just wanted you to know that I'm here to help in any way I can."

"I appreciate that, but I'm just not sure what you'll be able to do."

"And there's also some things I want to tell you. Mind if I sit in with you and Jen for a little while?"

That's all I need. My dad meant well, but he wasn't usually what anyone would call helpful. "I'm not sure if that's such a good idea, Dad."

He acted as if he hadn't heard me. "So, you got caught lying to the Feds, huh?"

Before I could answer, Connor was right beside us. He'd caught up without making a sound "What'd you get caught doing, Dad?"

"Nothing, Connor," I said, glaring at my dad. "Okay, let's go inside. We can talk for a few minutes."

We walked onto the patio and I met Connie. She seemed nice enough, although I doubted she had any idea what she was getting involved with in my father. Laura gave me a look that said *I'm sorry, there was nothing I could do.* She stayed outside with Connie and Connor while I went inside with Jen and my father. A few seconds later, we were sitting around the kitchen table. "Dad, you know you can't talk about any of this in front of Connor, right?"

"Well, you can't keep him in the dark, can you?"

"We don't, Dad, but he doesn't need to know everything."

"Got it. So, what happened with the Feds? Laura was a little sketchy on that part of it."

"There's nothing to tell. Initially, we were going to leave me out of it, which means I wouldn't have known what happened between Mark and Adam. So, when the federal agents asked me about it, I said I had no idea what happened. Unfortunately, they'd already set up the surveillance in my apartment, so they knew it was a lie." Because of what Max said, I wasn't going to tell my dad about Eddie.

"You shouldn't have said anything. Didn't your lawyer tell you that?"

We'd been talking for two minutes, and I'd already had enough. "Yes, Dad, my lawyer told me not to talk to them, but it's more complicated than that. I don't have time to get into it right now. Actually, we have to go over a few things, so—"

"Sure, I'll leave you to it, but there's something I want to tell you first."

I was out of patience and didn't care if he knew it. "What is it now, Dad?"

"Your mother probably never told you I came to see her a week or two after Mark disappeared, did she?"

"No, she didn't."

"Yeah, I guess she wouldn't. She never forgave me, either. I guess she wouldn't tell you guys something that might make me look good."

I wasn't in the mood to have a pity party for my father, nor did I have the time. "Dad, look, I really don't have time for this."

"I was worried about you guys, especially Adam. I was living in Cleveland then, but I had some friends who still lived here. They told me Mark's disappearance was becoming a pretty big story around here and that there were people who thought Adam was involved. I had a few friends who had some ties to some pretty bad guys. Not only the Mafia in Everton but all throughout the Northeast. I asked them to dig into Mark's background to see if there was anything that might help us out. I could tell your mother knew something, but she wouldn't tell me what it was. She was sticking to the same story. Mark hit her and then skipped town with some other woman."

I wanted to say that men skipping town with other women was a familiar theme in Mom's life, but I managed to keep it in.

"So, anyway," Dad continued, "these are the guys who found out about the gambling debts and the money he owed to a loan shark. There were a couple local bookies he owed money to, but a lot of it was to a loan shark out of Utica. I think it was ten grand if I remember right. I was the one who told the local police about those debts."

"Mom never told me that."

My dad nodded. "There was something else I found out from those guys. They told me Mark had some trouble with a woman he'd been living with. This was two or three years after his divorce from his first wife, and he was living up in the Syracuse area, a town called DeWitt, I think. They said the woman's daughter had accused him of molesting her. I never got the full story of what happened, as far as if the police were involved or if he ever got charged with anything, but I think the mother had a drug problem. Don't hold me to that last part, though. It was a long time ago."

I looked at Jen and our eyes locked. We were both thinking the same thing. If we could find this girl, and she was willing to talk, it would corroborate Jess's tape and eliminate any doubt Mark was a child molester. "Did you tell Mom any of that?"

"I did, and I remember her being very interested, but she never said why. At the time, I thought it was just because she loved him, but I guess it was because he'd done the same thing to Jess."

"Did you ever get a name, Dad?"

"No, unfortunately, and I can't go back and ask them now because all those people are either dead or senile." He chuckled as if that was funny. "I'm pretty sure Mark worked at Carrier, and if I'm not mistaken, so did the woman. Maybe you can find someone there who remembers her name."

"I doubt it. It was nearly forty years ago."

"You're probably right. Well, that's really what I came up here to tell you, Danny, and of course, to give you some moral support if I could." He started to get up and then sat back down. "Your mother was a good person, Danny. I know you know that already, and I suppose it won't help if I say I was a stupid bastard back then."

"No, it helps." I stared at my dad for several seconds, and then we both started laughing. "Mom always told us to keep a sense of humor."

My dad stopped smiling and grew serious again. "Before I left that day, I told her I wanted to get back into your lives if I could. I knew she wouldn't take me back, and I didn't want that anyway, but I wanted to be more involved with you three." He paused as if I was going to say something, but I didn't. "She told me it wasn't a good time. She said Adam wasn't ready yet, and neither was she."

I don't know what he expected me to say, maybe that I wished we could have done more together when I was a kid. I was thinking it, but I couldn't bring myself to say it. He had to have known I wasn't going to say anything against our mom. "Well, Dad, things don't always work out the way you want them to."

He looked at me for a long time. "Yeah, I think you're right about that."

I guess I was a lot more like Adam than I thought.

62

A few minutes later my dad went back out and Laura came in. One look at her face told me she wanted to know what was going on. I knew there would be a serious conversation about why I'd never told her about any of this before, but she knew better than to say anything about it now, especially in front of Jen. I filled her in on what my dad had just told us, and I also told her about the recording Mom made of Jess. I knew exactly what she was going to say.

"If you find that second girl," Laura said, "won't it support Jess's tape?"

"That's what we're hoping."

"Then why don't you just involve the police? They could probably find this girl, or I guess she'd be a woman now, couldn't they?"

Her question told me she didn't fully grasp the situation. Then I remembered she didn't know about Eddie yet. I was tempted to tell her, but it was just too risky. I couldn't imagine Eddie's involvement would remain an unknown for too long, but I didn't want the leak originating from me. It was partly because Max had asked me to keep it quiet, but I also felt like it could work to my advantage if I ever tried to contact Eddie directly. "Well, it's not really that simple, Laura. The police are working with the Feds, and they aren't exactly interested in helping us."

Laura was nodding, and I could tell the gears were turning. "So, you want to find her yourself?"

"That's right."

"But I guess I don't see how that's going to help if the police have no interest in helping you."

I almost said Eddie wouldn't want that information going public, but I caught myself. "Well, it could help because it could make it look like the Feds are going after two guys who helped bring down a child molester."

"And a potential murderer," Laura said, "Don't forget that. If you didn't show up, he would've killed Adam."

"That's what Adam kept saying in his video, and it's true, but since it didn't happen that way, no one cares. They're still going to go after us, but if we have *two* girls Mark molested, it could embarrass the hell out of them, and it might give us some leverage."

"What about an ex-wife? Was Mark ever married? Maybe she'd remember the name of the woman Mark was living with at the time."

It struck me as funny that Laura would think of that. It was a good idea but one we couldn't pursue. I wondered if the media had tried to contact Mark's ex. "Actually, my mom did talk about her a couple times. I don't think she and Mark had much contact after their divorce. Mom said she moved away and they never spoke."

"Did Mark have any kids?"

"A son, but we obviously can't ask *him* about it."

Just then my dad popped his head back in to tell me he and Connie were taking Connor for ice cream. Laura, Jen, and I hunkered around the table and talked about the best way to proceed. We all agreed we'd probably have to hire a private investigator to have any chance of finding this second victim. Jen mentioned Max would likely have an investigator or two in mind. But hiring an investigator, especially a good one, would be both expensive and risky. I felt like half of these guys were either former police officers or former federal agents, and upstate New York is a pretty small place. If we were going to try to surprise the Feds and perhaps even Eddie with this new information, the last thing I wanted was for them to hear we were using a private investigator to dig into Mark's past.

The conversation turned to doing something on our own. All we really knew was that Mark and possibly his girlfriend had been working at Carrier Corporation during that time period. We knew we'd have to find someone who worked with Mark that also remembered *her*. That would be hard enough if Mark had spent his entire career there, but since he'd worked there for only a couple years, it would be all but impossible.

We spent a half hour scouring the Internet. I used Connor's PC in the living room and both Laura and Jen used their laptops. Naturally, there were countless articles about Mark and the discovery of his bones at the golf course. In just two days the story had gone national. According to Laura, all the cable news shows had covered the story, focusing mostly on the murder and how my family managed to keep it a secret all these years. The stories revolved around Adam and Mom, but since they were both dead, there wasn't much to keep it going. There had been some coverage of the charges against me and Billy, but that didn't carry the same weight as parading the actual killer in front of the camera. The shows didn't have any information regarding my involvement that night, nor did they know what Mark had done to Jess. They followed the same basic storyline Adam's video promoted, specifically that Mark had struck my mother and everything followed from there. The story didn't appear to be headed toward long-term cable news fame, but I knew that would change instantly if they learned about Eddie.

We weren't able to find anything about Mark living in Syracuse, other than one article that mentioned he'd lived in a couple different locations in upstate New York. It said he'd lived in Albany and Syracuse before moving to Binghamton in the winter of 1977. We reassembled at the kitchen table around 12:40 and started talking about what we were going to do, if anything.

"Okay," Jen said, "what about this? And I'm just throwing this out there."

"Absolutely," I said.

"We drive up to Carrier, posing as lawyers. We could say we represent Mark Dolan's estate, claiming that some assets were recently released. We'll tell them we're looking for a woman identified only as someone that used to be in a relationship with Mark, and someone who also worked at Carrier."

"And we tell them what? That we have some money for her?"

"I don't think we have to get specific, but that's the implication."

"Why wouldn't we have her name?"

"We could say records were lost, but there's a mention of a woman from Carrier in the paperwork. Or we could say a relative of Mark remembers her and knows he wanted certain assets reaching her."

"Why now, though? Just because Mark was found?"

"Yes. We could say there were assets that weren't released until a couple days ago. You have to assume they heard about the story, so it will probably make sense."

"I don't know, Jen. It's not a bad idea, but we're going to get sent to human resources, and they're going to want a lot more information before releasing old records. And that's if they even still have them. What about calling instead of going up there?"

"We could try it, but I think showing up and looking like lawyers has a much better chance of success."

"I don't like it," Laura said. "The last thing you need right now is to get arrested in Syracuse for impersonating a couple of lawyers."

We discussed it for a while longer, then Jen excused herself to use the bathroom. She left the kitchen and headed up the stairs. Laura looked at me, and I knew I was in trouble.

"I can't believe you never told me any of this," she said. Anyone who heard her tone would have thought we were still married.

"Watching my brother get strangled and then hitting my future stepdad in the head with a baseball bat aren't generally topics you bring up at the dinner table."

"We were married for twenty years, Dan. I think there were plenty of opportunities to bring it up."

"I didn't *want* to talk about it, Laura. It was the most awful thing that ever happened to me. Don't you get it?" I could hear my voice rising, but the last thing I needed was an argument with my ex-wife.

She continued staring at me. "I just feel bad that I couldn't help you with it."

"Really? Because it sounds like you're pissed." It hit me then what was happening. Laura was hurt that I'd never told her. As soon as that thought came, it was followed by another. *Too bad.* I felt myself slipping toward that place I'd mostly left behind, that period in my life where Laura decided that screwing the guidance counselor was more important than me and Connor. I took a deep breath and shook it off as best I could. "I'm sorry, Laura. I should have told you, but can we talk about this later? Right now I need to figure out what I'm going to do."

Her expression softened. "I'm sorry. I know you don't need this right now." She was about to say more when we heard Jen coming back down the stairs. Laura stood from the table and headed into the other room before coming right back. "I forgot to give this to you, Dan." She tossed a small newspaper in front of me. "I picked it up a couple days ago. There's a picture inside of Connor standing on second base."

I looked down and saw it was a recent edition of the Tremon News. It was a little like a Pennysaver, but it covered local youth sports. There was a similar paper when I was growing up in Everton. Someone told me recently they were loading all the old editions online. As soon as that thought hit me, another one rolled into my head. "He was a coach!" I said, holding up the paper. "Mark always used to tell me he coached Little League! There had to be a paper like this in Syracuse, probably more than one. Maybe we can find someone from one of his teams."

"*If* he coached up there," Laura said.

"I'll bet you anything he did," I said.

Jen looked at me. "You said Eddie was in law school when Mark lived in Everton, right?"

"Yeah, either in law school or still an undergrad. So?"

"Well, that was 1978, and this would've probably been around 1975 or '76, so Eddie would've been too old for Little League, wouldn't he?"

"Shit, you're right. He probably would've already been nineteen or twenty at the time. Eddie might have played Teener League, though, which would have been around '72 or '73."

"Do we know where Mark lived in 1973?" Laura asked.

"I don't know—wait a second. Mark coached softball, too. I can remember him telling Jess that when he was trying to get her to play. And he didn't have a daughter, so he had to be coaching the daughter of one of his girlfriends."

"Okay," Jen said, "so we search Mark Dolan, softball coach, Dewitt. That's the town your dad said, right?"

"That's what he said, but he wasn't positive."

The three of us hopped back online and went to work. I hadn't even finished typing in my first search on Connor's PC when Jen shrieked from the kitchen.

"Oh, my God, Dan. Get in here!" I ran back into the kitchen where Jen had her laptop open on the table. Her eyes darted from the screen to me and then back to the screen again. "The Chronicle, June 24, 1976. Look." She pointed at the screen even though it wasn't necessary.

The monitor showed what looked like a screenshot of a local Pennysaver. Running along the left edge was an ad for Vito's Italian Deli. *6-inch subs just ninety-nine cents! Foot-longs a dollar seventy-nine! Daily lunch specials!* To the right of the advertisement was an article about Post 1900 winning the regular-season Little League softball title. Above the article was the team photo, complete with the names of the players and coaches. I didn't have to read the names to find Mark. He was a little heavier than when he lived in Everton, but there was no denying it was him.

"I don't believe it," Laura said. "Jen, can you zoom in on that photo?"

Jen clicked on the image and it doubled in size. It was obvious the paper had been scanned at a high resolution because the image was surprisingly clear. Mark's face was unmistakable. He was smiling, as was most everyone else in the photo. "The devil in the flesh," Jen said.

Looking at this photo was like taking another trip back in time. It wasn't as powerful as hearing Jess and Mom talking, but it was still pretty strange. I could almost hear Mark's voice as he walked into our house, announcing he had a Nate's pizza with sausage.

There were eleven girls in the photo, and they all looked to be about Connor's age. Mark was standing on one end of the team while another coach stood on the other. According to the names listed beneath, the second coach was James Schneider. There were two other coaches listed, but they weren't in the picture.

"The girl we're looking for has to be in this picture," I said. "He had to be dating her mother. Otherwise, he wouldn't have been coaching the team."

Laura was already back in her seat, typing away on her laptop. A second later she turned it toward me. "According to this, there are five James Schneiders listed in New York. Three are down near the city. Of those three, one's eighty-four and the other two are under forty. The fourth is sixty-five and he lives in Albany. The last one lives in DeWitt. He's sixty-seven, according to the site."

"How old would you say this guy looks here?" I asked.

"I'd say about thirty or so," Laura said.

"That would make him around seventy today," I said.

"So, we start with the guy in DeWitt," Jen said, "and then we try the guy in Albany if it isn't him. Do you want to call them or should I?"

"Let's think this through for a second," I said. "What are we going to say? Do we tell the truth, or do we have some kind of story? Chances are this guy's seen the news."

"I agree," Jen said. "Why don't we stick with the story about assets being released from Mark's estate? We'll tell them Mark left this woman some money. We don't know her name, but we know her daughter played on his softball team."

"That still sounds a little strange to me. Why wouldn't we know the woman's name?"

"Records were lost. A relative remembers the daughter played on his softball team. We found the team photo, and we're working backwards to find the mother."

"That would be a very unusual relative."

"True, but all we need is a name. Most people aren't that skeptical. They know Mark's remains were found a couple days ago. I don't think it's a stretch to think certain assets could get released after something like that."

"I don't know, Jen."

"What's the worst that can happen? He won't tell us? If that happens we start contacting these girls directly. One of them is bound to know something."

That gave me an idea. "Let me look at these names for a second. Laura, grab a pen and paper and write these names down, would you?"

I read through the list of names, leaving out the Schneider girl as well as the daughters of the other two coaches. After a brief discussion, we also left out the one set of twins. We all agreed if Mark had molested one of the girls, he probably would've molested the other. My dad didn't say anything about a second sister, but I made a mental note to check with him later. That left five girls we figured were most likely to be Mark's victim. I looked back at the picture, thinking there was a good chance Mark had probably stood near the child he was molesting. The girl directly in front of him was one of the five on our list. Her name was Colleen Sparks. I took a closer look and noticed something I hadn't before. Mark's hand was on her left shoulder, his fingers barely visible in the black and white photo. Then I noticed something else and a pit formed in my stomach. Colleen was the only girl in the photo who wasn't smiling.

Laura got out some cheese and crackers while Jen and I talked about the best way to handle the call. Jen offered to do it, saying she'd follow the basic idea she'd just outlined. We agreed to start with the James Schneider living in DeWitt, NY. If he turned out to be the one in the photo, she'd ask him if Mark had been dating Colleen's mother.

I did a quick search for Colleen Sparks and found a fifty-one-year-old Colleen Sparks-Baker living in Albany, NY. It was tempting to call her directly, but we decided to stick with the original plan. If Mr. Schneider confirmed it was, in fact, Spark's mother that Mark had been dating, and if we could determine she was now living in Albany, we'd probably drive up for a face-to-face meeting.

Laura said she was starting to feel too nervous, so she took the cheese and crackers outside while we made the calls. My dad and Connie had gotten back from the ice cream shop, and Connor was playing catch in the backyard with a friend from down the street. We decided to use the home line for better reception and also so caller ID wouldn't read Abbot. Laura had gone back to her maiden name, so it would show Talon. We practiced two or three times, and when Jen felt like she was ready, we each found a notebook. Jen's had the names of the five girls listed at the top. My heart was hammering away in my chest as Jen dialed the number.

"Hello?" a voice answered. It was a male, but he sounded younger, like maybe late thirties or early forties. Jen was angling the phone away from her ear, so I could hear everything.

"Hello," Jen said pleasantly. "I'm looking for a Mr. James Schneider."

"This is he."

"Hello, Mr. Schneider. My name is Jen Collins, and I'm calling from Collins and Talon Law Firm in Binghamton, NY."

"May I ask what this is regarding?" the man said.

I could hear the change in his voice, and I began to wonder if pretending to be lawyers was such a great idea.

"Of course. We're settling the estate of Mark Dolan, and we're trying to track down the mother of a girl who played on his softball team back in the mid-1970s. And we have information that you were also a coach?"

"Oh, you're talking about my father. This has to do with the guy they found on the golf course a few days ago, right?"

"Yes, that's correct. Is your father available?"

"Unfortunately, he's not. He passed away last summer."

"Oh, I'm sorry to hear that," Jen said. I wrote *get info for sister* on Jen's notepad. She read it quick and nodded. "That means it must have been your sister who was on the team then? Andrea, is it?"

"Yes, that's right."

"And do you happen to have her phone number?"

"I'm sorry, who is this again?"

"My name is Jen Collins, and I'm calling from Collins and Talon Law Firm."

"And why do you want to talk to her?"

"We're settling the estate of Mark Dolan, and we're trying to locate a girl who played on his softball team. Actually, we're looking for the girl's mother."

"Well, I'm not comfortable giving out my sister's phone number, but why don't you give me *your* number, and I'll pass the information on to her. If she wants to call you back, she can."

I tapped Jen on the arm and whispered, "Ask him if he knows which girl it was."

"Mr. Schneider, do you happen to know which girl's mother Mr. Dolan was seeing at the time?"

"Ah, no. I was only five or six-years-old when my sister played on that team."

"Was it Colleen Spark's mother by any chance?"

"Again, I have no idea."

I could hear his tone sliding from cautious to annoyed. "Leave him our number," I whispered.

Jen gave him her cell number and hung up the phone. "We can always try to find Andrea's number ourselves," she said.

"Why don't we try one of the other coaches first, one of the ones not pictured."

We looked back at Jen's computer and retrieved the names of the two coaches who weren't in the team photo. The first was a man named Michael Abrams, and the second was someone named Sandy Jester. Given that we were talking about the 1970s, and that the other three coaches were men, we figured Sandy was probably a male, as well.

Jen searched Michael Abrams and found several men living in New York State. We both agreed the most likely candidate was a sixty-eight-year-old man living in Fayetteville, another suburb of Syracuse. I flipped to a fresh sheet in my notebook. When Jen was ready, she dialed the number.

"Hello?" a voice answered. It was a female, maybe sixty-five or seventy-years-old.

"Hello," Jen said pleasantly. "I'm looking for Michael Abrams."

"Yes, may I ask who's calling?"

"My name is Jen Collins, and I'm calling from Collins and Talon Law Firm in Binghamton, NY."

"Oh, may I tell him what it's regarding? I'm his wife, and he gets confused in the afternoons."

Oh, shit.

"Absolutely," Jen said. "We're settling the estate of Mark Dolan, and we're trying to track down the mother of a girl who played on his softball team back in the mid-1970s. And we've learned that your husband might have also been a coach. The team was Post 1900 in DeWitt, NY."

There was a pause, and I feared the woman might have just hung up on us.

"Oh, that was a very long time ago, Miss Collins."

"Yes, it was and some records were lost. That's why we're working backwards to try to find this woman."

"Well, unfortunately, my husband isn't remembering things too well anymore, and I don't think he'd remember that information even on one of his better days. That had to be forty years ago."

"I understand, Mrs. Abrams. I'm very familiar with that type of situation. My father passed away four years ago from Alzheimer's."

It was a lie, and a risky one, but I thought it might work. If the woman believed her, Jen might have just created a bond.

There was another pause. "Well, I'm sorry to hear that. What was it you wanted to know about that girl, Miss Collins?"

I thought her tone had sharpened. I got the sense she might have sniffed out the lie or maybe resented that Jen had mentioned it at all.

"Well, um, we're settling the state of Mark Dol—"

"Yes, you said that. My husband has the memory issues, but I'm doing just fine."

Jen began fumbling her words, and I could tell she'd been thrown off. I pointed at Colleen Spark's name, hoping to get her back on track.

"Mrs. Abrams, I was wondering if you could confirm something for me. We think the girl's name was Colleen Sparks, and we believe Mr. Dolan had a relationship with her mother. Do you recognize that name?"

Another silence, longer this time.

"There *was* a Sparks girl on the team, Ms. Collins," she said, her tone turning harsher, "but her mother wasn't that bastard's girlfriend."

Jen stuttered again, and I couldn't blame her. That would've stopped me cold, as well.

"What did you say this was in regards to again, Miss Collins?"

"Um, Mr. Dolan died recently, and we're trying to settle his estate—"

"I'm not sure where you're getting your information from, young lady, but they just pulled the son of a bitch's bones out of the ground two days ago. He's been dead for thirty-nine years."

"Yes, I'm sorry, Mrs. Abrams. That's what I meant to say."

"What firm are you with again, Ms. Collins?"

"I—"

I could tell Jen was losing it. I also sensed Mrs. Abrams was about to hang up. "Tell her," I said. "Tell her who you are."

"Who is that?" Mrs. Abrams said. "Am I on a speakerphone? I think I've had just about enough of this."

"I'm sorry I lied, Mrs. Abrams." I could tell right away Jen had her confidence back. "My name is Jen Abbot. My husband, Adam, is the one who killed Mark in self-defense. That other voice you heard is his brother, Dan."

There was another pause, but this time I knew she wasn't hanging up. "Well, honey, let me tell you something. I don't care if your husband went over there, gave him a big hug and then blew his head off with a God damn shotgun. I'm just glad the monster ended up dead, so he couldn't hurt any more little girls." Jen squeezed my hand hard. I think it was mostly out of relief because she thought she'd blown it. "Now, why do you want to know the name of the family he messed with?"

Jen looked at me for approval, and I whispered, "Anything but Eddie."

"The FBI is coming down extremely hard on the people who helped Adam all those years ago, mainly because they can't prosecute *him*. He died last year. If we can find another girl that Mark abused, we might have something to fight them with."

"Another girl?"

"Yes, Mark molested their sister, which is why Adam went over to his house that night in the first place."

"So, you're banking on the hope the FBI doesn't want the world to know what a disgusting human being Mark was. Am I right?"

"You're exactly right," Jen said.

"I have my reservations, but I'm going to tell you the name of the girl anyway. Her name is Kelly Newman. Her mother was Mark's girlfriend for two summers, maybe longer. That's how long our daughter was on the team. Her mother wasn't the brightest bulb in the pack if you know what I mean, but she was a nice woman. She had some issues with alcohol and some other drugs, as well. I heard it was heroin at the time, but I don't know for sure. What I do know is that she was no match for that bastard, and he took full advantage of the opportunity. I'm not going to tell you what he did. I'll let Kelly tell you that if she wants to, but let me just say thank God for your husband. Sometimes God sends down angels to take care of his mistakes."

"Amen to that," Jen said. I was certain that somewhere Adam was cringing.

"I just wish he'd sent him earlier, but it's not my place to question. I think Kelly lives in Cortland now or maybe it's Homer, and she also got married. I think her last name is Johnson now. She and her husband ran a diner there last I heard. And it is Homer, now that I think about it. Not Cortland. I need you to promise me two things before you contact her, though."

"Of course."

"The first is that you don't tell her I gave you her name. She may guess, but I'll deny it. The only reason I told you is because I have no doubt you need help, especially if they don't know what kind of monster he really was.

I can't promise she *will* help you, but she might, and anyone who helped kill that bastard deserves all the help I can give them."

"You have our word," Jen said.

"The second thing is that you'll respect her wishes. I don't know exactly what you have planned, but she may not want to help you. She's living her life as best she can, and she may have buried all that stuff so deep it's not coming back up. I hope you can understand that and respect it. And be kind to her. I guess that's a third promise. Be kind to her because she's been through a hell of a lot, even after Mark moved away. Sometimes once darkness finds you, it's awfully hard to shake it off. You end up dragging it along with you, no matter where you go."

"We will," Jen said, "I promise you. Thank you so much for your help."

"Well, I don't how much I helped you, but like I said, I had to try." She paused again for a few seconds, and this time I really did think we might have lost the connection. "And, Mrs. Abbot, do me one more favor when the time suits you."

"Of course. Anything."

"Put some flowers on your husband's grave for me."

And right then a realization came to me hard and raw. It had started forming soon after the conversation started, but it hit home now with a painful thud deep inside. If my mother were alive today, this is how she would've sounded.

Summer

63

The last day of school was a half day, and it fell on a Thursday. Mr. Holt was in a good mood (as was everyone else) but his good moods were different from the other adults. Certainly, he was happier than usual, smiling more and all that, but you also felt like he was only one small step away from slipping into his other persona — the one that got off on humiliating children, and if he was lucky, making them cry, as well.

On that particular day, he avoided the short trip to psychoville, although he came pretty close when Big Mike wouldn't stop talking to Lisa again. I think had it been any other day, Mr. Holt would have used the incident as an excuse to lose it, but on that day he kept the beast locked up. Mr. Holt wasn't stupid, and I think he knew flipping out on the final day of school — when literally everyone was relaxed and happy — would have made him look bad in the eyes of the other teachers. I also think he'd been trying to keep a low profile since our mom's visit. There'd been a couple outbursts, but they were mild compared to what he was capable of.

When the final bell rang, I slipped out of my room — purposely avoiding Mr. Holt — and entered the screaming chaos that was the main hallway. It was a little like a Friday, crazy and euphoric, only that day it was ten times worse. A few of the teachers were standing in their doorways, smiling and waving goodbye to students as they rushed by, laughing and yelling their way toward the doors and the freedom beyond. I made my way out of the school and down the steps to the spot where I usually waited for Jess.

In the days following the incident with Mark, Jess wasn't herself. She spent a lot of time in her room and just didn't seem to be as perky or happy as she normally was. I think it was about a week later, right about the same time the police started showing up at our house, when she started acting like the old Jess again. I think that was when she began to realize Mark really had gone away for a while and maybe even forever. Jess was devastated that Mark would hit our mom, but despite that (and despite what he'd done to her) I think she still missed him. Mark had become a pretty big part of our lives, and it was weird to suddenly not have him around. I know I would've missed him, too, had I not watched him strangling Adam with my own eyes.

While Jess had rebounded, it was a different story with Mom and Adam. Both had become noticeably quieter since the incident, even withdrawn in Adam's case. He wasn't joking around like he usually did, and he didn't seem to have any patience with me or Jess. He was spending even more time at Julia's house, and when he wasn't doing that, he was fishing somewhere with Billy. Mom told me not to worry about him. She said he just needed some time. I think it was harder for Adam than it was for Mom because she'd been able to slip into protection mode. Yes, she had loved Mark and had planned on marrying him, and it was devastating for her to learn what he truly was, but she had three children to worry about. Two of them were still in elementary school and the third could easily be charged with murder if she slipped up. Protecting her children from the aftermath of that night had become another full-time job. She simply didn't have the luxury of coming apart. Adam worried about us and protected us, too, but it wasn't the same. I began to realize, even then, that what happened at Mark's house had affected him in a way I didn't fully understand. I think I went through something similar in the coming years, but at ten, the emotions were beyond my ability to comprehend.

I watched the door as Jess literally came running out of the school. She found me at the bottom of the stairs and flashed a huge smile. It was a smile that said *summer vacation* and nearly everyone was sporting it. I didn't see Matt approaching until he hit me on the arm.

"Hey, Danny," he said, smiling, "we made it. No more Mr. Holt."

"Yeah, that's right," I said, laughing. While I'd been waiting for that moment since the day he took over the class, I realized I hadn't been thinking much about it lately. I think it was because Mr. Holt had toned it down dramatically and also because he ignored me. But as I stood there with Matt that day, I realized that unless a teaching spot opened up in the sixth-grade (and Mr. Holt decided to take it), I was free of him forever. I decided to switch topics. "How are All-Stars going?" Six kids from J&F made the All-Star teams. Truck, Eric, and Justin made the A-team, and Matt, Chris, and Paul made the B.

"It's going good. We're 3-0 so far."

"Wow, you've already played three games?" It was sort of funny. I knew All-Stars had started, but since I wasn't on the team, Matt and I just didn't talk baseball much anymore.

"Yeah, we started playing last week." Matt glanced around like he was looking for someone. "Hey, I have to go. Maybe I'll see you around this summer."

For some reason I had the feeling that wouldn't happen even though Matt didn't live that far away. "Yeah, let's play some basketball sometime."

"Okay, Danny, see ya." He slapped me lightly on the shoulder and then disappeared behind a bus.

When Jess reached me, she was still smiling. I had a sudden flashback of the day she learned Mr. Holt was our new teacher. We were in the exact same spot where we'd first talked about it. I thought about Ms. Becker, wondering again if she would ever be back. I'd heard a couple rumors recently, neither of them good. But despite that, I figured she had to be coming back at some point—if not the fall, then maybe the following year. I thought for the hundredth time that God might allow horrible things to happen to people like Mark, but not to beautiful people like Ms. Becker.

"Hi, Danny," Jess said. "It's officially summer vacation." Her smile grew even wider.

I couldn't help but smile back at her. "I know. It's awesome, isn't it?" We turned and started walking along the fence, past the buses.

"Hey, Danny!" a voice yelled from behind me. "You better practice your hitting this summer!"

I turned back just in time to see Jason hop onto a bus and disappear. It was a technique he'd perfected in the days and weeks after the championship game. *The drive by.* After the game, and the one moment I'd rendered him speechless, he spent a full week avoiding me. Then he began implementing his new game plan. He'd think up some comment—usually something along the lines of how lucky we got that night—and then deliver it as he ran past me. The idea, of course, was so I couldn't come back at him with anything. Little did he know I'd lost the appetite for the everyday back and forth. I just couldn't bring myself to respond anymore. He'd worn me down, and in that regard, at least, I suppose he'd won. In that first week alone, he hit me with a few other gems, including that Hardy had the flu that night and even that the ump admitted he'd blown the close call with Matt at home plate. He'd deliver his line and then slink into the bathroom, or onto the playground, or in this particular case, the bus, before I even knew what hit me. I knew he was still hurting over the loss, so for the most part, I didn't let it get to me.

"That kid's a jerk," Jess said, her smile gone.

"Yeah, he is."

"You should beat him up."

I remember looking at my little sister, a bit shocked. I would have expected a comment like that from Adam but not from Jess. "Yeah, maybe I will." I wanted Jess to think I'd stand up for myself, but I knew I'd never do anything close to that. It just wasn't in my nature.

Jess stopped walking and looked at me, her eyes wide. I could tell whatever was coming next had nothing to do with Jason Billings. "I just thought of something, Danny. What if I get Mr. Holt next year?"

My mind fell back to our mother's recent visit to the school. I never told Jess about it, but I didn't know if Mom had filled her in. "That's not gonna happen, Jess. Mom would never let them do that."

"Are you sure?"

"Positive. Mom already told me she talked to the principal about Mr. Holt, so there's no way they'll put you in his class next year. Besides, Ms. Becker might still come back."

"Anna Krandall said she's still in a coma."

That was the same rumor I'd heard from Jackie. "Maybe, but I think she'll be back anyway."

I thought Jess was going to keep talking about Ms. Becker, but she surprised me again. "Do you think Mom is sad about Mark?"

"I think she is sad, but she also knows he was a bad person."

"I think she's sad, too. I think she misses him." She looked at me, and I could tell her mind was working again. "You didn't tell her what happened, did you?"

I realized right away what was bothering her. She was worried I'd told Mom what Mark did and that that was what led to their fight — the fight that made Mark leave. "No, Jess, I promise I didn't, but I think *you* should. I think she'd wanna know."

Jess nodded but didn't say anything. We continued in silence, walking along the fence that bordered the school yard. When we cleared the last of the buses, Jess grabbed my hand and I held it.

64

Sunday Afternoon

We headed out for Homer at 12:55. The tentative plan was to meet back at Max's office at 6:00, so that gave us plenty of time. There was some discussion on whether or not we should just wait and talk everything over with Max, but we opted not to. For one, we thought Kelly would talk more readily with us than with a lawyer or investigator, and two, I had an idea that what I was going to do with this information—if, in fact, she gave us any—wasn't going to have much to do with the law.

After a few minutes on the Internet, we learned Kelly and Andrew Johnson ran Alexa's Diner in Homer, NY, and had been doing so since 2001. They were open for breakfast and lunch only, so we figured they'd be closed by the time we got there. Luckily for us, there was only one Kelly Johnson living in Homer, and she lived at 26 Hadlow Drive, which appeared to be less than a mile from the restaurant. We decided to take a quick trip to the diner to see if Kelly might still be there, and if she wasn't, it was on to the house.

I wanted to take the more scenic Route 26 to Whitney Point and then Route 11 into the Cortland-Homer area, but in the end we chose Route 81 because it was faster. The muggy day had given way to afternoon showers, and it rained most of the way there. By the time we took the Homer exit, I was feeling both nervous and depressed—two emotions I didn't typically feel at the same time. It wasn't easy to ask someone to pull up a painful past and share it with the world, especially when it had been buried for a long time. I knew that truth better than most, and my past was nowhere near as painful as Kelly Johnson's had been. Five minutes on the phone with Mrs. Abrams was enough to convince me of that.

Alexa's Diner was on Lamar Avenue, which, according to our GPS, ran parallel with Route 81. Two quick turns after our exit and we were on the right road. "In half a mile," the electronic voice said, "your destination is on the right."

"Turn that off, would you?" I asked. There was something about the artificial voice making me even more nervous. Jen pressed a button and the voice was gone.

We kicked around a couple different approaches, but the only one that made sense was the truth. I would tell Kelly who I was and then ask her if she would help us. I had a basic plan forming for what I might do if she said yes, but beyond that I was flying blind. All I knew for sure was Eddie wouldn't want his father to be publicly exposed for what he was. I doubted he cared much about his father's legacy, but I knew he cared about how it would reflect on him. If he knew we could prove his dad was a child molester, our situation could improve dramatically. And there was also a chance it could go away altogether.

"It should be another quarter mile or so on the right," Jen said.

"Yep. I'm already looking."

"Listen, I've been thinking, and you probably have, as well. If Kelly won't help us, we could have Max put a private investigator on it. I seriously doubt Jess and Kelly are the only two girls he's molested. If someone digs back far enough, there has to be others. Maybe even family members."

I nodded as I continued searching for the diner. The street had been mostly commercial, but it was starting to bend residential. Stretches of modest homes were now mixing with laundromats and car washes. "I think you're right. I'm sure there are more, but maybe not as many as you think. Mark was very smart, and he was patient, too. He was in our family for well over a year before he tried anything on Jess. And we also need to be careful. Our leverage goes away if Mark's little secret goes public."

"What do you mean?"

"Let's assume Kelly is willing to help us. I think our best shot is to get this new information to Eddie privately, and then let him think about the consequences if it gets out there."

"There has to be people who already know. Mrs. Abrams knew what was going on, so plenty of other people must know, too, including the police."

"I'm sure there *were* other people who knew, but that was over forty years ago, and a lot of them are dead now. And for whatever reason, there were never any charges brought. There may be a few rumors floating around, but there's no proof of anything. And that's a far cry from having it talked about every day on the cable news shows."

Jen nodded. "That's for sure."

"Let's see what happens here, and then we'll talk to Max about it."

We drove past another row of houses and a small apartment complex. I wondered if maybe there was a federal agent pretending to live in one of them right now, perhaps making a complete fool of some other lonely middle-aged guy. The thought made me chuckle out loud.

"What's so funny?"

"I'll tell you later. There it is," I said, pointing.

Alexa's Diner was a one-story yellow structure with large windows running along the road side. It was built like a long, double-wide trailer with a slanted aluminum roof hanging over on both sides. A large white sign with *Alexa's Diner* in cursive blue letters was affixed to the top. The place wasn't much to look at, but then again, the best diners usually weren't.

There were several cars in the parking lot, and I could see people still sitting inside. I checked my phone and saw it was 1:52. My guess was they closed their doors at 2:00 pm. I pulled into the parking lot next to an old blue pickup truck and looked over at Jen. "We'll go inside and grab a seat at one of the booths. Then we'll ask for Kelly."

"Sounds good, but we better hurry. They close at two o'clock."

"How do you know that?"

"I saw the hours on the door."

"Show off."

We walked in the diner and were met by the familiar smells of bacon, toast, and coffee. I wasn't hungry, but the smell still made me crave a cheese and sausage omelet. We reached the small sign asking us to *Please wait to be seated* just as our waitress hurried by with two plates in her hand. One was carrying a short stack of pancakes, and the other had what looked like a club sandwich. It was hard to tell for sure. She was really moving.

"I'll be right with you," she said, forcing a smile. Her face was friendly enough, but her voice was saying *We close at two, and you walk in here at seven minutes of?*

Jen looked at me and whispered, "I guess they don't like last-minute customers."

I was about to respond when the harried young waitress was back. She looked to be about seventeen or eighteen and appeared to be on the tail end of her shift. She had a look that said *I've had enough for one day.* I saw another waitress on the other side of the room, but it looked like our girl had this side all by her herself.

"You just made it," she said, still smiling. "We close at two." Again, if you weren't paying close attention to her voice (or if you weren't all that observant), you might have thought she was happy to see us. "Are you going to be having lunch today?" She reached toward a stack of menus sitting near the cash register.

"No, just coffee today," I said.

This time we got a true smile. "Whew, I need to leave right at two today." She started leading us toward one of the open tables.

You have to love the honesty of youth, I thought. "Do you mind if we take the corner booth over there?" It was well away from the few remaining people and would be a more private place to talk, assuming Kelly was even here.

"Sure, go-head. I'll be right back with your coffees. Do you need cream?"

"Yes, please." I watched as she disappeared around the corner and out of sight. As we walked to our booth, a funny thought crossed my mind. I wondered if our waitress was the namesake for the diner. If my age estimate was right, she would have been a toddler when they opened it.

Jen climbed in on one side of the booth, and I climbed in on the other — the side facing back out onto the restaurant. No sooner did I slide in and get comfortable when our waitress whipped back around the corner, carrying two ceramic mugs, a carafe, and a plate of creamers. She slid the cups onto the table and had them filled with steaming coffee in record time. Not only was she in a big hurry, she'd been doing this a while — probably a couple years or more. I did some quick math. If she was seventeen now and had been here for two years, that was younger than the legal working age. The feeling she was Kelly and Andrew's daughter intensified.

"Sugars are on the table," she said, before turning to go.

"Is Kelly here today?"

"Yep, she's cooking today. Same as every Sunday."

"Could you ask her to come out here for a minute when she gets a chance?"

The girl looked at us more closely than before. I thought she was going to ask who we were, but she didn't. I was glad because I realized I didn't have a good answer. I got the feeling this wasn't exactly an unusual request, but more often than not, she recognized the folks who were making it.

"Sure, I'll get her, but it'll probably be ten or fifteen minutes. There's a few orders that just came in."

"Of course. No problem." As soon as she walked away, it hit me that I'd better have a good answer if she came back and asked me who we were. I didn't want to say my real name because if Kelly had been watching the news, she'd know who we were and might just slip out the back door. Just then our waitress came bouncing around the corner again. *Shit.* I looked at Jen and the answer came to me.

"She's actually really busy today," she said, no longer sounding all that friendly.

I knew exactly what had happened. She reported to Kelly that two people she'd never seen before — two people that walked in at 1:53 and ordered coffee — wanted to talk to her. With Mark being found two days ago, there was a damn good chance the visit was related.

"Oh, I'm Dan Talon, and this is my wife, Jennifer. I went to school with your mom, and I just wanted to say hello." I realized my mistake right away.

"Okay," she said cautiously, "I'll tell her, but she's real busy, so she might not be able to."

"Okay, no problem." On the way home, it would hit me how lucky I was. If that wasn't her daughter, there's no telling how she might have reacted, but the fact I knew probably convinced her I was telling the truth.

A minute later a large woman wearing shorts and an apron walked around the corner and headed down the aisle toward the table. Her brown hair, slipping hard toward gray, was pulled back into a short ponytail. She stood about 5'7" and carried an extra fifty pounds in her legs and backside. I tried to reconcile the woman approaching us with the young girl in the team photograph but couldn't.

"Here she comes," I said, being careful not to make eye contact until she got close.

Jen sucked in a deep breath to calm her nerves, and I did the same. The woman smiled and waved to a couple at another table and then worked her way all the way back to our booth. She fixed her eyes on me as she approached. It was clear she didn't recognize me, and she made no effort to pretend she did.

"Can I help you?" she said, still studying me.

"I hope so," I said, trying to keep my voice steady. I suddenly had the strong feeling we were going about this in the wrong way. "I'm sorry to stop in unannounced like this, Mrs. Johnson, but we needed to talk to you. My name is Dan Abbot."

"I thought your name was—" I could see in her eyes she'd made the connection. They'd turned from uneasy and wary to cold and calculating. She was trying to figure out why we were here and what we wanted from her. After a few seconds, she seemed to realize we weren't dangerous, and her shoulders dropped. "You're his brother," she said. "The one that killed him."

I nodded. "Yes, that's right. Adam was my brother."

She turned to Jen. "Who are you?"

There wasn't an ounce of nuance or subtlety to her words, but it wasn't because she was angry or because she was trying to be rude. It seemed to me she was a simple woman who'd had an extremely difficult life. I sensed things had been much better in recent years with her family and the diner, but I also felt like the scales hadn't evened out yet. I suspected they never would.

"My name is Jen. I was Adam's wife. He passed away over a year ago."

Kelly nodded. "Well, I sort a figured someone would come to see me eventually, but I didn't expect it would be you two. We're gonna close up shop in a few minutes. When we get everyone cleared out a here, I'll come back and talk to you. Should be about twenty minutes or so. Just yell if you need more coffee. It's on the house."

She walked back up the aisle, and I noticed she had a slight limp. Her gait was more like a waddle than a true stride. All in all, she didn't appear to be in very good shape. She reminded me of my father's sister who had diabetes. She died of a heart attack at fifty-nine, and I feared this woman might be destined for a similar fate. I watched her turn the corner, heading back toward the kitchen, and then I looked at Jen. "So far, so good."

"Absolutely. I was terrified she would tell us to get the hell out of here."

"Me, too."

Jen's eyes grew wide. "How did you know our waitress was her daughter?"

"I didn't. It was just a lucky guess, but it slipped out by accident. I panicked."

"Like me on the phone earlier."

"You did fine. Don't worry about it."

"Maybe we should start a private detective agency when this is over."

I laughed. "Yeah, that'd be a great idea."

Twenty minutes later the diner was empty except for me and Jen. Even the waitresses had scooted out and driven away. I was beginning to wonder if Kelly had changed her mind and slipped out when she came shuffling around the corner. She was carrying a carafe of coffee and a mug. When she reached our table, she refilled our mugs without asking and then filled hers. Jen had already moved over and Kelly slid in beside her with an audible sigh. The entire booth rocked as she sat down. She added cream and one teaspoon of sugar to her coffee before gulping down half the cup.

"It's been a long day already," Kelly said, looking up at me. "And no offense, but it didn't get any shorter when you two walked in."

"None taken," I said.

"Well, I've been thinking about what you might want, and I think I figured it out." She took another long sip of coffee. "Mind if I take a shot at it?"

"By all means."

"Against my better judgment, I watched some a the news coverage yesterday. They're trying to crucify that guy — Billy, I think his name is — for helping your brother all those years ago. And they'd like to do the same to you, but all they could get you for was lying to those federal agents. And you think if you can find someone that Mark abused, it'll help sway public opinion against the prosecution."

"That's pretty close. We already have one person who was abused, but we don't think she'll be believed, so we're looking for a second."

Kelly stared at me for a solid three seconds. "Well, I'm not gonna lie to you. You've got my interest. Who else did Mark get after?"

"My sister, Jess. Adam went over there that night to rough him up a little, or maybe a lot, and Mark tried to kill him. I showed up in the middle of it and knocked him out. I'm not exactly sure what happened after that. I suspect Adam suffocated him, but I don't think we'll ever know for sure.

Later that night, Billy helped Adam bury the body. That part I just found out about two days ago."

"Wish I had brothers like you two," Kelly said, without smiling. "Mine left when I was eleven. Mark wasn't screwing me yet, but he'd already started coming in my room at night when my mom was out getting high."

I had no idea what to say, so I just listened. I noticed Jen had started to tear-up despite her best efforts to fight it. I felt for her. A few short days ago, she knew about some long-ago secret that had almost no chance of seeing daylight. Now it was out and exposed, and she was sitting beside a woman who'd been repeatedly raped as a child. It was overwhelming.

Kelly put her hand on Jen's. "If those tears are for me, honey, you don't have to worry. I made peace with it a long time ago. If I didn't, I wouldn't be here. Trust me. The way I look at it, somebody's always got it worse. I'm not gonna tell you it was a picnic, but there are plenty who had it a lot worse than me." She took another sip of coffee and then refilled her mug. "Why don't you think your sister will be believed?"

"Jess died over twenty years ago, but my mother recorded her story when she was young. She was smart enough to know she might need it someday to defend Adam."

"And if you've got me, then people will believe Jess."

"That's about it."

"Well, I wanna help you, and I'm not just saying that because I feel like it. I owe something to you and your brother. Mark had left town by the time he went missing, as you know, but before that happened, I lived every day thinking he was gonna show up at my next softball game or find me on my way home from school to take me away somewhere. Then we heard that he'd disappeared. After a while, I began to realize he was gone for good, and I was finally able to relax. Or at least that's when I *started* to be able to relax. Anyway, the problem is my daughter, Alexa. She has no idea all that happened to me as a kid."

"She was our waitress, right?"

"That's right. She ran out to go to a movie with her girlfriends. She's a sweet kid, and I want her to get through high school before she learns about all that shit."

"So, no one around here knows about your connection to Mark?"

"There's a few. My husband, Andy, for one. There used to be others, but they've been passing away here in recent years. It was a long time ago, as you know. I ended up moving to Connecticut when my mom died. I had an aunt who lived out there. I was just thirteen at the time. I didn't come back until I was thirty-two, and there was nobody here in Homer that knew about Mark. I met Andy when I was working at a restaurant in Cortland. A few years later, we had Alexa and opened up the diner."

"It looks like you guys are doing pretty well for yourselves."

She smiled. "We do okay. It's not easy running a diner, but it's ours. You know what I mean?"

I nodded. I'd never had my own thing, but I'd always dreamed about it. Maybe now was the time to take the leap and start something. Of course, there were two big questions that needed answers. What in the heck was I going to start? And what kind of business can you run from prison? "Kelly, what if we can keep it out of the news? Does that change anything?"

"How in God's name are you gonna do that? It's all over the place right now and will be until the next big story comes around."

"Well, let me ask you something. Until today you were probably under the impression that Adam went to see Mark that night because he hit our mother, right?"

"That's what I saw on the news." She smiled. "I see where you're going. Not everything gets released to the media."

"Exactly."

"Especially with Mark's son being involved," Jen added. She realized her mistake right away and looked at me with wide eyes.

"It's okay," I said.

Kelly straightened in her seat. "What about Mark's son?"

I could tell right away she not only knew him, but there was some history there, as well. "So, you knew Eddie?"

"Yeah, I knew him. Not all that well, really, but I knew him. From what I remember, he lived with his mother in Pennsylvania."

"Well, you're not going to believe this, but little Eddie grew up to become a pretty powerful lawyer. He's the U.S. Attorney for the Western District of New York State."

"Jesus Christ." Kelly sighed and leaned back against the seat. The entire booth shifted again. She closed her eyes and brought her hands to her face.

"Kelly, are you okay?" Jen asked.

Kelly didn't answer for several seconds. Finally, she lowered her hands and let out another long sigh. "I'm okay, honey, but I'm gonna need something stronger than coffee to talk about this one."

Fifteen minutes later we were sitting in the back of Ray's Tavern, a dark, dingy dive about a quarter-mile from the diner. The bar smelled like stale beer and dirty mop water. It wasn't the kind of place I would've chosen to continue our conversation, but I wasn't calling the shots. On the bright side, there were no televisions and it was almost empty. Two college kids sat at the bar, sipping draft beer and eating popcorn. There were several tables and a couple booths behind the pool table. We found the one in the corner, as far away from the bar as possible. Country music—I think it was Waylon Jennings—played quietly through mounted speakers.

The last thing I wanted right now was a drink, but Kelly insisted. I ordered a rum and Coke and Kelly ordered a double bourbon on the rocks. Jen ordered an ice water and got away with it only because she was driving. A scruffy looking middle-aged guy in a Metallica tee-shirt delivered the drinks. I had a feeling it was Ray, but I didn't ask.

"Here you go, Kel," the man said, as he placed the drink in front of her. He dropped my drink in front of me with a quick glance and then took a much longer one at Jen as he handed her the ice water. Kelly saw me staring at him as he finally walked away.

"Don't worry about him. He's harmless." She turned to Jen. "It's the ones who don't give a looker like you the once-over that you need to worry about."

Jen smiled and blushed. I made a note to make fun of her later.

Kelly took a healthy sip of the bourbon and swallowed it with a small grimace. "I didn't drink for fifteen years. I had to give it up when I was trying to kick the other stuff. I still don't drink a lot, but every now and then I feel like I need one, and this is definitely one a those times."

I nodded and took a sip of my rum and Coke.

Kelly continued on. "Let's see. Where do I begin this part? It *could* be really long, but it doesn't need to be. And I know you folks have to get back, so I'll give you the short version."

"Whatever you want to do."

"It was October, I think, when my mom came home from work and caught me and Mark screwing in her bed. She'd stopped by the school to pick me up early, but I wasn't there. They told her I went home sick. We never heard her, so she caught us right in the act."

Suddenly, I was back in the doorway of my bedroom, watching Laura and McBride. Then Kelly's words from the diner came back to me. *Somebody's always got it worse.*

"She said she had no idea, and maybe she didn't, but I think she was just in denial. There were enough signs if she'd looked hard enough. Of course, that's not easy to do when you've got a needle in your arm every night. As you might expect, she went crazy, threatening to call the police and all that. I'll never forget Mark. He acted like a fucking professor, as calm and as rational as he could possibly be. He explained to her that they'd take me away from her if she did that. 'They don't let minors stay with heroin addicts,' he said, along with a bunch a other things. It worked. He scared her into keeping her mouth shut, at least for a while. I wasn't much help. By then, I was getting high every day—just weed mostly—and I'd also gotten used to being with Mark. God help me, there were times I looked forward to it. I thought it was normal.

"Anyway, Mark agreed to leave town and then disappeared. We heard lots a things. He went back to his wife in Pennsylvania. He moved to

Canada. Someone said he went to California, but eventually we heard he turned up just an hour or so down the road in Binghamton."

She paused and we both took the opportunity to take another sip of our drinks. I was already starting to feel the effects of the rum and told myself to slow down. The last thing I needed right now was to get drunk.

"My mom actually got cleaned up for a while. After watching her spiral down for so long, I never thought she could do it, but she did. I stayed with friends while she went to some rehab program in Syracuse. She was only gone a couple weeks, maybe three, which should a been the first clue it wasn't gonna last. But for a while anyway, she stayed off the heroin. She kept telling me she was gonna go back to school to be a nurse, and then we were gonna move to Connecticut to live near her sister. Like I told you, that's where I ended up."

Kelly paused again, and I could see she was getting emotional as she talked about her mother. She took another hit of the bourbon, and I noticed it was almost gone. She glanced over her shoulder for the bartender, but he'd slipped into the back room.

"At some point my mother started talking about going to the police. Never in front a me, but I'd eavesdrop on her phone conversations with her friends. She was getting her life together and was starting to feel confident about reporting Mark without losing me. By then I wasn't under Mark's spell anymore and was pretty impressed with what my mother was doing. I was still smoking pot every day and having sex with just about every boy I met, but I still loved my mom and wanted to be with her. Well, one a her stupid girlfriends told the wrong person what she was planning, and it got back to Mark. She had some friends that were absolute morons. He called my mother one night, and I heard almost the whole conversation. My mom thought I was asleep, but I snuck into her room and picked up the other phone. Mark offered to pay her some money — $10,000 — if she agreed not to go to the police. We were living in a shit hole at the time, and I'm sure my mom saw a down payment on a house with that money. I know my mom was gonna go to the police anyway, money or no money, but I'll get to all that in a minute.

"It was maybe a week later when we got a knock on the door. My mom had been acting all nervous that afternoon, so I knew something was up. She sent me to my room, but I snuck back down the hall and watched as she let a man into our apartment. I saw right away it was Eddie. He gave my mom a bag, and I watched as she dumped it on the kitchen table. It was more money than I'd ever seen in my life."

"Jesus Christ," I said, "Eddie delivered the payoff."

Kelly looked at me and smiled. "That he did."

65

By the time the bartender brought the second round of drinks, we'd confirmed that he was, in fact, Ray. According to Kelly they met a decade ago when they first bought their house. Kelly and her husband walked over when they wanted a drink, and Ray was a regular at the diner.

Three more college kids, two girls and one guy, had joined the other two who were still sitting at the bar. *To be young and in college again,* I thought. I wondered briefly if I'd go back if given the chance. I decided I probably wouldn't, but it would be a blast to do it for a month or two.

The shock of learning Eddie delivered a payoff for his father's crimes all those years ago had already worn off. Or I suppose if I really thought about it, it hadn't penetrated to the level of shock in the first place. With the insanity of the last two days, I think I realized anything was possible. This was just one more thing in a long line.

"Okay, Kelly," I said, "I guess I have to ask you something."

She picked up her fresh drink and took a long sip. She smiled and I could tell she was starting to feel pretty good. "Well, Dan, you go-head and ask away. I don't think you could surprise me now even if you tried."

I hoped she didn't order another bourbon. This was serious business, and the last thing I needed was for her to get drunk. She might agree to all sorts of things now and then wake up tomorrow morning wondering what the hell she was thinking. "Given what you now know about Eddie, are you still against coming forward?"

Almost as if she were reading my mind, Kelly looked at me, pointed to her drink and smiled again. "It doesn't matter how many a these I have, my feelings on that subject aren't gonna change. If I can get Alexa into college, or better yet beyond it, before she learns about this shit, then I'd be tickled pink. But I will say it does make a difference knowing that Eddie is being such a prick, given that he knew what his father was." She looked away for a moment. "I'm also not crazy about letting Billy sit in a jail cell for helping out your brother that night. How many years are they trying to get on him?"

"They're going for the max — fifteen years. I find it hard to believe they'll get that, but I also find it hard to believe they found Mark's body on a golf course or that Eddie became a federal prosecutor. So, who knows?"

"And you?"

"The max is five years. My lawyer says it will probably be half that if they're serious and probation if they're not. With Eddie involved to some degree, my guess is they're serious."

"And you said your sister's tape won't be enough?"

"Well, so far we're the only two who have heard it, but we don't think it will be. All they have to say is that my mother made it to protect Adam. And given everything else she did at the time, it's not really out of the question."

"What do you mean? What else did she do?"

I explained to Kelly how she made me and Adam practice that morning at the kitchen table. I also told her about all the things she did in the following weeks and months to protect the three of us. That led into a discussion about Adam's video.

When I finished Kelly said, "And the Feds heard all this because they planted bugs in your place?"

"That's right."

"Christ."

"Yeah, exactly."

"So, if they've got me, that makes Jess's tape the truth, and we can show the world what Mark really was?"

I nodded. "That's about right."

"And you'd also have something that could get little Eddie into a whole lot a trouble."

"I've been thinking about that, too. It would be awfully hard to prove, as far as anyone pressing criminal charges."

"And the statute of limitations would have to be long over by now," Jen added.

"I think you're right," I said, "but it could end his career as a federal prosecutor."

"If people believe me," Kelly said.

"That's right, and of course, it's risky as hell. He could come after you awfully hard." We all nodded, unsure of where to go from there. "Okay, I have another idea," I said, "but I need to ask you a couple things first."

"Shoot."

"Do you think anyone else might have seen Eddie the night he made the payoff?"

"Not that I know of. Certainly not anyone that knew who he was."

"Do you think your mom told anyone?"

"I doubt it. My mom's friends weren't the kind a people you'd wanna know you had cash laying around. There were a couple a women like her — good people that just got snared by the drugs — but most were lowlifes. They would have broken in and taken that money without even batting an eye.

Like I said, my mom's plan was to go to the police. That money was for us, and she didn't want anyone else knowing about it."

It occurred to me, and not for the first time, that this had to be the money Mark obtained from the loan shark—the money that made everyone stop looking for him. Since Eddie was directly involved, he knew where the money went and maybe even where it was from. Either way, he knew his dad hadn't skipped town because of it.

"Okay," I said, "my idea—if it works—would keep your story out of the media."

"I'm all ears," Kelly said, smiling.

Jen was staring at me and shaking her head. "No way, Dan. I know we were talking about it earlier, but it's too risky."

"Jen, everything we do from this point on is risky. Even if Kelly came forward and told her story, there are no guarantees. We can't prove Eddie's the one who delivered the money, which opens her up to all sorts of trouble."

Kelly chuckled. "Someone wanna fill me in here, since it sounds like we're talking about my future?"

"Dan's thinking about blackmailing a federal prosecutor," Jen said.

Kelly looked at me and smiled. In that moment she looked twenty years younger. I didn't think I'd have any trouble picking her out of that team photo now. "Dan, it's a good thing for you I'm married because I'm starting to like you more and more."

I smiled, hoping like hell I wouldn't blush. "Here's the situation. If we could prove Eddie delivered the cash, we could go after him hard. He'd have to resign, which would blow this whole thing up, but unfortunately that's not the case. We can't prove it, and Eddie just has to say you're mistaken about the ID. And that means we can't do it publicly."

Kelly leaned in closer. "So, you go to Eddie on your own and tell him to drop the charges or you're gonna go to the media."

Jen grabbed my hand. "And then Dan goes to jail for twenty years for trying to blackmail a federal prosecutor."

"Well, first of all, I won't be that blunt. Second of all, it will be his word against mine. I'm not going to let him record it, for Christ's sake."

"I like it," Kelly said. "Once you mention my name, he'll panic. You won't need to say anything about the payoff. I'm sure he'll know we can't prove it, but it sure isn't something he wants the world to learn about."

"But you have to know, Kelly, if it doesn't work or something goes wrong, your story is going to be everywhere. You'll have no choice but to tell the world what happened, and then in all likelihood defend it."

Kelly seemed to ponder this for a moment. "And you think if Eddie wants to make everything go away, he can do that?"

"That's what I think. Or at least he has some major influence. And I've been thinking about it all afternoon. I don't think I have any other options."

Kelly finished off her second drink, looked at Jen, and then back at me. "Lemme go talk to my husband about this. I don't wanna make any decisions without his input." She slid out of the booth and Jen followed her, probably thinking she would need to drive her. "You're fine, honey. I live just three houses down the road. Get yourself some chicken wings. They're really good here. My favorite are the barbecue, but the hot ones are good, too."

Neither one of us was hungry, but after Kelly left, we decided to take her advice and ordered a dozen barbecue wings. By now it was almost 3:30, and if I kept putting down rum and Coke's without getting anything new in my stomach, I'd be in trouble. And the way Ray made them—looking more like iced teas than Coke—I was already halfway there.

As soon as Kelly left, Jen started in about my plan to contact Eddie myself. She was right in saying it was extremely risky, but I felt like if I did it right, it was our best option. Jen kept telling me to talk to Max about it before I did anything. I told her I would even though I wasn't completely sure about that. I just couldn't envision how we'd be able to convey the information to Eddie without several more people finding out about it. And, of course, the more people who knew about it, the bigger the chance someone would leak it. And once that happened, it would be all but worthless to us. Sure, it might improve our situation by swaying public opinion, but both Billy and I would still be facing criminal charges. And there was always the chance it could backfire. Eddie would be on the warpath, and things might actually get worse, not only for me and Billy but also for Kelly. The deciding factor for me was that Kelly wanted to keep everything out of the media. If I could get to Eddie and talk to him directly, I felt like we could keep it quiet. I wasn't going to tell Jen this, but if Kelly gave me the go-ahead, I'd pretty much already made up my mind.

The wings were every bit as good as advertised, and I found I was hungrier than I thought. We had just killed the last couple when Kelly came waddling up to our booth.

"I see you two took my advice. They're good, aren't they?"

"They are *so* good," Jen said, wiping her mouth with a napkin.

Kelly slid into the booth next to Jen, and Ray came back around to see if we needed anything else. Kelly ordered an iced tea, and Jen ordered another water. I was glad Kelly didn't order another bourbon. It wasn't that she couldn't handle her liquor. In fact, she'd just downed about six shots, and if I hadn't been sitting right here watching, I wouldn't have known it. I just didn't want the booze to be even a slight influence. Whatever she decided could very well affect the rest of her life.

"Okay," Kelly started. "Andy feels bad he couldn't get over here himself. He slipped a disc moving a stove in the diner last week and isn't feeling so hot. He sends a handshake your way, though, Dan, and wishes he could a met you both. Maybe we can have you two up when this thing's over, and we can celebrate."

"We'd love that," I said.

"Absolutely," Jen added, smiling.

"He also said that 'he would fuck you up' if you messed with us. Those are his words, not mine." Kelly gave me a half-smile, but I could tell she wasn't joking. "He's 6'2" and goes about three hundred pounds, and he has a nasty temper, to boot, so please don't take that lightly. Alexa's his baby girl, and if something hurts her, it hurts him. You know what I mean?"

"I know exactly what you mean," I said, smiling. "And I promise I won't mess with you. I haven't lied to you, and I won't. There is a chance of this getting out, like I said, but I'd never do anything to hurt you intentionally or to deceive you."

"Fair enough, and I didn't think you would, but he made me promise to tell you that. Now, here's what we decided. We both like the idea a you holding this over Eddie's head privately. How you do it is up to you, although I agree with Jen that you need to be very careful. If something goes wrong, we didn't know anything about it, and I'd deny any knowledge of it."

"Of course."

"Now, don't say anything about me seeing Eddie at my mom's place. You don't need it for one thing, and I've got a feeling that information— more than anything else—can get me into a whole lot a trouble because I can't prove it. Just mentioning my name should be enough to accomplish what you're after."

"And if something goes wrong? Say it gets leaked by somebody?"

"Well, then I'm prepared to come forward and tell my story under oath. Alexa's gonna find out eventually, and like Andy said, it's not like she's a baby anymore. It's probably about time she starts learning what goes on in this world." She looked at Jen and then back to me. "I'm happy to say she's lived a pretty sheltered life."

"Well, I don't know how I'm going to be able to thank you," I said.

"Don't worry about it. You did me a favor thirty-some years ago, and I'm just happy to be able to repay it. I just hope it helps as much as you think it might. But I'm not doing it just for you. I'm doing it mostly for my mom because I know she'd want me to. She'd never be able to rest if she knew two men were heading to jail for helping take that sick asshole out a circulation."

Ray came back with our drinks and set them on the table. I asked him for the check and he nodded.

"I've got one more thing to tell you," Kelly said, "if you've got the time. I think it will help you understand why I've done things the way I've done them, and why I've made the decision to help you now."

"Of course we have the time," I said.

"About three weeks after Eddie delivered that money, or it might a been closer to four, my mom had a relapse. She went out with some friends and had a few drinks. Later, she ended up with a couple junkie friends, and they came back to our apartment. I was out at the time, no doubt getting high myself. Well, there was a guy with her friend that she didn't know very well. After he got my mom and her friend stoned out a their minds, he went through my mom's stuff and found about half the money. Thankfully, she'd been smart enough to hide it in more than one place. She couldn't go to the police because it was blackmail hush money to begin with.

"I think she thought she'd beaten it, and when she relapsed, it devastated her. Combine that with what she'd let happen to me and losing half the money, and she just couldn't take it. She went into work the next day — some shit hole restaurant she was waitressing at — and shot herself in the head behind the dumpster. There was a note waiting for me when I got home. It told me where the rest a the money was and exactly what to do with it. I hopped on a bus that night out to my aunt's house and never looked back. She thought she was doing what was best for me. Aunt Susan had her life together, and she loved me. I'm not gonna tell you everything was peaches and cream because it wasn't, but it was the best thing my mom could a done for me, and it's why I'm where I am today. There isn't a day that goes by that I don't wish my mom didn't do it, but I'm not sure we would a made it, and my mom knew that. So, I'm doing this for her more than any other reason."

"I hope you don't mind me saying," I said, "but I think she would've been awfully proud of you."

"Me, too," Jen said.

Kelly smiled. "Well, I appreciate you guys saying that."

Jen ran into the bathroom while I paid the bar tab. By now a couple different groups of men had wandered into the bar and started drinking. Two of the college-age boys came to the back and started up a game of pool. Ray had turned up the music, and it was easy to imagine what this place was like on a busy Friday night.

After Ray thanked us for the business and walked away, Kelly looked at me. "I can tell that Jen doesn't want you to do this, so lemme ask you while she's in the bathroom. What do you think you're gonna do?"

"For sure? I don't know. Jen wants me to run everything by my lawyer, and I just might do that. But I also might just tell her I'm doing that and then go see Eddie directly."

"How you gonna get him alone?"

"I actually haven't thought it through yet. I suppose I'll try to find out where he lives and catch him on his way into work, or maybe it would be better to catch him on his way coming home. I don't know yet. I don't think I can just request a meeting in his office, though."

"Whatever you decide to do, be careful. From what I remember, he was a prick, even at twenty-years-old. Now he's got all this power, and I'm assuming he's had it for a long time. He's not gonna be somebody to fuck around with."

"I think you're probably right."

"Wherever you talk to him, make sure he doesn't record your conversation. If you're patient, maybe you can catch him running into a Starbucks or a Dunkin' Donuts or something. I used to live with a guy who did a lot a private detective-type work. I even helped him. He used to watch people for a while to get their patterns. I don't know if that's an option for you, but you might learn he makes the same stops every day or at least every other day."

"That's a good idea, but like I said, I haven't even gotten that far yet."

"But be careful there, too. Following somebody's an art form in itself. If you're not good at it or if you're too obvious, you'll be noticed."

I nodded but didn't say anything. Just thinking about it was making me nervous. It was easy to say I was going to confront Eddie, but actually doing it was another matter altogether.

"Do me a favor, Dan, would you?"

"Anything."

"Lemme know your plan when you decide to do something. I'd just like to know what's happening in case Eddie hears my name and decides to do something stupid. I doubt he would, but you never know." She gave me her cell number and I loaded it into my phone. "Just make sure you call me from a safe phone, and I wouldn't consider your cell phone safe after what they did. It would probably be best if you used a friend's cell phone or even a pay phone if you can find one. And whatever you do, don't text me. If something goes wrong and they charge you with blackmail, there can't be any link back to me. Just so we're clear, I'll back you up and testify to everything I've told you, but I didn't know anything about your plans to contact Eddie. As far as I knew, you were gonna work it legally through your lawyer. Okay?"

"Got it, and I'll let you know what I plan on doing...once I decide myself."

Right then Jen came back from the bathroom, and the three of us began making our way out of the bar.

66

The trip back to Binghamton seemed to take almost no time at all. Both of us were still in a state of mild shock over what had happened. Spending the afternoon with someone who'd gone through what Kelly had was both depressing and strangely uplifting at the same time. It was like witnessing the entire gamut of human capabilities, from pure evil to the unshakable will to survive. There had been plenty of times in the last year when I was feeling sorry for myself, but my experiences were nothing compared to what Kelly had endured. It was even hard to lament over something as recent and embarrassing as Ally when I thought about where Kelly had been.

Much to my surprise, Jen hadn't brought up what she thought we should do with our newfound information. I think she was confident Max would shut down any thoughts I might have of traveling to Buffalo and contacting Eddie myself. Little did she know I'd already made up my mind to do it. It was simply a matter of when. According to Max, things would move fairly slowly from this point forward, so there was no immediate rush. But my gut was telling me to do it as fast as possible — certainly before my arraignment in two weeks. The longer this thing went, the more entrenched both sides would become and the harder it would be to change anything. There was also the chance some other woman would see Mark's name in the news and come forward with allegations of molestation. And if that happened, any leverage we might have had with Eddie would probably be gone.

Jen was driving, and I'd slipped into a short nap when I felt my cell phone vibrate. I pulled it out of my pocket and noted the time as 4:42 pm. It was a text from Max. I read it and turned to Jen. "Max says he can't meet with us until tomorrow afternoon. He says he'll text me tomorrow morning to confirm the time."

"That stinks. I'm dying to tell him about Kelly."

It occurred to me I should probably say something similar, but I decided to pretend I was going back to sleep. Inside, I was wondering if I could get to Buffalo and back in time to meet with Max. I figured it was doable if I could get on the road early enough. The big question was could I find Eddie and get him alone? I'd done some digging online, and I knew where the U.S. Attorney's Building was located. I figured it might be worth a try to get there early, get a good parking spot and wait for him to come into work. From what I could tell from Google Maps, there didn't appear to be a private parking garage. It looked like all employees, from the janitors to the U.S. Attorney himself, had to park on the street or in a parking lot and enter through one of the doors. And if I struck out catching him on the way into the building, I could always just go inside and ask to see him. Initially, I didn't think that was an option, but the more I thought about it, the more plausible the idea seemed. I knew Eddie personally, and there was a time when we were almost stepbrothers. Why couldn't I go to him to ask for help? He wasn't officially involved in the case, so I wouldn't technically be breaking Judge Tarver's conditions. Of course, it would be highly unusual, given the circumstances, but I was confident Eddie would see me. His first instinct might be to turn me away, but curiosity and possibly even a dormant fear would get the best of him. I could almost see his face turning an ashen white when his secretary told him Danny Abbot was waiting to see him in the lobby. I wondered what might go through his mind at that moment. I doubt he'd suspect we'd found Kelly, but he couldn't totally rule it out, either. Would I get an arrogant, defiant Eddie — a man who was finally getting a chance to revel in an Abbot's misfortune — or would I get a nervous Eddie who was wondering exactly what we'd managed to discover.

Either way, the conversation would be recorded, so I'd have to be extremely careful. I figured I could start by professing how much I loved his father and then work my way into what he'd done to Jess and the tape my mother made. That would rattle him, although he would never show it. And then I would move on to Kelly as definitive proof our mutually beloved Mark had had a serious problem. If he didn't lose his cool at that point, I would innocently ask if there was anything he could do to help me. I wouldn't get to call Mark a child rapist or watch Eddie's expression as I threatened to tell the family secrets to the world, but the innocent, ask for help approach might just piss him off even more. As long as I didn't make any threats, I wasn't doing anything wrong. Eddie would know exactly what I was doing, of course, but he wouldn't be able to do a damn thing about it. I wouldn't even have to get specific. The implication would be crystal clear. *Get the charges dropped or you're going to see me and Kelly having coffee with Ashleigh Banfield on HLN.* Of course, he might not be there at all, which could make for a wasted trip, but it wasn't like he lived in Chicago or Los Angeles. I could be there and back in under eight hours.

I was deep in thought when I heard Jen's voice again. "Are you going to answer me?"

"I'm sorry. I was daydreaming. What did you say?"

"I said you haven't changed your mind about telling Max, have you?"

"No. Like I said, I'll run it by him and see what he says. Hopefully, he'll have some good ideas."

Jen looked at me. I got the feeling she wanted to call my bluff, but she didn't. We passed by the exits for Binghamton and neared the ramp that would take us across the river toward her hotel.

"I don't know, Dan. I'm pretty tired. I didn't sleep well last night. I think I need to go back to the hotel and lie down for a little while, especially since we're not meeting with Max today."

"I think I'm going to do the same. Do you want me to drop you off and take your car? I can pick you up later."

"No, that's all right. I'll drop you off. That way we'll both have cars. Maybe we can have dinner at Laura's later."

"Yeah, three more hours with my dad is exactly what I need."

Jen laughed. "You should text Laura. Maybe he went back already."

"I doubt it." I started a text, but it was a response to Max. *OK, we'll talk in the morning. I was doing some research online. There are two US Attorney offices in Western NY. Where does Eddie work?*

A minute later I heard back. *Likely has an office in both Rochester and Buffalo but main one is Buffalo. Planning to stop by?*

Yeah I'm sure he'd love that. No, I was just wondering. Talk to you in the am. Thanks for today.

No problem.

Right then my phone rang. It was Connor. "Hey, bud."

"Hi, Dad. Where are you?"

"I'm almost back in town. What are you doing?"

"I'm just wondering what's going on. Mom told me some more stuff, but she said I should talk to you about it. Will I see you tonight?"

"Yes, definitely. I'm really tired, so I think I'm going to get some sleep first, and then I'll come over. Okay?"

"Promise, Dad?"

"I promise. I'll call you later."

"Okay. Love you."

"Love you, too. Hey, Connor?"

"Yeah?"

"Whatever Grandpa told you about your batting stance, just forget it. You're hitting too good to change anything."

Connor laughed. "Okay, Dad, I will."

I think if I hadn't already decided, hearing Connor's voice would have done the trick. There was a very good chance Eddie was driving this investigation. He was acting like a vindictive asshole and affecting everyone I cared about. And it was all because of an evil man who didn't deserve to be defended. Eddie had to be put in his place and soon. I was shuffling off to Buffalo, and I was pretty sure it would be tonight.

67

I decided to scrap my plans for a nap and headed over to Laura's for an early dinner with her, Connor, my dad, and Connie. Jen said she'd meet us later after taking a power nap. My dad had decided to stay an extra night after all. His plan was to take Connie to see Niagara Falls in the morning. I thought it was quite a coincidence we'd be heading in the same direction, but there was no way I was going to suggest riding together. Three-plus hours in the car with my dad would be slow torture, but more important, no one except Kelly even knew I was going. She had asked me to keep her updated, so I used my dad's cell phone to call her from Laura's. My initial plan was to be on the road by 8:15. That way I could get to Buffalo by midnight. I'd already made a reservation at a Fairfield Inn about ten minutes from the U.S. Attorney's Building. I'd leave the hotel around 5:50 am and wait in my car for Eddie to arrive. If he didn't show up by 8:30, I'd go inside and request a meeting, just to be sure I didn't miss him somehow. If he wasn't there, I'd leave a note and head back. I hadn't yet decided what I'd write in that note, but it would be enough to entice him into a meeting. Bottom line, it would concern him that I'd driven all that way out there just to talk to him.

Laura threw together some pasta and corn on the cob, and I cooked some chicken on the grill. Jen showed up at about 6:00 with a couple bottles of red wine. Connie turned out to be pretty talkative and funny, too, especially once she got some wine into her. My dad seemed quite taken with her, and I had a feeling "the break" he and Jan were taking was well on its way to becoming permanent.

I managed to get about fifteen minutes alone with Connor to fill in some of the gaps Laura had left. I asked her to join us for the end of the conversation, so we'd all be on the same page. My biggest concern, and Laura's, as well, was that he'd be harassed at school. Connor didn't seem worried, but he knew it was a possibility. We told him he could stay home Monday if he wanted to, but he insisted he wanted to go to school. I told him if kids started giving him crap, to just say, "You don't know the whole story yet," and walk away. I didn't know if that was too mature a response, but it was the best I could come up with. Laura said she'd call the school first thing and make sure his teachers were on the lookout for any problems. Connor was a well-liked kid, and he didn't have any real enemies that we knew of, so we didn't think it would be too bad.

I said my goodbyes around 7:15, claiming I wanted to get to bed early. I told Jen I'd call her in the morning to let her know about our meeting with Max. I hoped to be on my way home from Buffalo by then with an exciting story of how I terrified Eddie into submission. Connor walked me to the door, and I gave him a big hug and a kiss on the forehead.

I walked to my SUV, realizing I still hadn't told anyone I'd lost my job. The simple truth was I just didn't want to deal with it on top of everything else. I figured I'd tell Jen sometime tomorrow, depending on what happened with Eddie. Carolyn had been texting me, too. She saw the news and wondered if there was anything she could do to help. I told her probably not, but I'd call her in a day or two.

When I pulled into the bike shop parking lot, I saw a red Ford pickup truck in my usual spot. I could tell the car was running, and I could see a broad frame sitting behind the wheel. *Now what?* I thought. I hopped out of the Saturn and started toward the truck. Suddenly, I had the crazy idea it was Ally. She'd come to apologize for what had happened. As I approached the side of the truck, the door opened and Kelly leaned out. "Kelly, what are you doing here?"

"Sorry, I should a told you I was coming down, but I sort a decided at the last minute. You guys stirred up some memories today, and I kind a felt like taking a drive."

"It's okay. How'd you find my address?"

"Online. You're the only Dan Abbot living in Tremon, NY. I figured it had to be you."

"I was going to pack quick and get on the road. Do you want to come in?"

She pointed toward the stairs. "I'm assuming that's you on the second floor?"

"Yeah, right above the bike shop."

"Why don't we talk in the truck then. Stairs do a number on my knees, and I'm not exactly comfortable talking inside your apartment. You know what I mean?"

I nodded. Max told me the Feds had removed all the surveillance devices, but somehow that wasn't all that comforting. I walked around to the other side of the truck and climbed in on the passenger side.

"Sorry to just show up like this," Kelly started, "but there's something else I wanted to tell you before you left. And like I said, I wanted to take a drive."

"No problem at all." I couldn't imagine what she wanted to tell me, but I was starting to think it was pretty important.

"I should a just told you when we were at the bar, but I guess I was embarrassed, as crazy as that sounds. I could tell you about Mark because that was all him, but this other thing was my fault, too, so I was partly responsible."

My God, there's even more to this story?

"Maybe a couple months before my mom caught me and Mark in bed, Eddie came to stay with his dad. He started coming over to the apartment to see me before our parents got home from work. My mom's schedule was more flexible, but she was hardly ever around anyway."

It was obvious where this was heading. I didn't think anything could shock me at this point, but I was wrong.

"Well, after getting high together two or three times, one thing sort a led to another, and we slept together a few times."

"Jesus, Kelly, what were you, thirteen?"

"Yep. Just turned, in fact, and Eddie had just turned twenty. Our birthdays were only a week apart."

I had a disturbing vision of the four of them — Kelly, her mom, Mark, and Eddie — sitting down behind an ice cream cake while everyone sang happy birthday. I wondered if Mark knew Eddie was also raping Kelly, not that he would have viewed it that way.

Kelly continued on. "I don't blame Eddie because it was as much my fault as it was his."

"Kelly, you were thirteen. He was seven years older and in college, for Christ's sake. And if it wasn't for Mark's abuse, you wouldn't have even been thinking about doing that."

"Maybe so, but with Eddie I was probably the one who started it. He was pretty awkward, and I don't think he'd had much experience with girls."

"I understand where you're coming from, but come on. Eddie should've known better. You were still a child."

"I know, but I still feel responsible. It wasn't like he forced me, and I don't think he knew what was happening with me and his dad. At least not *then* he didn't."

"Kelly, I'm sorry. I just can't give him a pass on this. He wasn't fifteen or sixteen. He was a twenty-year-old man."

"I know. This just—" Kelly stared out the window for a few seconds. The silence stretched on, and I was about to say something when she spoke again. "I wanted you to know about this in case you needed it. I don't think too many men make it to his position without knowing how to fuck with people. And given Eddie's past, I'm guessing he's a little better at it than most. I think he probably shoved all those memories into a dark room somewhere in his mind and then bolted the door shut. He's probably convinced himself it didn't even happen. And the fact he's gone after you so hard—or is pressuring somebody else to—tells me he's not worried about you finding me. I'm hoping just mentioning my name will put him in his place, but who knows? Like I said, he could a convinced himself it didn't even happen. It wouldn't surprise me one bit."

"I think he remembers it, but I agree he doesn't have any idea we found you, or even that we're looking. He's going to be shocked when I mention you."

"I'd prefer to stick to our original plan and not mention the payoff or what I just told you. But if you get into a jam, I'd be willing to testify to all of it. I'd even be willing to take a lie detector if it came down to it."

"I don't think he'd ever let it get that far. For him, it's all about public image. He's pushing me and Billy around because he thinks he can. Thanks to you, he's going to find out he can't—not without suffering some serious blows himself."

"Just be careful and remember what I said. You don't make it to being a U.S. Attorney without—"

Just then an Everton Police cruiser turned the corner and passed slowly by. I thought they were going to stop in front of my apartment, but they didn't. We watched them continue down the road and disappear around the corner.

"How often does that happen?" Kelly asked.

"Normally? Never. But I haven't been home since I got arrested."

"If they drove any slower, they would a stalled."

"Yeah, that was pretty obvious."

"Okay, I'm gonna get out a here, so you can get on the road. You've got some driving to do tonight. Call me on the way if you need somebody to talk to."

I looked at her and smiled. "Thanks, Kelly, I will." I climbed out of the truck and headed for the stairs.

68

Two hours later I pulled up to the Dunkin' Donuts drive-through in Rush, NY. I'd spent most of the trip thinking about what Kelly had said about Eddie. She was right that I had to be extremely careful. One wrong move and I'd be heading to jail for a very long time. I was getting tired, so I ordered a large coffee with cream. I still had another hour and a half to the hotel. Jen had texted me about ten minutes ago, asking me where I was. She'd driven by my apartment on the way back to her hotel and didn't see my car. I was debating whether to lie or to just break down and tell her the truth when she called. "Hi, Jen."

"Hi, Dan, where are you?"

"You don't want to know." I guess I decided on the truth.

"Please tell me you're not on your way to Buffalo."

"Okay, I'm not on my way to Buffalo."

"I don't believe you, Dan. I thought we agreed to run it by Max first."

"That was never going to work, Jen. This has to go directly to Eddie, and I'm the only one who can do it."

"I'm against this, Dan. I want you to know that."

"Duly noted, counselor."

"This isn't a joke. I'm scared for you."

"I know you are, Jen, and I appreciate it, but you don't need to be. Don't forget, Eddie and I go back a long way."

"Things have changed a hell of a lot since you were kids. Eddie's out for blood, and he's in a position where he can get it. I'm sure I don't need to remind you that he's one of the most powerful men in the country now."

"I know and that's exactly why this is going to work. He doesn't want to give any of that up."

"I'm going to bed now because I'm exhausted. I hope you know what you're doing."

"I do, Jen. I'll call you on the way home tomorrow."

"Okay, love you."

"Love you, too."

I hung up the phone and took my first sip of coffee. A minute later I was driving up the on ramp to I-390 West. My mind wandered back to the recording of Jess and our mom. They had both sounded so young and so *alive*. I stared at the empty highway in front of me and replayed their voices in my head. Suddenly, I found myself standing in my mother's kitchen. It had been a very long time since I thought about the day Jess died. I didn't want to go there now, but I couldn't seem to stop it.

I'd dropped by Marcell Street just to say hello because I hadn't spoken to Mom all week. She was making supper on the stove—fried chicken and her famous green beans. Adam was on his way into town with his on-again, off-again girlfriend, Carleigh. Jen was still almost two years away from changing his life forever. I had planned to go out on a date that night, but I remember smelling the mouthwatering aroma and wondering if I should cancel and have dinner with them instead.

Mom was wearing her red cooking apron. She turned toward me and smiled as I walked into the kitchen. Her hair was down, which always made her look younger. It was moments like that when I still saw the beautiful young woman she used to be. She had just kissed my cheek when I heard a knock on the door. I remember thinking how loud the knock was and wondering if it might be Adam, but Adam wouldn't have knocked at all. At that time of day, early evening, he would've just walked into the house and yelled hello to announce his presence. When I got to the door and saw the two state troopers on the steps, my stomach began its slow crawl toward my throat. It wasn't just that they were there, it was the look on their faces— faces so young they looked like they might have come directly from their graduation ceremony. I think I knew even then that something terrible had happened, and they were the unfortunate souls who'd drawn the short straw. I wondered if something had happened to Adam. Maybe he'd gotten into a car accident on his way down from Syracuse. Right at that moment I was so certain Adam was dead that I couldn't even answer our mom when she asked who was at the door.

When the two young troopers entered the house and told us that Jess and her boyfriend, Wade, had been killed by a drunk driver earlier that day, I remember thinking it wasn't possible—that they'd made some kind of terrible mistake. After all, she was with Wade at his parents' lake house in Skaneateles, NY. They wouldn't have been driving anywhere. They were probably lounging around the house, admiring the view, or maybe Wade had taken her out on the family sailboat to cruise the lake. They wouldn't have been in the car on such a beautiful day with the gorgeous lake beckoning.

Jess and Wade had been seeing each other for just over a year, and we all had the feeling that an engagement ring wasn't far off. Adam and I loved Wade because he adored Jess. The fact his family had money didn't hurt because we felt like Jess would be well taken care of. Mom loved him for those same reasons and also because he seemed to be the antithesis of our father.

There was a picture of them sitting atop the armoire near my mother's front door — the same photo now hanging in my living room. I found myself staring at it while the troopers tried to explain that they didn't suffer. They were killed instantly they said, hoping it would ease our pain a little. It didn't then — the shock and probably more so the overwhelming instinct to deny — were simply too great, but I found some comfort from it in the months and years ahead. I think anyone who's lost a loved one prays that they didn't suffer. It's something to hold onto in the lonely morning hours when you have nothing else. The picture was taken just a few months earlier. Jess's long, blondish-brown hair, windblown and sun-bleached after a long day on the water, hung down and covered her shoulders. She was holding up a glass of white wine and smiling like she had the rest of her life ahead of her.

I don't know how much time had passed before I saw a sign for the New York State Thruway. It announced ominously that Buffalo was just seventy-eight miles away.

69

It was 11:53 pm when I unlocked my hotel room and stepped inside. I threw my bag on the floor and fought the urge to just tumble onto the bed. After going to the bathroom and brushing my teeth, I called the front desk and placed a wake-up call for 5:15 am. I figured I could get showered, dressed, and out to the U.S. Attorney's Building by 6:00 and still have time to grab a McDonald's breakfast. I saw the golden arches just down the street from my hotel. I turned out the light and started running through as many potential scenarios as I could think of. The last time I checked the clock it was 12:16.

When the phone began ringing at 5:15, I was certain I was lying in a hospital bed somewhere. I'd been run over by a large truck and airlifted to the nearest trauma center. I was beyond exhausted and my neck and shoulders ached miserably from the late-night drive. Finally, on what must've been the tenth or eleventh ring, I rolled over to the other side of the bed and lifted the receiver from its base. I closed my eyes and then jolted awake a minute or two later. I climbed out of bed before I could fall asleep again and stumbled toward the shower.

Thirty minutes later I was pulling into the McDonald's drive-through. I ordered a large coffee and two Egg McMuffins, and then I punched the address for the U.S. Attorney's Building into my phone's GPS. By the time I got off the highway and made my way to Delaware Avenue, I'd finished the first Egg McMuffin and nearly half the coffee. I told myself to slow down. I didn't want to have to go to the bathroom and miss my chance of catching Eddie on his way into the building.

I could tell I was nearing downtown Buffalo because the buildings were growing taller with each passing block. At this hour I had the streets mostly to myself. When my GPS told me I had five hundred feet to my destination, I turned it off and set the phone on the passenger seat. I recognized the U.S. Attorney's Building from the images I'd studied on Google Maps. It was a modern five or six story structure with blue windows and a smooth white concrete finish. Just before the building was an entranceway to a small parking lot. A row of trees, thick with late spring foliage, blocked a clear view, but it looked mostly empty as I drove past. I continued on, passing a set of glass doors at the top of a small staircase on the northeast corner of the building. Seventy yards later I reached the southeast corner where the main entrance faced the intersection of Delaware Avenue and West Mohawk Street. A small flight of concrete stairs, maybe five or six steps total, led to a covered landing sitting between two thick pillars. The actual entrance into the building was a revolving glass door flanked by a traditional glass door on each side. A wheelchair accessible ramp led away from the landing toward the other entrance.

When I reached the intersection, I took a right onto West Mohawk Street. As I passed by the south side of the U.S. Attorney's Building, I could see there were no entrances. I glanced to my left at another modern looking structure, a semi-circular behemoth I remembered from Google Maps as the U.S. Courthouse. The courthouse was heavily barricaded with bollards rising up from the sidewalk like a long row of concrete teeth. I had no doubt the pillars were reinforced with anchored metal rods, designed to deter anyone crazy enough to attempt a vehicular assault. There was no such security on the U.S. Attorney's Building, but I suspected there were armed guards sitting just inside the glass doors as well as state of the art security cameras panning the streets.

I found a large parking lot at the rear of the U.S. Attorney's Building, but I didn't see an entrance. I figured there had to be one, but it didn't seem likely that Eddie would park back there anyway. It occurred to me that he might use a private entrance or perhaps even have a driver. I turned around and headed back toward Delaware Avenue, knowing the front of the building was my best option. I took a left back onto Delaware and parallel parked between a white pickup truck and smallish BMW. From here, I could see both of the front entrances and also the driveway leading into the smaller parking lot. If Eddie drove down Delaware and pulled into that lot, I thought I had a decent chance of spotting him.

I lowered the driver side window halfway and turned off the Saturn. The light fog present when I first left my hotel room had already lifted, giving way to a crisp blue sky. In stark contrast to the muggy heat of home, the air here was arid and chilly. I bit into my second Egg McMuffin and started thinking about what I was going to say if and when I spotted Eddie. I had a basic idea, but I wanted to nail it down. I had to be ready because I'd probably get only one shot, and I'd have only a few seconds to do it. If I could get him alone, I could be direct. I'd tell him to stop the vendetta and let this thing die. Otherwise, all sorts of terrible truths would surface about his father. At some point I'd mention Kelly. If that didn't break him, nothing would, but I'd have to be careful. If he recorded me making threats on his smart phone, I could be arrested for blackmailing a federal prosecutor. I didn't know the penalty for that particular crime, but I suspected it was a lot longer than five years.

If I couldn't catch Eddie on the way in, I'd have to request a meeting. I was confident he'd see me, but I'd have to change my approach. I'd have to make it look like I'd come to ask him for help. Even so, once I mentioned Kelly's name, he'd get the message. If I'd talked to Kelly, then I knew his secrets.

I finished the last bite of my second Egg McMuffin and noticed the first pedestrian of the morning. It was a woman in her early thirties, dressed in a gray business suit. The way she carried herself reminded me of Carolyn. She crossed West Mohawk Street, then darted up the small flight of concrete stairs and entered through the revolving glass door of the main entrance. I checked my phone. It was 6:42. Her arrival was a harbinger of things to come. Over the next hour, at least two dozen people—many in business suits—walked up those same stairs and entered the building. A smaller number entered through the northern entrance. There was no parking directly in front of the building, but a couple sedans pulled up and dropped off passengers. None of them were Eddie. There were also numerous cars pulling into the parking lot. Most of the time I could see the driver but not always, and since many of the cars had tinted windows, I couldn't see into the back seats. As the flow of traffic increased, both vehicle and pedestrian, it became difficult to monitor all three entrances at once. When 8:00 am came and went, I was all but certain Eddie was already inside the building. I finished the last of my coffee and considered my options. I could wait here and continue monitoring the street, or I could go inside and ask to see him. It was an easy call. Catching him on the way into the building had always been a long shot, especially when I had no idea which entrance he used.

I stepped out of the SUV and locked it with the remote. I walked back to the crosswalk, checked for traffic, and headed across Delaware Avenue. I started thinking about what I'd write in my note if Eddie wasn't there, and in no time at all I'd crossed the street and reached the landing of the main entrance. I was so consumed in thought as I approached the far right door, I almost missed the small group of sharply-dressed people coming out of the building. They were on the other side of the revolving glass door and were clearly together, moving in a single unit like a pack of wolves. Positioned in the middle of three men and two women was the United States Attorney for the Western District of New York State. I saw Eddie first through the blue tint of the glass door and then more clearly as he stepped outside into the crisp summer air. He looked a lot like his online photo, but his hair was shorter now, and he looked like he may have lost a few pounds. He was smiling, and I couldn't help but notice the awkward arrogance that used to radiate off of him like a bad sunburn was nowhere to be seen. Nor did I see any signs of the "slightly off" Eddie I remembered from our brief encounters all those years ago. What stood just fifteen feet away from me today was a man who looked very much like he'd grown confidently into middle-age.

The actual sight of him had an inverse effect on me. I immediately felt *my* inner confidence slip. It felt like I was standing in the middle of a swimming pool that had just collapsed. I didn't know what or who I expected to see, maybe just an older version of the conceited jerk that spent an hour at our house thirty-nine years ago. Maybe he'd have a few wrinkles on his face or a head full of gray hair, but it would essentially be the same person. As I watched Eddie hold the door open for the two women, I wondered if maybe he'd fundamentally changed. Maybe he'd matured and mellowed with age. For most people that would be a positive thing, but right now — for me — it felt strangely ominous.

I watched as Eddie waited patiently for the two female members of their party to exit the building before following them onto the landing. The group waited near the stairs for him to catch up, and then they headed down the steps in unison. At that exact moment, I caught a glimpse of a large, black SUV pulling up to the curb where I'd stood only seconds earlier. Eddie and his entourage were clearly heading for that vehicle.

I stood frozen with one foot still on the landing and one foot in the doorway. For two long seconds, I was certain I'd watch them stroll down the stairs, walk across the sidewalk, and climb into the SUV. And then I heard Jess's voice, young and innocent and alive as she told my mother what Mark had done to her. It was enough to break my paralysis. I stepped back outside the building and began following them. They were already down the stairs and moving briskly toward the SUV. I had to say something now or it would be too late.

"Eddie!" I yelled, probably louder than necessary. My voice echoed toward the street, and all five people turned back to look at me. I could see the surprise on their faces, likely the result of hearing the U.S. Attorney called by his first name. I continued moving slowly toward them, staring directly at Eddie, when I felt the presence of someone approaching from my right. A man grabbed my forearm and stopped me cold.

"Can I help you, sir?" the man asked.

I turned to see a tall, well-built man in his early thirties, staring into my eyes. His expression said *I'm going to have you on the ground in less than a second if you give me even the slightest reason to do so.* I looked at him for another moment or two and realized he wasn't just saying it with his eyes, he was truly hoping it would happen. I turned back toward Eddie and noticed a second security agent standing on my left. It was then I realized they'd observed my actions at the door and reacted immediately as soon as I turned back toward the U.S. Attorney. I watched as Eddie's group continued on toward the SUV. One of the three men darted ahead to open the doors of what I could now see was a Cadillac Escalade.

Jen's voice was in my head. *Keep your mouth shut, and you might just get out of here without any further damage.* Then I heard Adam's voice just as clear. *You're not giving up that easily, are you?* I didn't come this far to chicken out now. "Eddie! It's Danny Abbot!" I felt the second man clamp onto my left forearm just as Eddie paused outside the Escalade.

"Come on," the first man said, pulling me back toward the doors. The second agent bumped into me, and I began a reluctant stumble toward the building. I wanted to tell them to get their hands off me because I hadn't done anything wrong, but I knew that would be a mistake. So far I'd been well within my rights as a citizen of the United States, but if I resisted, that would change quickly. We were almost to the doors when I heard Eddie's voice. I hadn't heard it in almost forty years, and it sounded very different from what I remembered. Instead of the arrogant, angry voice of a twenty-two-year-old Eddie, I heard the relaxed tone of a respected U.S. Attorney. His confident demeanor bothered me, but what upset me even more was that he sounded exactly like Mark.

"Hold on a second, Kyle," Eddie said, and the two agents stopped immediately.

They loosened their grips just enough for me to turn around. I watched as Eddie reached the stairs and started up. He stared at me as if trying to convince himself it was really me standing there and not some lunatic who'd simply heard the name Abbot on a cable news show. I could almost feel his mind trying to figure out why I was here. When he reached the top of the stairs, his expression changed to one of confused compassion. Here was a man he'd known long ago, someone who might've even become a part of his family if things hadn't taken a wrong turn. I was obviously here for help and he commiserated, but what could he do? It was out of his hands now.

It occurred to me Eddie knew he was being watched, not only by his group and the two security agents holding my arms but also by cameras picking up our every move. It also occurred to me this area might be mic'd up for surveillance purposes. *Be careful,* I reminded myself.

"Jesus, Danny, what are you doing here? Surely, you realize this is highly inappropriate."

"Eddie, I was hoping we could talk for a couple minutes. Do you think we could speak in private?"

"Actually, Danny, I don't have time right now. As you can see, I'm on my way to a meeting."

"This is only going to take a second." I glanced down the ramp toward the other entrance. "Maybe we could walk that way."

Eddie stared at me for several seconds. Just when I thought he was going to refuse, he looked at the first agent who'd grabbed me. "It's okay, Kyle. I'll speak with him for a minute."

Both agents released my arm. The one he called Kyle said, "Put your hands on the wall and spread your legs." I did what I was told. After he frisked me, a process which included a few hard groin pats, he nodded at Eddie.

"Okay, Danny, I have a couple minutes if you make it quick." He started walking down the ramp and I followed. There was no one on the sidewalk between the two entrances, which meant there was plenty of room for a private conversation. As we moved down the ramp, I noticed Kyle began to follow us, but it looked like he was going to stay back a little. "Naturally, I've heard about what happened in Everton. I've been kept abreast as a courtesy. What do you want from me, Danny?"

I was suddenly torn between approaching this the way I wanted to, and the way I felt like I had to. I couldn't shake the real possibility our conversation was being picked up and recorded, and that meant other people would be listening. If I threatened him and told him to call off the dogs, Eddie would have no choice but to call Kelly a liar and go after me for blackmailing a federal official. "Eddie, this might surprise you, but I loved your father. I fully expected he was going to be my stepfather."

"It's too bad Adam didn't feel the same way."

His voice was incredibly calm, almost soothing. I felt like I was confessing my sins to a priest. "Eddie, there are some things you don't know. Adam went over there that night because your father molested Jess."

"What? Jesus, Danny. I know you're under a lot of pressure right now, but this is ridiculous." Eddie had raised his voice and he'd also stopped walking. By now we were halfway to the other entrance. I glanced back and saw that Kyle had approached to within twenty feet. "I agreed to talk with you as a favor to an old friend, and you pull this shit on me?"

I was relieved to hear him losing his composure, but I also realized the conversation could be over at any moment. "Eddie, it's true. Jess told me first, and then I told Adam. That's why he went over there that night."

"That's why he went over there and murdered my father, you mean. Look, Danny, I agreed to speak with you because I know my dad was fond of you, but I think this was a mistake."

Eddie turned and started back toward Kyle. The security agent, who went about 6'3" and weighed around 230 pounds, began lumbering forward. Judging by his pace, I only had a second or two before I was either arrested or sent packing.

"I spoke to Kelly Newman yesterday."

I watched Eddie stop, pausing motionless, before raising his open hand to Kyle. I would have given anything to see Eddie's face at that moment. I imagine it was full of shock and maybe even fear. Kyle stopped abruptly and took a few steps back. Eddie turned around, his poker face intact. A couple seconds later, he reached me, and we continued walking.

"So, Kelly was telling lies again, huh?"

If Kelly was telling lies, you wouldn't have come back. "She was molested by Mark, too. In fact, it went well beyond that."

"We went through this forty years ago. There was never any evidence because Kelly was lying, and her mother was a junkie."

I noticed he kept his cool this time even though the accusation was much worse. I figured I'd seen the last of his temper. "Eddie, if this thing keeps going, it's all going to come out, whether it's —"

"That sounds a lot like a threat, Danny. Are you threatening a federal prosecutor?" The origins of a smile formed on the corners of his mouth.

"No, Eddie, not at all. I'm trying to keep this thing from going public. So far no one has picked up on it, but the longer it goes, the more likely it will come out."

"Not that I think there's an ounce of validity to any of these claims, but what would you have me do about it? I have absolutely nothing to do with this investigation. Like I said, I've been kept abreast simply as a courtesy."

This wasn't going as I'd planned. I thought one mention of Kelly, and Eddie would begin to crack, but that wasn't happening. I had his interest, but he appeared content to call my bluff. I had to give him what he wanted. I had to take this to the next level, and I was running out of time.

"Eddie, this thing's gone far enough. Your father was a child molester, and I think you know that. He tried to kill my brother, and he would've killed me, too. The charges against me are complete bullshit. Yes, Billy helped Adam bury the body, but Mark brought all of this on himself. There's no fucking way I'm going away for five years, nor will I watch Billy go away for fifteen without telling the whole story. And I mean the *whole* story, Eddie. Kelly told me everything."

Eddie stared at me, his face changing right before my eyes. In a matter of seconds, he morphed from a confident middle-aged man into the arrogant, insecure asshole he was beneath the façade. I suddenly felt like it was thirty-nine years ago, and we were all sitting around the dining room table on the night we met.

"You were always a loser, Danny. I suspected that even when you were a kid, and it turned out to be true, didn't it? Living in a dumpy three-room apartment over a bike shop? Couldn't even keep your marriage together, could you? That's a fine example for your son, but I suppose that was to be expected when your worthless father skipped town, and you were raised by a conniving bitch who covered up a murder."

It was all I could do to not drive his face into the concrete. The moment would have lasted only a second or two before I was knocked unconscious or killed, but it would have almost been worth it. Of course, I realized that's exactly what he wanted me to do. Hitting him was out of the question, but the gloves were off. There was no way this conversation was being recorded. Eddie was still staring at me, smirking. I looked him in the eye.

"My father might have been an asshole, but he wasn't a child rapist. And speaking of child rapists, Eddie, what's it like to have sex with a thirteen-year-old? Last time I checked, that wasn't part of the preferred background of a U.S. Attorney." Eddie opened his mouth to respond, but I cut him off. "You have two options, asshole. You can have me arrested now, and you'll see Kelly on *Dateline*, telling the world how little Eddie followed in his daddy's footsteps, or you can make a few phone calls to make these charges go away. And don't give me this bullshit you aren't involved because we both know you're driving this fucking ship."

I turned and walked toward my SUV, fully expecting Kyle to grab me. About halfway across the street, I glanced back and watched Eddie climb into the Escalade. Kyle was nowhere to be seen. I took a deep breath and got into the Saturn. As I pulled out onto Delaware Avenue, I could feel the eyes upon me through the tinted glass windows of the Escalade. I started retracing my steps back toward the highway. When the U.S. Attorney's Building disappeared in my rearview mirror, I grabbed my phone and called Jen.

70

I got home around 12:30 and met Jen for lunch near her hotel. The plan was to meet with Max at his office at 1:45. The trip back had been pretty uneventful, but I kept thinking I was going to be pulled over or run into some kind of roadblock. I suppose that was foolish since it would've been much easier for the Feds to just wait until I got back to Tremon before arresting me, but I still couldn't stop looking in my rearview mirror. I would've made it home sooner, but I stopped in Rush again and found a payphone to call Kelly. She was still in the thick of things at the diner, so I gave her the short version. She laughed when I told her how Eddie reverted back to an angry twenty-two-year-old right in front of my eyes. I suppose she was one of the only people alive who would've thought that was funny. If he were here, Adam certainly would've been another. She thought I did about as well as I could have and agreed we'd just have to wait and see if it worked.

Jen and I had lunch at TGI Friday's where Carolyn had started this nightmare of a week just five days ago. Over an enormous Cobb salad, I told her everything that happened. She was still a little mad at me, but she was mesmerized by my story anyway. When I told her about the long-ago relationship between Eddie and Kelly, her jaw literally hung open. After a lengthy discussion, we both agreed Eddie didn't have much of a choice. He had to do everything he could to shut this thing down or his days as a federal prosecutor would be coming to an end. Whether or not he could actually get the charges dismissed was still an unknown. The biggest question emerging now was how hard we should push if we didn't get what we wanted. Neither one of us had an answer to that one.

The other big question was how much I should tell Max, if anything. I figured he'd be furious to learn what I did, especially given I hadn't been upfront with him from the beginning. I thought there was a decent chance he might just tell me to take a hike. While I liked Max and didn't want to go looking for another lawyer, I was confident I'd done the right thing. There was only one way this situation could've been handled without risking a leak, and that was the way I did it. By the time our waitress brought the check, I decided I'd tell him the truth, minus the part about Eddie sleeping with Kelly, and the part about Eddie delivering the payoff. Again, the more people who knew about those two things, the riskier the situation became. I felt like Max could be trusted, but those were hard ones to take to the grave.

I parked my Saturn outside Max's office—further down the road than last time. Unlike the other night when everything looked deserted, the street was bustling with vehicle and foot traffic. We made our way across the street and into the lobby where a pleasant security guard told us to head on back to Max's offices. As we turned off the main hallway, a woman greeted us and led us into the same conference room where we'd met just two nights ago. It was ridiculous how much had happened in the last forty-eight hours. If someone made me guess how long ago our first meeting with Max had been, I would've said at least a week, maybe two. After we declined offers of coffee and water, the woman left us alone and closed the door.

Five minutes passed before Max walked in, smiling. Our last communication had come at 11:00 am when I was still an hour or so from home. He walked around toward the head of the table, staring at me the entire way. He sat between me and Jen, and only then did he turn away from me to look at her.

"Morning, Jen," he said, still smiling.

"Hi, Max." She looked at me, a touch uneasily.

His eyes were back on me now. "Morning, Dan."

"Hi, Max. It looks like you have some good news, or did you just win the lottery?"

Max laughed. "Funny you should say that. I *feel* like I just won the lottery."

"Please share," Jen said, now smiling, too. It was contagious.

"I just received a phone call from William McCall, and while nothing is official at this point, okay?" Max paused long enough for both of us to nod. "Apparently, your old pal, Eddie, heard the recorded phone conversation between you two for the first time last night, and according to McCall he found it to be pretty moving. Because neither of you had any idea you were being recorded, he believed your account of what happened. And even more important than that, he's extremely sympathetic. Those are the exact words McCall used."

Jen and I looked at each other. Her mouth was hanging open again, but it was forced shut by an enormous smile. For the first time—right there in my lawyer's office—I wondered what it would be like to kiss her. A sharp, painful stab of guilt traveled through me, and I looked back at Max before she could read my thoughts.

"I need you both to understand that all of this is completely off the record at this point." Jen and I nodded eagerly. "No official decision has been made, but Eddie has recommended that the charges against you be dropped completely and that the charges against Billy get greatly reduced."

"What's greatly reduced?" Given how happy Max seemed, I almost felt ungrateful for even asking.

"Less than a year of jail time. McCall didn't want to commit to anything, understandably, but he said it could be something like a year of just weekends at a minimum security location or possibly even just three to five years of probation."

I looked at Jen again and saw instantly that we were thinking the same thing. *There was absolutely no reason to tell Max what I'd done.*

"Jesus, Max," I said, "I can't believe it. That's incredible news. When will it be official?"

"McCall wasn't sure, but he hinted it would probably be within a couple days. I'd say definitely by the end of the week."

"My God, I'm stunned. I don't know what to say."

"I know. That's exactly how I feel. This is easily the strangest case I've ever been a part of, and we're only forty-eight hours in."

"What did you say to them, Max?" Jen asked. "You must have scared them somehow."

"Believe me, I'd love to say I did something to scare them, but I really didn't. I mean I had a conversation with McCall yesterday, and I pleaded our case, but that had nothing to do with this. Eddie wasn't even mentioned. This one is just weird enough it might be true. I haven't talked with my friend yet to see if he's heard anything, but it looks like Eddie simply had a change of heart when he heard your phone conversation."

Jen and I looked at each other, and it was suddenly all we could do not to burst out laughing. We actually did start laughing, but we held it in check just enough so it could be explained away by our excitement. I got the feeling Max was about to ask us what the joke was.

"Have you spoken with Billy's lawyer yet?" I asked.

"I left him a voicemail, but he hasn't gotten back to me yet."

"I probably shouldn't call Billy yet, right?"

"*Definitely* don't call Billy yet." It was the first words Max had spoken that weren't accompanied by a big smile. "Let's play this thing by the book until it's official, okay?"

"Got it." If he only knew just how far I'd ventured from the official playbook. I didn't dare look at Jen. If our eyes connected again, it would've been over.

Five minutes later we were standing outside his offices and heading for the Saturn. When we got across the street, Jen grabbed my arm and spun me toward her. She lunged forward and hugged me. I was surprised at her intensity, but I recovered quickly and hugged her back. Even through the guilt, which came almost immediately, I couldn't deny how nice her body felt pressing against mine.

"I was so worried about you, Dan, but you were right. I can't believe how dangerous that was and how stupid you were, but you were right."

I laughed. "Thanks, Jen…I guess."

Jen backed away and looked at me. "You know I'm kidding. It was a very brave thing to do. I don't think I could've done it."

"Yes, you could've. Listen, I want to thank you for everything you've done for me. I never would've been able to do any of this without your help."

"You know I would do anything for you, but I was just doing what Adam told me to do. He set everything up. I had the easy part."

Just the mention of Adam's name sent another barb of guilt into my chest. "I don't know about that, Jen, but I do know I couldn't have done it without you."

She gave me another hug, and I struggled to think of anything other than how warm she felt. I pulled away from her and said, "Let's go tell Connor."

71

Everything became official on Friday morning at 10:45. William McCall held a press conference at the Federal Building in Binghamton, which ran live on CNN, MSNBC, WNN, and FOX News. Max had given us a heads-up the night before, so Jen, Laura, and I watched the press conference together at Laura's house. Jen had gone back home to West Chester after our meeting with Max and then returned just this morning to hear the official word. I didn't want her to go, but I was sort of glad she did. These feelings had come out of nowhere, and I felt incredibly guilty because I still thought of her as my brother's wife. I couldn't beat myself up too badly, though. She was a beautiful person and an extremely attractive woman. We'd been thrown into a crazy, stressful situation, and I figured it was probably natural for feelings to form. But now that this ordeal was over, I assumed things would go back to normal. Jen would go back to West Chester and then, for better or worse, we'd only see each other two or three times a year.

I think we all would have been surprised to see the press conference receiving that level of national attention had Max not filled us in on a new development. Apparently, the news that Mark was Eddie's father was about to break. Max's contact wasn't sure if Eddie would make an appearance, but the news was definitely coming out. Max was surprised Eddie was making it public, given that the charges were being dropped. Jen and I, of course, assumed it had something to do with my visit. Later, the two of us surmised Eddie was worried everything would come out eventually, so it was better to get ahead of the story and announce it himself.

McCall started off the press conference by declaring all charges against me were being dropped and that Billy would receive five years of probation in exchange for admitting to his role in helping Adam bury Mark's body at Valley View Golf Course. He then announced that Eddie Daniels, the U.S. Attorney for the Western District of New York State, was Mark's son. McCall explained Mr. Daniels had been notified early on that they'd found Mark's body and had chosen to remain out of the public eye to help maintain the integrity of the investigation. He also stated Mr. Daniels had been kept abreast of developments as they unfolded, and now that the case was being closed, he wanted to make a statement. There was no mention of Ally's undercover operation, nor was there any mention that Mr. Daniels had been directing every single move since the very beginning. McCall opened a leather binder on the wooden lectern and began reading the U.S. Attorney's statement.

"Thirty-nine years ago my father was killed at his home in Everton, NY, during a physical altercation with Adam Abbot, who at the time was seventeen-years-old. Certain facts came to light during the course of this investigation that lead me to believe my father was largely responsible for the altercation and what occurred as a result. While initially it appeared that charges were warranted against Billy Kent for his role in the incident and also against Dan Abbot for misleading investigators, Mr. McCall and his team no longer believe that is the case. And after speaking with Mr. McCall yesterday, I concur. Thirty-nine years is a long time, and I'm extremely pleased that my father can finally be laid to rest with a proper burial. I want to commend all law enforcement agencies that worked on this case over the last two weeks, including the Federal Bureau of Investigation, the New York State Police, the Pennsylvania State Police, the Broome County Sheriff, and most notably the Everton Police Department. The extensive work performed by each of these agencies was beyond stellar and helped to bring closure to a great number of people, including me and my family. Since this is the first time people are learning of my connection to this case, I'm sure there will be many questions. I will address these questions through future statements and interviews. Thank you."

As soon as the press conference ended, we opened a bottle of champagne to celebrate. Both Jen and I took calls from my father and a couple other well-wishers. Kelly also called my cell phone and we talked for ten minutes. Now that everything was over, we figured it was safe to use our cell phones again. Still, we were careful not to talk about what happened with Eddie. She made me promise that Jen and I would come up to celebrate, and I said we would. She told me to bring Connor, and I promised to do that, as well. Max called to congratulate me and asked me to call him early next week so we could wrap up a few loose ends. I told him I would and then congratulated him on a job well done. He insisted he didn't do anything out of the ordinary but thanked me anyway. My respect for him had grown a great deal in the last week. A lot of people in his position, most in fact, would have taken credit for what happened and may have even fabricated a reason for *how* he made it happen. Max made no attempt to do that. He simply told me the truth and had no qualms basking in our remarkably good fortune. Just before we hung up, I asked him if I could call Billy, and he gave me the green light.

When Laura offered to open a second bottle, I decided to skip out. I promised I'd be back later for dinner and more celebrating, but I really wanted to see Billy. I wanted to make sure he was okay, and I wanted to fill him in on some of the things that had happened. I also had a question I'd been dying to ask him since the story first unfolded on Saturday. I had his address at my apartment, so I stopped there first.

As I walked into the kitchen, I saw the berries on the counter and thought again of Ally. Over the last few days my anger had faded to a low, glowing ember. Connor had already gotten over it, so I figured there wasn't much to stay mad over. Ally was just doing her job, and more often than not, she was dealing with bad individuals who'd broken the law. While I'd been forced to admit her attraction to me, especially what happened in the kitchen, was also just her doing her job, I was still holding out hope that maybe a little of it was genuine. I knew that was just wishful thinking, but that's the story I was going with.

I found the notebook holding Billy's address, then ripped the sheet out and headed for the door. I thought about calling him, but a face-to-face visit seemed like the way to go. I had a lot to tell him, and I didn't want to do it over the phone. I figured he'd be home from work today because of the press conference. I opened the door to leave and saw Jen just making it to the top of the stairs. My heart rate suddenly jumped.

"Hey, Jen. I thought you and Laura were going to get started on that second bottle."

"Laura wanted to run a few errands before Connor got home. Mind if I come in?"

I felt like there was something she wanted to talk about, like this visit wasn't just to kill some time. "Sure, come on in." I backed up, and she followed me into the kitchen before closing the door.

Jen smiled and pointed at the berries on the counter. "You guys made quite a few jars."

"There were actually more. I gave a few to Ally."

"Maybe she'll bring them back."

"She's probably already thrown them out."

"I don't know. Maybe she's planning to return them in person."

Jen was looking at me, and I thought she might still be feeling the effects of the champagne. I was suddenly feeling a bit light-headed myself. "Yeah, right," I said.

"It wouldn't surprise me one bit if she brings them back. She'll say it's because she wanted to apologize, but it will probably be because she wants to see you again. And who knows, she might even be hoping you try to find *her*."

I chuckled. "I don't think so, Jen."

"Why not?" Jen had been closing the gap between us. I was leaning against the counter, and she was only four feet away. "I think a lot of women find you attractive, Dan." She was staring at me but not smiling.

Oh, God. I didn't know what to say, so I just looked at her.

"And I would have to count myself in that particular category," she added.

She was only two feet away from me now. I had absolutely no idea how she got that close. I wanted to say something along the lines of *You're my brother's wife,* but something had happened to my vocal chords.

Jen continued on. "I think it's very possible that Ally's sitting at home, hoping you decide to track her down. And I know that because I was sitting at home the last few nights thinking the same thing. Except I decided I wasn't going to wait."

She was only a foot away now and closing. I couldn't wait any longer. "Jen, you're my brother's wife."

"I *was* your brother's wife, Dan. I will always love him with my entire soul, but he's been gone a year now, and you've been separated for even longer. Something's happened between us in the last few days. I think you feel it, too, but if I'm wrong just tell me."

"You're not wrong, but I feel like I'm betraying Adam."

"Adam told me a dozen times that if you didn't work things out with Laura, he wanted us to be together. I remember because each time he said it, I told him he was crazy. I never thought this would happen in a million years."

"Adam said that?"

"Yes. He said we were the two finest people he knew, and he wanted us to be happy. And you know Adam. It's not like he thought he and I would be together in the afterlife." I chuckled at that, and soon we were both laughing. "I missed you when I went home. All I could think about was getting back here to see you."

I stared at her, and before I knew what was happening, she'd closed the short gap and was kissing me. She pressed her soft lips against my mouth, and I felt her tongue searching for mine. I could feel her breasts—full and firm—pushing against my chest. I felt like I'd just been slipped some exquisite drug. A second later she was pulling me toward the living room.

The thought of contacting Billy popped into my head and was gone, buried in the depths of my consciousness where it would remain for well over an hour.

72

Jen gave me a long kiss and then smiled before darting out the door. I stood beside the counter in a state of mild shock over what had just happened. I'd been sensing an attraction since I'd returned from Buffalo, maybe even before, but I never expected Jen to come over and make the first move. I suppose she had to be the one to do it, though, because I don't think I could have. I still felt weird about Adam, but Jen seemed so sure about what he'd said, and I knew she'd never lie about that.

I shrugged it off, knowing I wouldn't be able to come to terms with it now anyway. I picked up the paper holding Billy's address. I had his cell phone number, too, but I didn't want to call him. I knew if we started talking on the phone, I wouldn't go to see him, and I didn't want that to happen. I wanted to talk to him in person. I punched his address into my phone's GPS, and it told me he was only about fifteen minutes away. I knew the general area, but I didn't think I'd ever been to his neighborhood. I grabbed a bottle of water out of the fridge and headed down to the Saturn.

By the time I pulled up to Billy's house, the sky had grown overcast. Rain was on the way, and I didn't think it would be a simple thunderstorm. It felt like it was planning to stick around for a while. There were several cars in the driveway and another two on the street directly in front of his house. The front drapes were open, and I could see the dining room table, but it was empty.

I parked behind a white sedan and made my way up the stone walkway. I was nervous, but I felt like Billy would be happy to see me. The inside door was open, so I knocked on the screen door and waited. A few seconds later, a woman came around a corner and approached the door. I recognized her as Billy's wife. I'd only met her a couple times, and it had been ten years or more since I'd last seen her. Her name came to me just as she reached the screen. *Karen.* She opened the door, and I could tell by her face she didn't recognize me.

"Hi, can I help you?" she asked.

"Hi, Karen, you probably don't remember meeting me. I'm Dan Abbot."

Her eyes softened and her mouth curved back into a huge smile. "Of course, I remember you, Dan. It's just been a long time. Come on in." I stepped into the foyer and she embraced me. I could smell wine on her breath. "Your ears must've been ringing. We were just talking about you."

"I'm guessing my name's been thrown around quite a bit in the last few days."

"It has, as a matter of fact," she said, laughing.

"All good, I'm sure."

"Absolutely. Now your brother…that's been a little mixed."

We both laughed hard. "Don't worry. It's been pretty mixed at my house, too." That triggered another round of laughter.

She led me through the small living room. I could hear muffled voices and laughter coming from what I assumed was a back deck. I was about to round the corner into the dining room when a large mass appeared in front of me. I recognized him instantly. It was Billy.

"Well, I'll be God damned," he said. "It's Danny Abbot."

He reached out and pulled me into a massive bear hug. I could smell the strong odor of consumed alcohol. By the smell and the way he was smiling at me, I suspected he was on the back half of a twelve pack.

"Hi, Billy," I said, smiling. Even though we were both middle-aged men, I still thought of him as my older brother's friend—someone much older than me.

He held me at arm's length. "Let me look at you, Danny." His eyes traveled lazily from my face to my feet and then back up again. I was like a nephew he hadn't seen in a long time. "You're looking awfully good, my friend."

As he was taking stock of me, I was doing the same with him. Unfortunately, my report wasn't as positive. He was carrying an extra thirty-five pounds, most of it in the vicinity of his stomach. He had a deep golf tan, which sort of made him appear healthy, but I had the feeling he was anything but. To me he looked like a heart attack waiting to happen.

"You're looking good, too, Billy," I said, mustering as much sincerity as I could.

Billy stared at me for a second and then started laughing. "You're a shitty liar, Danny. Now I know how the Feds caught you."

We both laughed. "Thanks, Billy. I guess I can laugh at that now."

"Come on back and have a beer with us."

Just then I heard a door slide open and the muffled voices I'd heard earlier were suddenly crisp and loud. Someone whooped and it was followed by a raucous round of laughter. I knew if I got dragged back there, Jen would be picking me up in a few hours to drive me home. "Actually, Billy, I just stopped by quick. We're celebrating at Laura's house, so I have to get back."

"Laura's? I thought you guys got divorced."

"Well, we did, but Connor lives there, and we still get along pretty good."

"Wow, that's impressive. Me and my first wife can't even be in the same room together, and that was almost thirty years ago." Billy laughed and I started thinking he might be more drunk than I initially thought.

"Listen, Billy, can we talk somewhere for a few minutes?"

"For you? Absolutely. I don't know what you did, but I know you did something. One minute I'm looking at fifteen years — and shittin' bricks by the way — and the next I'm being told it's time to go home."

I laughed. It was impossible not to. "Can we go somewhere private?"

"Sure. We'll go upstairs to my office, but let me grab you a beer first."

I was about to decline the offer, but I knew that wouldn't matter to Billy. I was getting a beer whether I wanted one or not. Billy came back with a can of Budweiser and led me up the stairs and down the hall to a small room facing the street. There was a desk in one corner with a chair that looked like it belonged to an old kitchen set. Cardboard boxes and piles of clothes were stacked everywhere, including on the chair and desk. Billy might've called this room his office, but it was obviously being used as a storage room. I suspected it had been years since anyone worked at that desk, let alone sat at it.

He lifted a box off the chair and dropped it on the floor with a dusty thud. Then he put his hand on the back of the chair, spun it around like he did it for a living, and slid it toward me. "Take a seat, my friend," he said. He pushed a pile of old jeans into the center of the desk and sat on the edge. "Well, Danny, I was gonna wait until tomorrow to track you down, but you saved me a trip. What the hell did you do to get us off?"

There was no way I could tell Billy I'd threatened Eddie — not while he had six or seven beers in him, and I suspected that estimate was conservative. He'd probably tell everyone he knew, starting with the crowd on the back deck. The last thing I needed was for something to get back to Eddie. "Actually, Billy, I didn't have to do anything. Eddie learned the truth about what happened that night — basically that Mark was trying to kill Adam, and that I showed up at the right time. I think Eddie realized if this thing got dragged out, it wasn't going to make his father look very good, so he cut his losses and made it go away."

"I guess I gathered that from the press conference, but I sort of got the feeling something else happened behind the scenes. I figured you must've done something. I knew damn sure Eddie wasn't just trying to help *us* out."

"That's for sure. He would've loved to send us away, but I think he realized that taking a hard line could've made him look bad."

Billy looked at me like he wanted to ask something else, but he didn't. "Well, whatever happened, I'm grateful." Billy finished off the last of his beer and set it down beside him. "Something tells me you didn't come over here tonight to tell me that, though."

"You're right. I didn't. I came over here for a couple reasons. The first was to thank you for helping out Adam that night. Sometime we'll get together over a few drinks and talk about what happened, but I know he couldn't have done it without you. So, thank you."

"I didn't do as much as you might think, but you're right. That's a conversation for another night. Maybe we'll play some golf and grab dinner somewhere. I think I'll be able to get it all out over the course of an afternoon." He smiled at me, and I could see he was swaying slightly.

"That sounds good. I'd like that."

"So, what's the other reason you came over?"

"I wanted to ask you something." I didn't expect to be nervous, but I suddenly was. I guess it was because I'd always been afraid my swing had been the one that killed Mark. I decided to just spit it out before the pressure could build. "Did Adam ever say anything to you about how Mark died that night?"

Billy stared down at the ground. After a few seconds, I began to wonder if he'd heard me. I was about to ask him again when he finally looked up. "It's kind of funny that you'd ask me that. When I first heard about them finding Mark at the golf course, I had trouble remembering much of anything. I mean it was thirty-nine years ago for Christ's sake, and of course, I was drinking that infamous night, which doesn't help the memory. Obviously, I remembered helping Adam, but the details just weren't there. When I started talking to my brother, things started coming back to me, but I don't think we talked about that specifically."

"When I left Mark's house that night, he was still alive. Adam never told me what happened. Well, he never told me anything I thought was the truth anyway. For the most part, he never wanted to talk about it."

"That part I remember," Billy said, smiling. "He never wanted to talk to me about it, either. Let's see. Off the top of my head, I don't remember him saying anything, but let me run through a few things, and maybe something will come back to me. That's what happened before when I started talking to my brother."

I didn't feel like going through everything that happened that night — not right now — but I got the feeling I didn't have much of a choice. "Sure, Billy, take your time."

"I remember I was sitting home watching TV, and like I said, drinking a couple beers. I think I was about to go to bed when my phone rang. It was Adam and he told me he needed my help, but he wouldn't tell me why. At first I thought he wanted to go see that asshole teacher you had, or was it Jess that had him?"

"You mean Mr. Holt?"

Billy chuckled. "Yeah, that was his name. Mr. Holt."

"You're kidding me, Billy. You guys went to see Mr. Holt?"

"Well, we were gonna. Adam had this elaborate plan all worked out."

As fascinated as I was, I knew we could get off on a huge tangent. "Let's come back to that one. Finish telling me what happened at Mark's first."

Billy almost looked disappointed. "Okay, so where was I? Oh…Adam called me and told me he needed my help. Had I known he wanted me to help him bury a body—his mother's boyfriend, for Christ's sake—I would've told him to fuck off." Billy laughed again and leaned back, almost losing his balance in the process. He threw his left arm out to steady himself, but he still came close to toppling off the desk. After a couple seconds, he continued. "He told me to pull my car up on the street behind Mark's house. There used to be a wooded lot back there, but it's gone now."

"I remember it. Jess and I used to play in there sometimes."

"Then you know how dark it got in there. We carried Mark's body through that shit. He was wrapped up in a blanket or something. That wasn't much fun. I can promise you that."

"I'm sure it wasn't."

"It seemed like we were making a ton of noise, stepping on sticks and breaking through branches, but no one ever heard us. Oh, before we did that, me and Adam got into it inside the house. See, that's something I didn't remember the other day. It's funny how the brain holds all this shit, isn't it?"

I nodded but didn't say anything. I didn't want to knock Billy off his story.

"So, I walked into the house and saw a body on the living room floor. Adam already had him wrapped up by this point. Naturally, I went ballistic. I think I almost walked out on him. Let me rephrase that. I *know* I almost walked out on him. We were yelling at each other, and Adam told me to 'Get the fuck out.' That's when I realized I had to help him. And it's a good thing I did because I don't think he would've been able to do it himself. Mark was a heavy son of a bitch.

"We got him through the woods and into the back seat of my car, and then we headed over to the golf course. That part was all my idea. I remembered that we'd been digging near the twelfth green, and I thought it might be an easy place to bury him. Adam was talking about throwing him in the river, but I convinced him my idea was better. I mean who would ever think someone would be buried on a golf course, right? So we headed over to the gate near Griffen Park…wait a second. You've probably already seen Adam's video, haven't you?"

"Yeah, I've watched it a couple times."

"Well, Adam pretty much covered everything we did. The only difference is he had my help instead of doing it by himself. And I'll tell you, I don't think he *could* have done it by himself. The two of us had a hell of a time getting Mark's body down into that hole. If Adam had tried to do that alone, he would've broken those irrigation pipes for sure."

I felt the need to hurry the story along. "So, what happened after you finished filling in the hole?"

"Adam ran up the hill to your house and took a shower while I waited for him outside. It started getting light out, and I was terrified a cop was gonna drive by and see me. When he came out, I took him to Julia's house and dropped him off. Again, it happened pretty much the way he said it did on his video." Billy looked at me, his eyes shining. "Wait a minute. I do remember asking him what happened at some point. I think it was when I first got there and we were arguing. Adam told me that Mark had done something to Jess. Then he said they got into a fight and that Mark tried to strangle him...or something like that. I don't think he ever said anything about you showing up, though. I learned that from my lawyer just a few days ago. And I don't remember him saying anything specific about how he actually killed him. But like I said, Danny, that was almost forty years ago, and what I just told you—about Mark doing something to Jess—that just came back to me right now."

An alarm went off in my head. I was already getting calls from the media, and I had no doubt Billy was, too. Eddie had done what I'd asked him to do. The last thing I wanted was Billy telling CNN that Mark may have done something to Jess. That would go against Adam's video and also the storyline everyone had adopted, including Eddie. "Listen, Billy, what you just said, about Mark doing something to Jess? You need to keep that under wraps for now, and probably forever. In fact, don't tell anyone. Not even Karen."

"Why not?"

"Because everything, including the charges getting dropped, is built upon Adam's video and the idea that Mark struck my mother. We don't want the Feds deciding to take another look at this thing. You know what I mean?"

"Yeah, I think I do. Okay, I won't say anything." Billy shifted again but managed to keep his balance this time. "What were you hoping to hear if you don't mind me asking?"

"I guess I'm not sure. I've always had this fear that Mark died after I hit him. You know...that I caused it."

"I really doubt that, Danny. What were you, nine or ten at the time? I doubt you would've had the strength to kill a grown man with one swing." After a short pause, Billy added, "And even if you did kill him, it's nothing to worry about. That son of a bitch certainly deserved it."

I smiled, thinking he didn't know the half of it. "There's no doubt about that, Billy." I was about to tell him I had to get going when Mr. Holt's face flashed in my head. I hadn't thought about him in years and found it almost impossible to believe Adam never told me about his plan to mess with him. "Oh, you were going to tell me about Mr. Holt."

Billy grinned. "That's right. Good ole Mr. Holt. Adam *really* hated that guy. So, yeah, he had this plan all worked out. Adam somehow found out where he lived. It was in the middle of nowhere, up behind the old machine shop on Reynolds Road. You know where I'm talking about, right?"

"Yeah, I think so." I had no idea.

"Anyway, his house was surrounded by woods. Adam's plan was to hide the car up the road, and then the two of us would sneak back through the woods to the house. When he got home, Adam was gonna throw a burlap bag over his head and drag him out behind his house—just hold him down for a little while and threaten him. Apparently, Holt lived alone. I have no idea how Adam found all this out, but he did."

I shook my head. "You guys were really going to do this?"

"Oh, absolutely. We even did a couple scouting trips to make sure we could hide the car so no one would see it. Adam was convinced they'd never be able to pin it on us. He said Holt was a huge asshole and probably pissed off a lot of people over the years." Billy paused and looked at me. "Wait a second. Didn't something happen with Jess, too?"

"Yeah, he terrified her and one of her friends one time."

"I remember Adam talking about that. He was gonna do it anyway because the guy was such a dick, but that thing with Jess was the final straw. I don't remember everything, but I know he had it all worked out. I told Adam I'd help him, but that I didn't wanna hurt the guy. Adam said he didn't wanna hurt him, either—just scare the shit out of him."

Billy smiled and for an instant I could see him and Adam as teenagers. "You dumb bastards. What if he saw one of your faces or had a heart attack or something?"

"Danny, thinking ahead wasn't one of our strong points back then." Billy laughed hard and picked up his beer to take another sip. He'd forgotten he'd already finished it. "But we had masks," he said. "I remember that, too. We had these old Halloween masks we were gonna wear."

"So, what happened? You never did it, right?" At that moment, I was a little afraid of the answer.

"No. Or if Adam ever did anything, it wasn't with me. I don't think he did, though. I think that incident with Mark woke him up. Plus, with the police around all the time, he realized it was way too risky. But had that not happened, he would've done it. I can tell you that. Adam was crazy about protecting you and Jess. I don't know why. You were both a pain in the ass from what I remember." Billy looked at me and smiled. Soon we were both laughing again.

I stood from the chair. It was time to go. "Well, I better get headed back. They're waiting for me at Laura's." After a bit of a drunken delay, Billy did the same. We headed back down the stairs and stopped near the front door.

"Danny, are you sure you can't sit down and have another beer with us? I know everyone would love to meet you."

I knew I should stay, but I wanted to get back to my family. Laura had texted me that my dad was passing back through, so he and Connie would be there tonight, as well. I'd also sent a text to Kelly and asked her to come down. "We'll do it another time, Billy, and we'll get out for that round of golf, too. I promise."

"Okay, my friend, it was great to see you again, and thanks for whatever you did. I know you're not telling me the whole story, but that's okay. Everything's okay tonight. You know what I mean?" He gave me a huge, crooked smile.

I smiled back at him. "I know exactly what you mean, Billy."

He gave me another bear hug, and then I was out the door, heading toward my Saturn.

73

A week later, Jen and I headed up to Kelly and Andrew's house for a barbeque. By then the media's interest had already begun to die down. For the first forty-eight hours after McCall's press conference, my phone was ringing constantly, but they finally realized I wasn't going to talk about it. Much to my surprise, and Kelly's, as well, no one tried to contact her. I did see Billy interviewed, once locally and once on MSNBC. He came off exactly as he truly was—a happy-go-lucky guy who'd helped a good friend in need a long time ago. He kept his word and never mentioned Jess. Of course, I gave him a call the day after our talk, just to make sure he remembered. Eddie issued a second statement a couple days after the press conference and then did two follow-up interviews with CNN. I was worried someone would ask about Mark's past, specifically about the allegations of molestation against Kelly in the 1970s, but no one did. I suspect rumors had reached them, but they probably weren't able to corroborate anything. I also think there were likely negotiations about which questions were on the table and which ones weren't. And when you're a United States Attorney, you have a lot more negotiating power than most. Plus, in this case, at least, it seemed to outside observers like both sides were on the same page.

When we arrived at the house, there were already several other couples there as well as a handful of younger children. Andrew made both of us a strong cocktail and then fired up the grill, a silver monstrosity that took up a quarter of their back deck. I watched in awe as he threw on what looked like half a cow and a couple of chickens. There was a table off to the side, holding what looked like an assortment of summer salads, including potato (my favorite) and macaroni. Jen slipped into the house to see if she could help Kelly while I mingled with Andrew and a few of their friends. The entire scene reminded me of the party Jen threw last year for Adam. In some strange way, it felt like Adam was there, like he was watching over us. And while the sensation wasn't quite as strong, I felt like Mom and Jess were looking down on us, too. It made me happy that the three of them were together again, but it also filled me with a heavy loneliness.

Over the next three hours, Jen and I ate, drank, and celebrated with Kelly and Andrew and their friends even though the four of us were the only ones who knew what we were celebrating. Kelly pulled me aside to tell me she hadn't told anyone about my meeting with Eddie and never would. We didn't know what Eddie would do if the full truth ever surfaced, but we agreed we didn't want to find out.

It was after eleven when Kelly found me sitting by the fire pit, alone. Most of their friends had already gone home, and Jen was in the kitchen talking to Alexa. Kelly plopped into the lawn chair beside me.

"How you doing there, buddy?" she said, grabbing onto my hand and holding it.

"I'm doing well," I said, noting my words were beginning to stick together. "How 'bout you?"

"I'm fine, hon." She pulled in a full breath as she settled deeper into her chair. The fire crackled and threw sparks toward the sky. We watched them burn and die out like tiny meteors. "Listen, I've been meaning to ask you. How did you and Jen find me?"

I remembered what Mrs. Abrams said about keeping her name out of it. I considered telling Kelly that my dad had found someone who remembered her, but I didn't want to lie. She'd risked too much for us. "Actually, Kel, I'm not supposed to tell you."

Kelly looked at me and smiled. "Is that right?"

I smiled back at her. "As a matter of fact, it is."

"What if I tell you that you don't have a choice?"

"Well, in that case I'd tell you that it was a parent from your softball team when you were a kid."

"Which one? Post 1900?"

"I'm not positive, but that's ringing a bell."

Kelly looked at the ground for a second and then back at me. "It was Mrs. Abrams, wasn't it?"

I laughed. "I can see I won't be able to hide anything from you."

She gave me the same wide grin she flashed on the day we met. "You're learning, my boy." After another deep breath, she said, "Mrs. Abrams was a nice lady and she was always talking to me, asking me how I was doing. She probably had some idea what was going on, but I doubt she knew everything."

I wasn't sure what to say, so I just waited. Kelly surprised me by changing the subject.

"So, what's the deal with you and Jen?"

I tried hard not to smile but failed. "What do you mean?"

"Nice try, Daniel, but I've been around too long. I see how you two look at each other."

"In that case, I'll plead the fifth." I was still smiling, but I didn't want to talk about it. I could tell by the way her expression changed that she understood.

We sat there for a minute, staring at the fire. Kelly threw another log onto the blaze and another horde of sparks rose in the heat. She let go of my hand and patted my leg. I'd almost forgotten she was even holding it.

"You know, this is the first time we've been drunk together," she said.

"You're not going to start hitting on me, are you?"

"Maybe after my husband goes to bed." We both started chuckling and it evolved into drunken laughter. "No, this might surprise you, Dan, but I sometimes get philosophical when I'm drunk."

She butchered the pronunciation, but I let it pass, knowing I'd likely do the same. "Okay, let's hear it. What's on your mind?"

"Did you ever think about how we're sort a trapped by our own circumstances, like we've each been dealt our hand, and there isn't a damn thing we can do about it?"

"Yeah, I actually have thought about that before. Many times. It's another way of saying that life isn't fair, and it starts right about the time you come out of the womb. And, Kelly, I think you know that better than most...if you don't mind me saying."

Kelly looked at me, smiling. "It just so happens that I *don't* mind you saying." As soon as she got it out, she started giggling again, and I joined her right away. We both had to work not to lose it all over again. "No, I think it's more than that, Dan. It's almost like we're just this consciousness or whatever you wanna call it, and we're stuck inside these bodies — whichever one you happen to get at birth. We're like prisoners in a way. Even Eddie's a prisoner, I suppose. You get stuck with a shitty brain or a shitty family and you're screwed — unless you can somehow work your way out of it, that is. Sometimes I wonder if it's all just a test."

I was doing my best to follow along, but I was getting tired. I just hoped Kelly wasn't about to start talking about reincarnation. "You're talking about our souls, right?"

"I guess in a way I am, and in a way I'm not. Souls sounds too religious, and what I'm talking about doesn't have much to do with religion. At least I don't think it does."

"I think you would've gotten along just fine with my brother. He wasn't much of a believer, either."

"Oh, I didn't say *that*. I've always believed in a higher being, although I'm not sure it's the same God everyone preaches about on Sunday mornings. I sure as hell hope *something's* up there. Otherwise, what's the point a all this shit?"

I nodded. "I'm with you there, Kel." Neither of us said anything for a while, and I started thinking it might be a good time to call it a night.

"I'm not ready to go just yet," Kelly said, "but I'm looking forward to seeing my mom again."

That feeling of loneliness was suddenly back in full force. "Me, too, Kel. I can't wait to see my family again."

We turned our gazes back to the fire, listening to the crackle of the dry wood. Eventually, Kelly broke the silence. "I'm thinking about having a little sit-down with the man in charge when I get up there."

"Is that right?" I asked, smiling.

Kelly's eyes glistened in the firelight. "As a matter a fact, it is." She stood up and patted my leg again. "I've got some feedback for him."

Epilogue

Mark's story died a quick death after Eddie conducted the CNN interviews. Two of the late-night news shows wanted to do a segment on it, but when I (and I assume Eddie) refused to be a part of it, they decided not to do it. I told them nicely it was simply too emotional, and we wanted to move on with our lives. I reached out again to Billy and asked him not to take part in any of those shows, either. I paid him a visit at work where I knew he'd be totally sober. A few months later, we got our golf outing in and had a fantastic dinner afterward with his wife and Jen. We never once discussed that horrible night thirty-nine years ago.

It didn't take me long to realize I was very much in love with Jen, but it did take almost a year before the feeling I was doing something wrong — namely, that I was betraying Adam — finally went away. Jen ended up selling her house and moving up here to live with me in my apartment. We got married in a quiet ceremony, which included just Connor and the Justice of the Peace. Those first months were pretty fun, and I think we both felt like young newlyweds just starting out. In a lot of ways I guess we were. Eventually, we decided we needed more room and bought a house. It seemed like a mansion compared to The Palace, but it was actually pretty modest. Connor doesn't have to sleep on the couch now, so naturally he was all for it. Laura and I had some good years together — even a few great ones — but I can honestly say I've never been happier. I still make black cap jam every fall and Jen still helps me. She doesn't like picking the berries anymore, but she still likes making love after we make the jam. I think I got the better part of that deal.

Connor is sixteen now, and he doesn't help me pick berries anymore, either. He's too busy with baseball and his girlfriend, Bethany. She's a sweet girl, and we all adore her. They seem very much in love, but they're so young I can't help but think one of them is going to end up with a broken heart. I have a bad feeling it's going to be Connor. Jen reminds me it's one of those things in life that can't be avoided.

My father's still going strong at the age of seventy-nine. My instincts on his girlfriend, Connie, were spot on. They got married four years ago and moved to North Carolina. I see them two or three times a year, which is just about perfect. I think I'd kill him if we lived too close to one another, but getting together every few months is actually nice. I feel bad he and Adam never reconciled before Adam died, and I know my dad does, too. Whenever he brings it up, I tell him Adam also wished they could have reconciled. That's not exactly what Adam said before he died, but I think it's probably what he meant. Of course, it's also possible Adam's looking down and blowing a gasket. I'm hoping that wherever he is he's softened up on the subject of our father. If not, I'm in deep trouble.

Laura ended up getting remarried, as well. In fact, she was the first one to retake the plunge. When she first learned about me and Jen, she sort of flipped out. There wasn't any justification for it, of course, but that's what she did. She started crying and told me she'd been waiting for me and hadn't been seeing anyone since breaking it off with McBride. That wasn't exactly true based on what I'd heard from friends, but I managed to keep that to myself. There were plenty of times, especially in those first awful months after catching the two of them in our bed, where I would have reveled in her anguish. I'm ashamed to admit that, but it's true. But so much had changed in my life since that terrible night, and I no longer harbored any resentment toward her—ninety-nine percent of the time anyway—so I felt really bad about it. Laura didn't speak to me or Jen for a couple weeks, but she came around eventually. I think the whole thing freed her up somehow because not even two months later she met her future husband at a local fundraiser. No one ever found out what happened that night with me, Laura, and McBride, which goes down as one of my prouder accomplishments. I guess it's fair to say I'm good at keeping secrets…and so are Laura and McBride, although they had the easy part.

Jen and I have stayed close with Kelly and Andrew. We travel up there about once every other month to have breakfast at the diner. We always make sure we sit in Alexa's section. She's a senior at Cortland State now and still waitresses every weekend. Sometimes we head over to their house afterward and have a beer or two. Occasionally, it turns into several, and we wind up having a cookout or getting wings at Ray's Tavern. We don't talk about Eddie or the past much anymore even though it's a bond we'll always share. Andrew has become one of my closest friends, and Kelly and I have become more like siblings that got separated as children. We give something to each other that was missing from our lives—not a vital piece, maybe, but something we both want. Something that makes us feel more complete. For me, I feel closer to Adam, Jess, and Mom whenever we're together, and I think Kelly feels the same thing with her mom.

Right around the same time Laura got remarried, I fulfilled a lifelong dream and started my own business. It was sub and pizza shop right here in Everton. I called it Everton Pizza. Jen and Connor declared it the most boring name in the history of pizza joints, but I stuck to my guns. Having my own thing was both fun and rewarding, but after a while it got to be a grind, just like anything else, I suppose. Last summer I found someone who was interested in buying the place, so I let it go for what I thought was a pretty fair price. During the four plus years I owned it, I met a lot of unique people and had some interesting experiences. One of those happened on a Saturday afternoon, about a month after we opened. I got a call from a group of teachers at none other than West Everton Elementary. They wanted to order two round pizzas and a handful of subs. At that point we didn't do deliveries, but it was a big order and they asked, so I decided to take it over myself. It was late August and most of the classrooms were open on account of the teachers getting their rooms ready for the start of the school year. I decided to stop by my old fifth-grade classroom, just to check it out. The room seemed mostly the same, but they shrank it down to about half its original size somehow. Of course, the desks were different. I don't think even Mr. Holt could have ripped the top off of one of the new ones. As an adult I look back and wonder what could have happened in his life to make him act like such an asshole. I also think about what Kelly said — about how we all sort of get stuck with some random brain and body in some random place and time. If that's true, and I think it is, Holt was certainly dealt a lemon. But raw deal or not, one thing's for sure. He shouldn't have been teaching kids in 1978 or any other year.

I can still remember the feeling I had that day when I walked in and saw Mr. Holt sitting at Ms. Becker's desk — how I immediately sensed that everything had changed. It wasn't until seventh-grade and the true chaos of middle school before I learned what ultimately happened to her. Jackie Neal approached me one morning at my locker between classes. Normally, she didn't even bother talking to me, but that day she looked upset and a bit forlorn. Jackie told me her mom said Ms. Becker had died after being in a coma for two years. It was a pretty big shock, but a short-lived one. So much had changed since fifth-grade, and we had a lot on our plates, most notably trying to survive until the weekend. I think most seventh-graders look back fondly at their elementary years, but they also realize they can never go back. Life has pushed them frantically ahead, and whether they like it or not, there's no stopping it or even slowing it down. Jackie and I were no different, but still, that moment caught us and we stared at each other silently. We weren't friends or even close to it, but as we looked at each other that day, I knew we were thinking the same thing. If given even half the chance, we would've locked hands and jumped back in time together, not only to see our beloved teacher but to go back to a period in our lives when we were still truly children. Because of Mark and the aftermath of what happened that night, I'd already gone a long way toward leaving my childhood behind, but it took Jackie breaking the awful news about Ms. Becker to make me realize it.

I drove by Barnell Field the other day on my way to grab some takeout from Jen's favorite restaurant. I was early, but instead of grabbing a drink at the bar, I pulled into the baseball field's empty parking lot and walked up to the chain-link fence near third base. It was a gorgeous June evening, and by then the reddish sun was losing its daily battle with the horizon. There was no game, so the field was deserted, save for the dozens of fireflies dancing above the outfield grass. I leaned against the fence and looked around. The wooden bleachers had been replaced by aluminum ones, and the clubhouse and dugouts were a different color, but other than that it looked the same as it did when I played there over forty years ago. It made me feel good to see that. In a world of almost constant change, it had remained one of those places you can hold onto — a place that's more or less the way you remember it from your childhood.

And when you're standing there alone, the memories flow fresh and hard.

Dear Reader,

Thank you for reading *For Ann*. If you can, please leave a review on Amazon or Goodreads. At the time of this printing, my titles (see below) are not available in brick and mortar stores. If you are interested, please visit the Amazon bookstore—ebook and paperback versions are available, along with excerpts.

Thank you,

Shawn Sprague

The Hills Report

Cable news host Eric Hills awakes to shocking news—a beloved American actress has been abducted. Hills begins planning his coverage when he's handed the biggest break of his career: an email containing a photo of the terrified movie star. It's the first in a series of direct communications from the brazen kidnappers. Overnight, Hills becomes the face of the story as WNN becomes the highest rated network on television. Professionally, it seems almost too good to be true, but other mysterious events will soon threaten everything he's ever worked for...and perhaps much more. Hills is suddenly faced with an impossible decision: run to the Feds for help or ignore the warnings and continue pursuing his life's ambition. Will he survive long enough to make a choice?

The Hills Report beat 3 major best-sellers in a blind market survey. Visit shawnsprague.com for details.

Jackson & Franklin
(Ages 13+)

Danny Abbot's fifth grade year is crawling by, but things change quickly when he loses his favorite teacher and makes the Majors of Little League all in the same week. Unfortunately, his new teacher turns out to be anything but friendly, and that's not the only bad news. A questionable maneuver has landed the league's two hardest-throwing pitchers on the same team. As the season unfolds, Danny must face not only his teacher but also a powerhouse team that's devouring the competition.

Note to readers of *For Ann*: *Jackson & Franklin* is an extended (and cleaned-up) version of the youth chapters found in *For Ann*. While it's definitely suitable for younger readers, it can also be enjoyed by anyone who played sports as a kid and doesn't mind taking a look back. **A youth edition, ages 8-12, is coming soon.**

The Pickup and Other Dark Tales

Shawn Sprague takes you on a chilling tour of the unknown in this collection of horror and supernatural tales. (Includes the novella The Pickup.) In Four Minutes, Sean Hendel awakes from a horrible nightmare telling him that he has just minutes to get his family out of the house. In The Pickup, Ben Kellerman heads into the heartland of Pennsylvania to pick up copies of his first novel. He couldn't be more excited to get his new books home, but he runs into an old girlfriend who has other plans for his afternoon. In The Weekend, Becca Thompson plans an elaborate getaway with her boyfriend but ends up driving into a nightmare instead. In The Shadow, Matt Hastings awakes to a strange shadow formation on his bedroom wall. As the morning unfolds, he begins to wonder if it's the reason he can't move. In The Flood, Jason Emory comes home from college to discover his neighborhood is flooded and his parents are missing. The stories in this brand new collection will keep you up late into the night...perhaps even staring at strange shadows on the wall. (63,000 words)

Three stories from this collection went head-to-head with three award-winning tales by Stephen King in a blind market survey and more than held their own! Visit shawnsprague.com for details.

The Weekend

Becca Thompson plans an elaborate weekend with her boyfriend but ends up driving into an unspeakable nightmare. The story also appears in the collection *The Pickup and Other Dark Tales*. (14,000 word novelette; Kindle only; $.99)

I want to thank Eileen Barr, Alyson Dearie, Kim Hay, Alyssa Milligan, Jody Mashlykin, Diana Miller, Caitie Sidebottom, Sheila Guido, Becca Gamel, Michele Hughes, Betsy Kosick, Sarah Evans, Doug Winegardner, Dina Barney, and Jen Wegman for reading early versions of the novel and providing valuable feedback.

A special thank you to Valerie Zehl, Abby Davis, Samantha Mastronardi, Gene Thomas, Karin Hannon, Tom Musa, and Colleen Gentile for their considerable assistance and for their patience with my never-ending questions. Also, I want to thank my good friends who helped with the FBI-related information (any errors or breaks from reality were all mine.)

I'd like to thank my immediate family: Mom, Dad, Janine, Stan, and Chris, who served as inspiration for much of the book. While there is a great deal of fiction mixed in, many of the stories in the novel (especially those that occurred in 1978) actually happened, either to me or my family or to close friends. Just so there is no confusion, my dad never left us. In fact, both he and my mom were always there for us and continue to be.

Lastly, I'd like to thank my wonderful wife for her still unwavering support. Kim, I couldn't have completed the novel (or anything else) without you.

Some of the cities mentioned in the novel are fictitious (including Tremon and Everton) while others are real. Liberties were taken with geographical details. Liberties were taken in other areas, as well. For example, the video sequence described from the ending credits of *This Week in Baseball* did not appear until 1979. Incidentally, the theme song is called *Gathering Crowds* and was written by British composer John Scott. While there are some good sports theme songs out there, for me, that one is hands down the best.

Shawn Sprague lives in upstate New York with his wife and three children and their dog, Sammy. He runs a small publishing company and coaches youth basketball. He is the author of three novels: *For Ann, Jackson & Franklin,* and *The Hills Report* and a collection of dark fiction entitled *The Pickup* and *Other Dark Tales.* Please visit shawnsprague.com for more information, or like him on Facebook by searching Shawn Sprague Author.

www.ingramcontent.com/pod-product-compliance
Lightning Source LLC
Chambersburg PA
CBHW031425240626
47154CB00001B/209